Also by Gigi Levangie Grazer

RESCUE ME

maneater

a novel

gigi levangie grazer

SIMON & SCHUSTER
New York London Toronto Sydney Singapore

SIMON & SCHUSTER
Rockefeller Center
1230 Avenue of the Americas
New York, NY 10020

This book is a work of fiction. Names, characters, places, and incidents either are products of the author's imagination or are used fictitiously. Any resemblance to actual events or locales or persons, living or dead, is entirely coincidental.

For information regarding special discounts for bulk purchases,
please contact Simon & Schuster Special Sales at
1-800-456-6798 or business@simonandschuster.com

Designed by Jan Pisciotta

Manufactured in the United States of America

1 3 5 7 9 10 8 6 4 2

Library of Congress Cataloging-in-Publication Data
Grazer, Gigi Levangie
Maneater : a novel / Gigi Levangie Grazer.
p. cm.
1. Hollywood (Los Angeles, Calif.)—Fiction. 2. Motion picture industry—Fiction.
I. Title.
PS3557.R2913M365 2003
813'.6—dc21 2003042566

ISBN 0-7432-5328-0 (export edition)

Acknowledgments

Thank you to the professionals: David Rosenthal, Marysue Rucci, Jennifer Rudoph-Walsh, Sylvie Rabineau, Stephanie Davis, Tara Parsons, and Scott Gray. Thanks also to my friends, Julie Jaffe, Leslee Newman, and Julia Sorkin. And thank you to my parents, Frank Levangie and Phillipa Brown, to whom I apologize in advance.

To my husband, a maneater's dream

maneater

One
The Meet

My God, the wedding was beautiful. So what if the bride with the translucent skin and white-gold hair (courtesy of the ex–gay-porn-star hairdresser with the pregnant Amazonian wife) had fucked every one of the groomsmen at one point or another in her short life.

Back up. Clarissa Alpert's life wasn't actually as short as she liked to let on. She deemed herself twenty-eight, which was a surprise to everyone who'd grown up with her in the relative impoverishment of the (Lower) Beverly Hills flats, where bungalow after bungalow had trudged only recently into the half-million-dollar range. In fact, she was thirty-one, but to her twenty-seven-and-a-half- ("halves" were still important to the boy) year-old bridegroom, the damaged scion of an old-money family, she was twenty-eight. Even her brittle-boned, anorexic, four-pack-a-day-smoker, Jewish mother, confused by the conviction of her daughter's lie, came to believe she had given birth to this unnatural force twenty-eight years ago.

Clarissa had set her sights on Aaron not long after dumping Sean Penn.

She hadn't really dated Sean Penn. However, Aaron Mason, of the Mason Department Stores, the largest midlevel chain in the South, idolized Sean Penn. Aaron, an SMU film school grad, was a nascent producer, new to Hollywood and its ways. Clarissa had discovered him tripping off the bus (in this case, out of his 2002 Bentley at valet parking in front of the Ivy). She always had had a thing for handicapped men, and finding one who happened to be driving her favorite luxury vehicle was enough to make Clarissa, confirmed atheist, a Sunni.

Clarissa had dated all kinds of men with various afflictions—they ranged from dyslexics to a blind Moby-knockoff singer for a techno band to a wheelchair-bound Emmy-winning screenwriter. Clarissa had found herself, unfortunately, in like-plus with the screenwriter: she had enjoyed wiping spittle from his face, she had treasured his incoherent affections.

But a screenwriter? And a television screenwriter at that? Clarissa was only twenty-eight (she insisted); she was not ready to give up the brass (platinum, Tiffany) ring quite yet.

Aaron's affliction was a clubfoot. Clarissa watched him like a tiger eyeing a fatted wildebeest as he made his way from his navy Bentley up the ziggurat-like patio steps of the Ivy to his awaiting table, where three men with chubby egos yelled obscenities into tiny cell phones.

The limp cinched the deal.

Their romance was short; two weeks longer, it could have been called "whirlwind." Clarissa squired her prized cabbage to parties from the graffitied, Ecstasy-laden banks of Silverlake to the gilded, coke-encrusted shorelines of Malibu. Aaron could not have known what hit him, though he may have known (as we'll later learn) that Clarissa had slept her way, without mercy, regret, mourning or conscience, through Greater Los Angeles. But he could not have known that she lied about her age, religion (Episcopalian at the Bel Air country club, Jewish at Hillcrest), mating habits, hair color, plastic surgeries, level of education, her mother's nose job, her upbringing, her downfall, her rehab stay(s), the number of pregnancies she'd experienced—three—without an actual birth, and that she lied to anyone at any time for any reason.

At least, in the beginning, he could not have known Clarissa was a sociopath-in-training, as common to L.A. as envy and palm trees. He could not have known, emerging from the relative norm that is suburban Georgia, that sociopaths are even more prevalent in Los Angeles than in Washington, D.C.—and more celebrated.

And here, Clarissa Alpert was very celebrated, indeed.

Prologue, or How This Whole Mess Got Started

10:42 P.M., New Year's Eve. The following was being scribbled onto a Le Domaine cloth napkin:

January 1, 2003, Wish List: Men I, Clarissa Alpert, being of soundish mind and incredible (aux natural!) body, would like to acquire this year:

1. Bruce Springsteen (too old, married, children [ugh], probably happy. Level of difficulty: 9+)
2. Peter Morton (rich, Hard Rock (Planet Hollywood?) restaurants, etc., divorced . . . rich, rich, rich, engaged. Level of difficulty: 6)
3. Ted Field (rich, heir, ext. rich, likes tall, skinny, beautiful blondes. Who are 18. Who have proof of being 18. May be difficult: 10)
4. Graydon Carter (ink-hasn't-dried-divorced, dozen or so kids). Powerful, underlined. Semi-British accent—yummy AND peculiar. Level of difficulty: 8+—P.S. Prefers classy girls with exquisite taste . . . UGH.)

Clarissa Regina Alpert was making up her yearly to-do list. Lists, she knew, were important to the goal-oriented life; writing them imbued focus and direction. She had learned this lesson from an ex-ex-ex . . . *ex* boyfriend bartender/actor/stuntman with a permanently curled lip who learned it from a Dianetics course at the giant, Smurf-blue Church of Scientology (which he'd joined to meet Tom Cruise, John Travolta, or, at the very least, Jenna Elfman, better known as "Dharma").

Clarissa tried to learn one tidbit of knowledge from every man she'd ever dated; though she was never a great student of school or life, she happened to be the Valedictorian of Men.

She had written her "Man List" every year, on the New Year, since she had turned eighteen (twenty-one). Most of her waking minutes were spent in the company of girlfriends, but this was one tradition Clarissa saved for her own company; planning her future demanded her full and immediate attention.

She scribbled on, using Larry the Waiter's chewed pen. She was on her third Kir Royale, and work was to be done . . .

"You a screenwriter?" said a voice. Male. (No one in Los Angeles who appeared to be a writer could be anything but a screenwriter. Poets and novelists, much like vampires, hate the sun. Even if it's shrouded behind a smog burkha.)

A gorgeous "hairless" was standing in front of Clarissa. "Hairless" or "Leos" or "Preschoolers" were terms Clarissa and her girlfriends used for men under twenty-five.

However, Clarissa looked not at his unmarked, eager face, but at his shoes.

They were not Prada. They were not Gucci. They were not even Kenneth Cole.

They looked suspiciously like Hush Puppies. *Vomit,* Clarissa thought. *Sherman Oaks studio apartment, music industry mailroom—or worse, agent-in-training* . . .

"You may leave," Clarissa said, and went back to her mad scribbling.

"Excuse me? You don't even know—"

"Go. Away. Now. Take your ball, go on . . ." She said, with the warmth of an injured cobra.

Poor boy; he looked shocked. He almost frowned, but, unused to the expression, settled for a pout.

He made the mistake of trying to talk again.

"Look, I've eaten at your table, *comprendez-vous*? Not interested." Clarissa cut him off.

"Bitch." But he used the invective under his breath; the Leo was afraid.

Clarissa emitted a proper bobcat hiss, her precisely bonded teeth briefly displayed.

Back to the list. This year, the list had taken on greater importance.

"Think, Princess," she said to herself. Clarissa checked her watch. She had many, many girlfriends but they weren't to be trusted with her secret list. Much as she loved and adored them, why should she give her friends any ideas? However, she had promised to meet up at the Playboy Mansion (Silicone Valley, Tits Central, Home of the Free and the Laid) with her girls later. There was much fun to be had there among the cheesy food, the failed sitcom stars, the dank, infamous grotto that reeked of semen, desperate laughs, and cash, and then, the endless river of gorgeous women, so many they had to be bused in, and all so aggressively beautiful that ugliness itself became a welcome commodity.

But right now, there was work to be done.

5 . . .

5. There has to be more than four.

Clarissa thought, out loud, "Have I dated everyone on the bicoastals?"

Larry the Waiter came by again, lanky as a rubber band. "*Si, oui,* affirmative—that would be a yes in any language," he said, and set down another champagne cocktail. Without having to be asked.

All men, Clarissa thought, *should be gay waiters.*

"You should know, Mother," Clarissa agreed.

Clarissa wrote a name down.

"Larry the Waiter knows all, Miss All-That-and-More. You've been sliding in here since you were legal."

5. John F. Kennedy, Jr. (rich, good family, married [unhappily?]. Dead. Level of Difficulty: . . . 8)

"Correction. Before I was legal." Clarissa loved Larry the Waiter. He was gay, smart, bitchy, and bald. A yummy combo.

"Listen, honey, if you don't land one of these jumbo jets soon, I'm going to tie a yellow ribbon around your head and declare you a national emergency."

"I'm not interested in landing just any foolish rich man. Where's the sport, I ask you?" Clarissa said. And then she added, softly, "There's a small part of me that wants to fall in love."

Weddings, babies, children, young mothers in SUVs, young fathers with rolled-up shirtsleeves, old fathers in wheelchairs, Clarissa was surrounded. Her world had grown up around her, and she was determined not to be left at the station labeled "She Was So Cute, Remember?"

Clarissa shook her head like a wet dog. She thought maybe she had reached her alcohol limit.

"Uh-huh. Which part would that be?" Larry the Waiter looked at her list and declared it "Sold out. This isn't the nineties."

Clarissa looked down the names. *Was he right? Gay waiters are always right.*

"Look, Sweetness. Do you want to end up here in ten years with fake lips and helmet hair toasting a guy with half a pancreas?"

Clarissa looked at him. "Not Clarissa. I'm not going to end up like a retired Breck girl." They stared down at the end of the bar. Two Clairol blondes in their forties, their lips wrapped tightly around numerous collagen injections, their noses a matched set of early eighties ski slopes, were laughing with practiced hilarity at something an older man with spotted hands and a gut spilling out over his elasticized waistband had managed to spit out.

Clarissa noticed that one of them had a rip in her nylons. She noted the scuffed shoes.

Clarissa was all too aware of this tragedy; it was her own personal Clarissa Regina Alpert nightmare. Los Angeles was known as the land of broken dreams (blah, blah). Saunter on your Jimmy Choos into any of the better restaurants—the standards, Spago, Mr. Chow, Nobu, Ivy, Chaya, Giorgio—the tyros––the House, Lucques, Chadwick—and there was always the table Clarissa avoided like the plague (or retail . . . or J. C. Penney . . . or Estée Lauder foundation), the table that was either closest to the bathroom or the kitchen, the one with the two women, 90 percent of the time overblonde, with delicate, oval faces that looked good when . . .

When.

They would eat their salad ("appetizer size, please") in tidy forkfuls and engage in the appearance of conversation that both were too tired for, and if you didn't watch closely (as Clarissa did, for she couldn't help herself—how many get to see their future so clearly?) you wouldn't notice that they didn't share eye contact, that they didn't laugh. That they got up to go to the bathroom at least three times, and they walked slowly, heads up, face set, knowing this, *this*, was no longer a dress rehearsal; that they always ordered three glasses of house chardonnay but never dessert.

That they were watching your table, watching you watching them. Running their eyes over you like a truck.

And you didn't blame them.

Clarissa shivered. She had to get married before the end of the year.

Her timeline was clear: she would be twenty-nine (thirty-two) in November; she and her lucky husband would have two children within four years; she'd be divorced by forty and still hot (thanks to Dr. Drew Franklin of the Beverly Hills Triangle) and living the good life while the nannied, tutored, personal-trained kids attended out-of-state boarding schools.

But if they fell in love, well . . . Clarissa wondered about the odds. She'd been in love once. Had she already used up her chits?

A plan. Clarissa always had a plan. (Important Subplot: Her father, the Horrible Teddy Alpert, was threatening to stop paying her rent. This meant two things: a. Clarissa would have to get a job. Impossible, because, as she told her father, "I am my own full-time job"; leaving: b. Clarissa would have to get a husband who had a job.) Also, Clarissa felt she was, at her age, walking around with an expiration date on her head.

The waiter took Clarissa's pen from her frozen hand and wrote these words:

6–10: AARON MASON.

He wrote it in all caps, as though the name were bigger than the sum of itself.

"Who?" Clarissa looked at him, hazel eyes widened with curiosity, greed . . . and hope.

"Your last hurrah. Read your trades, Missy Miss."

Clarissa drove her convertible BMW (the preferred driving instrument for young hot women with acquiring minds) to the all-night newsstand at Fairfax and Third and bought copies of the *Hollywood Reporter*, *Variety*, and a couple music trades, though she loathed anything having to do with the music industry. After she told the ancient cashier to keep her change in order not to touch his hand, she didn't bother waiting to read the papers. She sat in the open air of her driver's seat as homeless people beckoned.

"Quarter for a song?" a black man with aging dreads asked.

"I'll need more than that," Clarissa said. Clarissa loathed reading under the best of circumstances (in her defense, she did enjoy *Vogue* and *Cosmopolitan* and sometimes *Marie Claire*, when it didn't get all "intellectual"); she needed to concentrate.

He was taken aback; he thought he'd heard wrong.

"You want me to pay you?"

"Look, Frank Sinatra, Jr., okay, I'll give you a dollar to walk away from here *without* singing."

He took it.

And Clarissa found her man: Aaron Mason had bought something called the "underlying rights" to something called *The Gay Divorcee,* an old Fred Astaire–Ginger Rogers musical (*Ugh. I hate old musicals,* Clarissa thought) for $1.5 million, paid to the inheritors of the original play—

"One-point-five mill—!" Clarissa exclaimed. The number gratified her, then made her angry that someone would spend so much money on something that wasn't even in color.

Aaron explained, in the article, that among the things he loved growing up, "the lonely scion of a Forbes 500 family" (the reporter's words), was old musicals. And his very favorite was *The Gay Divorcee.*

"I adore old musicals!" Clarissa said. And then proceeded to the twenty-four-hour video rental store on the Strip, a place frequented by blow hounds on a bender, garden-variety insomniacs, and porn addicts. She instantly forgot about the Playboy Mansion and its gaudy clarion song.

Clarissa Alpert had homework to do.

Clarissa's mom was taking a dump in Clarissa's own bathroom; Clarissa hated this because waste moved through Clarissa's mother's body and came out the other end with little molecular restructuring: If she ate corn, out came a cob; if she ate carrots, deli salad it would be; if she ate steak (she rarely ate steak, or anything with more than 150 calories a serving, for that matter), out came a Hereford.

"Mom!" Clarissa shouted. Her voice was naturally scratchy, like Demi Moore after a week of screaming at assistants. Some found it sexy, some merely annoying. Clarissa picked up the remote control and rewound. She was on her seventh viewing of *The Gay Divorcee*; as far as she could see, the movie was about how tap dancing could lead to wedding bells.

"Wha'?"

Her mother always said "Wha'?" instead of "What?"

"You know what I told you about taking dumps in my fucking bathroom?"

"You should wash out that mouth, that's wha'."

"T! T! T! T! *What*!"

"Pffft."

This meant "Shut your mouth, dear daughter, you mean little cunt, or I'll cut you like a knife."

The problem was, her mother was hooked on a molten something called "Dieter's Tea." It contained an enormous amount of "natural" laxative, enough to clean out a 747 engine. Clarissa drank it once, after a Thanksgiving dinner—she was going to have sex that night with an entertainment attorney with an enormous shlong and bigger Mercedes, and though she loved a heavy meal, especially Thanksgiving dinner, she also loved sex.

She drank it, and almost laid a brick right in the middle of foreplay.

Oral foreplay.

The tea had made her sweat and cramp; she crawled to the bathroom, bent over like a halter-topped Quasimodo. The attorney never called again, except once that next morning, because someone had taken his favorite meditation CD, the one with the stupid monks or something, and he had to ask . . .

Well, of course Clarissa had taken it. She knew he wasn't going to call again (there's always a first time!) and she wanted to punish him.

Oh . . . what Clarissa learned from the entertainment attorney: Never drink Dieter's Tea before sex. Never.

Also: Big Mercedes, like the 600 series, drive more smoothly than the small, sporty models.

Her mother was addicted to the hideous brown, bark-tasting liquid; she drank it three times a day. Once Clarissa had convinced her mother to stop drinking the foul tea; her bowels got so badly backed up, Clarissa had to rush her to the hospital so a dashing Indian intern could stick a long, dark finger up her mother's tiny, crepey butt.

Clarissa subverted her own rules (don't date anything that can't get you into the VIP section of a premiere or table seven at Mr. Chow) and had three dates with the intern until realizing, on the traditional third-date screw, his dick had the circumference of a number two pencil. She was hoping he'd be a "Grower, not a Shower," to no avail. The shock was so great that Clarissa retired, staying home every night for a month, with only Oreos, Red Bull and vodka, and her Bunny Ears vibrator to keep her company.

Finally, her mother came out of the bathroom to face Clarissa's grimace, which wasn't what it used to be, because of the botox.

"Wha'?"

"What?"

"Don't star—"

Start! Clarissa screamed in her head. Her mother was Jewish Bolivian, the granddaughter of a Bolivian general, once very beautiful, still petite. Clarissa looked like a Chechen weightlifter downing steroids for breakfast when she stood next to her.

"Mommy, did you read the article?" Clarissa shifted gears smoothly.

"Leave that boy alone." Not smooth enough.

"So Not Supportive," Clarissa tried to whine, but she was not a natural; her whine came out more like a Volkswagen engine straining over the Sepulveda Pass.

"He's not going to marry you."

"Want a bet?"

"Wha'?"

"Bet. *Bet.* You want to bet."

"No gambling."

"Mom, it's not gambling. Look, he's having lunch at the Ivy next Tuesday." Clarissa knew this because, posing as a ditsy secretary who didn't wish to incur her boss' wrath, she had called every upscale restaurant on the west side to ask if they had a reservation under "Aaron Mason."

"I'm not going with you."

"Yes, you are. I can't invite my friends. They're either too hot or they're too evil—there'd be nothing left of him. He'd be man dust."

Her mother waved her hand, as she often did when she was agitated.

"Don't say that, Mom."

Her mother waved her hand again.

"I'm not going to use him, or ruin him, or whatever it is you think I do to men." Clarissa uncoiled herself from her red velvet couch, purloined from an ex-boyfriend's defunct nightclub (from whom she'd learned to always keep chilled vodka on hand). "I just want to meet him."

Her mother narrowed her eyes and gestured once more.

"Great. I want you to wear the black Armani suit, the silk one with the silver buttons."

Mom's hand fluttered up and down.

"It does not make you look fat. You couldn't look fat if you were fat—Jesus!"

Clarissa rose from the couch and strode to the bar (otherwise known as "the mantel") in her rented off-Robertson duplex; her apartment was a place where scores of girls like her settled until boys like Aaron (only less rich) married them. Clarissa had stopped counting the girls in her five-square-block neighborhood (Robertson to La Cienega; Beverly to Third) who fit her description when she reached into the thirties: 25–34 (same as the coveted, ideal 9:00 P.M. Fox TV audience), straight blonde or brown hair (if not naturally straight, blow-dried twice weekly), tallish, but not supermodel tall, drinkers of cappuccino (morning) and vodka (evening), and eaters of . . . not much. They lived off Daddy and Mommy, though their stipends didn't cover designer shoes *and* rent *and* subscriptions to forty-eight beauty magazines. And, lastly, they were jobless, or, at the very least, on the verge of being jobless.

And not at all worried about the prospect.

Their signature personality statement was that they never worried. About anything: poverty, war, dinner, children, grandparents, the melting of the polar ice cap.

Clarissa made two Belvedere vodka tonics (filling hers, first, with maraschino cherries—she liked only red drinks) and walked toward her mother, putting her large gold head (a friend once remarked that it belonged on the face of a coin) on her mother's tiny shoulder.

"Please, Mama." The clincher.

Her mother patted her head; Clarissa knew she was home free—her mother would never let her down.

On the fateful day, the most important day of young(ish) Clarissa's life, her short, skinny, black-lunged mother totally bagged out on her. Clarissa told her mother to "screw herself sideways" and hung up on her, but not before they made early dinner plans at Mr. Chow; Clarissa was *les screwed*—she couldn't have lunch at the Ivy alone; nobody had lunch at the Ivy alone. The whole point was to go with someone else, then pay no attention to them; she'd stand out like a sore pseudo-AMW (actress/model/whatever). Clarissa careened through her Palm Pilot like an Indy racer, determined to find the one name who would combine three important qualities: 1. relative attractiveness (i.e., a mousier, perhaps chubbier version of herself); 2. relative popularity (i.e., well known, well respected, *not* popular with men); and 3. relative desperation (i.e., someone who, on an hour's notice, could meet at the Ivy).

Well into the *R*s, Clarissa struck lunch-companion gold. Roberta Raskin, she of the shiny red locks, the doe-eyes, the six-foot (but with extra poundage) frame—she would do. Roberta was a partner in a big P.R. firm, in her early thirties, desperate for male companionship, but dull as an undernourished houseplant. Normally, Clarissa couldn't stand Roberta—all the girl talked about was some half-brained, quarter-dicked, hair-plugged television director who dumped her *five* years ago; the man was married to an uglier version of Roberta with *two* equally ugly kids, for God's sake. However, Roberta was always good for a party invite; she represented young comic talent, and that talent was becoming big and Roberta always remembered Clarissa whenever there was a premiere, or a soiree, or a Vicodin-addicted bachelor.

Inviting Beige Roberta turned out to be a stroke of genius. She was there on time, securing the perfect table outside (next to a bevy of older, anesthetized blondes with diamond watches as dazzling as their husbands' bank accounts), where they could see and be seen, and waited patiently for Clarissa, who showed up twenty-two minutes late.

Roberta, in her brown Jil Sander uniform, looking very Third Reich– chic, had eaten through the bread basket and sucked the lemon out of her iced tea by the time Clarissa waltzed in, wearing tan leather pants, a silk and cashmere Gucci sweater, and a bright pink face from her acid peel.

"Sorry, sorry, sorry!" Clarissa squealed, simultaneously taking note of the restaurant's seating arrangements and silently cursing the dermatologist who told her her pigletlike complexion would be perfectly normal in a half hour; she'd have canceled her check had she ever bothered paying him—she made a mental note to stop blowing him on their twice-monthly dates.

"Not at all—I'm putting out fires." Roberta set aside her silver Nokia. "You look fabulous."

"You think?" Clarissa asked, her eyes widening. She wondered why she didn't call Roberta more often.

And then, jogging Clarissa's memory, Roberta sang out a refrain almost as familiar to Clarissa as Bing Crosby's "Christmas Song": "He took out another restraining order."

Clarissa remembered why she didn't ring; she sank into her chair and thirty minutes of Roberta's married-with-children director-ex saga. She would have rather sat through the entire sixth season of *Murder, She Wrote.*

Clarissa was on her third iced tea, trapped in the haze of Roberta's nonexistent love life, when the midnight blue Bentley drove up, forever dividing her (relatively short) life into "Before" and "After."

In Clarissa's unpublished but popular underground "Rules of Dating," there was a list of cars she preferred (to be seen in). She did not know the difference between a Rolls-Royce and a Bentley and did not care; both makes were at the top of her list, in a three-way tie with the Mercedes V12, convertible or hard top. Porsches, any insurance salesman with a bank loan could buy. BMW screamed anal retentive, very possibly wife-beater. Range Rover said the man was trying a wee bit too hard to appear sporty; Clarissa loathed "sporty." However, the inevitable problem with the Rolls or the Bentley is the person driving it would be: a. Old. Old like Hefner old. Old like Fernando Lamas (if he's still alive) old; or b. A Rap Star. Clarissa was not attracted to rap stars. To her, rap and opera were in the same category: She could not understand a word, and she didn't like the clothes. Also, as good as she was at lying, especially about her background, she had difficulty contending she was African American, though in college she once told a USC football player/biochem major with irresistible, shiny onyx skin that her grandmother (a smaller, meaner, Yiddish-speaking version of her mother) was Creole.

Clarissa let out a gasp.

"You're right, I can't understand why he left me," Roberta snorted wetly into her napkin; her chin quivered like a landed goldfish. Clarissa would have slapped her under any other circumstances.

"Aaron Mason."

"Who?" Roberta whined.

"Shoosh," Clarissa said, sounding just like her mother, God Rest Her Soul. Not that she was dead. Yet.

Aaron Mason got out of his Bentley and walked up the stairs, and every pair of eyes in the restaurant was locked and loaded. This guy was the real deal—tall, dark, handsome, yes—but also, rich.

He wouldn't last long in this town full of maneaters. Clarissa would have to move fast.

Then she noticed the limp. Clarissa took one look at that limp and knew beyond anything she had ever known before that Aaron was the man for her. She mentally scratched every other power cock off her list; trapping Aaron would require her full concentration. She'd start popping vitamin C and echinacea. She'd get a B_{12} shot tomorrow, and wondered about an early flu vaccine; she'd need all of her physical strength and mental vitality.

"Peepers," Clarissa said. She shot up and walked off, one foot directly in front of the other, heel-to-toe, giving her hips sway and her plan momentum.

She cut a swath through the murmuring, heaving, ringing lunch crowd and realized (*"plus de luck!"*) she had screwed one of Aaron's lunch mates outside her friend's Malibu Carbon beach house two summers ago. He drove a Range Rover with a spacious backseat and surprisingly supple leather interior; she'd escaped with nary a rug burn. She had filed this particular tryst under BAF, for "Backstage Access Fuck"; he had just signed a lead singer from a forgotten band.

"It's so all about connections," Clarissa congratulated herself, as she crossed in front of Aaron's table, Vera Wang wedding dresses and ivory Manolos dancing through her uncrowded head.

Oops.

She stopped, midpounce.

"First rule, Princess," Clarissa admonished herself. "To get a man's attention: Ignore him."

Clarissa scooted around Aaron's table, looking off in the distance as though Prince William himself were flashing her from inside the kitchen.

"Clarissa!" She made the fuzzy-looking man at Aaron's table wait as she tried to remember his name. She remembered body parts so much better than names.

"Clarissa!"

Cone-shaped penis, hairy shoulders—hairy like Dan Haggerty, Grizzly Adams hairy . . . Jamie, Joe, John, Ian, Kyle, her mind scurried like a hamster through her mental Rolodex.

"Maxi!" She turned and greeted the man as though the last time they had seen each other was on a train platform before the Great War. Tooth enamel–peeling enthusiasm was the only acceptable greeting mode in Hollywood, especially in the case of enemies. The more hated the person, the more enthusiastic the greeting.

Clarissa traded a triple-cheek air kiss (new to California, but all over the Paris scene, according to French *Vogue*) and thousands of hellos with Maxi, her largish but well-shaped melon ass hovering at eye-level with Aaron Mason ("Mrs. Aaron Mason, Ms. Alpert-Mason, Mrs. Clarissa Antonia Alpert Mason, no hyphen . . . ," the names danced circle jigs in her head); her butt swayed with her every breath, as though carrying on its own conversation with the chain-store heir. Clarissa, expert at the ignore-him-until-he-throws-something-sharp technique, burned holes into Maxi the Agent's brain with practiced interest, all the while feeling every flicker of an eyelash off of Aaron, every tap of a toe against his shoe. As Maxi rattled on about his semifamous clients, his third-row-center Laker season tickets (Clarissa to Clarissa: *"Not impressed—everyone knows the only seats that count are on the floor, okay."*), his St. Barts boating scare, and his weekly basketball game with Clooney and Damon, Clarissa weighed the pros and cons of ivory versus eggshell, Queen Anne silk against four-ply satin, emerald cut versus brilliant versus solitaire . . .

"Have you met Aaron?"

Finally, you hirsute fuckwad, Clarissa smiled to herself, the words she had been waiting . . .

"Hello," Clarissa lowered her voice and raised her eyebrows, but not so much as to wrinkle her forehead. She smiled, dazzling Aaron with her . . .

"You have something in your teeth," Aaron's Georgian accent came out as flat as her mother's breasts (before the lift).

Oh my God, Clarissa thought, smoothly running her tongue over her not-yet-paid-off wonders of cosmetic dentistry, *he's rude! That's so me!*

"Maybe I'm saving it for dessert," Clarissa said.

Aaron smiled.

He had dimples, one higher than the other. A slightly chipped front tooth (*childhood accident? college fisticuffs? beer bottle cap mishap?*). A crease between his dark, full eyebrows made him seem deep in a world of shallow-end swimmers. His dress was prep school gone wrong, and, Clarissa felt, irresponsible for a young man of his means: He wore no-name sunglasses with a shirt that was too big and a tie a pinch too small and a sportcoat that would have been rumpled, given a nice ironing. He looked like a very bad Catholic boy.

And then there were his shoes, which were not shoes at all, but boots. *Cowboy boots!*

Not only wrong—borderline unforgivable.

Aaron Mason was a lump of clay (albeit a gorgeous lump of clay), but in Clarissa's hands . . . Clarissa ran her eyes over Aaron with the same speed and intensity she employed as a hardline shopper at the Barneys Annual Warehouse Sale. And long before she had assembled information on the label and material and point of origin of Aaron Mason's slacks (and guessed about his underwear—she'd bet her fall wardrobe he was a boxer man), Clarissa blessed Larry the Waiter. With a tweak here, a fresh coat of paint there, a good tweezing (wax?), a haircut by Chris McMillan, here was the new "Mr. Alpert."

Two

Aaron's Turn

Aaron Mason stood outside the Ivy, waiting the fifteen seconds it would take to get his Bentley (given the twenty-dollar bill in the valet's hands) and asked Maxi Reese the question:

"So, who was the proud owner of that amazing ass?" It was the first ass Aaron had seen west of La Cienega that looked properly nourished.

"Clarissa Alpert. She's great, really great, you like her?" Reese said. He had a sheen across his forehead that Aaron longed to wipe off. "She knows everyone in town—everyone—you talk about hooked up, you talk about living in the eye of the vortex, if it's happening, she created it. Dated all the big names, knows where the bodies are buried, memorized the numbers on the bank statements. A dolly, a real kitty. You should go out with her, I'll hook you up."

Aaron had no idea what Maxi had said, but for what he wanted, he felt it was positive. He begged off: "I'll call her myself, thanks."

"Absolutely, I'll set it up," Maxi said.

"A number. I just need a number."

"I'll call you right away—hey, I've got seats this weekend, you like b-ball, of course you do," Maxi said. *Anything he could do,* Aaron thought, *to get in a favor that Aaron would have to repay.* In two weeks of living in Hollywood, Aaron Mason had received more gifts and favors and offers, monetary, physical, legal, and illegal, than in the whole of his existence. The obligatory gift was, apparently, as much a way of life as the false compliment.

"You look terrific, those shades are totally popping, awesome rideage!"

Maxi yelled as Aaron got into his car. "Think about Jessie Beal—she's a natural. You want me to set you up with her? She's a total dolly."

Aaron turned up the old southern rock CD on his $14,000 stereo system, drowning out Reese with a guitar lick by a long-dead ax man.

He was thinking about that ass.

Three

The Shindig

Planning a wedding is difficult; planning a wedding without the groom's knowledge is near impossible.

Immediately after meeting Aaron, with a requisite cheek-cheek air kiss to Roberta, Clarissa bagged lunch and headed to the valet, barely bothering to glance as a diner (obviously an SOB—south-of-the-border, i.e., Orange County tourist) said, loudly, "OmyGod—Britney and Justin!" and an underaged, overnourished, undersexed, overbleached twosome bounded up the stairs, cooing like partridges.

After indulging in a brief detour to one of eight Starbucks on the three-mile drive home for a Venti Cap (bone dry—much-needed energy with the fewest calories—she'd need to fit into a Vera Wang wedding dress, after all), Clarissa hustled into her apartment and grabbed the plastic notebook out of her underwear drawer, shaking the cheap Victoria's Secrets and expensive La Perlas from its pages.

Clarissa stared for a moment at its shiny Barbie Playhouse–pink cover, the rounded edges of the notebook showing age and erosion of hope; she could have sworn she heard choral music (and in fact, she did—the Wedding March, on a personally burned CD, was making the rounds on her Aiwa stereo). This was Clarissa's *wedding binder*, stuffed with magazine clippings of bridal gowns and tiaras, computerized and graded lists of hotels, wedding planners, florists, valet parkers, caterers, party rentals, photographers, videographers, officiates (civil? Jewish? Episcopalian? Buddhist? Clarissa had covered all the religious bases for her phantom groom), party favors, bridal salons, wedding cakes, and *Town and Country*'s ten best orchestral pieces for background music; she had been filling the yellowing plastic sleeves with bits and pieces of information, each torn sheet carrying the weight of a ruined talisman. And on every page there were handwritten mantras in the margins: *"Settling Is Not an Option"*, *"Zip Codes Matter"*, and *"Do Not Date in the 818"* or *"Flirting Is Aerobic."*

Clarissa thought about the times she'd pulled the notebook out before, and not just to run her fingers over the pages in smitten reverie, not to paste another article about bouquet fads. No. She'd been on a third, fourth date with someone—the Young Turk studio executive on the cover of *Los Angeles* magazine, the video director with the blue goattee embarking on his first feature, the club owner with dreadlocks and an advanced degree in Latin—and inevitably, she'd find herself before the pink notebook.

And then there'd be the break-up.

So why did this time feel different?

Clarissa's hands were shaking; she popped an out-of-date Xanax (compliments of best friend number one, Gravy—you'll meet her later) to calm herself and the side effects of the Venti Cap, then set to work like a rabbi performing a circumcision on his first grandson; her concentration was total.

She speed-dialed (the numbers were programmed into her cell phone; in planning a wedding, one needed to be time-effective) the Bel Air Hotel, the Beverly Hills Hotel, the Peninsula, and that one on the beach in Santa Monica with the gorgeous atrium but unfortunate Frank Lloyd Wrong architecture. Getting married in a hotel would save her worrying about the caterer and the wedding planner; Clarissa was nothing if not efficient.

All the while, she checked the list she'd started years ago:

WEDDING PLAN FOR ME, CLARISSA REGINA ALPERT

1. Immediately book hotel. Like, right NOW!

She informed the concierge at each hotel that she'd prefer several dates: June 20 was her first choice, mid-July her second, and her outside choice, if Aaron proved a challenge, September 2.

She was congratulated on her upcoming nuptials (she accepted the congratulations with concomitant grace for the occasion); however, June 20 was not available at any of the hotels—she settled for June 27 and waitlisted her first choice.

She gave her mother's credit card number as collateral; there was no sense in risking her own credit.

2. Book florist.

Tough call. Her absolute favorite, Ernest Buterwald, knew her well; she had attended his most recent birthday party at Mr. Chows and had insisted to her beaus for the last five years that his were the only bouquets she would accept. However, he was beyond expensive, and she had to take Aaron's feelings into consideration; she guessed he might have a problem with $2,000 table arrangements (and of course, he'd pay) and she could (hardly) blame him. She applauded herself on her newfound frugality and called Floridita instead, a hungry version of the Buterwald (his arrangements had not yet been featured for the *In Style* wedding edition), and booked both June 20 and June 27. When the Filipino florist asked for the name of the groom, she was stymied for a moment: Should she actually use Aaron's name?

She told him it was George Clooney.

Clarissa listened to him cry like a Sicilian mother at her firstborn son's wedding, and made him promise not to tell a living soul, not even his Thai boyfriend with the pierced nipples; everyone who read *People* magazine knew George savored his privacy, and he was famously averse to getting married.

Floridita understood perfectly.

He asked if there was any way the wedding could be featured in *In Style*. Clarissa said she'd think about it, but she'd, of course, have to get George's approval.

Clarissa hung up, satisfied with her ability to think fast under pressure; she had never even met Clooney (unless one counts the time she ran into him (i.e., waited for him) outside a Porta-Potti at the premiere for *Batman and Robin*), but no matter. Even if word got out, Clarissa surmised, Aaron would only become more intrigued.

She looked down her list: music, wedding dress, bridesmaids' dresses, party favors (matchbooks, small silver frames, tiny floral bouquets). Wedding planning was a difficult enterprise; Clarissa would need support.

Clarissa thought that maybe it was time to tell her mother that her only daughter was soon to be married to a very rich, very on-the-rise, very cute—then she remembered she didn't actually have Aaron's phone number. Clarissa made a note to track it down.

Clarissa and her mother sat at the bridal section on the second floor at Barneys in Beverly Hills and watched as models sashayed down the runway in the latest bridal fashions. Clarissa still hadn't told her mother why they were attending the fashion show; she felt it was best to break the good news to her over lunch, after her mother was primed like a pig to slaughter by these visions in eggshell, the palest mint green, and ballerina slipper pink.

"Ju crazy," her mother announced, after ordering a beet and goat cheese salad with no onions, no goat cheese, no dressing, and no beets.

"I am not crazy, mother," Clarissa waved at a table of gaggling pregnant girls fighting over a plate of French fries like pigeons at a McDonald's parking lot. A year ago, hell, *six months* ago, the sight would have sickened her. Clarissa would have scoffed at the idea of giving up her life to a baby, but now it was not only chic—Madonna had singlehandedly deemed it so—it was *time.* Clarissa's eggs were twenty-eight (thirty-one) years old. Plus, there were all those cool, new pregnancy fashions to consider . . .

Clarissa smiled at the pregnant women and hoped soon, God willing, that would be her.

"I wish you'd stop saying that. It's almost like you don't believe in me."

"Wha'?" Her mother recoiled, her hazel eyes flashing hurt brightly, like the glass stones at the bottom of Clarissa's fishtank—the tank that had no fish.

"Don't cry."

"I believe in you (*ju*), my daughter. When you were five years old, you (*ditto above*) said you would be president."

Why oh why did her mother always bring up this stupid anecdote. Clarissa only said that because a little boy she had a crush on had said *he* wanted to be president. *Duh!*

"Mommy, you know I'm not the ambitious type."

The waiter brought the salad with nothing on it. He placed it before Clarissa—

"Am I screaming *eating disorder*?"

He moved it over and put the cheeseburger with potato salad on the side in front of Clarissa.

"Mommy, I need your help. You are an enormous pain in my shapely ass, but you have exquisite taste."

Her mother looked at the salad, a jeweler checking a suspicious diamond.

"Estupido."

She shoved the salad away. Clarissa looked at it; it bore the unmistakable sheen of olive oil.

"Eat, Mother."

"Eh." Her mother sipped her iced tea. Clarissa bit into her cheeseburger. The sensation was like biting into a night of hang-from-the-chandelier sex.

"Plus, you could help me lose a few pounds before the wedding."

Her mother perked up.

"A *few* pounds. I'll go hiking with you—maybe even do that thing, that—"

Clarissa moved her hands slowly in the air. The pregnant girls waved again, their arms packed into their black cashmere sweaters like boudin sausages. Clarissa thought about another advantage to getting pregnant: She could eat and eat and eat. Aaron seemed the type to want a healthy baby.

"Tai chi."

"Right, that China thing," Clarissa said (without the slightest attempt at politically correct terminology).

Her mother picked at her salad. Judging from the number of chews she took (twenty-four) with each bite, she was evidently feeling better. Any more chews, she was thinking too much; any fewer, she was anxious.

"So, you'll help me?"

"When do I meet this boy?" She said "this" like "thees." Clarissa fought the urge to stick a fork through her tiny, baby sparrow–like throat.

"Oh, mother." Clarissa shook her head. Sometimes her mother was more stupid than that little dog she carried with her all the time before it jumped out of her mother's old Mercedes convertible going after a tennis ball.

Clarissa had been rolled up into the teeny backseat like a pillbug at the time; in a fit of rage, she accidentally threw the ball onto Olympic Boulevard during rush hour traffic. How was she to know Adolfo would go after it? With the help of Manolo, her therapist, she'd put the guilt behind her. After all, she was the one who'd missed her Saturday 10:35 A.M. appointment with Anastasia, the Beverly Hills Eyebrow Queen.

"*I've* barely met him," Clarissa admitted, between bites.

Clarissa's next move was getting Aaron to call her. For someone with her experience, this was easy enough: She would have a be-all, end-all, if-you're-not-there-you're-in-rehab-or-nobody party. And not invite him.

It worked like a charm. No sooner was she halfway through the guest list when "Sasquatch," the hairy-backed agent, called.

"Maxi Reese on the line for Clarissa Alpert," his assistant squeaked; he sounded as though he were barely out of his school uniform.

"Speaking," Clarissa said. She smiled to herself, gave herself a mental pat on the back and the promise of a hot fudge sundae at Morton's.

"Clarissa . . ."

"Maxi."

"You're having a party."

"I am."

"Where's the love?"

"What do you mean? I was just about to invite you—"

"Can I bring someone?"

"Only if she's a model or an actress. This is not a party for ugly girls unless they're fantastically successful or famous and/or can help my career."

"You have a career?"

"I won't rule out the possibility."

"Aaron Mason."

"Who?" Clarissa asked. If she were smiling any harder, her face would've split.

"You met him the other day. Kind of an FOB, a real country boy, but rolling in the big green."

Fresh Off the Boat. "Oh, right. Him." Clarissa sounded adequately bored.

"So, I'll bring him, then—"

"You really want to?" Clarissa tried to convey a pout. "He seems, I don't know, troubled."

"You don't like him."

"He wears boots."

"C'mon, be nice. He's a foreigner." In L.A., anyone born between California and New York was considered foreign. "He's not familiar with our customs. I want to show him around—he doesn't know too many people. And he's a sweetheart."

"You need his money," Clarissa said.

"No. Maybe. Independent financing. You never know."

"Oh, all right, bring the FOB, just tell him the look is Rodeo, not rodeo," she said, with her most charitable tone.

Maxi snorted and Clarissa hung up and screamed so loud the mean Persian cat with one blue eye, one green, leapt in fear from the top of the red velvet couch, skidding onto the marble floor, emptying out its anal sacs and filling Clarissa's living room with a fragrance that was a cross between a hazardous waste dump and decade-old Easter eggs.

Clarissa reminded herself to take the cat to the pound; she didn't even like cats but she thought the idiotic thing looked nice against her couch, its white fur standing out against the red velvet made her living room look like a *Martha Stewart Living* cover.

On second thought, Clarissa thought, picking white hairs from her pillows, the cat was useful. If Aaron loved cats, all the better; if he didn't, in a show of loyalty after their engagement, she'd give the cat away.

Clarissa loved a win-win situation.

There were about a hundred and ten kinds of fucks. At a drunken girls' night out at the home of a budding socialite and her French director/repeat offender cheater fiancé, Clarissa and a group of friends (as in "she's my friend, but I don't like her"), energized by sugarless Gummi Bears and sugary Cosmopolitans, made a lengthy list of all the different types of fucks to be found in this world.

1. Lust Fuck. Totally obvious: You meet at a bar, you like what you see, you're drunk, he's drunk, you lie to each other about your a. age, b. salary, c. CDS (current disease status), you barely make it home (or, in some cases, out of the front seat of your car).

   The problem with Lust Fuck is the aftermath: mutual embarrassment and concomitant nausea. The embarrassment, if one is unlucky enough to actually run in the same circles as the lust fuckee, can last, oh, the lifetime of the average Great Dane: eight years. The nausea clears up by the next afternoon—sooner if one starts the day with a Bloody Mary or a screaming phone call from the fuckee's wife/girlfriend or, God forbid, mother.
2. Love Fuck. Okay, maybe you've waited the requisite three dates (in one case, Clarissa actually waited three *weeks*—the producer she was dating talked about their future together, talked about romance, wanted their first time to be "special"—he had a "nickel dick," the size of an infant's, preferred to do it only from behind, and wanted Clarissa to have a breast reduction—he liked only flat-chested women. Clarissa ran like a tourist at Pamploma.); you've discussed favorite foods (lobster, invariably); favorite movie scenes (uh, *Sleepless in Seattle,* Empire State Building, *Jerry Maguire, "You had me at . . ."*); favorite TV shows from the seventies (*Brady Bunch*) and favorite hit songs from the eighties (for Clarissa, anything by Duran, Duran, WHAM!, or Spandau Ballet).

   Then comes the moment. He pays the bill, hopefully with a gold card, if not platinum. ("Friendship is free, love costs," Clarissa often counseled.) He looks at you, giving you those puppy dog eyes that now seem deep and sensitive but in six months will morph into the realm of the shallow and defeated. And he says, "You want to . . . ," and you say, "Sure." And the sex is really good, not great, a B+ on the Simon England scale (the best lay you ever had, twelfth grade antiprom rave), and it doesn't matter that that's the best it will be, because you're already in love—even though neither of you will say the words out loud for months to come, or even ever—there is a sweetness to the night and the moment and, for once, you do not feel alone.

Oh. If you're really lucky—really, really lucky—there is laughter, unmitigated joy, the property of small children. And this laughter will see you through your first fight, your first deception, your first anniversary.

Clarissa and her friends agreed that the Love Fuck is few and far between, especially in Los Angeles, where the men are a. gay, b. pretending not to be gay, but, by the way . . . gay, c. married but, incidentally, gay, or d. asexual, in which case the girls would much rather hang out with gay. However, several of Clarissa's friends could remember the Love Fuck, back in high school or in junior high for the more "advanced" among them, usually a first love. Usually a Simon England.

Clarissa had deleted Simon (diagnosed ADD since the sixth grade; she'd loved that about him) from her Palm Pilot and her memory banks years ago, but every once in a while his polished facade would pop up in her brain like a tin can in the vast, empty Pacific, tormenting her with his lopsided grin, the kind found only in Labrador retrievers and $20-million action stars. She'd lost contact with Simon after their third break-up—they were in their early twenties then, callow graduates out of USC (Clarissa double-majored: Clothes and Cosmetics/Product), and they'd been an item, the couple to count on, since their senior year at Beverly Park High. She had broken up with Simon the first two times (first time: boredom; second time: an all-state running back), and then, the third time, he'd broken up with her. Clarissa never forgave him for the humiliation. He'd said, "And I quote," Clarissa told her friends, "'I don't think we're good for each other.'"

"Like, that's a bad thing," Clarissa had said at the time.

Now Simon was a big A & R guy at a major record company, dating people like Gwen Stefani and that new Latina *sensacione,* and every time Clarissa read his name (accidentally, of course) in *People* or *In Style* or *Us* or, say, any obscure trade publication, she felt disgust, followed closely by the tiniest stab of sadness. After several of these mishaps, Clarissa made her mother go through every magazine in the house every single month to rip out any mention of Simon the Egregious.

God, how she hated him.

Other fucks included:

3. Curiosity Fuck: As in "I wonder what that totally inappropriate guy would be like in bed." The Curiosity Fuck, for the uninitiated, differed from the Novelty Fuck in that the Novelty Fuck may or may not include the element of curiosity.
4. Boredom Fuck: "Do I watch the *Friends* episode where David Schwimmer gets caught in the leather pants for the eighth time, or do I fuck that totally inappropriate guy?"
5. Desperation Fuck: "It's been six months, and if I don't get laid in the next twenty minutes (by that totally inappropriate guy), I will actually let my mother fix me up with her best friend's amoebic son."

The fuck list goes on, from the Adventure Fuck (with the totally inappropriate guy who surfs fifty-foot waves off Baja and races up mountains wearing a Nokia and a buckknife) all the way to the Zamboni, Zionist, and Zucchini Fucks, involving hockey, religious fervor, and green vegetables.

Clarissa wondered what manner of category fuck Aaron would best embody. Not love, nor lust. Not boredom (they had the rest of their lives for that one). Oh yes, Clarissa nodded, the good old standby, Intentional Fuck, was raising its time-honored head. Clarissa was the master of the Intentional Fuck, the deliberate, willful, calculated sex act that concealed an ulterior motive, whether it was an invitation to a trip to

Mick "Sexy Grampa" Jagger's private Caribbean island or, in this case, the recitation of the marriage vows.

Sex with Aaron would start out as the Intentional Fuck, but with any luck, Aaron would end up where, like the uncharted wilderness, only one man had been before, the Love Fuck. Clarissa closed her eyes—the elusive Love Fuck—ingredients: bare skin, bold eye contact, hands clasped, three words spoken in tandem . . . the future almost too sweet to taste.

She wanted it. Again.

Clarissa opened her eyes and ran down a list of caterers for the wedding with her French-manicured index finger; she had a lot of phone calls to make and very little time. Clarissa was finding that planning a wedding was a thankless job.

The bronze clock held up by two naked bronze men posted 11:05; Aaron had still not shown up to the party. Sasquatch was there, holding court on an outside deck with a trio of teenage starlets following the yellow brick road to the WB Thursday night line-up. Sasquatch was known for his roster of young up-and-coming "talent"; everyone knew he was the first stop on the road to the briefest of celebrity shelf life.

Clarissa looked across the room at him and wished an immediate "spittle death" upon him—a cocaine-induced heart attack right on Tony B.'s deck. She pictured his tongue lolling to one side as his body pitched forward, then backward in his final dance.

She smiled.

Tony B. pinched her ass, bound in a thousand dollars worth of Gucci black leather. She hoped he didn't feel the giant tag that cut into her butt crack (making the act of sitting an impossibility).

"*Où es le* Fresh Prince?" Tony B. said. "Or should I say, Fresh Meat?" and hurled a biting smile her way. Tony B. was Clarissa's best friend in high school, the guy with the poorest parents (they lived in a fifties-style stucco apartment building, which they managed for shelter and a pittance) and most ingratiating personality.

He'd made it big in a dot.com three years ago; he'd come up with an idea to provide college students with term papers and accurate tests—

for a price. Tony B.'s plan was *brill*—with minor league start-up money from a dead grandma, he paid USC and UCLA students for their papers, and then, with the help of an elaborate e-mail system, he'd expanded his empire through the Midwest—University of Michigan, University of Chicago—to University of Pennsylvania and, finally, the East Coast—Harvard, Yale, Princeton, and it was all, incredibly, legal.

Now, Tony B. was rich, richer than anyone he'd grown up with. So rich, he no longer used his last name, which embarrassed him with its conspicuous ethnicity; he'd made fuck-you money, in the neighborhood of a telephone number (that is, high seven figures), a neighborhood anyone would like to live in.

"Fuck you with a brass instrument, and get me another drink."

"The party's fresh, Princess, but I fear someone just defiled my Frette sheets."

Tony B. always called Clarissa "Princess"—she loved him for that, and for the fact that he never *never* revealed her real age.

For it would reveal his, and being a media wonder boy was a substantial part of his appeal to the baby boom business world, the men and women who followed him around like a trail of newborn ducks after their mother.

"Why is he not here yet?" Clarissa practically kicked the floor.

Tony B. sniffed. "Maybe the *Variety* cover boy's not attending."

"Aaron wouldn't stand me up," Clarissa replied. "He's intrigued."

"Of course he is. He's the only man in town you haven't bunged," Tony B. said. "No one likes being out of the loop in our cozy little village." The deejay cranked Moby up to plaster-cracking volume; the floor was vibrating. Clarissa noticed a group of girls standing in a circle, swaying to the music in a raw, self-conscious display of young adolescence.

"When did you open a day care center?" Clarissa was not amused by the younger generation of females. They reminded her that she was a. fatter than they were, b. older than they were, c. not married, and d. hungry.

"Why do PYTs make me want to scarf peanut butter cups?" she asked.

"Bitter aftertaste . . . ," Tony B. admonished, as his gaze lolled on a gilded (gold-painted) bodybuilder hired to strike poses, wearing a thong and a sigh. Tony B. had a Golden Boy at every shindig—he called them the perfect party favor.

"Are you still here?" Clarissa asked, above the music.

"Sorry. I'm not myself—Ooh. Looky what the cat just blew in," Tony B. grinned, as Clarissa followed his eyes. "Your cute-as-a-button past has caught up with you."

Simon was here; on his arm was a famous blonde thing with the skin of someone just born with it. In the background, partygoers screamed as Tommy Lee powered a boat with Motley Crüe's most talented "member" on the big-screen TV.

"Simon?" Clarissa whined, "Que the fuck is he doing here?"

"I invited him," Tony B. replied. "It's not a party unless there's a significant level of discomfort." He sipped at his pink champagne cocktail, nonchalant. "Besides, he and I like each other, remember? We came this close to a quasihomosexual experience in senior year." He pinched his fingers together. Clarissa admired the sheen of his nails. Tony B. was always perfectly manicured.

"You know how nature abhors a vacuum?" she said.

"Oh. You know you don't hate me."

"I know, I love you," Clarissa sighed. She felt Simon's presence billowing up behind her like a big, fat moon—Clarissa was starting to panic.

"Tony. How do I look?"

"Bardot, 1956."

"I look old."

"No."

"Truth."

"Muy Barbarella."

"I have a gray hair."

"We'll shoot it."

"Clarissa?" the voice said, reaching out of the past like a theater hook, grabbing her by the throat and off the stage, her stage, her party.

"Simon."

Clarissa turned and looked at him. *Fuck him, he'd never looked better,* she thought. Even down to his shoes—this season's Prada loafers, in chocolate, a brave, almost brazen choice. Any man who bought Prada shoes bought them in one of three colors—black, jet black, and ebony. Except, of course, Simon.

And of course, his shirt, the latest Armani. *Wait,* Clarissa thought, *there's a weakness—his stomach is a little soft—or is it the lay of the fabric?*

She hugged Simon, curving her arm around his waist like a curious serpent. Simon had gained weight. Clarissa knew that he knew that she noticed; he knew that she noticed *everything.*

Somehow, the little extra flesh made him even more appealing. More vulnerable.

"You look lovely, you really do," Simon said, his voice still deep, still with the English accent, not lost in the fifteen years he'd been in Los Angeles. *Simon clung on to that accent like a lifeboat,* Clarissa thought, smiling at the famous blonde thing. Simon's handicap was that he could barely read; dyslexia had first been an embarrassment to him; now, it was a calling card.

"This is Penelope," Simon stated the obvious.

"Stating the obvious, Simon." Clarissa smiled and shook Penelope's tiny, fetuslike hand, covered with thumb rings and henna tattoos. The blonde thing with one name smiled back with all the warmth of an eel awakened from a deep, watery slumber.

"Would you two like a drink?" Clarissa slipped into hostess mode like a swimmer into a still pool.

"I don't drink," the blonde thing said.

Ugh, Clarissa thought to herself. *A twelve-stepper already, and can't be more than eighteen, nineteen—what is there to look forward to?*

"Perrier and lime, it is," Clarissa replied, "And Simon, one Kir Royale coming right up." And then she was gone, leaving Tony B. to deal with the detritus of the conversation.

If Clarissa had turned, she would've seen Simon staring after her, memory merging with the present, a confusion of desire and caution: *Clarissa had remembered his favorite drink. Clarissa still cared.*

However, she didn't look back.

Clarissa reached the bar after waging battle through the perfumed throngs, taking in each compliment thrown her way with the ease of the professionally lauded; the only thing that threw her was the (subtly overheard) conversation between several PYTs who could not have been over fourteen, even on their fake IDs. They stood with their bony arms on their nonexistent hips, looking ever so geometric, mouths pouty from sprouting hormones, skin dewy from early age and early dermatology visits, hair and nails shiny from the salon. They were already, Clarissa surmised, in training by their mothers (who looked like their jaded, slightly older sisters) to take over Clarissa's job, well, not job—*place.*

And they could not yet (legally) drive.

"I polish up the hood for ten, then I cir-cu-late the ball-age—," said PYT #1. "I don't leave anything on the table."

"Ugh—Waaaaaay time-consuming, Tiff," PYT #2 said. "I work it fast and furious. I pretend I'm hydroplaning through the racks for Tuleh at the Fred Segal sale."

"Spit?" the third one said.

"Spit," said the fourth.

"Spit."

"Swallow," said PYT #1. "Pure protein, zero carbs. It's totally Zone."

These girls, these young, sweet, barely unfolded flowers, were discussing blow jobs. Clarissa froze for a moment, reeling from two unwelcome revelations: 1. Girls who should have been satisfied with getting their braces off were discussing the finer points of oral sex, and 2. They were, apparently, better at it than she was.

Oh, was her clock *ticking*.

Ticking wasn't the right word. Her biological clock sounded like it was breaking down large, solid objects.

"Are any of you virgins?" she turned, asking the shiny-haired Lolitas. Three of the four nodded. "Of course," said the one whose name was: a. Tiffany; b. Brandy; c. Dakota; or d. Ashley. "How is that possible?" Clarissa asked. She was going down that road, she might as well drive on, despite the potholes.

"We only do anal," stated the other Brandy, in an annoyed, matter-of-fact tone.

"Passionfruit-ini," Clarissa said to the bartender, upon arrival; it was a plea. That would be number . . . four?

"Please?" the cheeky bartender implored. Clarissa sized him up like a jockey with a horse at the Kentucky Derby. Even with his curly gold locks and brown eyes, Clarissa figured he'd not quite qualify for Lust Fuck—maybe because her mind was elsewhere.

"Curiosity Fuck," Clarissa stated.

"Excuse me?" the bartender asked.

"Perrier and lime," Clarissa replied; she couldn't be bothered to explain her whole theory of life.

"Curiosity Fuck," a voice, confident and amused, said behind her. "Now that sounds damn intriguing."

Clarissa almost turned around, stopping herself at the last second; her inner voice (tonight, after a few drinks, it sounded like Natasha from the *Rocky and Bullwinkle* cartoon) saving her once again, saying, *"Don't turn around, dahlink. Just peek over your shoulder. SLOWLY."*

Which she did.

Standing there was Aaron Mason, her future husband. Alone. More handsome than she remembered.

Or maybe she was just more drunk.

"You weren't meant to hear that, obviously," Clarissa said. She reached over and straightened his tie. Again with the Catholic schoolboy outfit. And still with the boots.

"Oh, I think I was, darlin'." Aaron replied.

"Your drinks," the bartender interrupted, with the Perrier with lime and the Kir Royale; Clarissa almost bit the Curiosity Fuck's hand off.

"I know this is your party, and all," Aaron said, "but it looks like a sorry bunch of losers, pardon my French."

"'Losers' is not a French word. I know this, because I took four years of it in high school and am well equipped to locate a restroom at the Eiffel Tower," Clarissa said.

"I'm duly impressed," he said, bowing.

"It's taken you long enough," Clarissa shot back, smiling. "If you'll excuse me, I have to give my boy—my ex- . . . I have to give someone their drink."

"A Kir? Isn't that a girl's drink?"

"Hardly, Marlboro Man," Clarissa said. "Oh, I'm sorry to report we have no 'Bud' on hand—"

"Clarissa. My car is right outside the door. The motor's running."

"You call that a car? I call it a penis extension," Clarissa said, "Besides, I'm not leaving—I'm the hostess."

"And I'm the guest of honor."

"You're *what*?"

"C'mon, darlin'," Aaron put his arm around her waist.

"No . . . I can't . . . I'm not going anywhere." Clarissa was perturbed; the situation had spun out of her control.

Aaron grabbed the two drinks. "Where do I drop these?" Clarissa pointed toward Simon and the blondie. Aaron turned and walked toward them as Clarissa followed.

"Your drinks," Aaron said. He handed the Perrier to Penelope and the Kir to Simon, who accepted it with a cemented-on smile.

"My word," Tony B. said, sounding like a southern belle gone wrong.

"Aaron Mason, at your service," Aaron shook Tony B.'s and Simon's hands like a Republican at the 2000 Convention. He bowed his head toward Penelope.

"Anyone else feeling flush?" Tony B. said.

"Mr. B.," Aaron said, "this is a swell party, but I'm afraid I have to take Clarissa home. She's been a very bad girl, and it's past her curfew."

"My word," Tony B. repeated.

Clarissa shrugged and searched for a proper Clarissaism, finding none. Her eyes met Simon's briefly—but his emotions were hidden behind a wall of good manners.

And with that, Aaron took her hand, and they walked out of the party and into their future.

Four
The Wedding Party

Clarissa had four girlfriends in her inner circle—what she liked to call her "Star Chamber." She had named her group (also known in [less] certain circles as the "pussy posse") after a late-night, vanilla–Häagen-Dazs–powered viewing of the gorgeously bad Michael Douglas movie in which scowling, black-cloaked vigilante judges hunted down scowling, slippery criminals. The comparisons were obvious: Clarissa's girl gang lived in black stretch pants, were judgmental, and hunted down whatever (shoe, belt, nail polish) or whoever (cute guy, rich guy, unavailable guy) interested them.

Rules were essential to the Star Chamber—many of which went back as far as the fourth grade: *No Overalls (modified to Jeans) on Tuesday . . . No Getting Drunk on Monday Nights . . . No Visible Panty Lines . . . and No Scamming on Each Other's Boyfriends or any boy declared O.L. (Off Limits).*

When they got together, the seating arrangements were as specific as a Donald Trump prenup. Alexandra Hargrave, whom Clarissa considered her oldest (and she was, thankfully, one week older than Clarissa) and best friend, sat immediately to her right (her best side). An actress who went to business school for exactly one minute before she took up jewelry-making, Gravy, as everyone had called her since their preschool days at La Lycée, a tony Frenchish school in West Los Angeles, was the fifth daughter of an ancient, famous Beverly Hills plastic surgeon (was there any other kind?) who, as a seventeenth birthday gift, had bestowed upon his daughter a precarious pair of D-cup breasts. Dr. Hargrave was currently on his fourth wife; he'd recently given the same breasts to his sixteen-year-old stepdaughter. Five years ago, Gravy had the attention-grabbing domes removed—she called them "Las Pamelas," after the Star Chamber idol, Pamela Anderson—and had them replaced with her current "Courtneys," after Courtney Cox, also a Star Chamber idol—B-cup, low-key, under-the-radar hooters.

Gravy's favorite word was "bullshit."

Her second favorite word was "cunt."

Her third favorite word was "pharmaceuticals." As Gravy would say, "Some of my closest friends are pharmaceuticals." Paxil, Wellbutrin, Xanax, Valium, Clonopin, and Vicodin had all enjoyed extended stays at the Hargrave medicine cabinet.

Gravy, with a body like Olive Oyl and "statement" (i.e., *frizzy*) hair, was the smartest of the group; she could remember any phone number, spell any word, especially if it were medicinal, and she knew several languages, though she rarely spoke any except Rodeo-ese: Beverly Hills English.

Jennifer Ellenbach was Clarissa's second best friend; she sat on Clarissa's left (less telegenic) side: the Marie Osmond of the Chamber, Jennifer was the girlfriend every girlfriend needs: Jen would agree with anything any of the Star Chamber said at any time, and, more important, she dished out compliments like a Jewish mother at a bar mitzvah. Clarissa could be as fat as a blue-ribbon hog at a 4-H contest and Jennifer would insist she could be Kate Moss' less-zaftig twin.

In her spare time, Jennifer, who had the big brown eyes and long lashes of a young Robert Downey, Jr. (pre-waking-up-in-neighbor's-crib days), enjoyed wrapping gifts, writing upbeat letters with circles over her *i*'s to Death Row inmates, and baking dog biscuits for her pugs, otherwise known by the Star Chamber (without Jen's knowledge) as the Ugliest Fucking Dogs on Earth. She was, also, the proud owner of an extensive rubber ducky collection—it was the Star Chamber's darkest secret.

Though the Star Chamber would rip its own members front to back at the drop of a fake eyelash, Jen-E. was untouchable; the Star Chamber would not fuck with unconditional love.

Jen was a "soft center."

Polo Parker was named by her mother (a former model and heroin "survivor," now megahyper drug counselor), after the Madison Avenue label, not the sport; Polo was the Star Chamber Goddess. She was

Vogue-insert beautiful and a known accessories whore (examples: a. She named her shoes after members of the Royal Family; b. owned twenty-three "blue" purses—navy, not-quite navy, shade-beyond navy, azure, midnight, midnight sky, sky blue, etc.). At 5′4″, she was four inches and light-years under the supermodel barre, but with the locks of a Hindu deity, green eyes, and skin like a percent cappuccino, the worst one could say about her looks (and the Star Chamber was always on the hunt for the worst) was that, under stress, her thighs could become . . . even thinner. Polo was *Playboy*'s Miss May in some year in the early nineties—only one cup size away from being Centerfold of the Year. The Star Chamber often would hold Polo out as Male Bait during a night on the town—if you threw her out in a crowd, she'd always come back with four or five bites.

Alas, what the good Lord giveth, bad genes taketh away; Polo was not the healthiest specimen. She was constantly fighting the flu or a cold or that most dreaded of female companions, the yeast infection ("The Beastie Yeasties," as the Chamber referred to the affliction).

"Truth. Do I smell like sourdough?" was often the first question she asked at a Star Chamber event.

Clarissa had given her a nickname: "Polio."

Polo would squeeze in next to Gravy, her closest ally—incredibly, the one with the most time and patience to deal with her "issues." Clarissa had a theory that Gravy only had patience for Polo in order to, one day, get her into bed; Clarissa believed Gravy would one day admit she preferred to eat at the "Y."

Clarissa had a ton of theories—she thought of herself as the guru of the Star Chamber—the Oprah of the skin-deep set. Point of fact: Clarissa was the backbone of operations for the Star Chamber: Without Clarissa, the planner, the organizer, the glue, this group would not exist.

The fifth (wheel) of the group was also the scariest: Suzee Chambers was the Freddy Kreuger of the Star Chamber. Everyone in the Star Chamber disliked Suzee, and as an added plus, they were also afraid of her. Suzee had a tongue more like a saber than a serpent's tooth—it could arbitrarily make sashimi of opponent or friend. But keeping Suzee in the group kept Clarissa's mind sharp; maneuvering around Suzee and her evil was like playing chess with Kasparov.

There had been a vote once, many years ago, when the earth was cooling and Mark Goodman was the "hot" VJ, as to whether Suzee should be allowed to stay in the Star Chamber. This was after a gruesome incident regarding someone's boyfriend and a Love's Baby Soft–perfumed mash note. The votes were cast, in secret (*right!*), and the votes were tied. The truth was, each of the girls had a soft spot for Suzee; Clarissa would never forget that it was Suzee who had showed her true kindness with a new Sean Cassidy T-shirt when her parents separated the first time.

Also, Suzee loaned out designer shoes, a key aspect of enduring friendship.

Clarissa likened Suzee to a candied peel, the sugared lemon or orange peel half-covered with dark chocolate that one ate when desperate (like, starving to death at base camp on K2 or way PMSing). Bitter on the outside, slightly less bitter on the inside.

The Star Chamber's ages ranged from twenty-eight to twenty-eight (thirty-one); they were the last vestige of the Generation Xers, suckled at the MTV teat, reared on designer labels, raised by boomers who resisted growing up themselves. Theirs were mothers who, thanks to the gym, their trainers, plastic surgeons, dermatologists, vigilant dieting, and disposable income, competed on an even playing field for the attentions of their daughters' boyfriends; their divorced fathers, able to afford both sports cars and new hair, dated their best friends. The Gen-X progeny/offspring was half a generation behind technology. Though they chattered into individually colored Nokias, duly clipped on their Blackberrys in the A.M., toted designer Palms with clever, furry covers, and never sent an actual posted letter in their lives, they were not completely in sync with the true computer generation, the boys and girls of Generation Y. Cloaked in "names," hiding behind fake boobs and altered noses and hair dyed so often since their early years they could not accurately guess the color they were born with, there was no reason for these girls to be comfortable with themselves; they did not know who "themselves" were. But the Star Chamber did manage to intuit, somewhere inside their prepackaged facades, that even at their relatively young age(s), they were obsolete.

Gravy took one look at Clarissa at the Star Chamber postparty wrap-up (breakfast at the Polo Lounge—so out of favor, it emerged, suddenly, white hot) and said one word:

"As someone with an advanced degree, I can tell you that your little fairy tale reeks of bullshit."

Granted, her expression contained more than one word, but Clarissa heard only the important one.

"This is me, Clarissa Regina Alpert, begging to differ," Clarissa protested. "Aaron walked—no, strode—into the party, took me by the hand, dragged me off—"

" . . . like a caveman. A cro magnon?" Gravy said, "I didn't see a thing. Therefore, it never happened."

"You were drunk."

"Of course I was drunk." Gravy was *always* drunk at a party. "That doesn't mean my senses were impaired."

"Clar, that's so *Officer and a Gentleman,*" Jenny volunteered. "But you're the un–Debra Winger, and Aaron's even more handsome than Richard Gere. You two look perfect together."

"What color hair does Aaron have, Jen?" Gravy asked.

"Oh, like, a light brown—sort of blondish."

"Jet black," Gravy said.

"You still read the trades, Gravy?" Clarissa asked.

"See, I totally saw him," Jenny replied, good-naturedly. "He looks like he really likes you, Clarissa."

Clarissa thought Jenny might start crying.

"Am I late?" Polio turned up, looking like "Gwyneth Who?" in bell-bottomed yoga tights and a Miu Miu tank. Worse than her phenomenal legs were the breasts—smaller than Clarissa's twins but as perky as a ray of fucking sunshine through a raincloud.

"Coffee?" the waiter asked.

"No, I don't do caffeine. Tea, green tea," Polio said.

"Hi, Sweetie," Gravy said. "You're peaked." Gravy put her hand on Polo's forehead. Clarissa performed an eye roll.

"What's wrong this time?" Clarissa asked. She tried to sound annoyed, her specialty, but really, she was curious. Polio always had some interesting, exotic-sounding malaise.

"My new holistic doctor said no caffeine, no dairy, no alcohol, no sugar, no wheat, and no sex," Polio said. "We're going to dinner at Giorgio's this Saturday."

"But, Polo . . . you won't be able to eat the orrichiette, or drink the Pinot Grigio," Jen offered up the obvious. "He must be really cute—you don't give up simple carbs and alcohol for ugly."

"No hanger appeal," Polo replied, "but I want to try him on, anyway. He could be an accessories sponsor." A "sponsor" was a man who would buy expensive things for Polo.

"Dumb fuck," Gravy said. "You can't go out with one of your doctors again. Doctors are insane, that's why they're doctors." They all shuddered, having just gotten over the last M.D.—a tiny obstetrician who kept calling Polio "Mommy" in bed.

"I'm getting married," Clarissa announced. Why not? If she waited for a lull in the conversation, she'd grow whiskers out of her ears.

"You've found Mr. Alpert?" Polo asked, rubbing her tiny nose.

"As an attorney, I can tell you're lying," said Gravy.

"You're not an attorney, you went to business school for exactly one minute," Clarissa continued. "And, whatever, it's true—Aaron just doesn't know it yet."

"Should we have a special 'Get to Know You' dinner?" Jennifer asked.

The girls just looked at Jennifer.

"Clarissa Alpert," Gravy declared, "you are certifiable," pouring a pint of maple syrup on her French toast. Like half of the *Cosmo* readership, Gravy was a recovering anorexic, making up for twenty-two years of intense calorie counting; she once told Clarissa the calorie count of a meal of six ounces of fried reindeer butt cheek, in case she ever made a trip to Reykjavik. Clarissa was convinced Gravy was some sort of mad genius, like the girl behind the J. Crew catalogs.

"I so admire your determination," Jenny said.

"She's as ambitious as Hitler," Gravy said.

"So I guess you don't want to be the maid of honor?" Clarissa said to Gravy.

"Oh my God," she replied, her eyes welling up in a bout with sincerity. "Really? I've never even been a bridesmaid."

"That's because none of us are married," Jen volunteered. "You're going to be the most beautiful bride." And now Jen *was* crying.

"So when are you going to tell him?" Polio coughed.

"Grasshopper, do not question the Way of the Teacher," Clarissa replied. "After I get everything planned, I'll tell him. It'll be so much more efficient that way."

"You're so not a rules girl," Polo said.

"Have you seen the women who wrote that book?" Clarissa said. "Rules are for fools. I'm a feminist, not a pugilist."

"A pugilist is a boxer," Gravy said.

"Well, I'm not that, either."

"You're really doing Aaron a favor," Jen said. "You know how men hate the idea of planning a wedding."

"But if you need any help," Gravy said, "we're here."

Polo hocked up phlegm, in support.

"What about Simon?" Jen then asked.

Clarissa nearly choked on a piece of toast.

"You know, your Default Man," Jen said.

"Simon *who*?" Clarissa replied. The matter was put to rest. The girls hugged Clarissa and spent the rest of the breakfast discussing their fantasy weddings and chocolate, their two favorite topics.

"What have I missed?" Suzee said, pushing her spiderlike frame into the booth, exactly one hour late.

The rest of the Star Chamber looked at each other, and then, in the silent agreement of longtime friends, they said, "Nothing."

Truth: Clarissa had not slept well the last night; she could not put a French-manicured finger on it, but something was bothering her. She had awakened with her jaw clenched and her hands curled up like lobster claws, and she hadn't even had an argument with her mother in a week.

While wiping sleep and Maybelline from her eyes, she thought about the night before.

Aaron had taken Clarissa back to his home. Up at the very top of Doheny Drive; it had belonged to an old movie star who was famous for dancing or singing or . . . Clarissa forgot, and it still looked like a strawberry ice cream cone, down to its pink marble foyer; the place was right out of a 1930s musical. He'd offered her champagne, which she'd accepted, and popped open a bottle of Cristal for her, and cracked open a Bud for himself. Clarissa had not been wrong about his drink of choice.

"They say if you listen closely, you can hear Fred Astaire tapping down the staircase," Aaron said, his mouth dangerously near the back of Clarissa's neck, lips soft, breath warm. And clean. She was happy his breath was clean, but not minty. She hated minty breath. *What hideous secrets were those breath mints covering up, anyway?*

"Fred . . . ," Clarissa said.

"Astaire?" Aaron said. "You've heard of Fred Astaire, Clarissa." His accent came out slow; she enjoyed the feel of his voice rolling down her spine.

Clarissa's nether regions were tingling. They hadn't tingled in, what? Six months? A year?

When had they last tingled?

Cease! she said to herself. She waved a hand at Petunia, her pet name for her clitoris—she was determined not to fall into bed with Aaron tonight.

"No offense, little girl," Aaron said, in a soft drawl. "You're probably too young to have heard of him."

Clarissa snorted, but, fortunately, not loud enough to hear.

"'Chance is the fool's name for fate,'" she replied.

Aaron looked at her, ambushed by her sudden clarity. "Clarissa. That's a famous line from *The Gay Divorcee.*"

"I may have seen it, a long, long time ago," Clarissa said, nonchalant.

"I love Fred Astaire," Aaron said. "I can't believe you know that line."

"He's sort of cool," Clarissa shrugged. Of course she had heard of Astaire; she had first seen him in a movie when she was about three years old, and her grandmother, her father's mother, had actually danced with him at a coming-out party, but sometimes Clarissa just felt like being contrary.

She was just not Clarissa if she wasn't contrary.

"A lot of my childhood was spent in bed; the only movies my mother allowed me to watch were black-and-whites," he continued. "*The Gay Divorcee, Top Hat . . .*"

Clarissa nodded. Until two days ago, she would have had no idea what Aaron was talking about.

"Aaron—if you tell me what your favorite Broadway show from 1972 is, we'll be friends and compare handbags, but I'm outtie here."

Aaron laughed. "Pass. I don't know Broadway. Only black-and-white."

Aaron had shown Clarissa around his property, the back lawn that stretched out and down a rolling hill like a lush green blanket, at the bottom of which was a white, ornate cabana where Clark Gable could easily have traded kisses and bon mots with Jean Harlow.

Which is precisely what Aaron and Clarissa did.

"You're cute," Aaron said, fondling the skin on her upper arm.

Clarissa wished he'd stop. Yes, her skin was soft, but her upper arms reminded her of Easter hams.

"You're borderline attractive," Clarissa replied, easing away from the arm fondle. How did men know exactly where to touch a woman to elicit the most negative response? Upper arms, inner thighs, under the chin . . .

"Clarissa."

Oh, Clarissa liked the way Aaron said her name. He said it as if every syllable mattered.

Aaron flipped a switch on an outside control panel. Music came on. A man's voice, soft and romantic, was singing . . .

"Why did you pretend not to invite me to your party?" Aaron asked. His hand slipped to her waist as he leaned in and turned her body—and just like that, they were dancing. *Adult* dancing. Clarissa, in her tight leather pants and stilettos, somehow followed.

"I beg to differ, Mr. Mason," Clarissa said. "Why did you show up pretending it was an afterthought?"

He dipped Clarissa, his face a breath from hers. Clarissa, who had overindulged on the chicken satay at Tony B.'s, winced at the thought of her pants splitting—and having to pay for them.

"Why am I so intrigued by you?" Aaron asked. He stared into her eyes, shocking her. Here was a man, Clarissa felt, who was unafraid of confrontation. In Los Angeles, men and women did not look each other in the eye unless they were exchanging vows. Or insults.

They turned, again. Her head tilted back as he spun her.

She felt weightless. She felt elegant. She felt defensive.

"Why am I so bored?" Clarissa responded.

Aaron smiled. "Haven't you read the back of the trades? There's a million actresses and models in this city just waiting for my call." He circled his arm across the view of the city below. And then curved it back around her body.

"Hand models, commercial actresses."

Aaron laughed. "Do you smoke?" he asked.

"Never," Clarissa said, "unless you have a cigarette."

"Are you always this circumlocutional?" Aaron asked.

"Only when I wish to make a good impression," she replied.

Aaron spun her again, blissfully unannoyed by what could be considered Clarissa's most annoying quality—her personality.

"You're something else, Clarissa. I'm just not sure what."

Clarissa smiled to herself. She and Aaron had jumped the first hurdle of the relationship like seasoned athletes; they definitely had chemistry. The meet at the Ivy was not a fluke.

Oh. And she made a note to look up the word "circumlo . . . ," "circumal. . . ." *Oh, fuck it,* she thought. *He's not after me for my brain.*

The song ended. Aaron held Clarissa against his chest, their fingers still entwined. Clarissa's heart was beating too fast; she realized she was panting like a Yorkie.

"I'm not used to this," Clarissa said.

"What? Dancing? Exercise?" He held on to her. Clarissa was aware of a small bead of sweat languidly rolling down her spine. "Undeniable sexual tension?" Aaron smiled. "You have to get out more."

And then he grabbed her ass.

"You'll pay for that," Clarissa said.

"I'm sure I will," Aaron replied.

Clarissa smiled and pulled him out of the large potted plant she'd pushed him into.

"Why do you limp? For effect?" Clarissa asked, as they made their way back to the big pink house. The slight pause in Aaron's gait that had disappeared during their dance had returned.

"It's a little embarrassing," Aaron said.

"I love embarrassing. I trade in embarrassing."

"Fine," he said. "I was born with a clubfoot."

Clarissa squelched the urge to jump up and down. She had found a man with the perfect handicap—obvious to the discerning eye, but not life-altering.

"Is that a turn-off?" he asked. "Some women, you know, have a problem with it—although it's fairly common, I mean, one out of one thousand live births . . ."

"On the contrary," Clarissa said, curving her arm inside his, her hand curling around his bicep, "without your limp, you'd be nothing to me."

Aaron's mouth dropped open—he threw his head back and laughed.

"Now, about your wardrobe," Clarissa continued.

"Wardrobe?" Aaron stopped. "You mean, my clothes?"

"Cowboy boots, out. Helmut Lang, in," Clarissa said. *If he could like her personality,* she thought, *she might as well go all the way.*

"Who?"

"We'll stop by Fred Segal Melrose, a genius personal shopper named Brett Brooks, best friend to Winona, he should get a Nobel in fashion. While we're in the neighborhood, a real haircut is in order—Laurent, McMillan, Art Luna—do you belong to a gym?"

"I play basketball—"

"Right, so we'll set you up at Sports Club L.A. for basketball, that's where the Lakers play for fun, and we'll sign you up at the Warehouse, that's where the indie types reign. We should do that this weekend, although boxing's pretty hot right now, but that's, like, at a smelly place in Koreatown. I recommend we ride out that phase."

"Anything else?" Aaron said.

"Yes, of course," Clarissa said. "I'm so glad you asked. We need to throw a party. You have the perfect venue—and the right party will put you on top of the schmoozing circuit."

Aaron just looked at her.

"I'm going to teach you everything you need to know about living large in L.A.," Clarissa said. "How much do you know about season tickets?"

She put her arm around Aaron's shoulder. "Don't worry, Aaron. I'll take care of you."

"I'm not worried, baby," Aaron said, looking into Clarissa's eyes (*again!*). "I'm petrified."

* * *

Aaron was staring at his bathroom medicine cabinet. All of the products, which he'd purchased at a pharmacy when he stepped down onto West Coast soil just weeks ago (*Was it weeks?* Aaron thought. *It seemed like dog years.*) seemed so common now—plain wrap soap, disposable razors, the first shampoo he'd seen on the shelf. These items had a temporary feel, they belonged to a visitor, a tourist, someone who was just passing through. Clarissa had taken one look at his bathroom (after, evidently, having rummaged through his belongings) and vowed she would stock it with something called "Kiehls" before the week's end.

Tonight, for the first time, Aaron felt like there was a chance he would belong, long after the time he had been given to make it here—six months. In six months, his plan was to find a director, have a workable script, be well on his way to producing a feature film—

But he wanted more than six months. The minute he had stepped off the plane, he had wanted that rarest of entities: a long-term commitment from this town. And in order to have that, he needed direction.

And tonight, he had found his road map.

She was all curves.

Aaron thought about that body. Clarissa was L.A.'s own Varga Girl, his physical ideal since the age of six, when he spied his first *Playboy.* "I'll take care of you," Clarissa had said. Aaron knew she was a born manipulator—the prettiest girl in high school, all grown up and heading in the direction marked "Eligible Bachelor." He'd seen it before, many times—at home, in college—but at least Clarissa was more than the grand total of her physical package—she had a personality, a spark. She was dangerous, as reckless as she was sexy. Aaron was a man who chose his words with care, who'd never had a speeding ticket, who read the instruction booklet that came with any new electronic purchase. Taking chances was not in his life's repertoire. Taking chances was all Clarissa knew.

And yet, Aaron felt safe because he was mentally prepared. Clarissa would navigate the rocky terrain for him, would steer him away from making a fool of himself, would plant him in the right places at the right times. And in return, Aaron would be her partner for however long the ride. He had what she wanted (money) and she had what he wanted (access and adventure)—neither of them would get hurt.

Aaron washed his face with the soap that smelled like dishwashing detergent for the last time—Kiehls was just around the corner.

Clarissa had promised her mother that after breakfast she'd go on a hike in picturesque Temescal Canyon, high above Sunset Beach and its unwashed, oiled-up masses. Clarissa found herself actually looking forward to this foray into the quasi–great outdoors, as she sped west on Sunset, cutting off midwestern tourists and Middle Eastern bus drivers alike. She and her mother hadn't been hiking, in, well . . . uh . . . they'd never actually been hiking. What she didn't bargain for was that her mother's friends, whom her mother called the Three Musketeers, would be along for the trip, cackling and complaining and bragging. Clarissa christened them the Three Wizened Crones. They couldn't make up their minds or their faces. Between them they'd had eight eye jobs, ten face-lifts, countless tummy tucks, and enough bovine collagen to build a Texas-size herd.

"Why didn't you tell me your friends broke out of the retirement home?" Clarissa asked, in hearing range of the grayed objects of her derision.

"I don't owe you a 'splanation," Clarissa's mother drew herself up to her full 5′ 2″, then skittered uphill like a beetle.

The worst part, which was difficult to pinpoint, was that these sixty-year-old women were in better shape than Clarissa. Much better shape.

"You should spin, sweetheart, like I do," one of them, the one with the rhinestoned cap and red runny lips offered, as Clarissa plopped her five-ton ass down on the trail, heaving like a skid row drunk. Runny lips went on for five minutes about the wonders of spinning, but since Clarissa hated bikes, exercise classes, and Spandex, she could safely deduce that spinning was not in her future.

Clarissa gave the old bag the finger, which went unnoticed. Or ignored.

"No, no, no. This one, she should jog," the second one piped up, she of the chic silver-gray hair and too young capris; from behind, she looked like a twelve-year-old with an old butt.

"Jogging's good for the ticker." *Ticker?* thought Clarissa. *Who are these people?*

Clarissa's mother clucked, "It's bad for the knees."

"It's terrific for the ass, though," this one turned around, pointing at her small, old ass. "Take a look at that, huh, girls? You could balance a plate of rugelach on this butt."

"She should have more sex," one woman countered. "Sugar and I are still hitting the orthopedic, three times a week. I can't sleep without my orgasm."

Clarissa felt like barfing.

On the ride home (Clarissa's car had been "booted" again for unpaid parking tickets), Clarissa stared at her mother, hoping she would drop dead. *Why doesn't she ever drop dead when I want her to?*

"I know wha' you're thinking," her mother claimed, talking above the Tito Puente CD.

"Trust me, you don't."

"Is natural to be jealous of your mother," her mother said, reverting to her habit of talking about herself in the third person, the maddening domain of antique movie stars like Debbie Reynolds or Elizabeth Taylor. Clarissa tried to remember whether they were still alive or only on *Entertainment Tonight.*

"Your mother, she has been taking good care of herself, aha." Her mother clucked her tongue against her teeth as if agreeing with something someone else had said.

"Mom, seriously, I was just sitting here hoping to God you would die."

Her mother shrugged her tiny shoulders. "Is natural. I wished my own mother, rest in peace, would die, too."

Why was her mother so understanding? It made Clarissa hate her even more; how could a person be as annoying as a tick, and at the same time, as agreeable as a retriever?

"Your father and I are dating."

"Oh, *please.*"

"He feels terrible."

"Oh, pullllease."

"I can' talk to you about this." And she turned Tito up.

It's not that Clarissa's father was a *bad* person. Just because he ran a telemarketing concern selling siding and fax toner to seniors, just because he had cheated on his wife for twenty-three of the twenty-four years they were married, just because he spent time in prison when Clarissa was a child (her parents said he was on an extended business trip to the Bahamas, but he arrived back home, after more than a year, sans tan), all of this did not make him a bad person. What made him a bad person, in Clarissa's mind, was that, on the eve of her junior year at Beverly Park High, he cheated with her *best friend from high school,* someone her father had known since they were *two and a half.* Someone who had celebrated her seventeenth birthday not two weeks before Clarissa found them in *her* bed together, nestled among an adolescent entanglement of stuffed Disney characters and Sylvia Plath poetry.

Okay, it wasn't really Sylvia Plath—it was the slim book of Love Signs for Scorpios.

Whatever.

Clarissa got over the shock (of seeing her father's pickled ass), with the help of an obnoxiously grand clothing allowance and a brand-new orange-red BMW.

She never told her mother, not because her father, naked, on his knees, cried tears of contrition and begged his only daughter, only child (as far as she knew) not to. She just couldn't bear to bring her mother pain on that level. Even when her mother complained daily that Teddy, her dad, was spoiling her, that Clarissa was spending too much on clothes at Neiman Marcus and Saks, that she didn't need *three* credit cards, for the love of God, at age sixteen. Even when Clarissa and her mother got into awful shouting matches, so loud that the neighbors called in the B.H.P.D. officers enough times that Clarissa knew the names of their children.

Clarissa never told.

Her parents divorced after her mother's little discovery, what Clarissa called the "Laker Cheerleader Incident," in which her father was found to be dating not one, not two, but *three* Laker cheerleaders. The girls are small, small like Herve Villechaize, despondent midget, small, and so her father claimed to her hysterical mother (so furious that she couldn't stop shaking to light a cigarette and started *eating* one instead) that dating a Laker Girl wasn't like dating a life-size human being—that three should count only as one.

Clarissa was impressed with his logic and his stamina (after all, he was in his fifties at the time). Nonetheless, she was proud of her mother for pulling the plug on her longstanding, but not upstanding, marriage.

But that didn't mean they ever stopped dating.

As serendipity would have it, the marriage broke up around the same time Simon had made the infamous "We're not good for each other" statement. It seemed the Alpert women could not hold a relationship together, but Clarissa blamed her parents for the demise of hers—after all, how was she supposed to know what a trusting relationship was? She had grown up watching her mother rifle through pockets after the endless days at work, through the wallet on those golf weekends, through crumpled bills hidden in locked drawers; she had grown up accustomed to the sound of muffled anger and the sensation of unseen tension. She knew how it felt to walk into a room and suddenly not be able to breathe, her chest constricting under the weight of a phantom argument.

"See?" she would say to her therapist, the one she called Ms. Manolo, after her extensive, inappropriate, spike-heel collection. "It's no wonder I'm fucked up."

Manolo would nod her head with appropriate gravity, but Clarissa knew she was mentally calculating how many nutty patients she would have to see to buy more shoes.

Therapy hadn't helped at all. Clarissa swung from one "relationship" to the next like a femme Tarzan through the urban jungle of men. The girl knew how to keep up appearances, how to fake a smile, a laugh, happiness, and, finally, an orgasm. But Clarissa did not have the first clue about how to have a relationship. She was a Manipulant Savant—a girl who could get a man—but not a girl who could keep one.

Clarissa climbed out of her mother's convertible, dragged her beaten body upstairs to her duplex apartment, and collapsed for the rest of the afternoon.

Five

Baiting the Trap

Clarissa awakened to find the fluffy white cat sitting on her face. And remembered how depressed she felt. And why.

Simon. Simon, who had been at her party, watching her with eyes that knew and were the first to appreciate all the better parts of her body. Simon, who still had that ridiculous faux accent. Simon, who was there as she stood next to Aaron (and the ghost of Fred Astaire) trading cashmere-covered barbs and measuring chemistry, even though he wasn't. Simon, her soul mate.

Soul mate? Clarissa thought. *How about the itch that won't go away?*

Fucking Simon.

"Oh, boo-fucking-hoo," Clarissa admonished Clarissa as she tossed the cat on the floor and plucked white fur from her teeth.

She pulled herself from the red velvet couch and looked at her body in the huge antique mirror hanging in her dining room. The mirror, a baroque piece, had come from a friend with an antique store on Melrose in West Hollywood who'd been shot by his lover/business partner last year; she'd received it on consignment, and, well, no one had ever asked for it back, so . . .

Clarissa moved in front of the mirror, posing like Madonna on her eighth comeback. She thought she looked . . . good. Not just hoochie-mama, phat-phresh good, but life-partner, meet-the-parents good. Clarissa was blessed with her father's broad shoulders, her mother's small waist, her Jewish grandmother's ample boobs and longish legs. So what if she carried a little extra on the backside; in a town full of pinched faces and buns the size of grapes, she was a real woman, full of body and opinions and eccentricities, and though she seldom showed it, heart.

Aaron was damned lucky to be marrying her.

"Shit!" Clarissa cried, running into the bedroom. She and Aaron were having their first official date tonight. She was supposed to meet him at Orso's at 7:30 and she still hadn't Googled him.

Clarissa Googled every man she'd dated in the past five years; she was always looking for that extra piece of information that could give her an edge in the dating game. Once, she had found out that a potential date, a guy she met through Manolo, was an ex-con.

She had still gone out with him—she couldn't care less about the ex-con thing ("Manslaughter can happen to the nicest people," Clarissa said.)—he had a body that Calvin Klein himself would've posted bail for. In which case, he would have been found under "B," for "Bail-worthy Fuck."

Aaron Mason's name elicited 1,645 Web pages.

Clarissa squealed. A new record. She ran to get a box of Twizzlers and chewed her way through an hour of fine print.

The fine print revealed three things: The first was that Aaron's name was actually *Joseph* Aaron Kingsley Mason IV. The second item was that Aaron's family, the Masons of Mason Department Stores (based out of Colene, Georgia, pop. 22,001) were rich. Clarissa called Tony B. to confirm.

"What's a NASDAQ?" she asked.

"Stock exchange—Princess Honey, I'm so proud, are you reading a newspaper? Have you sullied yourself with the business section?"

"If a company is listed on the NASDAQ, what does that mean?"

"It's a big company. I'm feng shui-ing my shoe closet—I'll call you back."

The third item? The third item was something else, altogether.

"Sean was . . . powerful," Clarissa lightly fingered the rim of her glass. "He called me his muse. He said, I'll never forget this, he said, 'C—Sean always called me 'C'—'C, you are to me what that incredibly beautiful girl with the nose was to Van Gogh.'"

"You mean the destitute, one-legged, syphilitic prostitute?" Aaron asked.

"No, silly," Clarissa said. "The other girl—the one with both legs." She put her hand to her throat, as though catching herself. "Listen, I really don't like to talk about our relationship."

Bless the Google gods. Clarissa had found a recent *Variety* interview with Aaron, in which he had stated that Sean Penn, the sour-faced actor-director whose recent movies (i.e., anything post–*Fast Times at Ridgemont High*) Clarissa had no hope of understanding, was not only his favorite actor of *all time*, but also his favorite director. Clarissa wondered what that meant for her future. *Why couldn't his favorite actor-director be Tom Hanks? That seemed so much safer.*

"Good," Aaron said. "Let's talk about something else."

Clarissa nodded sadly. She sipped at RazOrgaz Numero Three (crushed raspberries, raspberry liqueur, and vodka and hovering at 224 empty calories) and wondered just how many she could drink during pregnancy. "Absolutely," she said.

"So . . . how long did you date Sean Penn?" Aaron asked.

Clarissa smiled. "It wasn't how long we dated . . . it was the, ah, what's the word?"

"One-night stand?" he smiled. There were those dimples, again.

"That's three words, Pumpkin," Clarissa corrected him. "No, it was the . . . intensity."

Now, Aaron nodded sadly. "Yeah," he said. "I don't think I can keep up with that."

Clarissa agreed, "Maybe not."

"I mean, I know I'm fascinating—who wouldn't be fascinated by a rich guy with a handicap—but Sean Fucking Penn?" Aaron shook his head."Another," he called out to the passing waiter.

They sat there for a moment, in the red leather booth where so many other couples with so many other lies drank away their moments.

"Clarissa," Aaron said.

"Yes?" Clarissa was still upset over her break-up with the amateur pugilist-actor/director.

"Are you Jewish?" he asked.

"On occasion."

"My mother's Jewish," Aaron said.

"I am so incredibly Jewish," Clarissa said. "Aaron, can we start fresh?" She clutched his elbow. "Can we just pretend there was no Sean, that you and I are here, in this booth at Orso's, and . . . there is no past."

"No past?" Aaron said. "Clarissa, from what I hear, you're all past."

"Look at me," Clarissa said. "Look me in the eyes."

"I'm looking," he said, squinting. "You have crazy eyes."

"My mother has crazy eyes," Clarissa said.

"Acorn. Tree. It's all coming together," Aaron said, "So, what's your mother like?"

"Dead," Clarissa said. She tried to cross her toes, difficult to accomplish in her strappy Gucci sandals. Her foot started to cramp. Aaron mistook her soft moan for a bruised heart.

"Oh God, I'm sorry," Aaron said.

"It's been twenty years," Clarissa said.

"You were so young."

"To new beginnings." Clarissa raised her glass.

"*New* beginnings?" Aaron asked. "Why does everyone say that? Shouldn't it just be 'beginnings'?"

"Aaron."

"Yes?"

"Tap the glass or suffer the wrath of Clarissa."

Aaron tapped her glass. Too hard. He was tipsy. A sweet, pink trickle of RazOrgaz ran down her arm, soaking forever into her cashmere Loro Piano. This was very bad, for it meant she'd have to pay for the sweater.

Clarissa smiled at Aaron's klutzy effort. *That,* she thought, *can be fixed.*

As they stared into each other's eyes in a fit of intimacy (hers crazy, his squinty), Clarissa ran down Aaron's physical attributes like keys on a Steinway: wavy hair (slight thinning at the crown? No biggie), strong jaw, wide shoulders, flat enough stomach, excellent bank, respectable height, bad left foot. She couldn't tell how long his legs were, but she thought they were at least average length, which was good, as she hated short-legged men. And would never procreate with one.

"Ugh," she shuddered.

"Is it my breath?" Aaron said. "You should get a whiff in the early morning. Like, say, Saturday morning." He said this in his best Groucho

Marx impersonation (which happened to be terrible), his eyebrows dancing up and down.

"Short-legged dental students," Clarissa said.

Aaron laughed. "Don't ask me how, but I understand perfectly." He ran his finger down her arm.

"I like your laugh," she said. It wasn't a guffaw, and yet it didn't hold anything back. It was unafraid, confident, warm.

"That's good, because you're funny," Aaron replied.

"I'm funny?" Clarissa asked. "Funny amusing or funny strange?"

Aaron looked at her. "Clarissa. You're funny. You're like Lucille Ball with a rack."

Clarissa had never thought of herself this way. She just stated her mind as often and as openly as possible. Words passed through her mouth, unencumbered by thought.

The waiter walked past their table, giving them the hairy eyeball. They had been there an hour without ordering dinner.

"Maybe we should actually order food," Aaron said.

"I always forget about food after the third drink. It's the original liquid diet," Clarissa said. "Of course, I forget about driving, too, and where I left my clothes."

Again, with the thinking-out-loud thing.

Aaron looked at her and laughed. "See?" he said. "That's funny."

After their dinner, Clarissa did a full-body yawn, sticking her breasts out like flesh beacons, and declared that she had never been so tired in all of her twenty-eight-year-old life—she was pleased to see the disappointment on Aaron's face; she knew he'd been on the verge of inviting her over to his place again. To finish what they hadn't even started.

The check came. The waiter, who heretofore had been semihelpful, was now ready to wallpaper their living room and wash their dogs. "Will there be anything else?" he asked, panting after the big tip. Clarissa thought she saw him wink.

"No. That's all, thanks," Aaron replied. He pulled out his wallet; without looking at the total, he deposited a black credit card on the bill.

The waiter looked at the card and hustled off as fast as his toe shoes would allow. Clarissa looked at Aaron and strategized. This was her first black American Express card sighting, the commerce equivalent of spotting the elusive white leopard in the bush, of playing paddle tennis with J. D. Salinger. Clarissa needed to play her next move exactly right.

She chose to ignore the card. *"When in doubt, ignore,"* said her inner voice, with a Marlene Dietrich basso.

Aaron dropped her off twenty minutes later, and Clarissa gave him a brush on the cheek with her full mouth, and she knew that the rest of the night, all he would be thinking about was how close those lips had come to his, and what they would taste like when they did.

And perhaps, why she had kissed every other frog in the western hemisphere, but not him.

The voices were like acrylic nails on a chalkboard.

"Why the fuck hasn't he called me?"

"Clarissa, don't be so needy."

"It's been three days!"

"Hei-nous."

"Why don't you just call him?"

"Why don't I just . . . *what*?"

"Call . . . him?"

"Jen, sometimes you are just so . . . *Jen*."

"Are you *high*?" Clarissa asked. "I'm not putting myself *out there*."

In their first emergency meeting that week, the Star Chamber sat side by side at Z. Salon on the Sunset Strip, their faces covered in paraffin wax like characters in an Ed Wood film, their feet soaking in hot water and lavender bubbles, their fingernails buffed by delicate Vietnamese girls, whose solid gold bracelets twinkled like wind chimes with every swipe. Emergency meetings were called by the Star Chamber only for circumstances requiring immediate attention; for example, a bad dye job (like the time Gravy bleached her tips and looked very eighties MTV–reject, sans shoulder pads and beaded gloves), a heinous (or incredible . . . or, frankly, just any) date, or a celebrity sighting (preferably a "Friend" or Brad Pitt sighting—both would garner double bonus points for the lucky recipient, good for a free drink).

There were approximately three emergency sessions of the Star Chamber called per week.

"That doctor I dated last week?" Polio started. "Total flatliner."

Gravy went to punch her, but Clarissa held her arm back. The Vietnamese girls took note, chatting back and forth with each other in their native tongue.

"Que es your problema?" Clarissa asked.

"Her love life is my problem—she throws herself at any object that has an M.D. trailing behind it."

"At least I have a love life, Hard-up. You haven't been laid since butterfly clips."

Polio's time line was always based on fashion trends.

"Maybe I'm choosy," Gravy said.

"Maybe everyone else is," Polio replied.

The Vietnamese girls picked up steam, their sentences overlapping each other like engines at the Indy 500; Clarissa thought they sounded like chipmunks on Benadryl, but then she thought that of every foreign language except, maybe, Dutch, which sounded like a bulimic episode in an echo chamber.

"Do you mind?" Gravy asked the girls. "That's extremely rude."

"Grave, don't say that," Jen said. "They came here on boats, you know." She smiled at the Vietnamese girls, who smiled back, then resumed their chatter.

"I don't care if they came here in a soap dish. They're talking about us," Gravy complained. "Talkie, no tippie." Gravy turned to the smallest one. The girl smiled and nodded as though Gravy had just complimented her hair.

"My throat hurts," Polio said.

"Can we get back to the topic at hand?" Clarissa insisted. "Why hasn't he called? Have I lost the 'Clarissa touch'? I haven't had a guy not call me back since . . ."

"Candies."

"Correction. Original Candies."

The girls let out a communal hush, a verbal bow to the Dating Goddess.

Jennifer looked at Clarissa with her puppy face. "Maybe he's just been busy."

"Well, I'm extremely busy, too, and I've had time to call."

"So why haven't you?" Polio asked.

"Because I've never called a guy first . . ."

"Simon," the Chamber said, in unison.

"Game player. Like every straight man in Los Angeles, they date like they're playing Monopoly." Every word Gravy said sounded as though it was shot from a gun.

"Who are you? Reading Railroad?" Polio sneezed.

"Marvin Gardens," Gravy replied. "Everyone wants Marvin Gardens. Solid investment, on the high-end side, but not overpriced."

"I'm thinking of dating my gardener," Jennifer said. "He seems like a nice person."

Clarissa felt Aaron was neither extremely busy nor a good Monopoly player.

"Maybe . . . ," she couldn't get the words out. They caught in her throat just like that time Fonzie couldn't say "I'm sorry" to Richie Cunningham after the misunderstanding over the red-haired girl.

"Maybe he just doesn't like me," Clarissa finally said.

The Star Chamber looked at each other like the first time they heard John Kennedy, Jr., had died. Shock, despair, disbelief.

"No way," the Star Chamber choir sang.

But Clarissa couldn't help wondering as she stared at the saddest image in the world—an empty answering machine.

Well, not really empty. There were seventeen messages, but none was from her new fiancé-who-didn't-know-it-yet. Half the messages were old, dating back to last year. Clarissa was sentimental—she liked saving messages from old friends and C-level celebrities. She had an answering tape collection that dated all the way back to babydoll dresses, sparkle dust, and Hole. When she was feeling blue, she'd replay some of her favorites:

"Clarissa, if this is Clarissa—I, ah," said the British actor with the floppy hairdo, "it seems, I ah, have your name and, ah, number written on my, ah, inner thigh."

Pause.

"Can you tell me, I, ah, hmm," he stops for a moment, flustered. "How did it get there?"

"Oh, baby, baby," said the boyhood pal who grew up to be a constantly strung-out character actor. "Oh, baby, baby, baby . . ."

That one went on for *five whole minutes*.

"Bitch, you laid some motherfucking smack down on a brother," said a wrong number. "Why you play me like dat, ho?"

At least, Clarissa thought it was a wrong number.

She was in the middle of the gentle, erudite sitcom comedian's message, one she had never returned, of course (he was old enough to be her father's younger brother, and frankly, not as attractive), when the phone rang.

She went to pick it up—then smacked her own hand. She was determined *not* to be available. The only way to win this game was not to play.

The machine picked up.

"Clarissa?" A man's voice, from a car. Radio on. Broken up by tall buildings and airwave range. "Clarissa, are you there?" A pause. Clarissa stared at the machine, her hand hovering over it—

"I didn't know if the number still worked—"

Simon. Simon was calling her. Simon.

"I was wondering if we could get together—it was nice to see you the other night, you look . . ."

The line broke up.

Fuck! Clarissa thought. *How do I look? How do I* look*?*

The phone rang again. Clarissa picked up, breathless and nonchalant at once: "Ye-ess?"

"Clarissa."

"Hello," Clarissa purred.

"It's Aaron."

Clarissa made a hissing sound.

"Are you okay?" he asked.

"And?" she said.

"And, what?"

"And, what do you want?"

"Well, I was calling . . ."

"I'm very busy right now." Clarissa looked around her living room. Magazines, nail clippers, hair pins, half-eaten Snickers. She was her very own sorority.

What was she doing?

"What are you doing?"

"I'm working on my . . ."

Sometimes Clarissa really did wish she had a job, just so she could actually be busy. She thought of all the "careers" she'd had—interior decorator (painting her mother's bathroom); hostess (fired for dating patrons, causing a scene when several had reservations on the same night); antique store salesperson (one week, falling under Clarissa's personal "Don't Ask, Don't Tell" policy); and receptionist (two hours, from 9:30 to 11:30 in the morning, at her dad's office—her own father fired her after finding her asleep under the desk, earphones strapped to her head, playing C & C Music Factory's "Gonna Make You Sweat" over and over).

" . . . novel?" Ooh. She liked the sound of that.

"You write?"

"Doesn't everybody?"

"Well. I certainly . . . I don't want to disturb you."

"Too late."

"God, you're difficult."

"God, you're catching on."

"Clarissa, I was calling to ask if you wanted to go to the Laker game tonight."

Now, Clarissa was hurt. "This is really last minute."

"I know, I'm sorry. I just got the tickets."

"As I see it," Clarissa said, recovering. "You have two problems: One, I have plans, and two, I hate baseball."

"Basketball," Aaron said. "Extremely tall, predominantly African American athletes slamming a large round orange sphere into net hoops at either end of a one-hundred-fifty-foot court."

"Rudeness: Rich, spoiled, semihandicapped heirs who call four and a half hours before a date," she replied.

"You're absolutely right. Mea culpa; maybe some other time."

Clarissa allowed a pause to linger in the air, a noiseless censure.

"Hello?"

"Six-thirty."

"What's that?"

"Don't ask me to repeat myself." She hung up.

* * *

Clarissa spent the first two quarters of the game against San Diego (at least, she thought it was San Diego—it could rightly have been San Antonio), fighting vertigo as she watched, sitting next to Aaron, from a SkyBox (he'd received comp tickets from MGM). SkyBoxes were the latest salvo fired in the ongoing war to prevent the rich from having to mix with the hoi polloi; there were about twenty of them, scattered at nose-bleed height. They were minitheaters, equipped with cappuccino machines and private bathrooms and, strangely, television sets with which to properly view the concert or athletic event one has bothered to actually leave the comfort of one's home to attend (where, surely, the SkyBox patrons had SUV-size television sets galore). Formally attired minions would bring anything from warm sushi to cold peanut butter cookies—or even the other way around. There was every condiment, every accoutrement, every wish fulfilled, every whim attended to.

The view?

The view sucked like a hooker with a quota, in the immortal words of Rodney Dangerfield, or like some other old guy. Clarissa's father may have said it.

Watching a basketball game was like taking a bad turn on Sony Playstation II. The players, these large, regal examples of manhood, became miniaturized, like cartoon characters, and even then, one could see only the tops of their heads. Forget telling the players apart by their features or the numbers on their jerseys; if you were in a SkyBox, you had to rely on 'fro dimensions.

Finally, Clarissa couldn't take it anymore—being suspended in the air several stories up, with nothing between her and God and the basketball court but two feet of glass . . .

"I feel sick," she said.

"I know, they are losing pretty badly," Aaron said. "But they can still pull it off . . ."

"Aaron, lunch, lunch, Aaron. Have you met?"

"You need some Pepto-Bismol?" He waved a freshly baked chocolate chip cookie in the air. "Coats, soothes, protects—kind of like yours truly."

He smiled. Despite the line, Clarissa had to fight to ignore the charm of his emerging crow's-feet, the sure sign of a ladies' man, according to *Cosmo,* May issue.

"Drive me home," she said.

"But . . . it's not even halftime."

Clarissa looked at Aaron. "I don't give a rat's ear if it's the last game of the championship season." She wondered if she were quoting Chick Hearn accurately. "If I stay here one more second, given what I know of physics and something to do with velocity and air current, my lunch is going to land with impressive tonnage on Jack Nicholson's head."

Aaron looked over the two-foot pane of glass. Jack was sitting on the floor, stories beneath them.

"Maybe you could hit his girlfriend, the one who looks like a pair of nail clippers," Aaron suggested.

They were halfway to Aaron's Towncar when she heard the familiar, stomach-churning refrain.

"Clarissa, Babycakes!"

That voice belonged to her father; he seemed to have a patent on the word *Babycakes*.

"Teddy." He liked to be called by his first name.

"Honeybaby, have you met Apricot?"

Apparently, Apricot was the name of the child standing next to him, not more than nineteen, holding a large cup of beer. With her bright red hair and shiny features, Clarissa thought she looked more like a persimmon than an apricot.

"She's an exchange student."

Clarissa, in a moment of horror never before experienced in human history, realized that her father would now want to be introduced to Aaron. She had been hoping to avoid this exchange until after the wedding.

The four stood there for what felt like several Alpert family Thanksgivings.

"Aaron, this is Teddy." Clarissa said, hoping if she didn't clarify that Teddy was her father, maybe no one would mention it.

"Teddy, this is Aaron."

They shook hands.

Aaron then introduced himself to the fruit.

Then they all looked at Clarissa.

"Okay, 'bye," Clarissa said. She tried to grab Aaron's hand, but Teddy moved faster—he got a tight grip on her in-the-dark-fiancé's arm.

"What do you think of the game?"

"Well, I was enjoying it—"

"She drag you off?"

Clarissa stared daggers through her father's head and realized he'd had a new row of hairplugs embedded in his scalp. She couldn't take her eyes off the tiny tufts of wiry-looking hair; he looked like a middle-aged cactus.

"Clarissa's not feeling well."

"Would you kids like a drink?" Teddy asked, like a host at a Jewish singles dance.

"This 'kid' is about to throw up," Clarissa said, sweetly.

"No, thank you," Aaron said.

"You want to grab a bite to eat?" Teddy said. "There's that great sushi place on Main."

"No." Her dad was always into the latest sushi place, as though the eighties and his forties had never ended.

"We're full of junk food, thanks," Aaron said. *How come he sounded so fucking cheery?* Clarissa thought.

"How's your mother?" Teddy asked.

"You should know—aren't you two dating again?" Clarissa looked at Persimmon or Apricot or some pitted fruit–named girl.

"She started making demands again. You know your mother."

"Like what? That you stop being an asshole?"

Aaron looked confused. "I thought your mom was dead," he said to Clarissa.

"People make mistakes." She shrugged.

"Clarissa, that's not nice," Teddy said.

"Teddy, neither are *vous*."

Not exactly true. Her father was very nice, unless you happened to be married to him, sired by him, selling to him, or negotiating with him. Then, he was an asshole.

"It's not my fault," Teddy said to Aaron.

"I'm sure it's not," Aaron replied.

Teddy and Persimmon walked away, her Jimmy Choo knockoff heels click-clacking along the waxed floor, a siren call for over-the-hill lover-boys.

Now, Clarissa really felt sick.

"Nice man," Aaron said. "Have you known him long?"

"He's my dad," Clarissa said.

Then she threw up a junk food medley on Aaron's shoes.

She loved that they were Helmut Lang.

Planning the wedding was going exceedingly well; Clarissa congratulated herself on her organizational skills. The hotel was booked, the dress was on hold (she knew "people"), the bridesmaids' dresses were going through their first set of alterations, the caterer was planning a summer menu, the floral arrangements were dispensed with—all that was left was the honeymoon.

And the groom.

Clarissa went over her notes with her girls at the 323rd Emergency Session of the Star Chamber called in the last six months. The setting: Gravy's (mom's) house; sustenance: mini Milky Way bars (energy) and mimosas (vitamin C!).

Gravy: "Sexual chemistry?"

Clarissa: "Check."

Jennifer: "Sense of humor?"

Clarissa: "Check."

Gravy: "Straight?"

Clarissa: "Affirmed."

Polo: (cough).

Clarissa: "Check."

Gravy: "How affirmed?"

Clarissa: (Ignores question.)

Jennifer: "Good driver?"

Clarissa: "Check. *What?*"

Jennifer: "It is important."

"So what can we do for you?" Gravy asked.

"I'm on the second stage of the manhunt . . ."

The girls let out a collective "ooh."

"I need suggestions. The next move is vital to the operation."

The Star Chamber had garnered many theories throughout the years (since fourth grade at Rodeo Elementary) on how to best pursue, catch (trap), and, God willing, hang on to a man, even if that man happened to be, at the time, a ten-year-old boy tripping over his Converse high-top shoelaces. Item: The *Wild Kingdom* Theory of Mating, forged after hours of watching reruns (and ogling the preternaturally musclebound yet hapless assistant Jim: "And now, watch as Glistening Manmeat Jim tries to untangle himself from the clutch of the deadly water-dwelling Anaconda"). Tenets: 1. Identify target/prey. Done; 2. Identify social/daily habits/interests of target/prey (Halfway Done); 3. Entrap prey through any means necessary (To Be Done); "any means necessary" may be interpreted as "any means sexually."

"You haven't been too available?"

"No."

"You've turned him down for a date?"

"Well, no."

Gravy made a sound like that buzzer on that annoying game show.

"You've mentioned other men who are interested in you, in a casual, passing manner."

"Yes."

"Who?" Jen asked. As though it were a surprise.

"Sean Penn."

"Really?" Jen said. "Isn't he married? They seemed so happy."

Clarissa felt the session was going nowhere fast. She thought about the throwing up on Aaron's shoes incident—*could vomit have diminished her chances at marital bliss?*

"You need an identity," Gravy said. "Something that sets you apart from the pack."

"He says I'm funny," Clarissa offered.

"You could direct?" Jen said. "Everybody directs."

"Men don't like funny," Gravy said. "If men liked funny, my best friend wouldn't have three speeds and an adapter."

"Or maybe . . . you could be a scientist," Jen said.

"Aaron claims to like funny," Clarissa said.

"That's just sick," Gravy said. "What a mind fuck."

"Just be yourself, girl," Polo said. "Your self is your best angle."

Clarissa looked at her. "Thanks a fucking lot, Polo."

Clarissa sat with Aaron at breakfast the next day, taking in amusing sights at the Peninsula. Aaron had called Clarissa way early in the morning (like, before 10:00 A.M.) and insisted on taking Clarissa out to make up for the other night's multicolored debacle; however, he told her, he'd make sure to wear an old pair of Converse, just in case.

Clarissa had informed Aaron that breakfast at the Peninsula was a ritual in Hollywood, as sacramental as picking up high-class hookers at the bar in the Peninsula after 7:00 P.M. Here was an agent, spic and span, hairless as a newborn, flattering a nervous writer; there was a film producer, now old and fat, but, still, defiantly, tan as a brick, waxing filthy tales of pursuit with an FOB—every other word starting with an "F" and ending with an "uckingscumbag."

The waiters danced their little dances and sang their little songs of the specials and hoped that someone, anyone, would ask about their latest script/project/five-and-under.

And then there was Clarissa and Aaron, who to the observer's eye appeared the classic new couple—hurrying to finish each other's sentences, picking at their blueberry pancakes, she pushing a hair from his eyes, he pulling out her chair. So fresh there was almost a dew about them.

But as Clarissa was pushing the hair from Aaron's eyes (hazel, if you must know), she was weighing the benefits of being direct with her fiancé-to-be. Instead of playing games, Clarissa thought she should be frank; after all, Aaron had sat up half the night after the basketball game stroking Clarissa's hair as she dieted (vomited) four pounds off. Food poisoning really was the dieter's best friend; the Star Chamber was very jealous to hear of her weight loss, and had demanded to know where she had eaten lunch that day.

"Where would you like to go on our honeymoon?" she asked, as she looked over the breakfast menu like a starving refugee. For the next few days, she had her "Get Out of Jail Free" card—there was nothing she couldn't eat.

"Vladivostok," Aaron replied.

"Interesting." Clarissa said this as though something heavy were sitting on her tongue.

"Haven't you ever wanted to go someplace dangerous? A little off the beaten track?"

"Like, east of La Brea?" Clarissa said, referring to the Los Angeles basin, where one could find pawn shops and Army-Navy stores. "Aaron. I have to plan our trip right away. Where is the one *romantic* place you would like to travel to?"

Aaron looked at Clarissa. "Oh, I get it. You're being funny. Again." And then he started laughing. "You know, people warned me about you. They said you were a little . . . kooky."

"Aaron, darling, I'm serious as a bad peel."

Aaron scrunched up his face, confused. "But . . . when you say 'our honeymoon,' that's like a joke, right?"

"Aaron, don't make this difficult. I just asked you a simple question. You don't have to answer if you don't want to."

"It's a loaded question."

"Why?"

"Well," Aaron said, "for starters, we're not getting married."

Clarissa touched his face; he was getting red. "You're blushing," she said. "That's so cute."

She took a bite of a scone, brushed the crumbs from her mouth. "Anyway, my mother says that Maui is still the place to go, but then there's that new Four Seasons on Kona—"

"Clarissa, please, we're not getting married. We barely know each other."

Clarissa took Aaron's chin in her hand and squeezed lightly as though she were addressing a five-year-old.

"Aaron, if you don't like Hawaii, just say so. Maybe we'd do better someplace more exotic, like . . . Bali."

Aaron sat back, his eyes wide and frightened, flipping side to side like a fish caught in a net.

"If you think we're getting married, you're crazy," he said, with impressive finality.

Clarissa looked at him and smiled; she finished her scone.

Aaron was still insisting that they weren't getting married as the valet drove his Bentley up.

"Aaron, honey, we don't have to get married if you don't want to." Clarissa hopped in the passenger side and snuggled into the soft leather.

"Good."

"I mean, I would never, ever force anyone to marry me."

"I didn't mean that you would . . ."

"Of course you didn't mean it," Clarissa said. "I could get married any time I want to."

"I know," Aaron said.

"I told Sean no; I can certainly turn you down," Clarissa continued.

"What do you mean, turn me down?"

"Well, I'm not even sure we should be thinking about marriage."

"But that's what I said."

"We barely know each other."

"Exactly."

"You're right," Clarissa agreed. "It's a bad idea. I mean, you could be hiding things from me. What if you're gay? What size tux did you say you wear?"

"I'm not gay," Aaron said. "I don't wear tuxes."

"How do you know?"

"How do I know I'm not gay or how do I know I don't wear tuxes?"

"The invitation says 'formal attire,' Aaron."

"*Invitation?* I never—this is ridiculous. You're just trying to confuse me."

"Oh, I understand, you don't like formal. But think about the photographs," Clarissa said. "Hold on. I have to write that down—a photographer, I need a photog . . ."

Aaron put his hand on hers. "You need a lot more than a photographer, Clarissa. You need a psychiatrist."

"Oh. I see. So that's it, then," Clarissa said. "We're never getting married. Well, you don't have to beat me over the head."

"Clarissa, I didn't say that."

"You said you didn't want to marry me."

"I didn't say that."

"So, you do want to marry me?"

"Christ. I'm not ready to get married. I just got here!"

"So you're saying that you do want to get married to me, but you're not ready yet, which is sort of inconvenient for me, because, frankly, I don't have a huge window of time."

Aaron just stared at her, his mouth open wide.

"What?" Clarissa said. "Is there a problem?"

"You know, you're the most emotionally unstable girl I've ever met."

"All's fair in love and war," Clarissa said. "And this is revolution!"

If he could quote one Fred Astaire movie, she could quote another. Aaron looked at her as though she had barfed up roses. But he still was not swayed.

"You'll find I'm just a little bit smarter than you think, Clarissa. I wasn't born the day before yesterday, you know."

Clarissa just smiled and patted his hand. Because before Aaron knew it, he would be encased in the quicksand of Clarissa's singular logic. The more he insisted they weren't getting married, the more Clarissa twisted out the possibility of marriage, as though squeezing water from a rock. She'd find the droplets of possibility—and before long, she'd have a puddle. A bathtub. And then a pool. Then an ocean. *Who needed advice from the Star Chamber, now?*

And by that time, Aaron would be drowning in it.

"Are you allergic to roses, because if you are, we could just do silk flowers, they're incredibly lifelike." Clarissa said, as they turned down Little Santa Monica.

"Clarissa!"

Six

(Stuffed) Animal Magnetism

The Star Chamber, brought together to try on bridesmaids' dresses at Neiman Marcus, applauded Clarissa's fine work. Clarissa was, after all, a virtuoso of manipulation, nonpareil.

"How's the sex?" Gravy asked, then, "Oh my *God*! Whose back is that?!" She was pointing at her reflection.

"I think it's going to be amazing," Clarissa said.

"*Think?* What is this *think*?"

"We haven't actually done the deed."

Gravy turned, slowly, and looked at Clarissa, her head cocked at an angle like the RKO dog.

"Are you waiting for the honeymoon?" Jen asked. "That's so romantic."

Gravy snorted.

"God, no," Clarissa replied. "We've only known each other, like, two weeks."

Gravy turned and looked at her back again, reflected in the floor-length mirror. "I recognize that back. That's my mother's back!" She sat down on the ground; she appeared to be drowning in taffeta. "Just kill me, now."

"Hi, girls," Suzee stalked in. She threw her tiny Prada bag into a corner and whipped a dress off a hanger—it cracked like a bolt of lightning. Suzee often seemed accompanied by special effects. "Clarissa, lovey, I heard your prenup has ten chapters and a bibliography, is that true?" The words dripped off her tongue like tiny drops of mercury.

Clarissa looked at Suzee, melting her, mentally, like the Evil Witch in *The Wizard of Oz*.

"Evilina has arrived!" Gravy said. "Meow to you, oh cuntish one."

"There will be no prenup," Clarissa stated.

"That's not what I heard," Suzee said, bouncing out of her mean little black heels and mean little black dress.

"Everyone has a prenup these days," Jennifer offered. "Even people who are truly in love."

"Oh my God," Suzee said. "Could this dress be any uglier?"

"Dearest, that's not the dress," Gravy said. "Those are the cake icers you call boobs."

Gravy was right—Suzee's boobs did resemble unripe bananas.

"Odious," Suzee spat.

"There will be no prenup," Clarissa declared, again.

"Ladies," Gravy stood and bellowed, "place your bets."

"1995 Vuitton tote, mint condition, on Suzee," Polio piped in, coming in from her latest round of fetal pig cell injections (something about a burgeoning skin condition; this time, Clarissa was afraid to ask).

"Wait a minute. What's with this 'mint condition'?" Gravy intoned. "We're not selling cars, here."

"I'll go last summer's Versace scarf on Clar," said Jen.

"A scarf?" Gravy said. "Why not just bet, like, one Manolo slingback?"

"It's more like a cover-up," Jen protested.

"You mean a pareo," Polio said, without coughing.

And then she did.

"Throw in an eyeglass case, for fuck's sake," Gravy said. It warmed Clarissa's heart to see how her oldest friend bullied others in the (questionable) name of Clarissa's honor.

The ever good-natured Jen shrugged. "Fine with me—what're you throwing in?"

"Veto on your jewelry line, Gravy," Suzee said, slipping out of the bridesmaid's dress. "I only wear names."

"I'm thinking of a name right now," Gravy said. "It starts with a capital 'B' and ends with a . . ." She started scratching her arm.

"C'mon, Alexandra. Tell the audience what I'm going to win," Polio said.

Gravy took a dramatic breath, "The year is 1994. The look: An . . ."

"Animal print!" Polio yelled.

"For goddamn . . . let me finish!" Gravy yelled back. "The look: Animal print. The designer . . ."

"Dolce?" Polio squeaked.

"Valentino," Gravy said. Her newly waxed brows did a jig.

No one said a word. They knew the dress. Picture the finest Italian hand-spun silk, gathered from the mountains of Umbria; black and white zebra stripes descending from the shoulder in waves, floating weightless to the red-carpeted ground. Clarissa had stepped into the dress once—it had felt like stepping into a glass of milk. Cool and delicious and high in calories.

They'd all fantasized about wearing it.

They'd all fantasized about having someplace to wear it to.

"Hello? Insider trading!" Suzee screamed at Gravy. She turned to Clarissa "Are you pregnant?" she demanded.

Clarissa just smiled. Truth? She was surprised and pleased Gravy had so much faith in her; she hoped she was up to the challenge.

"I am so winning that dress," Polo said to Gravy. "It's belonged to me since the first time I almost stole it from your closet."

"Well," said Suzee, regaining composure. "The good news is, per the second amendment to the Star Chamber Constitution, section four, Simon England is totally free and clear. I think I'll make a run for him."

Clarissa smiled, her very expensive teeth grinding into very expensive dust.

"With my blessings," she said.

As she scrubbed the already clean Spanish Anfora mosaic tiles in her bathroom (she had begged her father to buy them for her for her twenty-eighth (thirty-first) birthday, and had been slipping on them ever since), Clarissa was daydreaming about what kind of death would be appropriate for Suzee, the Alger Hiss of the Star Chamber. Staring at her bathtub, Clarissa thought about drowning. However, she felt a watery death wasn't "impactful" enough for Suzee's demise. She needed a "statement death."

Clarissa got out a piece of paper, sat down on the cold floor and made a list:

1. Fire: Burn Suzee's house down. Matches. Oil can. Involves heavy lifting.
2. Car crash: Cut Suzee's brake line. Note to self: Have to find out what a brake line is.
3. Hanging: Encourage Suzee to tie a rope around her neck, fling one end over a rafter, and jump from a rickety chair. Rafters?

Clarissa sighed. Inspiration, that whimsical, teasing wraith, was failing her.

She arose and moved to her bedroom, but not before shredding her "kill Suzee" list in the garbage disposal. If there was one thing she'd learned by watching *The Billionaire Boys Club* over and over (those boys put the "Q" in cute!), it was "destroy any list with the word 'kill' on it."

She then lit three patchouli-scented candles (her aromatherapist had told her it was an uplifting, soothing scent), set them in a circle around her, crossed one leg over the other, spread her hands over her knees, and closed her eyes. And waited. And waited.

Clarissa had learned how to meditate at the behest of her mother, the aerobicized chain-smoker; she had gone to a class of five or six women, all of them with ample disposable income and time to be "spiritual." She was given a mantra (long forgotten) and a prayer to intone at the beginning and end of each meditation (never bothered to memorize). Her teacher, a "spiritual guide" with a face like a ripe tomato and the earnestness of a trained seal, seemed disappointed with her progress—Clarissa had slept through all three sessions.

Like many things that required sustained effort, TM was not for Clarissa.

On rare occasion, Clarissa felt the need to journey deep inside her flinty pretense, past the age-old hurts: teenage anger, childhood disappointments, fetal traumas, to a place inside of her where no lies were ever told, no judgments articulated, no manipulations stirred.

It took a while to get there.

Instead of answers, questions rose before her like eager hands, bursting from the ground that was her subconscious mind. Clarissa knew she was supposed to ignore this "brain chatter" and allow her mantra to drown out distractions, but instead, she opened her eyes and thought about the questions: *When will there be a reliable instrument for permanent hair removal? Why don't men get cellulite? And, last, Was she, Clarissa Alpert, still in love with Simon England?*

Clarissa thought about her relationship with Simon. She remembered the first moment of the first day she met him in her senior year in high school. He was fresh from London, new to the school, new to (excuse the oxymoron) Beverly Hills culture. Clarissa and her friends deemed him Simon England after hearing his accent; to this day, no one, including Simon, can recall his true last name. Simon was already a fearless dresser, but not in the sense that he dressed like a trendsetter, no. Simon would come to school in suits. Beautiful suits—a few cashmere Savile Row handed down from his grandfather and father, an international law expert—tailored to fit his narrow-hipped Roger-Daltrey-at-Monterey-Pop-Festival body. He had a pin-striped Hugo Boss and a silver-blue Armani, paid for by a job deejaying at all-night parties and raves; the suit that pushed Clarissa into demanding a date with him—white linen with a paisley shirt—was straight out of Abbey Road London, circa 1972.

Sometimes Simon would even wear a silk ascot; he had a collection of antique canes.

On special occasions, he wore a cape.

Even at sixteen, Simon had style.

Clarissa sighed.

She wondered if she could ever love Aaron, the future father of her children, the way she'd loved Simon. The way she hadn't loved anybody since the day he had said goodbye to her, the day she knew what she had suspected all along—that, she, Clarissa, Queen of All She Surveyed, was unlovable.

Manolo the Therapist had told her that the root of her relationship problems stemmed from Clarissa's relationship with her father.

"Like, duh," Clarissa had said.

"Listen to me," Manolo had cautioned. "You are doomed to search out meaningless and empty encounters and relationships unless you come to terms with your father."

"Come to terms with him?" she said. "Does that mean I have to converse with Mr. Creepy?"

Clarissa had loved her father to the near exclusion of everyone, including her mother, until her twelfth birthday, when she figured out the rules of life.

She had written them down.

"The rules of life," the twelve-year-old Clarissa wrote, "as per Clarissa Alpert, Age 12 (as of today)."

Her father had forgotten her birthday and had taken a girlfriend out on his boat instead. He had forgotten he was still married to Clarissa's mother. He also had forgotten that the bank owned his boat.

"Don't show your feelings."

She had overheard her mother screaming at him over the phone, then shattering the receiver. Her young girlfriends had heard as well. One of them sat Clarissa down and told her what she already knew: Her father was a cheater.

"Don't expect anything from anyone."

Her mother spent the rest of the afternoon with a smile ripped into her face; Clarissa would never have known she was unhappy.

"Don't ever let anyone break your heart."

Later that day, after her friends had left and the birthday cake had been ceremoniously thrown out so that Clarissa wouldn't eat the leftovers (which she did anyway, diving into the trash after her mother went to sleep), she and her mother went shopping.

Her mother spent $8,000 that they didn't have at Tiffany on a platinum and diamond tennis bracelet for herself. She bought Clarissa her first set of diamond earrings, half-carat studs. The price tag was about $1,500.

"Get everything you can."

After that eventful day, Clarissa picked up on every nuance, every set of behaviors of the women around her. Whether married, separated, divorced, stay-at-home, or career-oriented, they made practical decisions based on surviving with their pride intact. If that included buying an $8,000 bracelet to ensure that one still was "somebody," so be it.

She noticed merchants always referred to her mother as "Mrs. Alpert," whether on Rodeo or miles east of La Cienega—and she knew exactly the price her mother was willing to pay to keep that moniker.

Her parents made up later in the week after an exchange of harsh words, tears, and one more trinket, but by that time Clarissa already had learned her lessons well. And, by her thirteenth birthday, she was a card-carrying, full-blown femme fatale.

"Get them before they get you."

The phone was ringing. Clarissa rose from her modified lotus (modified in that she was lying down) and raced to the phone. As she picked it up, she realized two things: a. She had run to the phone. This was odd because she hated any form of any exercise, and she *never* ran for a call, and b. her cheeks were wet; Clarissa had been crying.

She knew it was Aaron before she answered.

"I just realized something," he said.

"You can't live without me."

"I've never been to Disneyland."

Clarissa smiled. "Tonight?" she asked.

"I'm downstairs," he said.

She screamed like she should have on her twelfth birthday, a scream of joy, of opening presents on Christmas morning (even in a Jewish household, like Clarissa's, she being more "Jewish" than Jewish), of being at the top of the roller coaster before it plunges.

She didn't even bother changing her clothes.

The day was full of firsts for Clarissa.

Clarissa and Aaron walked into Disneyland with almost $500 and walked out with over a dozen stuffed animals (all of which had been named by Aaron), not counting the number he gave away to passing children, despite Clarissa's admonishments. (She thought the children—the snot-cheeked little crumbsnatchers one finds in public venues—might consider this pied piper of the furry set a potential threat; as she pointed out to him, no one gives away anything for free. At least, no white man.)

But Aaron shook his head at her as though she had said something really sad, like, say, "*Elle Decor* has gone out of business" or "Brad Pitt shaved his head" or "Bikini waxing has been found to cause uterine cancer."

Aaron's stuffed-animal fetish emerged quickly, popping to the surface like debris from a shipwreck; his first purchase was a small Piglet at a store on Disney's "Main Street, U.S.A." It had caught Clarissa's eye momentarily, and she mentioned she'd had one as a child. Aaron pretended to go to the restroom and bought Piglet, presenting the stuffed toy to Clarissa as though it were a furry three-and-a-half-carat emerald-cut diamond.

Clarissa loved it.

She loved it all the way to the fifth stuffed animal, and then stopped loving it. But by then it was too late—Aaron had grown attached.

"Look at the eyes on this one," he'd say, holding up a terrifying raccoon.

"It's so soft," he'd say, stroking a tiger.

"Do you want your mommy?" Aaron said to a baby elephant.

"What's Piglet thinking?" Aaron asked, as they walked out of their third store, holding two full bags—animal heads popping out, their shiny marble eyes like children watching their parents, hoping a fight is averted. Clarissa had grown more silent with each purchase.

"Piglet is thinking that Mr. Aaron may be out of his fucking mind."

"Oh, that couldn't be Piglet—Piglet doesn't swear."

"Okay," said Piglet, through the perturbed blonde woman. "Mr. Aaron? How do you spell fetish?"

"Do you think I want to have sex with my animals?" Aaron asked.

People were staring.

"Talk through the fish," she demanded.

"The yellow tang or the puffer?" he asked.

"That one."

Aaron picked a fish out of the batch, a giant neon yellow tang.

"It's a little difficult. Mr. Tang has no vocal cords," Aaron said. "But he doesn't like to talk about it."

Clarissa tried to hide her smile.

"I don't care," said Piglet. "You think this is easy for me? I mean, I barely know you, and here you are, buying up every stuffed toy in the store."

"I'm going to give most of them away," Mr. Yellow Tang claimed.

"Not most of us!" the animals protested.

"Mr. Yellow Tang. Are you too weird for me?" Piglet asked, serious.

"You have to understand, Piglet," said Mr. Yellow Tang. "When I was growing up, I didn't have . . . I was different. I had no feet, so I couldn't go to school. I was an only yellow tang; I had no brothers and sisters. My parents swam off every day . . ."

Clarissa watched Aaron with the eyes of someone who understood.

"I had three friends, Moe, Larry, and Marcus Aurelius."

"Aurelius?" Piglet asked. "Don't use that word near an open flame."

"They were a panda, a poodle, and a bear. And even though I was a yellow tang, they loved me."

Clarissa reached out and took Aaron's hand, and they strolled, all of them, to New Orleans Square toward "Pirates of the Caribbean," which, as it turns out, was Mr. Yellow Tang's favorite ride.

Piglet, on the other hand, was too afraid of pirates to open his eyes.

"Yellow *What*?" Gravy asked.

"What happened to Curly Joe?" Jen asked.

"That's sort of way beyond the point, Jen," Clarissa said.

Clarissa was on a three-way conversation with her best mates.

"Okay, okay. So, he likes these . . . stuffed animals . . . in a cute way?" Jen asked.

"More like an acute way," Gravy said.

"Verdict?" Clarissa asked. She was in a hurry.

"Adorable," Jen said.

"As your most educated friend, I can tell you he's whacked," Gravy said, "but Zoloft-able."

"Good enough," Clarissa said.

"Just make sure he doesn't spend all his money on these things. It feels like we're traipsing into dangerous Jean Kasem territory." Jean Kasem was the blonde, white version of Grace Jones married to small, dark, *Billboard* deejay Casey Kasem. A "Jean Kasem" was known as a scary rich person in the Star Chamber catalog of sayings. She was often featured in *213,* the Beverly Hills free press—and the girls found her frightening. Gravy claimed she was really a man.

Clarissa hung up and went back to soaking in her tub. Walking through Disneyland carrying bushels of "friends in fur," as Aaron called them, had taken its toll on her body, and she had another date with Aaron—at a new Frenchish place on Beverly Drive.

Tonight was the third-night qualifier; Clarissa wanted to be in peak form.

* * *

"What do you mean you don't want to sleep with me?" Clarissa almost screamed. "It's our third date—the third-night screw is sacred."

Aaron was not budging; Clarissa was experiencing "blue clit."

"I don't believe in the third-night screw," he said.

"But it's like, internationally sanctioned."

"Clarissa, how can I explain this? I wanted to ravage you the moment we met. Right there at the Ivy, on the table, right on top of those crispy French fries."

Clarissa smiled. The big-ass-in-face gambit had worked.

"And then I wanted to, again, when you threw that big party for me and pretended not to."

Before Clarissa could protest, Aaron held up his finger to her mouth. "Yes, you did."

Clarissa sat back and pouted. "But because we waited," Aaron continued, "all these many . . . hours, I find that I, almost inexplicably, care about you." He looked at her. "Therefore, I don't want to sleep with you. I want to take my time. The buildup is half the fun."

Clarissa suddenly got up from Aaron's bed, where they had completed the perfect makeout session, and started pacing.

Phase Two of Operation Fucknight had begun in the entryway. They had just returned from Phase One: a *très* romantic dinner at Valentino. After much consideration, Clarissa had chosen the venue for the lighting and the wine list. She had wielded superhuman powers in abstaining from the world-class tiramisu—tonight, she had to be in fighting shape. She had to be the Muhammad Ali of the bedroom.

They had just entered his darkened mansion; Aaron had closed the door behind them. From behind, he quickly slid his arm around her waist. And then he started kissing her neck, gently pushing her head to the side as his lips brushed her collarbone.

Clarissa tried to turn to face him, but he held her, grinding everything he had into her backside . . .

And "everything" was a full plate.

He whispered into her ear, "You smell so good—Oh my God, Jesus, you smell so good . . ."

Clarissa's legs were literally melting underneath her; Aaron was a neck kisser. And a talker. And a grinder. It was the Stereo Aaron Experience.

How much luck could one girl have?

She pointed upstairs with a lust-weakened arm, but she wasn't sure how she would get there, given that her legs were useless—until Aaron lifted her and carried her up the winding staircase and into Nir-fucking-vana.

They were entering Phase Three.

Not so fast.

Minutes later, sitting back on Aaron's bed, Clarissa's head spinning, her mouth parched, she could not see; Clarissa couldn't understand what she'd been hearing—everything had been going so well—he was the most wonderful kisser, not too wet, not too dry—she had even caught him with open eyes, staring at her.

"What am I going to tell people?"

"The magazine?"

"The Chamber—my girls—what am I going to tell them? They expect results from me—I can't let them down—they'll be so disappointed, their little faces, they're like children—you have to give me something, a spin, anything."

"Your friends are that interested in your sex life?"

"Of course. Aren't yours?"

Aaron thought about this a moment. "Only meaningless sex. If it's meaningful sex, they cower in their beers or their bongs." Aaron patted a spot on the bed, next to him. "Our sex life is between us, young lady. Now, come here."

Clarissa wouldn't budge, partially because she was confused. "Define meaningful sex."

"Meaningful sex: I, Aaron, say I'll call you tomorrow, and I do, before *Nightline.* I sleep over at your place, and I'm still there for the *Today* show and eye boogers and 'How do you like your coffee' chitchat. I make plans for a Friday night before Monday's been put to bed."

Clarissa wasn't buying it. "Joseph Aaron Kingsley Mason: You're not attracted to me."

"Clarissa, I want to take this slowly. How did you know my whole name?"

"Google. And don't say 'take this slowly.' The last guy who said 'slowly' to me sported a cashew in his pants."

"Well, not to worry. Mine's more like a filbert."

Clarissa sat next to Aaron and leaned back in his arms.

"That's a girl," he said.

"You think I'm fat," she said, her head popping up.

"Healthy."

"You think I'm *healthy*?"

"What's wrong with healthy?"

"What's wrong with healthy? You might as well call me 'pleasantly plump' or 'junior plus'!"

"You're a beautiful girl, you've been beautiful since the first day of adolescence, and you know it."

"I still hate you," she said, feeling quite the opposite.

"Look, honey," Aaron said. "I grew up in Georgia; in Georgia, we like breeders, understand?"

"You're grossing me out. Tell me you never had sex with any form of livestock."

He grabbed at her thigh and squeezed. It was not altogether unpleasant, but Clarissa still smacked his hand.

"If a girl is too concerned with what's going in her mouth, you know you got trouble in the bedroom. The girl who doesn't like to eat, doesn't like to eat. If you get my drift."

Clarissa got the drift. She smiled. "I've never been a picky eater. But more importantly." She poked him.

"I pride myself on my eating habits," Aaron replied. "Let's pick out a pair of pajamas and get into bed."

He got up, opened a large drawer for her filled with cotton and silk and cashmere pajamas.

Clarissa selected a light blue cashmere set.

When she was done changing, Clarissa joined Aaron, slipping next to him in bed like they had been performing this routine for fifty years. She half expected to see his dentures in a cup on the nightstand.

They spooned and he put his arms around her . . . and they cuddled. Clarissa suddenly felt shy. Cuddling, for her, was the true intimate act. She couldn't even remember the last time a man really hugged her. Sadder still, she couldn't remember the last time she missed being hugged.

Clarissa suddenly felt very sorry for herself.

"Do you mind if someone joins us?" Aaron said.

Clarissa twisted to look at Aaron. "I knew it, I knew you were going to turn into—" She spun out of his reach.

Aaron pulled the yellow tang from under the covers.

Clarissa shook her head and rolled back into his arms. Moments passed.

"Do you want our children to sleep in our bed, or out?" he asked.

Clarissa kissed him. "Those brats? They can sleep in the garage."

She hoped he didn't hear the crack in her voice.

They lay there for a moment; Clarissa timing her breath to his, finding comfort in his slow, steady rhythm.

"Did your voice just crack?" Aaron asked.

Okay, so the whole stuffed animal thing was a risk. Aaron wanted to see just how far he could test Clarissa, how much she'd be willing to play along with his (relatively banal) eccentricities—and so far, she'd passed with flying colors. But after all, he hadn't asked her to screw herself with her own foot or bleach her poophole or any of the things he'd heard regarding the needs of the successful L.A. bachelor, stories that he'd picked up at the Sports Club L.A. locker room from that agent at C.A.A. who always wore a red bandana on his head and a wedding ring that looked like a handcuff and from the sitcom producer who wore Hawaiian shirts like jerseys and seemed so proud of his erstwhile crack addiction.

So Aaron had an obsession. Easy for any cut-rate therapist or 1-800 psychic to get to the root of; he'd grown up on the Mason compound, with few friends and parents who were absent by dint of alcohol or infidelity or choice or just plain old neglect. When he was hospitalized as a toddler to correct his handicap, he was given a teddy bear—which he'd kept until he left for college. He realized that his beer-guzzling, good ol' boy roommates at SMU might raise an eyebrow at a guy who slept with anything but a buxom cheerleader whose major skill was holding a beer can and a lit cigarette in one hand while administering a handjob with the other.

When he got out of school, he'd headed straight to Los Angeles, and the less control he felt over the outside world, the more furry friends he would add to his collection; he would bequeath them names and birth dates and personalities. He liked their smell and their feel.

Okay, so he was a little weird. But he likened his habit to the collection of hubcaps and beer bottles he'd seen at other bachelor pads—without the sharp edges and potential tetanus shots.

Confession: When Aaron moved to L.A., the first thing he wanted to do was go to Disneyland, but he had no one to take, and he felt stupid going alone.

Until Clarissa came along, who seemed game for anything not involving blood or mucus or ugly footwear.

Disneyland.

Aaron had received word that morning that a director was interested in the project—a director who was older, who had a track record, whose last job wasn't a video or a commercial or something with a III at the end of the title.

The director had called Aaron directly; he wanted to talk writers. He wanted to get started right away.

And Aaron had felt like celebrating. And he found himself calling Clarissa.

The girl who produced lists of the coolest restaurants and nightclubs and publications and insisted Aaron wear comme des garcon cologne gasped (in a good way) at the prospect of going to Disneyland.

Few things could have made Aaron happier.

Aaron was finding he was more serious about Clarissa than he thought he could or should be—he missed her throughout the day—to the point that a pretty face or potent figure would only bring hers to mind. Sure he could have fucked her on their last date—he wanted to fuck her. But he had decided, over a plate of lobster ravioli (and much to his own surprise), not to go through with it. Clarissa was more to him than a fuck—she was an inspiration.

She motivated him—to stay in L.A., to make his life here work. And maybe one day, he would be successful enough, and she would love him enough, that she would understand and forgive why he did what he did.

After she kicked his ass.

Seven

Kickin' It Up a Notch

Detes!" Gravy said, breathing heavy, her face red and puffy like a drunk Santa. "Details—in-depth, up to the minute, news at eleven—I'm going to die!"

"She can tell us . . . when she's ready," Jen said, closing her eyes and tilting her head back, as though avoiding passing out.

"Take the hill, you gaping holes!" a voice like human sandpaper screeched.

Clarissa stared straight ahead, sweat dripping from the top of her forehead and up into her nostrils, defying what she had understood from two years (repeated) of high school physics.

The Star Chamber was six minutes into Dominatrix Lola's Spin Class at Crash Gym on Sunset. Clarissa, who'd sworn never to spin, had been recruited by her peers, whom she would *never forgive*.

"Silence, lemurs!" the dyke teacher with the enormous quads wrapped tight in black Lycra yelled. She wore a brilliant yellow belt around her waist; she looked like a very bad gift.

"This is important shit!" Gravy yelled back, as she tried to pedal harder.

There were forty people in the 10:00 A.M. class at Crash, a testament to the teacher, the students, or to unemployment levels in the southern California entertainment industries.

"Please don't get her mad," Jennifer huffed. "She likes to make people cry."

"I heard she's an actual dominatrix—but only on weekends," Clarissa said.

"She's not a dominatrix, doink, she's a bookkeeper at MGM," Gravy wheezed.

"Pick up the pace, ruminants!" the dyke teacher yelled.

Polo had just walked in, late and luxurious of gait, as though she had been fucking in the broom closet just thirty seconds before.

"Her Royal Whoreness has arrived," Gravy said.

Polio smiled and sat her plasticine self on a bike behind Clarissa and spritzed on cologne. The dyke teacher (it's okay—she called herself both the "dyke teacher," and "Dominatrix Lola") said nothing. She, like anyone who came into contact with Polo, was sporting a crush.

"So, 'rissa—particulars?" Polo asked.

"Ixnay on the intercourse-ay," Clarissa said. Her thighs were chafing against the bike; her seat was angled so she felt as though she was losing all feeling in her genitalia. It was much like having to sit through a recent John Travolta movie.

"No way," Jennifer said. Then, shifting her weight, she added, "This can't be good for my 'ginie."

"Third-date screw," Gravy demanded. "What happened to the third-date screw?"

A man in front of Gravy turned and shot her a look. Gravy, in her usual mature fashion, stuck her tongue out at him, wiggling it like a fat earthworm.

"He's gay, 'rissa," Polio said, sitting on her bike, not bothering to pedal. "Your man is stone-cold homo. He's smokin' pole."

"After class," Clarissa managed to say, "I'll explain—after class."

"I can't feel my labia!" Jen cried.

"Do I look flush with excitement, comrades?" Gravy said. "Fred Segal has accepted my spring line." She showed off a pair of tiny earrings—one said "1," the other "2."

"What spring line?" Polo asked.

"I have no fucking idea. But I'll have one by the time spring gets here. I figure there's enough numbers out there to keep me busy. I'm calling it Smarteez. It's going to feature all kinds of mathematical symbols—pi, the isosceles triangle, $E=MC^2$—"

The Star Chamber was sitting at the juice bar at Crash suckling yogurt-alfalfa-wheatgrass-carrot smoothies and munching down protein bars and unidentifiable muffin-type items with gusto—taking in more than double the caloric expenditure of their spin class.

"I let you guys down," Clarissa said. "I don't like to let my people down."

"You could never let us down," Jen reassured her.

"Speak for yourself," Gravy said. "I say he's a Mormon, and I don't even know what that is, and, by the way, who needs it?"

"Look, genius," Clarissa said. "Aaron said . . . he just didn't want to have meaningless sex with me."

"Gay as the day is long as a two-dollar bill a rainy day Rosie O'Donnell," Polio said. "But under no circumstances Kevin Spacey." And then, she coughed.

"Gay is as gay does," Gravy agreed.

"He's not gay," Clarissa said. "He presented a fine argument against the third-date rule."

"Well, you can't marry him, I mean, *force* him to marry you until after you sleep together. It's un-American, even if he is a member of the Rip Taylor clan," Gravy said. "And besides, you don't have much time if you're going to make your June wedding."

"Why don't I sleep with him, then report back?" Polo laughed. And then coughed.

Clarissa did not laugh. She and Polo had "shared" on several occasions (although not at the same time—Clarissa would never be seen naked in the same room with Polo, *are you crazy?*); it was not an experience she wanted to relive.

"He's such a romantic," Jennifer said. "He's so . . . Rick Springfield."

"Girls. Aaron talked about our children," Clarissa said.

The Star Chamber looked at her. No one said a word. No one seemed to be breathing. "Our children," Clarissa repeated; it sounded like a mantra. The girls sat in silence, digesting this crucial bit of information. And then, Gravy spoke: "He said the 'c' word?" Her voice was just this side of "quivering mass of envious jelly." Clarissa was pleased.

"Children?" Jennifer said. "Oh, Clarissa, are you sure?"

"Am I sure? It's not like he said 'chowder' or 'chicken.'"

"I have never heard a man say that word," Polo admitted. "Never. Not even when they see children playing in the street. They'll say 'Look at those . . . material objects . . . playing basketball.' Or if their sister just had a baby, they'll say 'My sister just dropped off a package.'"

"Try asking them if they have nephews or nieces—you might as well ask if they have herpes," Gravy said. "They get this look on their face—like . . . bad refrigerator smell."

"I find Latin men are much more open about children," Jennifer said. She looked at them. "Don't you?"

"Latin men?" Gravy said. "Like who? Ricky 'Don't-Ask-Don't-Tell' Martin?"

Clarissa had only heard a man mention children once before, and that was in high school, when such words could be spoken and not taken seriously. Simon had said the word to her. She had waited fourteen years to hear the word again.

"Girls," Gravy said, banging her smoothie on the table. "We are going to a wedding."

They all screamed.

However, there were two items that needed clearing up before "Here Comes the Bride": 1. Aaron had to pop the question; and 2. Clarissa and Aaron had to have sex. If Clarissa had learned anything in life, it was that one had to test-drive a car (even a Mercedes) before buying. Clarissa was willing to compromise her future—but not her future sex life. If said Mercedes had a flat, no gas, engine trouble, or preferred a male driver, Clarissa wanted to know.

And time, as Gravy so aptly stated, was of the essence. Clarissa had less than two weeks to get Aaron to propose—or at least to believe that he'd proposed. There was a phrase Clarissa had heard that was used in the movie business—"suspension of disbelief." Aaron had to be sucked in (pardon) fast, much like the unwitting audience at a Renny Harlin film; if Aaron suspended disbelief that he would marry Clarissa, then Clarissa could take their relationship to the next step.

And so, as desperate times call for desperate means, she resorted to a joint meeting with her parents.

Clarissa wrote a list of meeting places that could be considered neutral, as her parents had just broken up for about, oh, the millionth time (if millionth is a word) since the late 1960s. Clarissa wondered if Camp David were available for a weekend rental.

She nixed Nate and Al's (her dad's favorite) and Spago Beverly Hills (her mother's); she drew a line through Santa Monica Pier (too proletariat) and Hillcrest Country Club (too exclusive). Clarissa was at a loss, until she remembered—court number three at the Beverly Hills public tennis courts—a meeting place all involved could agree upon. Clarissa hated tennis but loved the short (*not pleated, thank you—they make me look like a bison who's wearing a pleated skirt*) skirts. Her mother loved tennis, was not a great player, but looked gloatable in both a visor and pleats, no mean feat at her age or any; her father loved tennis and was a great player but looked ridiculous in shorts—he was, at his age, all knees. Thus, the playing field for both parental units would be even.

Clarissa waited, growing impatient, in the parking lot; she was about to call Gravy to complain when her mother pulled into the parking lot blaring salsa music.

"Thanks for showing up, Mama," Clarissa said.

"I hate heem, your father," her mother said. "But I do this for you." She hopped out of her sports coupe wearing a pleated skirt with a matching shirt, socks, tennis shoes, and visor, all in bright orange and so brand spanking new she crackled with every step.

"Also, you look extra cute and extra citrusy in that Izod outfit and you want to rub it in," Clarissa pointed out.

"Also, that," her mother said. "So, what's this meeting about, Clareesa?"

"Great news, you'll find out," Clarissa said. "There's Teddy."

Teddy drove up fast in his single-guy sedan, screamed to a halt, and jumped out as though he had been bitten by a rattlesnake; he grabbed his racket and a set of balls and strode toward them with an enormous amount of annoying "old man" energy. Her dad had become the type of man who could be seen at tennis courts and high school tracks around the country: "I'm still viable!" the old guys practically screamed with every step, every holler. "I can still take you on!"

"Edward," her mother said, as he approached.

"Sweetie," Teddy replied. He'd always called her mother "Sweetie." "You look radiant, as always," he said. Clarissa couldn't tell what her mother was thinking, but she noticed color fill her cheeks. "Ugh," Clarissa said, under her breath.

Teddy kissed her mother's hand.

"And how do I look, Teddy?" Clarissa asked.

Teddy looked at her. "You feeling okay, kiddo?"

"Christ," Clarissa said. "Let's walk to the court. We only have forty-five minutes to decide my fate."

Clarissa first played on her mother's side of the court, against her father, and then switched halfway through. She may as well have been reading the *Star* or picking polish off her nails, something worthwhile and redeeming—neither parent ever hit a ball her way. In fact, her mother and father seemed to forget she was on the court altogether. Finally, Clarissa sat on the bench on the side of the court, watching the ball connect more times than she could count until her parents took a water break.

"You're killing me out there, Sweetie," her dad said, as he took a swig off an enormous Evian bottle, then handed it to her mother.

"You just going easy on me, Eduardo," her mother smiled. She took a ladylike swig off his water bottle.

Clarissa rolled her eyes. "Okay, now that we're exchanging bodily fluids, can we discuss my future happiness, please?"

Her parents looked at her as though shocked to see her sitting there.

"Can it wait?" Teddy said. "We're almost done with this set."

"No, it can't wait, Teddy," Clarissa said. "I need you two to have an engagement dinner for me and Aaron."

"Oh my God!" her mother screamed and hugged Clarissa.

"Babycakes!" Teddy said, and then, with the tiniest bit of paternal interest crossing his brow. "How well do you really know this guy?"

"Well enough to get engaged," Clarissa replied, "Saturday, ten people, Mom's house, around eight is good." She stood quickly, before objection or whine or practicality issues could reach her ears; she brushed off her rear. "Don't let me down—your future grandchildren are depending on you."

Then Clarissa hugged them both and blew them both kisses and walked off; she had work to attend to.

"I thought your parents were divorced," Aaron said.

"They are, but they still sleep together," Clarissa replied. She bit into one of a thousand bacon-wrapped melon balls that her mother had put out on silver platters.

"So, what's the occasion?" Aaron asked.

A loud noise came from the kitchen, something quickly followed by an exclamation mark.

Jennifer jumped up—"I'm going to check on that . . . thing"—and headed, courageously, for the kitchen.

Clarissa looked at Gravy, who was sitting sideways on an overstuffed chair fondling a tall drink. She had a flower in her hair, which was almost as annoying as it was stupid.

"The occasion?" Gravy asked.

"Yes, the occasion, for this get-together," Aaron said.

Gravy looked at Clarissa. "The occasion."

"Aaron, can't anyone have a dinner party without an occasion?" Clarissa said. "Gravy, take that flower out of your hair, please."

"Do you like my flower, Aaron?" Gravy asked.

"It's very nice. It's . . . festive."

"It's very gardenia," Gravy agreed.

"Five minutes ago it was festive; now it's feeble," Clarissa said, five minutes meaning one year. She popped another bacon-wrapped melon thingie in her mouth and wondered about the rationale behind mixing meat with fruit just as the doorbell rang. Clarissa smiled at Aaron and rose and headed for the front door.

Evil Suzee was there; standing next to her was Simon.

"Darling!" Suzee exclaimed.

Clarissa grabbed Suzee and pushed her into the broom closet inside the hallway.

Simon raised his hand, confused; he was wearing a thumb ring.

"I'll be right back," Clarissa said to him. "Good shoes."

Simon looked at his feet as Clarissa shut the door.

"What the hell are you doing?" Suzee spat, as Clarissa crowded into the closet and turned on the overhead lightbulb. Several of her father's heavy winter coats were still hanging as though waiting for their owner to appear; Clarissa thought about going through the pockets.

"You can't bring my Simon to my engagement party," Clarissa said. "It's a declaration of war. We have rules."

"You said I could bring a date," Suzee hissed. "Simon is my date. Now, let me out of here."

"Simon is not a date. Simon is a chapter in the Clarissa Regina Alpert history book—three chapters, tops."

"Aaron and Simon will have to meet sometime. I don't see why you're so upset, unless, of course, you still have feelings for him." Suzee smiled. She looked like a happy boa constrictor. "And if you do have feelings for him, well, you shouldn't get married, right?"

"Fine," Clarissa said. "I'll just sit them on opposite ends of the table." She started to open the door.

"Clarissa?" Suzee said.

"What."

"Simon is the greatest kisser *ever,* don't you think?" she said.

Clarissa smiled at Suzee as she stepped out of the closet.

And then shut the door and locked it from the outside.

"Kids," Teddy walked into the living room, "how's the drinks?" One of Teddy's eyes was almost swollen shut; what could be called his hair (after all, he paid for it) on the left side of his head was standing at attention. He looked like he'd been in a wrestling match with a Kitchen Aid.

"I'm dry," Clarissa said, as she rushed into the living room, straightening her Dolce Gabbana skirt. Suzee's screams were faint but audible; she ran over to the stereo and turned up her mother's Cubano music, bobbing her head like a dashboard Dalmation. Gravy shot her a questioning look, which Clarissa ignored. "Who's—" Gravy tried to ask, again.

"Neighbors," Clarissa said.

"Let me help you, Mr. Alpert," Aaron said, getting up.

"No, no," Teddy put his hand on his shoulder. "You'll have plenty of years to wait on this one."

He said, meaning Clarissa.

Aaron looked at Clarissa, who wrinkled her nose at him. Aaron narrowed his eyes at her, which only made him look cuter. And slightly near-sighted.

"'sides, you don't want to go in there, son," Teddy said, shaking his head. "Wish me luck," he said, over his shoulder, as he took a deep breath and went back into the kitchen.

"Who was at the door?" Aaron asked.

Clarissa looked at him, "Tell Gravy about your pet project, the musical. I think it's going to be a big hit. Do you think it should come out in the summer or Christmas or what?"

"Clarissa, who was at the door?" Aaron said.

"What door?" Clarissa asked.

Aaron shook his finger at her. "You know very well . . ." The doorbell rang again. Clarissa thought about Simon, whom she'd left out on the porch, in the cold.

"That door, Clarissa," Aaron said.

She sprang up, but not fast enough to beat Aaron.

"Allow me," he said, jumping up. "You keep an eye on your parents. Dial 911 if you smell blood or sulfur." They could now hear her parents shouting at each other above the kitchen fan. Clarissa's mother was saying things in Spanish that, even with her limited understanding, Clarissa knew weren't "Good evening" or "Would you care for some sour cream with your salmon skin appetizer?"

Clarissa sat down like a bag of rocks; the jig was up. It was too late to stop Aaron; Gravy sat down next to Clarissa, who had now found herself gulping down the last of Aaron's drink and fishing for the pineapple bits.

"C, what is up?"

"Suzee brought Simon," Clarissa said, picking her teeth with the toothpick.

"Mmm. So . . . where are they?"

"Suzee's in the broom closet. Simon is about to enter with Aaron. My life is very close to falling apart, and I'm not even close to being drunk enough to ignore it."

"This is quite the engagement party."

"Thank you."

"Your father mixes a nice beverage."

"Clarissa?" Aaron said, as he walked into the room. "Your friends are here."

Clarissa closed her eyes and turned toward Aaron's voice. She opened them up to Jennifer, standing next to a Latino man with a thick mustache and very white teeth, and wearing a large, white cowboy hat; he had the dignified yet rustic air of someone who worked well with his hands. "Clarissa," Jennifer said, "this is Pablo. I told you about him."

"Hi," Clarissa stood up. She didn't remember Jennifer mentioning any man at any time in the last two years, up to and including a Pablo.

Pablo took his hat off and bowed.

Her mother's Cubano tape ended; Suzee's lungs seem to have cleared, and now she continued her annoying screaming jag. A glass shattered somewhere in the vicinity of the kitchen.

"Is everything all right?" Jennifer asked.

And then, another glass.

"Ooh. That sounded very Waterford to me," Gravy said.

The doorbell rang again.

"Would you care for a melon ball, Mr. Pablo?" Clarissa offered, picking up a silver platter.

Simon walked in with artillery, the equivalent of the "smart bomb"—a dozen peach-colored roses.

"Simon!" Clarissa shot up as though she had a pack of Energizer bunnies up her ass.

Aaron unfolded himself from the couch and stood at proper manly checking-out distance.

Simon kissed both of Clarissa's cheeks. "I ran down to the corner flower shop two miles away—I remember how your mother loved pastel roses."

"Hey, Simon E.," Gravy said, toasting nobody. "This has become one hell of an engagement party."

Fucking Gravy, thought Clarissa. *Already the loud, inappropriate drunk.*

Simon looked at Clarissa. "Engagement party? Suzee didn't tell me . . ." He looked around for his date.

Clarissa interrupted, "You remember Gravy, Simon." As though that should explain everything.

"And I believe you've met Aaron," Clarissa said, turning toward her (almost) fiancé.

Simon looked at Aaron. They wore competing smiles. Simon tilted his head. "Did I?"

"Did you?" Aaron said. He smiled, without expression. "The other night, at that party." He sounded as disinterested as a weather reporter in Tucson.

"I meet so many, many people. One forgets," Simon said. "Anyway, a pleasure . . ." He looked at him as though searching for something insignificant, a dropped dime.

"Aaron. Aaron Mason."

"Right."

The handshake lasted about a minute, until Clarissa, in a feat of distraction, caught her dress on fire with Gravy's cigarette lighter—a gambit that had worked in the past without the bother of second- or third-degree burns. Aaron threw his coat over her and bravely patted her down with his bare hands while Simon threw a glass of water on her, which ruined her hair but was oddly refreshing, nonetheless.

And then it was time for the entrée.

Teddy and Clarissa's mother fought the rest of the night, she hurling her native, melodic South American swear words at him, a string of which could be translated, according to Pablo, as "half-penised son of a rooster." Teddy calling her, among other things, "a Bolivian nutbar" and "hotheaded headjob." Neither of Clarissa's parents sat at the table with the rest of the guests for more than thirty seconds at a time; Clarissa paid no attention to them unless she needed another drink or one more serving of her mother's mashed plantains; her attention was focused on Aaron and Simon and keeping them from exchanging information or blows.

Aaron gamely moved through various topics of conversation; he listened with practiced interest as Gravy, who maintained her perfect record of getting just-this-side-of-sloppy drunk at parties, described the latest in platinum versus white gold crucifix trends; he conversed with Pablo in halting high school Spanish about the pros and cons of perennials versus biennials; he even managed to calm Suzee after the closet incident, by offering her a Scotch and a cigarette and a sympathetic ear. Suzee almost forgot to be her extreme, cruel self with Clarissa, but this did not keep her from trying to turn the most minor detail into an ancient history–Simon and Clarissa story. Clarissa pinched her several times under the table, and then was forced to stab a fork in Suzee's thigh (hitting only bone) to prevent her from "sharing."

While Suzee cleaned up (a modicum of blood), Simon regaled them with fables about music industry travails—like a practiced raconteur. *It seemed,* thought Clarissa, *that he had been taking Richard Burton lessons.* Whether it was the one about Madonna and the long bus ride up a cliff in Majorca or the item about Minnie Driver flubbing back-up vocals for a local white reggae band, every story required him to jump from his seat and pantomime voices and reactions. He managed, as is often the case with industry people, to be both entertaining and annoying at the same time.

But still, he looked good.

Jennifer and Pablo sat next to each other, and Pablo would stand when Jennifer would leave the table, and hold her chair out for her, and listen attentively to her Ugliest Dogs on Earth anecdotes, though it was clear his comprehension of the English language was pretty much relegated to traffic signals.

All in all, the dinner was a success; by ten the guests were so engrossed in conversation that no one noticed that: a. the fireworks in the kitchen had died down to the occasional shout and murmur; and b. dessert, Clarissa's mother's famous flan, which Clarissa hated but her mother had insisted on making, had not been served.

Clarissa was about to get up to check when Aaron offered instead. "I want to bring my plate in," he said. He kissed her cheek.

Gravy looked at Clarissa, who looked at Jennifer, who looked at Polo, who would have looked at Suzee, but she sneezed instead. "Does your mom have cats?" Polo said. Simon left the table to get his smokes, the brown, imported kind that smell and taste like unpaved road.

Jennifer gestured for Pablo to join him—Pablo nodded and smiled, flashing white teeth the size of small boulders.

The girls were left alone.

Suzee emitted a genuine sigh.

"Aaron's not real," Gravy said. "He's a close facsimile of a human being."

"He's perfect," Jennifer said. "For you, I mean."

"There's something very wrong with that man," Suzee said.

"You mean, the fact that he's in love with me?" Clarissa said.

"For starters," Suzee said.

"Score?" Clarissa asked.

"Two to one," Gravy said. "The roses are nice, but Aaron's definitely on the gold medal track."

Aaron walked back in the door, still holding his plate. His skin looked ashen, his eyes glazed over and unfocused; he appeared to have witnessed death. "Aaron? Is it food poisoning?" Clarissa asked.

"Do not go in there," he said, sitting down.

Clarissa started to get up—he put his hand on her wrist, stopping her.

"I mean it, Clarissa," Aaron said. "You don't want to see . . ."

"Is it the flan?" Gravy asked.

Aaron shook his head, just as Teddy and Clarissa's mom blew into the living room, helping each other carry a large, unwieldy, ovum-shaped flan; their manner suddenly as cheery as blithering morning talk show hosts.

Clarissa realized her mother's blouse was improperly buttoned; it looked like a three-year-old's first attempt at dressing up.

"Oh my God," Clarissa said.

"Right there on the chopping block," Aaron whispered in her ear.

"But . . . wood absorbs!" she whispered.

Moments later, Pablo and Simon reappeared, and Pablo suddenly spoke. "I'd like to make a toast," Pablo said, in perfect English. He looked at Clarissa's mother and said something in Spanish, to which she nodded and smiled.

His voice had a deep, tranquilizing quality; his native tongue sounded like a lullaby. "In my country, when two people love each other very much, as I see you, Clarissa, and you, Aaron, do, there is only one thing to do. And that is, to get married. I am so privileged to be here today with your wonderful friends and family to witness your love and your commitment. You have touched my heart and my soul. I only hope that one day, I am as lucky as the both of you. Salud!"

Clarissa and Aaron smiled at Pablo as he raised his glass to both of them, and everyone raised their glasses at once, moved by the toast that none of them, except for Clarissa's mother, fully understood. Clarissa looked at her mother, whose eyes were shiny, wet with tears that had not yet fully formed; her mother did not bother to speak—she knew there was no need for translation.

Even Suzee wiped a tear from her quasireptilian eye.

"Ah, hell," Aaron said, standing (and almost knocking his chair over in the attempt) and raising his glass. "To Clarissa, who has managed to confuse, delight, annoy, repel, and fascinate me more than any woman I've ever known."

"I was there first," Simon said, into his drink.

"Shush, mister bitter ex," hissed Clarissa, and it occurred to her: *Simon, a nondrinker, was drunk.*

"Simon," Gravy said, "don't be a sore loser."

"Clarissa, I love you," Aaron said.

The Star Chamber filled the room with a collective sigh that sounded chorale in its intensity, and everyone (except Simon, who was busy looking sour) clinked their crystal glasses (her mother's "good stuff"), careful to include every person at the table, and then, at once, like a famished army, set to ravaging the flan.

Later, after what could have been the worst dinner party ever recorded in human history, Clarissa asked the question.

"Repel?"

"Only half the time," Aaron said, as he helped her put away the dessert plates; her parents already had gone to bed. The same bed. "The other half, I'm fascinated."

"So you're, like, half right," she said.

"You know, Clarissa, where I come from . . ."

"That state that's shaped like a boot?" Clarissa said.

"No," Aaron shook his head. "That's a country—Italy."

"The one that's bigger than Alaska."

"There is no state bigger than Alaska," Aaron said, his eyebrows meeting together in the state shaped like perplexity.

"So, geology was not my best subject."

Aaron laughed. "Georgia," he said. "Georgia. Where I come from, it's traditional that the man does the asking."

Clarissa continued to dry, rubbing a nonexistent flan stain from the china; she had lost her nerve to face him. Aaron's sleeves were rolled up; she noticed the sculpted quality of his forearms, the hair, as he put his arms on either side of her—dark, with a hint of curl; these forearms would age well. Those were very Pierce Brosnan forearms.

Aaron put his arms around her, pinning her to the kitchen counter; Clarissa, turning, pretended to struggle.

"Where I come from, Aaron, southeast Beverly Hills," Clarissa specified, "the woman who waits for the man to ask is what we call 'single.'"

Aaron was suddenly very close. She noticed the shaving spots where he'd missed; she noticed his breath was warm and inviting and his gaze was unwavering and confident and unafraid. And suddenly, she felt weak.

Then she snapped out of it. "Aaron. No fucking around. Did you mean it," she asked, "when you said that . . ."

"No. I'm just drunk and jealous," Aaron said.

Clarissa's eyes widened. Aaron laughed.

"What the hell, Clarissa," Aaron said. His eyes were serious, his tone sober. "You like me, I like you . . . I'm not a guy to let opportunity slip away—and you're not the girl who's going to do that either. Let's go for it."

"Starter marriage?" Clarissa asked.

"No. The real thing," Aaron said.

And then, they kissed. And kissed. And kissed.

"Don't," he said, as they came up for air, "for God's sake, don't touch that chopping block."

The guests lingering in the living room wondered what the laughter was all about.

Eight

Past Imperfect

3:04 A.M.

Tap.

A knight on a white horse racing through plush fields. Ooh. Has to be the English countryside.

Tap. Tap. Tap.

The knight jumping off his horse, sweeping his cape back and facing the fair maiden, who looks a lot like Clarissa with excellent hair and makeup, reclining on a bed of rose petals.

KNOCK—KNOCK, KNOCK.

He looks down at her, lovingly, then puts on a top hat and starts to tap dance.

BUZZ.

"Shit!" yelled Clarissa. She threw the beanie bag off her face—the one filled with lavender seeds to help her sleep (though she rarely needed help—she just needed to block out sunlight until noon). She looked at the digital clock with the T-shirt draped over it—3:06 A.M.

There could be only one answer. Well, two answers: 1. A polite rapist; 2. Booty call.

BUZZ.

Clarissa sighed and pushed her body out of bed, wrapping herself in a Frette cashmere robe she could ill afford but strongly felt she deserved.

She walked through the living room to the front door, but only after completing a proper nose/hair/teeth check in the large antique mirror.

"Clarissa!" someone howled. Clarissa smirked. She enjoyed that someone would care enough to howl her name.

She looked through the peephole.

There was no one there.

She looked again.

Still no one. She listened. Rasping sound; labored breathing. Clarissa wondered if someone were masturbating on her front steps. She wondered if she would have to clean up the aftereffects or if the gardener actually would be there on Tuesday like he was supposed to be. And then, she wondered if it were her father having a stroke, attempting to bid a tearful goodbye to his only daughter.

She thought about going back to bed and checking at a decent hour.

She thought about it again.

Opening the door (with the chain lock still attached), she looked around. A mound of something wearing European men's cologne was curled up on her doorstep.

Whatever it was appeared to be more asleep than dangerous.

Clarissa poked at the thing with her boa-feathered slipper. The thing groaned—an accented groan.

"Simon!" Clarissa said. "Get up!"

Simon looked at her, wounded and helpless and yet still very put together.

"I'm sick," Simon said.

"Not on my doorstep, you're not," Clarissa said. "What the hell do you think you're doing? I was asleep!"

She knelt to help Simon up, almost losing balance herself, as her slippers had three-inch heels and no patience for physical endeavor.

"I'm sick in love," he said, looking up at her.

Clarissa looked at him. "Come on in," she said, smiling.

Several pints of excellent, hot Coffee Bean and Tea Leaf faux-Kona later, and Simon was ready for short conversation intermittently interrupted by his passing out.

"Sorry," he said, as he awoke the second time. "I just—I see you with that . . . are you serious, Clarissa?"

"Simon, Aaron and I are getting married." Clarissa was not above rubbing it in.

"Clarissa. He wears boots—*cowboy boots.*" Simon said this like a plea.

"Fixable," she said. "He's not broken, Simon—he's not you, in other words."

"He's not you, either, Clarissa," Simon said. "He's so sub-Urban Cowboy—that's not who you are."

Clarissa looked at Simon. "Aaron is trying, Simon. He is . . . the other day, he wore Helmut Lang loafers."

"Alligator?"

"Patent leather."

Simon shook his head, sadly. "What happened to us, C?" he said, putting his head on her shoulder as they sat side by side, watching the nonexistent flames in the never once used fireplace, where minisized candy wrappers gathered like foil moths.

"You broke up with me," she said.

"You first."

"Yes, but I had a good reason."

"He was rude and very tall, if I remember."

"I was young—" she said, then, "ger. Young-ger."

"Does Aaron know how old you are?" Simon looked at her; his eyes were rolling around like balls on a pool table. Clarissa nodded, "Of course."

"Does Aaron know your age?" he slurred. He was sounding very Dudley Moore, very *Arthur*esque.

She nodded again, "Yes."

"Does Aaron know what year you were born?"

She shook her head. "No, he doesn't—I can never go more than three questions with you."

"I know that," Simon said. "So what are we going to do, Miss Clarissa?"

"About what?"

"About us."

Clarissa put her hands out to warm them by the "fire." She needed a moment to collect her thoughts, which were scattered and moving slowly, like old lab mice.

"Simon. There is no 'us,' " Clarissa said. The words coming out with a confidence she wasn't sure she felt. "I haven't seen you in ages, and then you show up, expecting me to be waiting around for you. Meanwhile, you've been dating anything with a one-octave range. Do you want something to eat? I'm starving."

"I'm so over that life. I'm tired, Clarissa. I want to . . ." His train of thought derailed.

"You want to what?"

"You know."

"There's very little I know—but what I do know, I'm sure of. And I'm sure that Aaron loves me and that we are getting married."

"Clarissa, we fit . . . ," Simon said, gesturing with his hands, drunkenly coaxing his fingers into a web. "I should've realized it earlier—I just always figured you'd be out there . . ."

"Waiting for you?" Clarissa said.

"You don't wait for anyone, Clarissa."

"You want something to eat?" Clarissa was tired. Being tired made her hungry. Being awake made her hungry, too. *Being* made her hungry.

"Sure," Simon said.

"Great. Tommy Burger's on La Cienega—I want one of those double-double things, and, I don't know, some kind of milkshake."

"I can't drive. I think I parked on a Volkswagen."

"God, I need to go to bed." Clarissa looked at the clock, which was running either twelve minutes fast or slow—either way, it was after four.

"Right," Simon said. "Can I stay?"

"Simon."

"Please, Clarissa. You can't send me out there tonight. Look at me."

Clarissa looked at him. He looked harmless enough—he had on his best harp seal expression.

"I'm going to sleep," she said. "I'll see you in the morning. Like, after *The View.*"

"Not even a kiss?" he said, as she got up. "Not one little, bitty, teeny, weeny good-night kiss?"

"You lost me on the teeny, weeny," Clarissa said. "And I was this close." She pressed her fingers together.

"I'll tuck you in," he said.

And then he closed his eyes and passed out, again.

Clarissa looked at Simon, her old boyfriend, passed out on her couch. And proceeded to undress him.

She couldn't help it.

First came the shoes. Gucci.

Then the socks. Black, cashmere/silk weave.

The pants. Prada spring line.

The wallet. Vintage Gucci. ($250 in cash; Clarissa kept a twenty. Okay, two twenties—after all, she was letting him sleep over.)

The underwear? Calvins, of course.

Clarissa awakened Simon with a pot of leftover Coffee Bean and Tea Leaf, which wasn't nearly as sublime six hours later.

"Good morning," she said. She sat next to him, trying different poses before finding the most sultry "I just emerged from my boudoir" pose.

Simon opened his eyes and shaded them from a nonexistent ray of sunlight. Clarissa was reminded of how cute he was when in pain.

"Clarissa," he said. "What happened?"

Clarissa's face dropped, until she realized that that action was aging. "What do you mean, what happened?"

"What are you doing here?" He started looking around.

"This is my apartment," she said. "I'm supposed to ask you that question, which I did, at three o'clock this morning."

"Oh, God," Simon said. "What did I say—I was so drunk."

Clarissa glared. "You weren't so, so drunk."

"What'd I do?" he asked. "We didn't . . ."

Clarissa just raised an eyebrow.

"We did?"

"Did we *ever,*" she said.

"Oh."

"Oh. That's it?" She closed her Frette robe over her cleavage—he didn't deserve a peek. "You asked me to come back to you."

"I did?" he said. His eyes blinked, which seemed to hurt—he rubbed his forehead.

"And I accepted," Clarissa said, "So now, we're back together. I think we should start calling people, don't you?"

Simon looked puzzled.

"Don't tell me you don't remember anything . . ." She started inching her fingers up his thigh. "You kept saying I was the best you ever had."

"I did?"

"Did you *ever*," Clarissa said. "Now listen, Aaron's coming over this morning. I'd like to tell him in person—so if you could just, you know—"

Simon was up and gathering his pants, his socks—and then, suddenly, he stopped. "No. I'm going to stay. Just in case."

Clarissa looked at him. She shook her head. "No, no," she said. "I can handle him."

"You don't know him that well, Clarissa. Now, I'll stay and take care of this situation—this is my doing. You . . . go do what you have to do."

"Simon," Clarissa said, "listen to me. I'm fine." She picked up his shoes and put them in his hands. "I'll call you when it's over, okay?"

"I'll just wait outside, in my car. If anything happens, I'll be right here."

"No!" Clarissa said. "Simon, look, I was just kidding about last night. Nothing happened."

"Clarissa." Simon touched her face. "We both know it was fantastic."

"It was?" The way he said it, she almost believed him.

"Oh yeah. It's all coming back to me now," he said. "In fact—" He gestured toward her bedroom.

"You know what?" Clarissa said. "I just realized. I have a doctor's appointment. It's an emergency."

"Are you okay?"

"I'm fine. It's just . . . my mother. She's not well." Clarissa steered Simon toward the door.

"Her heart?" Simon said.

"Yes," Clarissa said. "Apparently, it's shrinking."

Simon nodded, absorbing the disinformation. "Clarissa. I think we could really make it work this time."

Clarissa looked at him. "You're not just saying that because I'm not on the block anymore."

Simon smiled. "C. I'm all grown up now. I know what I want."

Clarissa smiled and sent him out the door and stood there, scratching her head.

* * *

"All grown up now?" Gravy grumbled. "He is totally Peter Pan without the tights."

"You don't think he outmanipulated me, do you?" Clarissa said. "I mean, is that possible?"

The girls were at Tiffany, picking out a proper engagement ring. Gravy, nursing a hangover and the usual postparty shattered sense of self, would have worn sunglasses over her entire body were it possible.

"Clarissa. Look," Gravy said, "Simon is beyond cute—he's the posterboy 19–24 demographic boyfriend. But he's never going to grow up."

"I like the canary, don't you?" Clarissa said.

"The one that costs one hundred twelve thousand dollars?"

"Too much?" Clarissa asked.

Gravy held up her hands. An emerald cut 2.5-diamond solitaire on her left, a round-cut 1.75 surrounded by baguette diamonds on her right. "Which one?" Gravy asked. Clarissa looked at her. "Which one do you like better?"

"I'm not sure," she said. "I'm really not sure—how can I not be sure?"

Gravy put her bejeweled hands on Clarissa's shoulders. "The rings, Clarissa. I'm talking about the rings."

Later that day, Clarissa and Aaron listened to the wedding planner with a face like a sock drawer in a light pink, softly lit room just off the patch of grass where they were soon to be married. Aaron, determined for his wedding not to be cookie-cutter, asked a barrage of questions: "How many guests can we invite?" "Can we do In-and-Out Burger instead of salmon?" "'Freebird' by Lynyrd Skynyrd instead of 'The Wedding March'?" The wedding planner never blinked or sighed, her smile never waned. Instead, she would rephrase Aaron's questions and put them to Clarissa, who held Aaron's hand as she led him down the path of wedding planner reasoning—the other end of which would be their wedding, as richly mundane as anything he feared.

Afterward they drove back to Aaron's home—and walked the spiral stairs to his bedroom hand in hand, Clarissa repainting the walls in her mind, settling on color schemes and updates and room "themes."

Aaron turned Clarissa to face him. And started to undress Clarissa. Slowly.

Really slowly.

"Ah. What's with all the buttons?" he asked.

Clarissa cursed her new ivory silk blouse with its impossible buttons. She sighed and ripped the blouse off.

"Nice," Aaron said, appraising her ample wares.

"You'd better be worth it," Clarissa replied.

He smiled and slipped off her lace thong and draped it over his nose; she laughed and picked it up, tossing it across the room.

Then Aaron pushed her back against his bed, raising her skirt and slipping both hands under her, pulling her lower body up toward his face . . .

"Holy shit," Clarissa sighed.

They cozied into an hours-long session of lovemaking, of bare skin and clenched hands and bold eye contact and no thoughts whatsoever of hunger or thirst until long after Jay Leno had introduced his last guest.

Afterward, Clarissa lay back, exhausted, arms and legs open, and floated in the aftermath of what she had captured: The elusive Love Fuck.

She turned toward Aaron, lying beside her, and appraised the arch of his nose, the curve of his full lip.

"How many rooms?" she asked.

He didn't open his eyes. "Eighteen. Why?"

"We have seventeen more to go."

Aaron smiled.

Nine

Here Comes the Prenup, uh, Bride

The morning of Clarissa and Aaron's wedding, Clarissa stepped into her Vera Wang gown in the hotel room at the Bel Air, surrounded by open champagne bottles and fruit baskets; there was a knock at the door.

Clarissa's mom scurried to get it; Clarissa wished she could knock her ugly hat off, but her mother was hell-bent on wearing the Pepto-pink satin number with tiny mother-of-pearl beading; it looked like she was wearing a giant pastry box on her head.

When her mother came back, a chihuahua-in-the-headlights look on her face, there was a man behind her, stepping gingerly.

"Clareesa," her mother said. Her accent was pronounced, her voice louder than normal, even for a Bolivian Jew; Clarissa knew this meant bad news.

"What is it?" Clarissa turned to the man. He had the superofficious look of an accountant during a bad tax year. He wore wire-framed glasses and was carrying a briefcase in one hand and a sheaf of papers in the other.

"My name is Keith Slocum," he said. "I'm the Mason family attorney." He tried to shake Clarissa's hand; she waved it away in a swift, frenzied arc, as though swatting a fly.

"I suppose you must know why I'm here," Slocum said. He looked as though he were accustomed to being swatted.

Clarissa took a step back and flipped her newly ringed hand out; her mother stuck a glass of champagne in it.

"So. Aaron sent his family attorney over," Clarissa smiled. "Let the games begin."

She drank down the glass of champagne. Beckoned for another.

"His family has some papers they would like you to sign." Keith set his briefcase down.

Clarissa sniffed at the air, nose wrinkling, as though a small rodent had died in the vicinity.

"I'm not signing anything," she said. She took off a glove, waved the glass (again) at her mother. "Hup hup," she said, demanding another. Her mother complied.

"I think you'll find this quite fair."

Clarissa took off the other glove.

"Perhaps you're deaf as well as nearsighted," she said. "I am not signing anything." She removed her shoes, silk eggshell, pointed toe, three-inch-heel Jimmy Choos.

She placed them in the attorney's hands.

"Prenuptial agreements are par for the course these days," he said. "I assure you there's nothing untoward . . ."

Clarissa slipped off her nylons—Calvin Klein nude shimmer control top sandal toe—and placed them neatly on top of the shoes.

Keith the attorney, head of the varsity debate team at the University of Philadelphia, magna cum laude graduate of Yale Law School, was losing his place in his line of reasoning. Socrates had nothing on Clarissa Regina Alpert.

"Please, I'm supposed to get your signature," he started to plead. And, like a spider catching a Pity Fuck fly, Clarissa knew she had him; she recognized his change as a show of weakness. She'd seen it many times throughout her dating career: "Please go out with me." "Please don't tell my wife." "Please don't hurt my credit rating."

"Mother, kindly escort this . . . lawyer person out," Clarissa said, as she turned her back. "Can you get my zip?"

"Clarissa—"

"Mother, my zipper," she said.

"No! I will not unzeep!" her mother proclaimed.

"Lawyer person?" Clarissa asked, turning her back.

"Stubborn!" her mother yelled.

"Miss Alpert, my client is only trying to protect his family interest. I'm sure you can understand," he said, shifting his weight from side to side, his voice getting higher.

Clarissa finally unzipped herself.

"Oh!" said her mother, sitting down on the loveseat, fanning her face.

Clarissa, in her La Perla bra and thong panties, turned to attorney Keith Slocum and stated what was now the obvious, "Clarissa Regina Alpert does *not* sign prenups."

And then she unhooked her bra and handed it to him.

"I'm sorry to hear that," he said, clutching her lingerie to his chest.

"It denigrates everything I stand for."

The attorney stood there, not moving; he was in no hurry. "I respect your . . . opinion."

"Mami!" her mother cried up at the coral-colored ceiling. "Take me!"

"Mom," Clarissa said. "Please. Sit down." She turned to the lawyer. "Tell Aaron I love him," she said, while escorting the stunned man, still holding her shoes, nylons, and bra, out the door.

"Would you like to have lunch sometime?" Keith the attorney asked.

"No," Clarissa said. "Oh, and tell Aaron . . . I loved him. Say . . . *loved,* okay? Past tense. Very important."

Then she grabbed back her girl things and shut the door.

Clarissa's mother looked at her and shook her head.

"What? Tell me you're shaking your tiny little pea head because you're disappointed in him, okay?"

"You're naked!" her mother screamed.

Clarissa walked slowly to the bathroom so as not to spill her new flute of champagne. She worked her way into an oversized robe and instantly felt superior.

"Why you so stupeed? Everybody has prenup these days!" Her mother jumped so fast off the loveseat her hat blew off her head.

Clarissa picked it up off the floor, brushed it off, then threw it out the window.

Her mother ran to the window as though a baby had fallen out."My hat!" her mother screamed. "Two hundred dollar, my hat!"

Clarissa sat back and picked up a magazine. “Mother, I really wish you had some faith in me.”

“I go tell everyone.” Her mother picked a piece of imaginary schmutz off her dress and sucked in her nonexistent stomach. She looked like a small female version of Fidel Castro.

“Tell who what?”

“No wedding,” her mother said. Her voice sounded like it was caught on barbed wire; she fluffed her hat hair.

“Mommy. Of course there’s going to be a wedding,” Clarissa intoned. She went to her mother and put her arm around her shoulders, bolstering her.

“Sit down, Mama,” Clarissa said. “Have another cocktail.”

Five minutes later, Aaron was at the door. He looked so delicious in his tuxedo that Clarissa almost started to cry, and then remembered she had spent $500 on her makeup.

“Mrs. Alpert,” he said to Clarissa’s mother, and kissed her on the cheek. “I hope I didn’t upset you.”

“Oh no,” her mother said, waving her arm at Clarissa. “She threw my hat out, my daughter.”

“It was ugly. It needed to fly.”

“I’ll get you another hat,” Aaron said. “But you look beautiful without it.”

“My hair,” her mother said.

“Gorgeous,” said Aaron.

Clarissa thought she saw her old, wizened mother blush.

“Now. You.” Aaron turned to Clarissa. “What’s this about you getting naked in front of the family attorney?”

“He was rude.”

“My God, what would’ve happened if he’d been nice?”

Aaron looked at her mother. “Can you excuse us, Mrs. Alpert?”

“Mom,” Clarissa’s mother said.

Clarissa rolled her eyes so hard, it hurt.

“Mom,” Aaron complied.

“Leesen to heem.” She pointed at Clarissa. And walked out. Clarissa knew that walk—her mother tried to strut like a peacock but looked more like a quail.

Aaron turned to her.

"So."

"So."

"You're not signing."

"I'm not."

Aaron sat down. All of a sudden he looked much older than his age. Like, thirty.

"Clarissa, come here." He held out his hand.

"No."

"Come here."

She sat down next to him.

"I want you to close your eyes," he said.

"Why?"

"Because I asked you to."

She did.

"Now. I want you to visualize something—and I want you to tell me the truth about what you feel."

"Okay," she said, though she thought this exercise strange; it reminded her of abortive meditation attempts.

"You and I are newly married," Aaron said, "and we don't have any money—we're just starting out."

Clarissa smiled.

"Really picture this, okay?"

She nodded. She stopped smiling.

"I'm driving a . . . Toyota. You drive a Mazda, or a Ford."

"Explorer?"

"Used."

"Late model?"

"Mid-nineties."

"CD player?"

"Clarissa." Aaron took a beat, then continued. "We eat dinner at restaurants at most a few times a month—places like El Torito or Coogie's. We go to movies less than that—maybe twice a month. We clip coupons, we fill our own gas tanks, we pay our own bills, balance our own checkbook. We go to the park, we go to museums. We do things that don't cost a lot of money. We don't shop. We dream of having children, when we can afford them."

Clarissa took a deep breath.

"Now. The question is: Do you still love me?"

Clarissa's eyes were still closed. "Are you still really cute?" she asked.

Aaron put his hand under her chin and brought her gaze to his. "Clarissa. I need to know . . . If I weren't rich, would you still love me?"

She looked at this man sitting in front of her. And she took a deep breath (and almost hyperventilated).

And then she kissed him.

The answer was in her kiss.

Twenty minutes later, Clarissa was walking down the aisle. Without a prenup.

Of course, she almost tripped when she saw Simon—(fall '89 Issey Miyake suit, Armani tie, bowler hat on his lap (risky!), alligator shoes—sitting on the left side, third aisle, directly behind her aunt Margie, the one with the kidney thing.

She barely noticed him.

Ten

Postwedding Wrap-up

Lidigike, whadigat thediga fudiguck idigis Sidigimodigon dodiging heredigere?!" (English translation: "Like, what the fuck is Simon doing here?!")

Clarissa was standing in the enormous muted-peach ladies' bathroom at the Bel Air, just off the enormous muted peach ballroom, screaming at the pussy posse (the Star Chamber's secondary nickname). Just as the more resplendent folks can flit between several of the finer classic languages (French, Spanish, Italian) with ease, the Star Chamber had an amazing knack for switching from West Valley American (like, duh, y'know, whatever) to "gee" language, which actually utilized the letter "D" as much or more than the forlorn "G."

"We all know who's behind this," Gravy said.

Bang. The door blew open.

"That Simon is absolutely divine!" Suzee sauntered in like a Lipizzaner on a Donny and Marie Christmas special.

"Didn't you lock that door?" Jen asked.

"Bidigitch!" Gravy enthused.

"*Ms. Bidigitch* to you, Gravy." Suzee smiled. "I was perfectly within my rights to invite Simon. Did it not say 'plus one' on the invitation?"

"Plus one does not mean Clarissa's ex—"

"It did not say 'plus one, except for anyone Clarissa may have dated.' Jesus, half the men here would be exempt."

"You underestimate me, Evil," Clarissa said. "I'd say it's more like two thirds." Clarissa was coming to her senses. This was, after all, her day, her shining hour, and damned if she was going to let some mean, spiteful bitch (even if it was one of her closest friends) ruin . . .

A familiar voice asked, "Can I help?"

The Star Chamber turned to see Aaron, hands in his pockets, standing back on his (good) heel like a too-handsome-and-therefore-doomed F. Scott Fitzgerald antihero.

"Christ," Gravy said.

"Oh, he didn't show," Aaron replied. "But a couple Apostles are busting a move . . ."

"I love it when you talk ghetto," Clarissa said, gluing herself to Aaron's arm and guiding him from the ladies' room.

"Are you going to tell me what happened?" Aaron asked, once they were out of gossiping range. His expression alone could force a confession out of a cold war spy. "We share everything now, Clarissa. Including secrets."

And then Clarissa saw a pink hat running her way—evidently, her mother had retrieved the $200 visual offensive from the ground-floor gardens.

"Clareesa, where you beeen (like bean). Plize (please), the receiving line!"

Clarissa looked at Aaron. "It's nothing, Aaron. I promise." And she surprised herself; she meant it.

Events at the receiving line, however, proved fatal to Clarissa's conviction. Clarissa stood next to Aaron, taking in her guests' best wishes with the cool acclimatization of a young Grace Kelly. She felt like a princess among her subjects. She had planned for this moment her entire life, had been groomed for a *Town and Country*–worthy wedding and little else, in fact.

Clarissa sighed with the satisfaction of a life's work well done. Two hundred of her closest, dearest (richest) friends under one roof, and their envious eyes were all on her. She looked down the row at her beautiful bridesmaids (Gravy, pulling up her dress; Jennifer, wiping mascara from under her perpetually damp eyes; Polo, sneezing into her gloves; and Suzee, a smile pinned to her face and the wild-eyed animal expression of a woman whose friend had married before her) and handsome grooms, all of whom Clarissa had recommended to Aaron because of the short-notice factor (Maxi Reese, the agent, whose cell phone had rung with the theme from *Batman* during the ceremony; Tom Sizeman, who created the hottest nightclubs in L.A. and whose last name was a matter of accurate reporting; Jonesie Morris, a recording executive with a reputation—the only black student in Clarissa's graduating class in high school (his father was a well-known professional opera singer); and Tony B., who couldn't stop laughing. Clarissa had slept with all of them, including Tony, on one of his few forays to the "dark side"—his term for heterosexual sex).

"You holding up okay?" Aaron asked.

"I wish I could get married every day," Clarissa said, as she turned to her mother's aunt, accepted her best wishes, and wondered if the extremely tight-faced woman had a knot of old skin at the back of her head.

"Simon," Aaron said. He was facing Simon, who was standing in line. "How are you?"

"Congratulations," Simon said to Aaron. "The best man won and all that. Clarissa's an amazing girl. One of a kind."

The exchange was far too cordial for Clarissa's taste.

"If there were a mold, someone please break it, right?" Clarissa said. False modesty was not her favorite pastime; she thought all modesty false.

Clarissa wanted Simon to move on, but he seemed firm in his stance.

"My first love," Simon said.

"We're practically cousins," Clarissa said.

"Geez, Simon, you're only the third person to say that to me," Aaron replied, brushing away the deeper meaning with a light touch. "I got very lucky today."

Clarissa buried her face in her husband's shoulder.

"Best wishes, C," Simon said. He pecked her on the cheek, leaving a delicate wet spot, like the kiss of a baby. He smelled of pine and Neutrogena bath gel and teenage memories.

Clarissa left the wet spot. She greeted the next guest and wondered when she could get a drink.

* * *

A few snapshots from the reception:

1. Gravy, after four drinks and a hit of Ecstasy, making out with Clarissa's uncle Bob, a sixty-year-old proctologist with a roadkill-inspired toupee.
2. Polo, in an ass-cleavage-baring Versace slip dress, being closely monitored by an army of fifteen-year-old boys boasting tuxedos and pubescent erections.
3. Jennifer, standing shyly off to the side during the tossing of the bride's bouquet; the bouquet, magically, as though carried by a sympathetic wind current, landing in her soft hands.
4. Suzee tripping Jennifer after she catches the bouquet.
5. Jennifer ripping the bouquet back from Suzee, yelling, "You want a piece of this?"
6. Tom Sizeman pinching Clarissa's ass as she slow-dances past him with her father.
7. Jennifer throwing up in the bathroom, still clutching the now-wilted bouquet.
8. Jonesie Morris asking if Clarissa wanted to pull a "Sonny Corleone" (meaning, to go off and fuck, *not* meaning get ambushed and murdered by mobsters).
9. Clarissa's mom dancing with Aaron to the strains (and it was a strain—the band was only so-so) of Henry Mancini's "Moon River."
10. Simon break-dancing on his back to Wild Cherry's "Play That Funky Music" while Suzee, his date, looked on, dismayed.
11. Aaron and Teddy talking in the garden, smoking cigars, and taking in the night air.

Almost three in the morning, and Clarissa, still in her wedding dress, sat back on her bed in the honeymoon suite, her eyes closed, concentrating on the memories she would have the rest of her life, the ones she would tell her children and grandchildren.

She thought of the stories her mother and grandmother had told her—how her parents had met, fallen quickly in love, had married within weeks over their parents' protests. How her grandmother, as a teenager, had run off with a peasant boy she'd known for two nights who later became a war hero.

But Clarissa was not so young, and though she and Aaron had chemistry, she had doubts. "Is Aaron the One?" she'd asked her reflection, partially hidden behind a Biore pore strip.

Or was he just "the One" she had managed to drag, semiconscious, under the huppa?

She looked up to see Aaron coming out of the bathroom, humming something Sinatraish. Clarissa wondered if the humming would get on her nerves after ten years and suddenly felt the urge to do a Carl Lewis and race out the door.

She jumped up from the rose petal–covered bed. Aaron started sneezing.

"Allergic," he said, scooping up the rose petals and tossing them into a pillowcase as Clarissa stepped into the bathroom, rocking sideways in her Jimmy Choos. She was not taking the shoes off, either.

"Are you alive?" Aaron said. Clarissa had been inside the bathroom fifteen minutes.

"Maybe I drank too much," she said.

Clarissa had her overnight bag out on the Italian marble sink. Inside was the usual: toiletries, razor, makeup bag, hairbrush, her mother's hand lotion, turkey baster.

Turkey baster?

"Hey Mrs. Mason, your husband's getting tired," Aaron said.

Clarissa smiled. She had managed to pee without taking off the dress. She wondered how she could have sex without taking it off.

Clarissa came out of the bathroom. Aaron already had set up a few of his stuffed animals. He and Clarissa had negotiated terms for their wedding night—they had agreed on three stuffed animals to share their honeymoon bed.

Aaron was naked, except for his briefs, which had little pictures of Tweety Bird on them. Several condoms were awaiting orders on the nightstand.

"I like the shorts," Clarissa said, as she walked over.

"I like the dress," Aaron said. "I'd like to check out the workmanship on the beading."

"I'm going to sleep in it," she said, as she slid into bed. "I'm just not ready to take it off."

"We'll manage," Aaron said. They lay face-to-face.

"I admire your tenacity," she said.

"I admire yours."

"What else do you admire?" she asked. She liked this game.

"I admire your lips." And he kissed her. "I admire your skin," he said, and he slid his face down her neck. "I admire your gumption," he said, kissing her cleavage.

"Which one is Gumption?" Clarissa asked.

"I admire you," Aaron said. "I admire my wife."

Clarissa blushed. She seldom blushed. Her eyes hit the nightstand and the gold condom wrappers. "And I admire your Magnum," Clarissa said.

There were sparks, flames, fireworks, and, afterward, lit cigarettes in a nonsmoking room.

And then, Clarissa locked herself in the bathroom for a half hour while her new baby-faced husband slept like a well-spent log.

Her next act should be explained this way: Clarissa knew she was going to be pregnant within the year. So what was the point of waiting? She was a practical girl, above all else. The baster was a stroke of genius Clarissa had read about in an article where a pro–baseball player involved in a paternity suit (shocking) accused one of the "girlfriends" he met on the road of using a turkey baster and a used condom filled with sperm to get pregnant.

And so, after volunteering to throw out the used condoms, instead of merely flushing the hapless yet valuable-on-the-open-market sperm, Clarissa took her turkey baster (boiled yesterday for twenty minutes to kill any bacteria—the first time she'd actually used her stove—then placed in an airtight, Ziploc pouch), sucked out Aaron's sperm and . . . well . . .

Clarissa lay back, still in her wedding gown (she was, in this happenstance, true to her word), inserted the baster and walked her legs up the bathroom wall into a half-cocked shoulder stand. And there she waited, her billowing ass against the cold tile, picking out names that would sound good with "Mason."

Then she realized that the only thing that had been missing from her wedding day was Aaron's parents. They were supposed to have flown in that morning, having missed their flight the day before. The elder Mason, Joe Three (so called, in a particularly regional way, after his father and grandfather), was an excellent businessman; he'd expanded his grandfather's corner five-and-dime store into the third-largest chain in the United States; however, alas, he was notoriously tight with a buck. Cinnamon, Aaron's mother, despite the spicy moniker, appeared colorless to Clarissa's big-city eye. In every picture she'd seen of her (new) mother-in-law, she looked like Betty Crocker. Or Lady Bird Johnson.

Clarissa made a note to remember what state they lived in. She wanted to impress her new family.

She also made a note to counsel the Masons on the benefits of owning a G-IV or V or whatever, number one being that no one who owned a private jet ever missed a plane. Clarissa had many plans for her new family; she felt sorry for them that they didn't enjoy their money more. She would enrich their lives—and deplete their money market funds. Joe Three and Cinnamon would love her.

Clarissa was slightly bothered that Aaron hadn't mentioned anything about his parents' absence. Then she smiled. Of course Aaron hadn't said anything; he didn't want to put a cloud on her day.

Because Clarissa had been looking forward to meeting her in-laws.

Eleven
Not the Fairy-tale Ending

Clarissa awakened to find Aaron packing his bag; she noticed he already had packed hers. She congratulated herself on acquiring such a thoughtful husband.

"Puffy?" she said. Puffy was the nickname of one of Aaron's animals, a small brown bear.

Aaron smiled, the grin of someone with a tantalizing secret.

"Why are you packing already?" Clarissa asked. She swung her legs over the side of the bed.

She was still wearing her wedding dress.

"Well," Aaron said, as he zipped up his Tumi overnight bag. He looked at her. "I've got . . . news."

"News?" she said. "You mean good news. Because when someone just says 'news,' Aaron, it usually ends with a death or a car fire . . . or . . . ," she looked at him with eyes so narrowed she could not see, "another woman."

"Oh my God, no. Not another woman. I can barely handle you." He started laughing and pacing, and Clarissa seriously thought it was intervention time. Plans began to form in her head for the three weeks Aaron would be out of town in rehab. Canyon Ranch would be nice, maybe that new place in Baja.

"Clarissa. There's no best way of putting this. I've been disowned."

Clarissa was not familiar with near-death experiences. She had never experienced a heart attack or a near-drowning or a knife-wielding relative. But she was convinced that her palpitating heart, her hyperventilating breath, and the sudden lack of oxygen was adding up to her first brush with the other side.

She woke up on the floor with a pillow under her feet and Aaron fanning a room service napkin at her head.

"Clarissa?" Aaron was saying. "Clarissa?"

"The lights . . . I can't see . . ." She struggled to sit up; Aaron supported her back against the bed.

"You dropped like a sack of bricks. I've never seen anything . . ."

"Water. I need some water."

Aaron ran to get tap water from the bathroom.

"Evian?"

"We drank it all."

"Room service."

Aaron made a Teddy face. As in, Clarissa's dad. It was a face that had done something dishonest. "Ah, I don't think that's a good idea."

Clarissa sighed. "Aaron? Are we dining and ditching?"

"Does that mean that we've spent the night in a one-thousand-dollar suite and ordered five hundred dollars worth of champagne and hors d'oeuvres and we're running out on the bill?" he asked.

"Yes."

"Oh, okay, then. Yes." Aaron checked his watch.

"How long do we have?" Clarissa asked. It was as though she were inquiring about the weather or someone's summer cold.

Aaron checked his watch. "Five, six minutes, tops."

Clarissa struggled to her feet (still wearing the Jimmy Choos).

"The wedding dress . . . ," Aaron said.

"I'm not taking it off."

"It's too conspicuous."

"Well. That's your problem, isn't it."

"Clarissa, be reasonable."

"Aaron," Clarissa said, tipping over bottles of champagne, collecting the warm, flat drops into a leftover glass. "I am being reasonable."

In fact, Clarissa was surprisingly calm. She had read about people who remained stoic in the face of disasters, like a devastating earthquake or airliner crash. She was glad to see that in the face of her personal horror she was still able to think clearly.

Clarissa refused to take off the dress, but agreed, finally, to slip a Bel Air bathrobe over her silk and lace confection. The shoes stayed.

Aaron grabbed their luggage. "I'll get the car," he said. "I mean, granted that it's still there."

"What?!" Clarissa barely had a chance to protest, as he kissed her on the lips; if she hadn't been so angry with him, she'd feel like Audrey Hepburn to his Cary Grant. Suddenly, Aaron ran back into the room, as the elevator rang . . .

And he ran back out, clutching Mr. Tang. "Never leave a man behind!" he yelled, running down the hallway.

Clarissa had never seen a human being so full of life. It made her sick.

The elevator doors opened and Clarissa stepped inside, squeezing in between two room service waiters and a full breakfast tray. The smell of overpriced coffee and thirty-dollar waffles brought tears to her eyes.

She had been so close.

Clarissa curved her head over the side of the Bentley. Her mouth felt alternately dry and watery, her stomach churned hungrily, her head pounded like the inside of a boom box. Aaron put his hand on her shoulder as he drove them east on Sunset, further and further from her dream.

She shrugged his hand off like a virus.

"Clarissa. Remember what we talked about? Before the wedding?" Aaron asked.

Clarissa remembered. Her mouth filled with a liquid that tasted like sewer runoff.

"Christ, Aaron," she said. It sounded like she was speaking from three feet under water. "If I'd known there was the vaguest possibility that this was going to happen . . ."

"What? You wouldn't have married me?"

She didn't answer.

"Oh, that's just great."

"Of course I would've married you," Clarissa said, crossing her fingers. "I just wouldn't have made it public."

He smiled. "There's the superficial little twat I know and love."

"Are you going to tell me what happened?" Clarissa said. "I mean, is this why your parents didn't show up?"

"Oh, they were here."

He turned onto La Brea. Clarissa was getting more and more uncomfortable the farther east they rode.

"What do you mean? I never saw them. I'm sure I would've noticed your mother, what with that hairdo . . ."

"Don't make fun of my mother."

"Betty Crocker."

"Clarissa."

"Just . . . spit it out."

"When you didn't sign the prenup, they skipped the wedding and went to Universal Studios instead."

Clarissa pictured Aaron's burly father crammed into the back of a tram with a load of Japanese tourists.

"That's so wrong."

"And they disowned me."

"That's even more so wrong," she said. "I had such plans for them. I could've made their lives so much better." She couldn't understand how people could live somewhere in . . . in that state they lived in when southern California was right here. They could go to Universal Studios every day of the week, for crissakes.

"Where are we going?" Clarissa asked.

"Well, I have to congratulate myself," Aaron said. "I anticipated this maneuver."

"And so you . . ."

"Rented an apartment."

"What about your house?" Clarissa sat up. "What about Ginger Rogers and Fred Astaire?"

"My parent's trust."

"The pink staircase?"

"A memory."

"The rose garden . . ." The words came out soft as a newborn's breath.

"Buh-bye."

"Well, at least you still have the car," Clarissa said, sitting back.

"Not after the weekend."

"Oh my God," Clarissa said. "You are so fucked."

"Correction. *We* are so fucked," Aaron said. "And I've never felt better in my life."

They drove up a narrow driveway off a Hollywood street above Franklin. An apartment building rose above them, fifties deco style, strangled in ivy. The sort of place, Clarissa thought, that horrid, overenthusiastic acting students rent out in packs.

"Here we are," he said.

"Here *you* are," she said. "I'm not getting out of the car."

"Look, Clarissa, you married me for better or worse."

"I didn't know worse was going to happen so soon. Worse is supposed to happen, like, thirty years from now, when you get cancer of the ass or something."

Aaron got out of the Bentley and crossed over to Clarissa's side. Each time Aaron tried to open the passenger-side door, Clarissa yanked it closed.

"Clarissa, this isn't cancer of the ass." Aaron shook his head. "We're just starting from scratch—lots of people start from scratch!"

"I am not starting from scratch! I don't know how to start from scratch! Aaron—I don't want to know what *scratch* IS!"

People were staring out their apartment windows. A couple hung over the balcony, looking at the girl in the robe ("Is that a wedding dress under there?") and the boy in the tasseled loafers and navy blue sweater who looked like Biff in a high school reproduction of *Death of a Salesman*.

The girl suddenly looked up and greeted the couple with a pampered, lotioned, French-manicured middle finger.

"Look at these people," she screeched. "They all look like . . . wannabe soap actors!"

Someone threw a leather sandal at the Bentley.

"Ugh! Birkenstocks. Get it away from me!" Clarissa yelled, "I'm calling my mom!"

Clarissa sat on her rump and speed-dialed her mother while Aaron unloaded the car. The answering machine came on, playing a 1970s trumpet ballad by Chuck Mangione. Clarissa made the same high-pitched sound whales make when they're mating and waited for the beep.

"Mommy, it's Clarissa. There's been an emergency," she said. "Aaron is poor."

She hung up and called her father. She hesitated for a moment before dialing—mainly because she'd forgotten his number and had neglected to put him on speed dial. Her father changed his home phone number every month to avoid the IRS, creditors, and girlfriends' attorneys.

Clarissa realized that her father had many of the same habits as Pablo Escobar, the Colombian drug lord.

Finally, as Aaron watched from the upstairs balcony (she heard him introducing himself to their—*his*—new neighbors), she remembered her father's phone number and dialed.

Something answered. Clarissa wasn't sure if it were an actual person. It had a mechanical tone, like a computer.

"Who is calling?" the voice asked.

"Clarissa. Your—Teddy's daughter."

"One moment."

Clarissa waited. The sun was just coming out from behind white clouds that on any other day would've been beautiful. She guessed it was about 9:00 A.M.

"Babycakes!" her father exclaimed. "What a wedding!"

"What answered the phone, Teddy?" Clarissa asked.

"Oh, that's my new system," he said. "You like it?"

"Try one hundred eighty degrees opposite. Hate it."

"It's my new computer system. See, even if I'm online, the computer answers for me."

"You're online? Why?"

"Sure, I got 64 RAM, 156k—I'm working on getting DSL, it's a little tough on the Westside . . ."

"Teddy . . ."

"I've been chatting with this cutie over in Finland. You should see this gal—six feet tall, a total knockout. Plays the drums. She's an actress, too, a few pornos, but not the hard stuff. Nice kid."

"How old is the child, Teddy?"

"Oh, nineteen, twenty, at least."

"Sorry about Apricot," Clarissa said. Trying to be nice took the last bit of her energy. She closed her eyes and tilted her head back. She thought she might have a nosebleed anytime soon. "I heard she took off with Slocum."

"That's okay," Teddy said. "I got the feeling she wasn't really serious about our relationship, anyway."

"Oh yeah?"

"She kept . . . borrowing stuff."

"Like?"

"A painting. Silverware. Personal checks."

"Okay, so, Dad?" Clarissa said. "I'm having a problem."

"Is Aaron okay?"

"Aaron's fine."

"I like that kid."

"Uh-huh."

"Nice kid, good boy. You got lucky, there."

"He's been disowned."

"Yikes," Teddy said.

"Yikes?" Clarissa replied.

"That's too bad," he said.

"Yes, it is too bad," Clarissa started crying. "It is really too bad, like I'm hemorrhaging diarrhea too bad."

"You need some help, Babycakes?"

For once, the nickname did not make her cringe.

"Hey, Moneybags!" she yelled up to Aaron, who was now, from what she could see, smoking a cigarette and enjoying a bowl of Cheerios with his new friends. "C'mon! We're going to see Teddy!"

"I'm not asking him for money."

"Well, guess what? I am." Clarissa's dad always paid the rent on her lousy duplex apartment off Robertson. She didn't see why he wouldn't put them up in a nice house now that she was married and legitimate.

"I won't accept any money from Ted."

"Aaron. I believe in you. I believe in this marriage. But I don't believe in living below the poverty line."

"We wouldn't be living below the poverty line. Jesus."

"Aaron, I just want a different housing situation. After that, I'm fine." She lied. She wasn't fine. She was lower . . . Lower middle class . . . below where she was *before* the wedding. She thought about her gifts. She couldn't possibly put her new china and silver in that apartment.

Teddy was standing in the spacious living room of his Century City Towers condominium wearing silk pajamas and a smirk. Behind him was an office filled with computer equipment and the heavy air associated with cigar smoke and aging Lotharios. There was a smudged outline on the wall where a painting had hung recently. "I thought about your little problem, Babycakes. And the best way I can take care of you," Teddy said, "is by not taking care of you at all."

Clarissa took a step back. Aaron held her up by her elbow and guided her to one of her father's purple velvet chairs. Teddy's decorating taste after the divorce from her mother veered toward Hefner Lite.

"Teddy. What the hell are you talking about?"

"Goddamn, this is the best thing that could've happened to you, sweetheart. Don't you see that?" He sounded excited, like he had just won a longshot bet on a horserace. Or, more likely, a mud wrestling match between two of his girlfriends.

"I can't see at all, Teddy. I'm going blind from stress, I swear to God." She "searched" for Aaron, blinking her eyes.

"The best time of my life was when your mother and I were starting out from nothing."

"Don't say that word!"

"What word?" Teddy asked.

"Nothing," Aaron said.

"I told you not to say it!" Clarissa cried.

"Why not? It's true." Teddy looked at Aaron. "Can I get you a Mary?" Teddy was already sipping a Bloody Mary with a celery stick poking out of it. He was so seventies television, Clarissa wanted to scream.

"I'm fine, sir."

"Good boy."

"Can we cut the convivial crap?!" Clarissa screamed. "My world is coming to a rapid-fire end! I'm going to wind up eating out of cans from the 99 Cents Store!"

"She's always had a sense of the dramatic, my girl," Teddy said.

"I can see that," Aaron replied.

"Do you have a plan, son?" Teddy asked him.

"Not so fast with that 'son' shit, Teddy," Clarissa said.

"I've got a job lined up, starting Monday."

"A producing job?" Clarissa asked, the hope in her voice as three-dimensional and tangible as a freight train running through her father's living room.

"A production assistant job. The director's paying me three hundred a week."

Clarissa howled. "A P.A.?!" She spit out the words like she'd swallowed Listerine instead of apple juice.

"Clarissa. What's wrong with being a P.A.?" Aaron replied. "I have to start somewhere."

"What about the *Gay Divorcee*—what about the deal . . ."

"You know about development. It could take years to get the script right. I have to find something now."

"Get the script right?" Clarissa said, her head spinning like a Chuckie doll. "Aaron, no one *cares* about getting the script right!"

Something beeped.

"Oh, that'd be my gal from the Ukraine," Teddy said. "Talk about a hot-button topic . . . If you'll excuse me."

He shook Aaron's hand and patted Clarissa's cheek. When she tried to bite his index finger off, Teddy shook it at her, his face growing red. The computer continued to beep.

"Clarissa, it's time you grew up. I wasn't much of a father to you. But now," he said, sucking in his stomach, "it's time for some tough love."

And he ambled back to his computer.

"You want to know about tough love, Daddy?" Clarissa yelled, springing from her chair. "Tough love is when I report your creative finances to the IRS! *That* is TOUGH LOVE!"

Her father waved as Aaron steered her to the front door.

But not before she ran into the kitchen and grabbed all of her father's forks.

"Ha!" she said to Aaron. "Let him try to eat, now!"

Twelve

Hey, Poverty Is Cool

Clarissa insisted Aaron drive her to her mother's house on South Beverly Drive, the house she'd grown up in after her father had made a little money. Though it was in Beverly Hills, it was not a showplace—it was a one-story, thick-walled California bungalow.

And it was home. Clarissa looked at the house and burst into tears. Again.

"There are benefits to not being rich, you know," Aaron said.

"Name one," Clarissa pouted.

"You don't have to hang out with other rich people," he said.

"Are you coming?" Clarissa asked.

"Only if you refrain from asking your mother for financial help," he said.

"Great. I'll only be a second," Clarissa said. She got out of the Bentley and strode up the walkway, past the ubiquitous wrought-iron gates that adorned so many California bungalows.

As she waited for her mother to answer, she noticed a light blue Cadillac partially hidden by the brightly colored bracts of the bougainvillea streaming over her mother's driveway.

"Mama?" she said, after waiting a few moments. "Mama?"

Her mother answered the door. She was wearing tap pants and a silk camisole. Her legs were fit and tanned, but with a Raisinet quality.

Clarissa refrained from comment, however. She was too engrossed in the fact that a man was sitting on her mother's couch. A black man. A young black man with a portable keyboard on his lap.

Clarissa recognized him immediately as the keyboard player in the wedding band; they were known as the "Sky Rockets" after the song "Afternoon Delight."

Clarissa was impressed that, under the circumstances, she was still able to remember minor details.

Clarissa had a number of choices, all of which were skittering through her brain like images from a moviola: a. Ignore the young black man; b. Act cool; c. Cry and throw up; or d. All of the above, plus ask Mom for money.

Clarissa chose "D." First, she ignored him.

"Mama," Clarissa said, walking past the young man. "Did you have a good time last night?"

Her mother looked at her. "Oh, yes. Clareesa, *esta es Roberto—*"

"Bobby," the young man said. Though she was in the first phase of action (ignoring the young man), Clarissa could not help but notice he was a stone cold fox. Lust Fuck.

"Aha, so. Mama, did you get my message?"

"Oh, Clareesa, I been busy this morning," she said, chuckling as she walked into the kitchen, her marabou slippers tap-tap-tapping along the oversized, orange-red Mexican tiles.

There was no sound more annoying than her mother's chuckle; she sounded like a trapped macaw.

"My whole life, she's been busy," Clarissa said to Bobby/Roberto. Oh. And. He was not wearing pants. So much for phase B, acting cool.

"Is that a hotel robe?" he asked. "Sharp."

Onto phase C, the crying and vomiting portion of the morning.

"Mama, Aaron has no money," Clarissa said, sniffling into her terrycloth sleeve.

"What you mean?" her mother asked.

"What *do* you mean?" Clarissa said.

"Yes, what you mean?" her mother asked again.

"Mother. Have you ever met a participle?"

"Café?" her mother asked. Clarissa nodded. Her mother made incredible coffee. Clarissa remembered, as a child, hearing the machine grinding coffee beans her mother had picked up at a South American grocery store on Pico. She was grateful for the stability of this small habit, especially as her universe was falling down around her.

They sat across from each other, sipping their coffee from porcelain cups in a moment of welcome silence.

Except for the Gap Band riff from "You Dropped a Bomb on Me" in the background.

"He is a wonderful lover," her mother said. The way she pronounced lover ("loooover") made Clarissa nauseous. It was as though the word had eight syllables instead of two. She made the same mistake with the word "vagina."

"Mama," Clarissa said, steering the conversation back in the proper direction—toward herself. "I need your help, your advice, and, most important, your money."

"Wha' happen?"

"Here," Clarissa said, picking something off the floor, "You dropped your 't.'"

"Ha ha," her mother said. "You want money, and you making fun of your mother. Not very brigh', Clareesa." There went that "t" again.

"Mama, Aaron was disowned. He only has the clothes on his back. He's starting a job on Monday, Mama, an *actual* job," she continued. "He was supposed to be a producer. He was supposed to be rich. What am I supposed to do now?"

"You love him?" her mother asked.

"Yes." Clarissa nodded.

"Then, you figure it out," her mother said, getting up from the table. "Your father and I, we started out with n—"

"Don't say that word!"

Her mother looked up to the sky.

"He rented this horrible apartment in Hollywood with all kinds of undesirables. Mama, it's got a carport!"

"Clareesa, you know how you say, 'Mama, you don' believe in me!' 'Mama, have faith in your daughter!'" Her mother was looking at her, a hand on her hip, unlit cigarette between her fingers. She looked like someone Ari Onassis would have dated.

"Yeah . . . ," Clarissa said, trying to grab the cigarette out of her mother's hand. She hated that her mother still smoked—half her family in Bolivia had died of lung cancer. She also hated that her mother's reflexes were faster than hers—she'd never been able to grab a cigarette from her mom.

"Well, I believe in you. I know you and Aaron will make something muy beautiful together."

"You're not going to give me any money?"

"I don't have a lot of money, Clareesa," she said, lighting the cigarette with a sterling silver lighter, a gift from her father. "An' I think this will be good for you."

And that, she could tell by her mother's impatient tone, was that. Her mother walked out of the kitchen. Clarissa followed.

"Couldn't you have faith in me *after* you support us for a few weeks—until I get this sorted out with his fucker parents?"

"Clareesa, Roberto and I, we are going to get pancakes—Roberto wants pancakes. You and Aaron want to come?"

Roberto/Bobby was not in the living room. Clarissa heard a shower running. She pictured Roberto and her mother getting married; she pictured herself with a thirty-year-old Gap Band–playing stepfather.

"I think we'll pass."

"Okay," her mother said. "Please. Give my son-in-law my love." She kissed Clarissa on the cheek and walked off, leaving a scented trail of Virginia Slims and last night's Chanel No. 5.

At least, Clarissa thought, she was happy.

A compilation of "A Typical Day in the Life of Clarissa, Premarriage":

1. Get up in the morning. "Morning" loosely defined: anywhere from 8:30 (construction outside window, called police, apparently perfectly legal, can't be helped) to 11:59 A.M. (phone call from mother).
2. Breakfast. "Breakfast" loosely defined: depending on contents of refrigerator and/or purse. Could be bowl after blessed bowl of Special K (the cereal with the commercials that feature a girl with legs like knitting needles talking about "cottage cheese" thighs), dry or, God willing, with low-fat milk (nonfat milk = water plus chalk). A piece of fruit, like a Fruit Roll-Up, or cherry-flavored Gatorade. Or tropical fruit Life Savers. Enough coffee to awaken a Vicodin addict from a

sleeping jag, or, like, a person who's been dead for twenty years.

3. Read the *New York Times*. Cover-to-cover.*
4. *Just kidding.
5. Speed-dial and/or IM Star Chamber. Wake up, if necessary. Plan day. This takes approximately one hour.
6. Day: a. If ridiculously healthy or hideously hungover, start with yoga class with hairy-backed Lothario instructor. Leave after approximately nine and a half minutes (recommended workout as per book *Ten Minutes to the Perfect Body*). Half minute not important, as "perfection" is a subjective term, after all.

   Or: b. Lunch with Star Chamber. Eat at one of three places: 1. Ivy Robertson (if one of the Star Chamber has access to current or ex-boyfriend's credit card); or 2. Chaya off Robertson, if one is fat and likes small portions of green stuff; or 3. That Euro place on the Sunset Strip filled with men named "Fazoul" and "Zxcyzx" (roughly) who will, after a few required moments of flirting (fifteen to twenty minutes, not counting eye contact), happily pick up the Star Chamber tab.

   Lunch lasts approximately two and a half hours.
7. Downtime: Shopping; M.A.C. for makeup (three times a week); Agnes B., Madison for shoes, etc.; or facial (throw a rock in Beverly Hills, you'll hit a facialist); or highlights/blow-dry (see above; insert "hairstylist" for "facialist"); or eyebrows (see above, ad infinitum).

Every once in a blue moon, or when the girls were so bored that the idea of a "tequila back massage" at the Four Seasons on Doheny brought a yawn, a Star Chamber member would suggest attempting something of a physical nature or doing something to expand one's mind. Like, say, attending a poetry reading. Or reading a newspaper where the front-page article wasn't about Melissa Rivers' water-retention problem. Some sincere soul in the Star Chamber (Jennifer) once suggested going horseback riding. But Polo, ironically, was dead set against anything having to do with horses. Her mother, an avid horsewoman, was a classic fifty-footer; from fifty feet she was a sun-kissed, slender beauty; up close her skin was creased, puckered, lined, webbed and sagging.

Also, as Gravy pointed out wisely, horses "stink like horseshit."

Clarissa liked to take a nap every day, which used up the remainder of her downtime.

8. Dinner: Top three choices: a. Stouffer's Lean Cuisine—anything at all resembling pasta—in front of the twenty-four-inch Sony TV (thanks, Teddy) watching *Ally McBeal*, *Friends*, or current reality-type show with attractive male contestants; b. Mr. Chow's (see "Lunch," under credit-card reference); or c. a fabulous date. A FabD8 meant the guy had that elusive element: potential. Potential meant: good shoes, good hair, good height (not too, too short or too tall), good teeth, good breath, good job and/or good inheritance/name, and good fashion sense. Polo, especially, liked a well-turned-out man.

   The Star Chamber had about three FabD8s between them in the last five years.
9. Sleep. Somewhere around midnight; later if there was a party to attend.

   There was always a party to attend. Clarissa hadn't gone to bed before two in the morning since oversized shoulder pads.

And, now, "A Typical Day in the Life of Clarissa, Postmarriage" (Day Two):

1. Awaken at seven. See (current) husband off to work. Take a moment to cry and create murderous scenarios involving family members. Go back to sleep in rank bedroom of disgusting apartment in horrible actors' workshop building.
2. Awaken at 10:00 A.M. (or other, more reasonable, hour). Check on convertible BMW to see if: a. stolen or

b. scratched by horrible struggling actor-type's Mazda. Cry some more. Notify two members (Jennifer and Gravy) of Star Chamber of tragic turnabout in life.

3. Cry. Visited at around noon by Star Chamber (everyone except Suzee). Polo sneezes as she walks in the door, screams "Who has a cat?" knowing full well that Clarissa has had a cat for about eight years and sits outside on the balcony for remainder of visit (two and a half hours). When she finally leaves (for her allergist) her face looks like a bad case of diaper rash.

   Unanimous Star Chamber verdict (Jennifer abstaining from vote and going on about "true love" and "money doesn't matter" and other nonsense): Leave before sunset.
4. Now around six. Too late to leave before sunset. Also, need gas in BMW and gas card canceled by mean, ugly father.
5. Cry. Attempt to make dinner out of a can of tuna fish and Kraft Macaroni and Cheese. Burn the orange stuff (cheese?) after misreading directions. Start all over.
6. Cry.
7. Bang on apartment wall when couple next door start acting out scene from *True West* at approximately same decibels as Metallica playing live from a shower stall.
8. Receive page from (current) husband: "Home l8. Love you. Miss me?"
9. IM husband back: "Ih8U."
10. Call (anonymously) the police on apartment next door. Claim to have heard gun shots.
11. Sit in horrid living room on now crowded red couch (stuffed animals) eating gooey tuna fish casserole with burned edges (burned edges: actually better than edible).
12. Cry.
13. Fall asleep on couch.
14. Awakened by husband* planting kisses all over face, yapping excitedly about new position, something about responsibilities, trust, rapport. (*Current version.)

Husband (at present) tells Clarissa he loves her so much and is so proud of her. And he is very tired.

He falls asleep in her arms, cooing over the soft underpart of upper arm flesh.

15. Make vow to starve to death.
16. Disengage gingerly from sleeping husband; cover him with a wrap (cashmere, prior life) just so he doesn't freeze to death and present another problem.
17. Finish off macaroni and cheese casserole.

Aaron was starting to feel himself again. The Bentley, the mansion in Bel Air, the black American Express—none of it was him. The motorcycle, which cost him less than half of one of the Bentley's bumpers—now, that was him.

He was excited by his job. Working as a P.A. for the director not only paid what few bills he would have, but provided on-the-job experience—that is, when he stopped having to pick up dry cleaning and baby-sitting the director's Yorkie. But he was willing to bide his time; the director had agreed to show him the ropes, to let him sit in on meetings, listen in on phone calls, to reveal, step-by-step, how to develop a script from one line, or even one word. He hadn't been paid one dime yet for his deal on *The Gay Divorcee,* but he'd explained that he needed living wages and the director found a way to get him paid. Aaron figured he had more than six months for the deal for *The Gay Divorcee;* he and the director were on the verge of finding a screenwriter that the studio would agree upon. Aaron had everything figured out, and he would do it on his own.

And he had a wife who would help him, support him along the way. Soon, with any luck, they'd be out of that apartment and into a house in the hills, and his first movie would be in preproduction, and all would be forgiven.

Or not.

After a couple of weeks of living dangerously, Clarissa had learned several things: Food For Less charges half what Gelsons does for canned tuna; a used Honda 260 motorcycle (husband's means of transportation) is, contrary to the TV commercials, *not* sexual catnip attracting bikini-laden babes; doing laundry requires a Ph.D. in logistical math; doing laundry in a crowded apartment building requires the stealth of a Mossad spy, the cunning of a Mafia lawyer, and the criminal instincts of a cocaine cartel lord; Taco Bell makes excellent burritos that couldn't be less Mexican; discovering K-Mart, Target, and Sav-On is to the hardcore shopper what discovering the lost city of Atlantis is to the dedicated archaeologist; and, of course, rich *is* better.

"Obviously. But how much better?"

This was the question Clarissa, her mouth full of massive, greasy onion rings, put to Simon, over a lunch of crab cakes, aforementioned onion rings, and mayonnaise-drenched cole slaw at The Palm.

"That depends," Simon said, staring across the heavy wooden table at Clarissa, "on whom you're sharing it with."

"Nonanswer, sir," Clarissa said. She tasted the crab cakes. She hadn't had any real food (i.e., restaurant food) in almost fourteen days. Which is why she agreed when Gravy suggested she and Clarissa have a friendly lunch with Simon and then forgot to show up. Clarissa IMed her, using her text sign for screaming: :-@. Clarissa, now a (currently) married woman, almost didn't go through with the lunch date. Then she saw the plates of Cadillac-size steaks dancing by, she smelled the onion rings, and before she knew it, Clarissa was sitting across from the one person who could ruin her life (besides herself and, maybe, her mother—and, also, her father), placing her order before her sizable ass even hit the wooden bench.

"Simon. Was there a reason you wanted to go to lunch with me?" Clarissa asked. "Granted, I'm fascinating, and you certainly qualify as an N.F. . . ."

"N.F.?"

"Nostalgia Fuck," Clarissa said, "but I did just get married like," she checked her watch, "ten minutes ago."

"I ran into Alexandra. She told me the story." He said it as though someone important, like Brendan Fraser or Elizabeth Hurley, had died.

"The story being . . ."

"Your . . . husband . . . has no money."

"Currently."

"He may never have any money."

"No, I mean, he's my current husband."

Simon smiled. If mathematically calculable, he was nineteen times cuter than in high school. Like Julio Iglesias, he had aged well. *Why do laugh lines and a few grays look so good on a man?* Clarissa thought to herself. *Why is scruffy appealing on a man but terrifying on a woman? Why are men allowed to fart while scores of innocent women implode? Why do men's suits hide every bulge while women's clothing is a veritable advertisement for cellulite?*

"Clarissa?"

"I'm sorry, what?"

"I was asking . . . ," Simon sounded annoyed. "Are you happy?"

"Oh, very happy. My god, these frikkin rings are like sex with a stranger."

"In your marriage."

Clarissa knew what he'd meant. "Simon. I believe in Aaron."

"That's . . . that's great. Good for you."

"I believe that he'll talk sense into his parents."

"And if he doesn't?"

Clarissa looked at Simon. "Are you familiar with the marriage vow, Simon? The part that goes, I'm paraphrasing, "for better or worse," something, something . . ." In truth, Clarissa had tried to get that part excised, but Aaron objected.

"Clarissa, you know you can't handle 'worse.'" Simon shook his head and smiled. "Love, I'm surprised you've lasted this long."

Clarissa was surprised herself. She was surprised that she had smiled at the couple next door that very morning. She was surprised that her BMW had embarrassed her, for all around her now were Toyotas, VW Rabbits, Hondas, and not one of them was shiny and newish, like hers. She was surprised that she secretly enjoyed comparison shopping.

She was surprised that she felt a gnawing, growing contentment. Not happiness—"happy" was something else altogether. But there was one thing she was not: unhappy.

And this bothered her. This had to be changed.

After lunch (and dessert, and cappuccino, oh, and biscotti, and, of course, those tiny, pillow-shaped buttery mints), Simon walked Clarissa outside The Palm onto Santa Monica Boulevard and a web of construction. They waited in silence for her car among the tractors and bulldozers and uprooted road. Clarissa hoped that no one she and Aaron knew would recognize her; she did not want Aaron to find out she had been to lunch with the only ex-boyfriend she still harbored feelings for.

And harbor feelings she did. She sifted through thoughts in her brain while valet parkers scattered like dung beetles in search of patrons' Mercedes, SUVs, BMWs, and the occasional Lexus (out-of-towner or screenwriter).

She ran down pros and cons as she watched Simon pay for her valet, as he insisted.

Simon is smart, worldly, gorgeous, and confident.

Also, he has a nice nose and long legs.

His ears are a little wide, probably a problem as a young child, less problematic as an adult with hair.

Aaron is smart, not worldly but earnest, cute, confident, and, also, her husband.

She heard Suzee (pin-size version, in a devil's costume, sitting on her right shoulder), wondering what either of them wanted with her.

Jennifer (tiny, dressed as an angel, sitting on her left shoulder) maintained that any worthy man would find Clarissa irresistible. She also complimented Clarissa on her new shoes, a real find at Tracey Ross on Sunset. Pre-poverty-stricken marriage.

"And so I've decided to become a Buddhist monk."

Clarissa looked at Simon. "Orange is so not your color. You're a 'winter,' Simon, not an 'autumn.'"

He was standing by her car, holding the door open for her. His Cadillac Escalade, the "it" car of the moment with the rap music crowd, was idling behind the BMW. Clarissa knew that Simon knew she hadn't heard a word he'd said in the last few minutes.

"I remember when you did my colors," Simon said.

"Mr. Hall's bio class," Clarissa said. "I hope you're still using my extensive 'season' knowledge."

Simon smiled. Clarissa fought the urge to trace his laugh lines with her tongue. "Good try, 'rissa. But you've been somewhere else, and I know I wasn't there with you."

Several of The Palm's (show business) clientele were waiting for Clarissa to get into her car so they could hurry back to their offices to berate their assistants in person. Clarissa hopped into her BMW and Simon bent over her as he pressed the door closed.

"Clarissa," Simon said, as he brushed her cheek with a kiss. "I still . . ."

He hesitated, then gave a slight shake of his head, which sent his mop into a stir, and swallowed the rest of the sentence; Clarissa started screaming out the window at him.

"What? I still *what*?!"

But Simon only half smiled in a halfhearted way and waved and headed toward his Escalade while the restaurant patrons honked and yelled epithets until Clarissa finally pulled out into traffic, flipping the other drivers the bird, wondering what had become of people's manners and believing that polite society had come to an end.

"I still?"

" . . . comb my hair with my fingers to better resemble Hugh Grant in *Four Weddings and a Funeral.*"

"Oh, I love that film," Jennifer said. "It's a total alternative-to-suicide movie, like *Sleepless in Seattle* or *The Mummy.*"

"It was a joke," Gravy said.

"Girls. Please. I think we know what this means." Polo spoke. Then sniffled. "Spring colds are the worst," she had told everyone. Though it was not spring, and judging from her hives, not a cold.

Clarissa had placed a bet on that tick disease. Polo always had to have the disease of the moment.

"He still loves her," Gravy said. "Anyone with half a brain knows that."

"He does?" said Jennifer. And then she added, "But . . . Clarissa's married, Grave."

"These things can be fixed," said Gravy.

The Star Chamber was having its First (and hopefully *not* annual) Fund-Raiser for Clarissa at Polo's mom's house in Old Brentwood, a standard issue faux colonial that housed more servants than occupants.

Everyone present (the Star Chamber—except Suzee, who was still in the dark about the state of Clarissa's marriage—and a couple of their mothers and cleaning ladies) was encouraged to give money to support Clarissa in finding new, more appropriate living quarters. The girls, headed by Jennifer, who had just taken her real estate exam (third time's the charm!), had found a small, cute "starter" house in West Hollywood, just off Doheny. As entertainment, Jennifer sang "Memories" while a housekeeper played piano (Polo's mother had paid for lessons so the woman could entertain by playing Broadway show tunes during dinner parties), then they had a slide show where the new house's brass bidet was prominently displayed.

But Clarissa was not happy. She hissed across the table at Gravy, who was busy cutting her rubber chicken breast.

"This fund-raiser is as embarrassing as the time I passed gas in the middle of the SATs," she said.

"Not as embarrassing as your score," said Gravy.

"And not as embarrassing as your zip code," Polo pointed out.

An elegant, dark-haired woman in a pink uniform bent over Clarissa, whispered something in her ear, and grabbed her hand. Clarissa's face went bad-makeup-job red.

"Polo," Clarissa said, mortified. "Clementina just handed me a twenty." Clementina was Polo's nanny growing up, and was now her mother's maid and best friend. She wore one-carat diamond earrings and drove an older Mercedes—both gifts from Polo's mom.

"She cares," Polo said.

"I do think Clarissa's place is cute," Jennifer said.

"You're not a good judge of 'cute,'" Gravy replied. "We've all seen your dogs."

"You don't think my dogs are cute?" Jennifer's face dropped like a famous name at a West L.A. dinner party.

"Okay, listen," Clarissa said. "This fund-raiser idea is really, really sweet."

"It's not sweet," said practical Gravy. "Remember the fourth amendment to the S.C. Constitution."

"'We will always come to each other's aid in a time of physical, emotional, or financial crisis,'" said Polo.

"Even if it's borderline, like, Suzee gets hit by a UPS truck," Gravy added.

"I did the flowers," Jen said.

"And I've never seen more beautiful arrangements," Clarissa said, "but I do not need a fund-raiser."

"We've raised fifteen hundred dollars toward your first and last," Gravy said.

Clarissa looked at her.

"So, this place has a garden?" Clarissa replied.

At the end of the afternoon Gravy gave Clarissa the check and they sat around Polo's patio drinking her favorite color—red cocktails of questionable origin and ingredients. The scene reminded Clarissa of high school, of coming home early (like, before first-period class) and raiding the liquor cabinet and making "punch" from rum, vodka, gin, and Kool-Aid and talking and swimming naked until it was dark—or until someone walked through a sliding-glass door. The parties often were broken up by paramedics (cute!) streaming through the backyard.

Clarissa missed those carefree days of summer, fall, winter, and, ah, spring.

"Just, thank God you're not pregnant," Gravy said, rolling over on a blinding-white chaise lounge onto her stomach. She stared up at Clarissa while she stretched her back. "That would really screw your shit up."

Clarissa nodded, slowly. After drinking the mysterious red concoction, her movements were slow and her thoughts slower. And then a picture emerged. Honeymoon night. The turkey baster. Legs spread against bathroom tile.

Clarissa must have looked momentarily nauseous.

"'rissa?"

"No, no. Of course not." Clarissa shook her head.

"C." Gravy sat up. This was not easy, as she was drunk and lying on her stomach. She attempted to roll over several times and finally fell to the ground.

Clarissa didn't notice.

"I am so not pregnant," Clarissa said. "I mean, one time—what are the odds?"

"At your age?" Gravy said. "About one in five hundred."

"But I'm not at my age," Clarissa pointed out.

Gravy climbed back onto the chaise. It was like watching a one-legged man climb Everest.

"There's no way," Clarissa said.

She stared at the half inch left of her red drink. And put it down. "Absolutely No Way."

Thirteen

Way

The two pink stripes on the EPT test said otherwise.

Clarissa was sitting in her bathroom staring at the test she had peed on that morning. She stared through breakfast, through Regis and Whomever, through her midmorning latté. She had missed IMs, ignored the phone, had not yet called the police on her next-door neighbors.

"How could this happen to me?" she said, ignoring the fact that she engineered the feat.

"How could this happen to you?" Gravy said. "How could it *not* have happened to you?"

The girls were having lunch at Morton's. Gravy was the first person Clarissa called. Gravy was always the first person Clarissa called.

"If you plan on having it, I'm throwing the shower," Gravy insisted.

"It's not an it," Clarissa said. "And of course I plan on having it—I mean, I am married."

"Oh, right. I'm blanking," Gravy said. "Oh, Christ." She made a face. "Does this mean you stop drinking coffee?"

"No."

"Sugar?"

"My best friend?"

"Alcohol?"

"I'll get back to you."

"Smoking?"

"I don't smoke," Clarissa said. "You smoke."

"Good. Because you'd never have the strength to quit. And then you'd have one of those teeny, wrinkly babies."

"I guess I'll tell Aaron tonight," Clarissa said. "I don't know how to say it, you know—it's so different from high school. You know, 'Hey, asshole, I'm knocked up and you better pay for it, because I spent my allowance on Jordache jeans.'"

"Then it's not different at all," Gravy said. She was still mad that Aaron had made Clarissa give back the money from their fund-raiser. Except she hadn't. The girls insisted she keep the money and buy something useful, like a D&G shearling winter coat for those biting cold southern California Januarys.

"He's not an asshole," Clarissa said. "And even if he were, for argument's sake, he is the father of my child."

"Oh, here we go." Gravy rolled her eyes. "The Madonna complex."

"Jesus' mom or the dancing one with the cute husband?"

"Both. Was Jesus totally hot or is it just me?"

They sat and started to eat their ahi tuna salads, dressing on the side, which they each emptied out over their salad.

"Fuck. Is raw tuna okay to eat if you're pregnant?"

"You've been pregnant thirty seconds. Don't worry about it."

But Clarissa was. "I don't want one of those parasites eating my baby's eyes." She pushed her salad away. Gravy just looked at her and shook her head.

"So, what happened to that guy Polo set you up with?" Clarissa said, needing a change of subject.

"Washout. Irreparably damaged."

"Maybe you're too picky," Clarissa said.

"Maybe." Gravy replied. "And maybe you're sounding like my mother."

As Clarissa drove home, she realized Gravy was right—she did sound like someone's mother. Maybe because she was becoming someone's mother.

She looked down at her belly and laughed.

She stopped laughing when she thought about stretch marks. Her mother often complained about stretch marks, claiming all was right up until the eighth month, when she suddenly woke up with a map of the U.S. tributaries on her swollen abdomen.

Stretch marks were genetic.

Clarissa pulled a U-turn to drive toward her mother's place. She needed reassurance.

Big mistake.

"Are you sure it's (eet's) Aaron's baby?" her mother said.

"Who are you? Evil Suzee's evil twin?" Clarissa said. "What are you talking about? Of course it's his baby."

"Because I know you had a lot of the sex before," her mother clucked. "How long you pregnant."

"Everyone needs a hobby, Mother," Clarissa said. "You wouldn't let me collect porcelain dolls, remember?"

"Pfft."

Clarissa sat and watched as her mother, puffing a Virginia Slims, ironed her father's shirts. She had insisted on laundering them herself during their marriage; she saw no reason to give it up afterward. She claimed she found it relaxing. Clarissa thought that she just wanted to still feel needed by her father.

The thought made her stomach curl and her hair churn.

"Okay, okay, *lo siento, mija,*" her mother said. And then she sniffed. "Roberto, I think he is married."

"Who?"

"Roberto, please. Come on, get with it."

"Oh, that musician guy?" Clarissa said.

"He was a perfect undercover looover, you know." Her mother sighed.

"Mom. Please," Clarissa said. "Don't sigh. You can talk, but please, no sighing."

Her mother sat down and sighed. "I think he's married, with two children (cheeldren). On the down low."

Clarissa was at a loss for words for maybe the second time in her life. "On the *what*?" she finally spit out. *When did her mother become J-Lo?* she thought to herself.

"My daughter," her mother suddenly said, her skinny fingers clutching Clarissa's hand. "I am so happy you have this baby."

"Really?" Clarissa said. "Even if I'm only hazarding a guess at who the father is?"

This was, thankfully, sarcasm. After all, it was no longer high school. Or college.

Or junior high, for that matter.

"Oh, yes," her mother said. "I will be perfect grandmother. I go to Neiman's and Saks this today afternoon, pick out some nice outfits."

Clarissa thought about maternity wear. She thought about Cindy Crawford in maternity wear . . . she thought about dieting. She thought about purging. She wondered if she could have liposuction at the same time as the delivery.

"You will be a perfect grandmother, and I'll be a . . . ," Clarissa couldn't end the sentence.

"Wha'?"

"I'll be a . . ." Clarissa thought. "Oh my God. I just realized."

She looked at her mother with panicked eyes.

"Your mom was a terrible mom. You were a terrible mom. Do you know what this means?"

Her mother shrugged.

"It's totally genetic!" she wailed. "I'm going to be a terrible mom!" And she dropped her big head onto her mother's tiny shoulder and cried.

Clarissa felt better after her mother deposited a wad of cash on Liz Lange maternity clothes for her. Even though she was barely six weeks along, she looked forward to wearing the black tights with elastic waistband and ballet slippers, and various other trappings of motherhood.

That night.

Clarissa ran home to her actor's workshop apartment house with the notion of making the best homemade meal she'd ever experienced: her grandmother's specialty, potato kugel. Her grandmother, a bellicose woman given to outbursts of a political nature, seldom visited; she was too busy picketing grapes at the local supermarket (she hit the manager with her picket sign) or laying her big body down in front of tractors to protest the building of a nuclear plant (more than once).

But one evening, when Clarissa was about eight, her grandmother made her potato kugel; she said she'd watched her own mother make the rich, buttery dish once a week. Clarissa watched her slice the potatoes so thin they were almost transparent. She watched as her grandmother popped the kugel into the oven, then watched as the butter melted and bubbled, browning the potatoes.

She wished that she, too, could witness this transformation every week, but her grandmother said keugel was bad for the cholesterol, and too work intensive besides. Even at that age Clarissa wondered if anyone would ever love her enough to cook for her again and again.

Clarissa's memories collided with her present: a bag of unwashed potatoes on her kitchen counter.

She looked at them and suddenly felt very tired; she decided against the kugel. She grabbed the small, round pepperoni-shaped magnet with the phone number from the refrigerator. Pizza would do just fine.

Aaron came home at 8:30 that night to half a pepperoni pizza with extra cheese and a wife who was already asleep, dressed in new black tights and ballet slippers, rolled up in a snoring ball on the couch.

As Aaron covered Clarissa with a blanket, she awakened with a snort, a thin line of drool seeping from her mouth into the pillow.

"You still live here?" Clarissa said, wiping her mouth with her sleeve like a six-year-old.

"It's not that late, Clarissa—it's only eight o'clock," Aaron said, as he started picking at the pizza.

"Eight?" Clarissa looked at the digital clock above the television set. *Friends* was on.

Why was she so tired?

"You looked so peaceful. I'm sorry I woke you up."

"Aaron, we have to talk."

"Oh, I see," he said. "It's the talk, huh?"

"What are you talking about?" she said.

"I know what you're going to say," he said. "So why don't you just save your breath."

She looked at him. "You know what I'm going to say?" *How would he know what she was going to say?*

"Of course I do." Aaron rose, went over to the kitchen. This involved about three steps.

He got a beer out of the refrigerator and snapped it open. The noise reverberated through the small, cardboard apartment.

And Clarissa started bawling. Aaron looked over, surprised.

"Hey," Aaron said. "Oh gosh, I didn't mean to make you cry, Jesus."

Clarissa just shook her head, vigorously. She looked like a windshield wiper on high.

"I just . . . look, I know you haven't been happy these last few weeks," he kept talking, faster. "It's understandable. I mean, we barely know each other, we get married, and then I lose all my money."

Clarissa looked at him with her puffy eyes and sniffed with her snotty nose and started bawling all over again.

"Clarissa," Aaron said, "please stop crying. I can't take it when a girl cries."

Clarissa heaved like an old drunk.

Aaron, confused and desperate, put his arms around her, squeezing the breath from her body.

Clarissa started hyperventilating; she sounded like a seal going after a fish. Aaron, completely at a loss, jumped up and started flapping his arms, trying to distract her.

Then he clapped his hands in front of her face.

Then he hopped on one foot.

Then he flipped over on his back and shook his limbs.

And Clarissa started to laugh.

"Get the fuck up, you imbecile," she gasped.

Aaron got up on the couch and sat next to her. She looked into his young, worried eyes.

"You don't know jack," Clarissa told him.

"You don't want to move out?" he said.

"Yes, of course I want to move out, what do you think I am, an idiot?" she said in one breath. "But that's not what I had to tell you."

He looked at her, cockeyed, like a Labrador retriever waiting for a "sit" command.

"Well?" he said. "What is it? Did your mother die again?"

"I'm pregnant."

Aaron did not move. He did not blink. He sat there on the couch as still as a statue.

"But . . . ," he finally said.

"But nothing. Apparently it is possible."

He nodded. And then, as quick as a young man with a minor handicap could, he leaped from the couch and started dancing around the living room.

"I take it you're happy," Clarissa said.

"I take it I am!" he yelled. And he took his wife in his arms and danced around the living room and picked her up by the waist and twirled her until her head spun and she demanded to be put down.

And despite her better judgment, Clarissa started to feel happy as well.

Aaron slept soundly that night, curled up between his wife and his "animals" (he bade each of them a "good night"—every single night—and, this night, he also informed them of the good news).

Clarissa, on the other side of the bed, slept fitfully; like any soon-to-be mother, her head was filled with worries.

Will Prada ever do a baby line?

Who do I bribe to get baby into a private preschool?

What if baby's nose is big like Teddy's, and we have to wait sixteen years for a nose job? Is there a way to get it done sooner?

But mostly, she was worried about money. They had argued over Clarissa going back to her dad for money; finally, she'd agreed not to broach the subject with her father.

However, Clarissa didn't have any intention of keeping their agreement; no blood had been exchanged, no pinky promise made. She knew her rights.

The next morning, in the wee hours (about 9:00 A.M.), Clarissa was on her way to her father's office to beg, on her hands and knees if necessary (as long as there was ample carpeting), for money. No child of hers was going to be swaddled in plain-wrap diapers.

Her father, dressed in a pinstriped suit and yellow tie, with freshly dyed red hair, looked like a broken-down daytime talk show host who had just secured a part in a Broadway revival of *Music Man*.

"Babycakes, whaddaya say?" Teddy said, as he sauntered into the lobby.

"I'm pregnant and I need cash," Clarissa replied, as he escorted her into his office. She saw no reason to make small talk. He was only her father.

"Good to see you too, Babycakes," Teddy said, as he closed the large, wood-paneled door behind them. His office was entirely wood-paneled. It looked like a ski lodge.

Teddy had, as many do, more money than taste.

They sat across from each other, father and daughter, staring across an abyss as wide as the Sargasso Sea, or her grandmother's ass in her later years. Finally, Clarissa spoke.

"How does a pregnant lady get coffee around here?" Clarissa said. "Can you have that old biddy out there wipe the dust off her ass and get me some joe?"

"No caffeine," Teddy said. "You're going to be a mother now, Clarissa. You need to be responsible."

"You remember my name. That's good," she said. And then, it occurred to her. "Responsible? You're telling me I need to be responsible? Who died and made you a parent?"

"That's my little girl. Always with the smart mouth." He went to get a cigar out of his humidor. Then realized the error of his ways; Clarissa smiled. If he lit up, she could lecture him at will.

Teddy sat there, chewing the cigar slowly. "Don't get one of those things, those tests."

"What test?" Clarissa said, herself getting rather testy.

"One of those, ah, whaddayacall—where they figure out the sex. And if it's a bad egg."

"Amnio."

"That's no good. I saw it on Lifetime." His owlish eyes got very big. "They stick a needle in your gut, right there."

He reached over and poked her stomach. Clarissa recoiled, smacking his hand, which always seemed to be balled up in a fist.

"And don't tell me what it is, boy or girl," Teddy said. "I don't want to know. You know, people didn't used to know these things. It used to be a surprise. That's nice."

"Dad?" Clarissa asked.

"Teddy," he said.

"Dad, you're going to be a grandfather, for fuck's sake."

"No cursing in front of the baby."

"Look," she said, "what the hell difference does it make that I call you 'Dad'?"

"The kid can call me Teddy, too," he said.

"Dad," Clarissa said, after a big sigh. "Your hair. Maybe I should be calling you 'Big Red.'"

Teddy looked behind him, into a big mirror hanging behind his desk, over the bar. He smoothed it back.

"I think it looks good." He smoothed it back again. "I look like that guy."

"Ronald McDonald," she said. "Howdy Doody?"

Clarissa desperately needed coffee. She was having trouble concentrating. She was so stressed by being with her father she thought she might lose her hearing—she'd read "It Happened to Me" stories in *Cosmo* about young women losing their senses after enduring extreme mental or physical strain, like during war or living in an actors' workshop apartment and eating tuna three days a week.

"You have to breast-feed, you know," Teddy said. His expression turned serious. She could tell, even though his last face-lift killed nerves around his forehead so that he was left with only one expression: surprise. He looked like a white, middle-aged, male Connie Chung.

"Did you just say 'breast'?" she said. To tell the truth, the thought of some little monster hanging from one of her gorgeous breasts, dragging them to the ground, made her sick.

"Well, you have to," he said.

"Mom didn't breast-feed me," Clarissa retorted.

"We didn't know any better. Now we do."

"This is really none of your business," she said.

"Breast is best," her father replied.

Clarissa didn't bargain for her father having this much interest in her newly forming baby's life. She didn't bargain for him to have *any* interest in it.

"And another thing," Teddy continued. "No alcohol."

"Mom drank a martini every night that she was pregnant with me."

"We didn't know any better," he said again. "Besides, did you ever get through college?"

"You didn't go to college."

"We're not talking about me. We're talking about you and the baby."

"Dad. Teddy. Are you going to give me money or not?"

Her father looked at her, the red plugs on top of his head lined up like tiny soldiers.

"Of course, Babycakes."

Clarissa jumped up and kissed him on the cheek before she knew she was capable of the gesture. Teddy smiled and kissed her back and hugged her as though it were a completely normal act. As though they hugged all the time.

Clarissa held secretly to the feeling (and the big check her father gave her) as she bolted down the stairs of his office and into her car. She wondered if the baby would change everything for her, would make everything right in her life. He/she/it had already brought Clarissa a hug from her father, which had happened only in childhood and on special occasions, like when he'd pay her.

She understood, finally, why the poor women she'd seen on the streets and in news stories had so many babies—because there was hope in children.

Also, apparently, poor people had too much spare time, no satellite, and fucked like rabbits.

Clarissa suddenly realized she was carrying her own leverage, not even six weeks old; she figured that if she'd had so much luck with her own, stubborn, hair-plugged father, she may as well try her hand at a much bigger target: Aaron's parents.

She would phone Joe Three and Cinnamon as soon as she got to her horrible-living-conditions apartment.

"No," Clarissa said out loud, narrowly averting a collision with an old man crossing Fairfax. "I'll fly in to see them."

If only she remembered what state they lived in.

Fourteen

Evil Suzee Appears, and All Goes Wrong

Clarissa was looking feverishly through the Yellow Pages (stolen from her next-door neighbor's apartment—they had left their door open) for a travel agent when someone knocked at the door, rat-a-tat-tat, bracelets jingling with every knuckle crack.

Clarissa didn't know why, but the knocking made her anxious—it sounded like Death on Fen-Phen.

She slipped off her Prada slides (thanks Mom!) and tiptoed over to the door.

A heavily lined eyeball had affixed itself to the peephole. Clarissa slunk back, her heart jumping into her throat (her heart tasting like the pepperoni from last night's pizza). She chewed her knuckle to stifle a scream.

"Clarissa, Lovey!" a voice sang out. "I know you're in there, doll, your beemer's warm."

"Damnfuckshitpisshell," Clarissa said under her breath, and jumped around in a fit, as though the gray pile carpeting (apartment standard) were on fire.

"Come, come, come! Brush your teeth and let me in," the voice said. "I brought the tote!"

The doorknob started shaking; Evil Suzee was not to be denied entrance.

"Charming," she said, stepping into Clarissa's living room, dining room, entryway, and kitchen.

It was all, sadly, one room.

"I brought the tote—remember our prenup bet? I always make good on my promises," as she handed Clarissa her Louis Vuitton bag. "I heard Aaron was disowned; maybe you can sell it," she said, with the cheerfulness of a Hallmark Christmas greeting card, as she stared at the life-size 1940s movie poster Aaron had affixed to the living room wall with chewing gum. "I love what you've done with the place—it's not at all like the projects. I don't know what people are talking about."

Clarissa could have sworn she saw venom dripping from Evil Suzee's fangs.

"Coffee?" Clarissa asked. She wanted a chance to spill it all over Suzee's vintage Chanel suit. She looked like someone's wealthy aunt. It was much too old for her, but she was bargaining, someday, to get onto a best-dressed list in some, any, fashion magazine; it was her life's work.

"No thanks, dear. I don't do instant," she said.

"All right, Evil. Who told you? Give it up," Clarissa said, setting down the bag. She chose to forgo the polite conversation route; her head was aching from the repression of the homicidal urge.

"You know I can't reveal my sources," Suzee said. Her eyes fluttered like Scarlett O'Hara at a debutante ball.

Clarissa noticed the little bags of fat under Suzee's eyes. Genetic aberrations. She had two years, tops, to correct the problem. Clarissa concentrated on the bags and rubbed under her own eyes, knowing this would make Suzee the Spider crazy.

Suzee narrowed her eyes at Clarissa. "What are you doing?" she said.

"Who told you about my new . . . ?" Clarissa couldn't say it.

"Your, er, quaint living arrangements?"

"Don't say 'er,'" Clarissa said. "No one says 'er.'"

"Er," Suzee replied. "I think I will take that cup of coffee. You must have one of those 'I "Heart" L.A.' mugs lurking in the kitchenette?"

Clarissa held her tongue, almost having to do so with her thumb and forefinger, and took the three (four, because her legs were shorter) steps into the kitchen. She banged through the cheap faux woodgrain cabinets looking for the Geary's china that went so well with Aaron's Old Hollywood abode the day she picked it out for their wedding registry, well before Aaron even knew about their wedding.

She found a small coffee cup with a delicate floral design and a gold rim; they'd reminded her of her grandmother's coffee cups—the ones her mother would throw at her father when she got angry at him. They lasted all of six months in their house, for china rarely bounced.

She took the cup down from the cabinet with the door that never closed.

And spit in it.

"Do you take milk or cream?" Clarissa called out, after pouring the coffee. "Milk is fine," Suzee said.

Clarissa eyed the remnants of the morning milk from the white cat's bowl.

And poured it into the coffee.

"I forgot to ask you about sugar," Clarissa said, bearing Suzee's coffee into the living room/dining room/entry. Suzee was sitting on the edge of the red couch as though it was covered in dog shit.

"Thanks, no," Suzee said. She bared her reptilian tongue and sipped at the coffee.

Clarissa gave her the first smile of the afternoon.

"Jennifer spilled," Suzee said, after savoring the last drop. "She cried like a baby when I cut her open." Suzee peered out over the coffee cup. "Kidding, Sugar. I just love metaphor, don't you?"

"Why would she tell you?" Clarissa asked, nervous about Jennifer. She hadn't heard from her that morning; perhaps Suzee *had* cut her into pieces and scattered her body parts all over the city.

"Because I told her to tell me or I wouldn't be her friend." Suzee raised an evil eyebrow halfway up her forehead.

"Right," Clarissa said. "Brilliant." Jennifer was like everyone's baby sister. All you had to say was you wouldn't be her friend anymore, and voilà. *Suzee v. Jennifer* in the Information Wars was an unfair match.

"You want to give me the royal tour?" Suzee said.

"Don't go having one of your annual orgasms, Suzee. This situation is so temporary it's already ended," Clarissa said.

"Not a divorce, I hope," Suzee said. Her eyes sparkled.

Clarissa was gaining speed and courage. "As a matter of fact, we've recently come into a windfall—we're planning on moving out as soon as I find an appropriate space."

"Did someone die?" Suzee asked.

"No, sorry, dear," Clarissa said. "Someone got knocked up."

Suzee's face made a grimace before she quickly swallowed her expression. "Ahhhh! Congratulations!" She flew over on her bat wings and hugged Clarissa to her bony chest. Clarissa felt like a fly dancing with a black widow. She disengaged herself. "Thanks. No one really knows yet, except Gravy." Clarissa could have killed herself for that comment—she had just given away the whole store.

"I hope you don't get too fat," Suzee said, smiling, inching her way (all ten inches) to the front door. "Oh, and the nausea thing, sometimes that lasts the whole nine months. And, you know, pregnancy is really ten months, not nine, that's a fallacy." Her bony, veined hand was on the doorknob. "And you know what they say about girls versus boys during pregnancy. Girls hate their mothers, naturally, so they make them fat and ugly, and boys love their mothers, so they just give them cystic acne." Suzee licked her always dry lips. "I'm sure that won't happen to you."

"You're a gem," Clarissa said.

"No. You're a gem." And Suzee blew Clarissa a kiss and flew out the door. Clarissa saw the silver cell phone in Suzee's hand before the door even shut. Clarissa ran to her purse in a blind panic. She wanted to tell the rest of the Star Chamber the good news before Suzee ruined it for her. It was time to speed-dial.

Gravy already knew, but was sworn to secrecy. Next one on the list: Jen: "Hello?" On the first ring. *Someone,* Clarissa thought, *was certainly waiting by the phone.*

"Jen, it's Clarissa—I'm—"

Clarissa heard a clicking sound come through the phone line.

"Hold on, C."

"No!" screamed Clarissa. "Damn it!" Her strategy sucked; she had used up too much time with "It's Clarissa."

Jen clicked back. "Oh my God! Congratulations! I'm so so so happy for you!"

"Fuck!" screamed Clarissa.

"You already gained ten pounds?" Jen asked.

Clarissa pressed conference, speed-dialed Gravy for backup and grabbed her Blackberry, IMing Polo at the same time.

"Suzee just told me about the skin thing—it'll clear up in no time," Gravy offered, as she ate crackers in the background.

"Fuck again!" Clarissa screamed. "Curse you, Evil Suzee!"

The Blackberry beeped. Polo had written: Ihrd! RUSck?

"Fuck squared," Clarissa said. "Excuse me, girls," she continued, "I'm going to go curl up in the fetal position."

"You know," Gravy said, her mouth full, "I heard pregnancy lasts ten months."

Clarissa hung up on everyone and turned off the phone.

Clarissa woke up with her face plastered onto the Yellow Pages, hovering over "M" for massage. She stared at the advertisements for Full Body Massage with Thai and Russian girls and closed her eyes and thanked God that she was born in such a great country where a girl with no prospects but a nice rack had a reasonable shot at marrying someone rich, even if it seemed like a shitload of trouble at the moment.

Clarissa figured she should make travel plans to see Aaron's parents in person—she didn't feel the impact of a grandchild, their first, would register as deeply by phone.

She called a travel agent, asked what state the city of Colon or Callin or whatever was in, and made airline and hotel reservations (she didn't want to be a burden, after all).

Aaron came in, carrying a package.

"Oh my God, Aaron. What are you doing home?"

"Why? You have another man in here?"

"No, I just . . ."

"I'm kidding." He handed her the package. "Open it."

"For me?" She ripped it open like a tiger with a rodent.

A necklace. Delicate gold lace with tourmaline and pearls. It was beautiful. And Clarissa could never wear it. It would never fit around her neck.

"For Mother's Day," Aaron said.

"But Aaron," Clarissa looked up at him, and gently, as though addressing a child, "it's not Mother's Day—and I'm not a mother yet."

"Since when do you care about details when it comes to gifts?"

"Point taken," she said. She looked at the handiwork. "This was expensive."

"I put it on layaway. What a concept. I've never used layaway before."

"Aaron. It's beautiful. It's really so beautiful."

"Do you love it?"

"I love it," Clarissa said, not loving it at all but filled with a new sensation: gratitude.

She looked at him. "How many rooms in this place?"

Aaron smiled. "Three."

"We've got two to go—"

The third time they made love that afternoon, the phone rang. Clarissa begged Aaron not to get it, but as he was on the clock with his boss, he had to pick up.

It was Teddy.

"It's Teddy," Aaron said, mouthing the words.

"I'm not here," Clarissa said.

"She's not here," Aaron said, into the phone. And then his expression changed.

"I think you'd better take it," Aaron said. "He's only got three minutes and one quarter."

Clarissa looked at Aaron. "That is so not funny."

"Neither is a middle-aged white man sitting in a jail cell comparing tattoos with gang members." And then he paused. "No, wait a minute. That is funny."

Clarissa picked up the phone.

"Dad?"

"Teddy."

"Teddy. Where are you?"

"I don't have much time." Someone hollered in the background; Clarissa had never heard anyone holler before. Yell, yes. Scream, absolutely. Hollering was something else, entirely.

"What's that noise?"

"Lunch."

"Tell me you're at Hillcrest at a bar mitzvah party."

"I'm at Fourth and Grand."

"Oh, fuck."

"I need bail money. Ten thousand dollars."

"I don't have ten thousand. I don't have twenty dollars, you know that."

"The check I gave you."

"But, see," Clarissa whined, "that's the point, Dad. You *gave* it to me."

"I need it to bail me out."

"You have more—you have to have more, you're my father."

"Of course I have more," he paused. "Before they search the apartment. Under my computer. There must be about five hundred or so."

"Five hundred?" Clarissa would have sat back, but she was already lying down. "Tell me there's five hundred thousand under your computer."

"You have to move fast. They're going to freeze my accounts."

"Freeze your accounts? What about me? What about this baby?"

"I wish I could help you out, Babycakes, I really do."

"Dad. How'd this happen?"

"My former partner."

"You mean your partner."

"Nah. I got tired of him. Always complaining about stuff."

"Like what?"

"Like paying less in taxes than he wanted."

"What?"

"Creative financing, like you said. I'm a creative guy, Clarissa, you know that."

"Dad."

"Yeah."

"I'll come down, bail you out."

"That's my girl."

Clarissa hung up the phone and looked at Aaron.

"I'll get my coat," he said.

"No," Clarissa said. "I don't want you to come down. It's too embarrassing."

"Are you kidding? It's not embarrassing." He smiled. "It's family."

"Family *is* embarrassing," Clarissa called after him.

* * *

They posted bond and picked up her father at downtown L.A.'s Central Jail and Aaron and Teddy greeted each other like old war buddies who had been separated by miles and years and wives and children. All the way back to Teddy's apartment he and Aaron chatted as though nothing unusual had happened; they discussed the stock market, the Lakers versus the Knicks, the best place in town to get New York–style pizza. They discussed every topic except the fact that Teddy was probably off to the Big House again.

After they dropped Teddy off at his Century City condo, Clarissa made a vow to herself to visit Aaron's parents in the next few days. If no one else was going to be an adult about the situation, at least she was.

There was no way she was spending one more pregnant month in that apartment.

The hard part was not letting Aaron know that she was getting on a plane to Atlanta and staying overnight.

Okay, that was the easy part.

The hard part was getting Gravy to come with her.

"I don't go places where they still use V05."

"Culturist."

"I'm a sophisticate. You know that." Gravy once had been called a sophisticate, in their high school yearbook, and had *never let go of it*.

"Let it go, Gravy."

"No. It's all I've got."

"Agreed." Clarissa took a beat. "So, you're coming?"

"Of course. It sounds like fun, watching you make a fool of yourself in front of the in-laws."

"Why are you such a bitch?"

"It's a skill, a talent, built up over many years. Also, I wasn't loved as a child."

They smiled at each other. "Have your bag packed by tomorrow at eight A.M.—we're on the nine-thirty flight."

"Jesus. I just hope I'll be able to get a decent Bloody Mary on the plane," Gravy said.

* * *

"So, honey, I was wondering if it's okay to sleep over at Gravy's tonight," Clarissa asked Aaron. He looked at her, confused. "She needs me to nurse her through—she just had that . . . girl thing fixed."

Aaron made a face. "Oh, geez."

"Yeah. Some sort of growth—"

"Oh God, oh—" Aaron put down his Frosted Flakes.

"Yeah, in her—"

He waved his arms and got up and scrambled toward the bathroom.

"So, is that okay?"

Aaron made a grunting noise.

"Thanks, honey, I really appreciate it, and so does Gravy." Clarissa paused, crossing her fingers behind her back. "So, I'll see you tomorrow when you get back from work. But if you want me, I'll be on my cell."

Aaron grunted again. Clarissa laughed. Men were so anxious to get into women's privates, but they could never bring themselves to talk about them. It was a party stopper, a surefire way of getting anything a girl wanted. Saying the word "vagina" was like using a handgun, only cheaper and less violent.

Clarissa drove over to Gravy's house early and dragged her out of bed; she looked like Courtney Love in the early preop, pre–Oscar party years. A.M. was not her favorite half of the day.

"You owe me," was all she said before Clarissa turned the shower on her.

Clarissa stared straight ahead in her business-class seat (And why not? She was a pregnant lady, now. Her mother, who'd unknowingly paid for the tickets, would never want her in coach) and thought: *People always say, "The flight was uneventful." Why did her flight, her first in two years, have to be so . . . fucking* eventful? Gravy, who insisted upon lugging an oversized bag on board, was cranky with the flight attendants, who, in turn, schooled her on the finer points of bitchery. When Gravy called out, "Oh, waitress," and shook her tiny, empty bottles of vodka at a woman in uniform, the flight attendants cut off her honey-roasted peanut ration and her liquor supply, which meant she'd go hungry and surly the remainder of the flight. And after Gravy complained about the in-flight movie in, ah, rather unladylike terms ("I hate that fucking [insert actor name to avoid possible lawsuit or angry letter from public relations maven]. He's so fucking sincere, plus it looks like his face got caught in a grain harvester"), and one of the flight attendants threatened to strap her down in her seat with her oxygen mask, even Gravy had to admit to being impressed.

Gravy left the flight exclaiming that she, herself, should consider becoming a flight attendant—she was (obviously) a natural for the job.

Clarissa had tried to ignore Gravy's outbursts, even attempting to meditate through the bumpier part of the flight, a storm over the Colorado Rockies.

However, the most she could do was visualize Aaron's parents welcoming her with open arms and open wallets. She had brought gifts for them—an Armani tie for Mr. Mason, and an Hèrmès scarf for his wife.

She had taken the Armani tie from her father's closet while searching for the big five hundred dollars and the Hèrmès scarf from her mother's underwear drawer (months ago, just in case). She figured her father wouldn't be attending a lot of formal dinners or business meetings where he was spending the next year (or so, depending on how good—read: pricey—his lawyer was). Not a lot of suit-and-tie activities, very few conference calls, and her mother hadn't worn the Hèrmès scarf since the day she decided scarves were worn only by old women.

The plane surged and rattled and Clarissa patted her belly, reassuring her very own passenger.

Gravy looked at her and smiled. She held her hand out and Clarissa grabbed it.

"It's going to be okay, Mommy," Gravy said. The plane wheezed. "Motherfuck!" screamed Gravy. "You so owe me!"

Fifteen

Meet the (Grand!) Parents

What?! They don't know you're showing up?" Gravy, wearing a scowl and oversized jet-black Chanel sunglasses, was dragging her mock-Prada overnight bag through the Atlanta airport.

"Never discount the element of surprise," replied Clarissa, trying to hide her growing nervousness. "'Sides, they're going to love me, how could they not?"

Gravy wheezed while Clarissa looked around for the car rental. All she could see were blondes with big hair and bright-colored dresses, shoulder pads and chunky jewelry; it was as though she had gotten caught up in a Miss America travel-day excursion; she swore, any second, she would run into Bert Parks.

"How could they *not*?" Gravy asked. "Allow me to count the ways." She stopped and put her fingers in the air, counting off: "One. You're older than their son; Two. You married him without a prenup; Three. You're not *exactly* an extra on *Dallas,*" she said, nodding her head toward the Kodachrome blondes. Who were everywhere. They seemed to be proliferating, like big-haired guppies.

"That will be all, Cindy Adams," Clarissa snapped, referencing the semifamous, arrow-tongued gossip columnist with the kabuki hair. Clarissa stopped to check her phone. No calls. She finally saw the Budget Rent A Car stand. "Let's get us a convertible." She felt a convertible would cheer her up—they always did.

"You have a credit card that works?" said Gravy, trudging behind. She stopped to light a cigarette, flouting the obvious NO SMOKING signs.

"No," Clarissa said, "but my mother does."

"And she knows you're using it, of course . . ."

"Not."

Gravy smiled and shook her head and blew smoke. An old woman in a pink suit made a face at her and pointed at the sign. "One puff!" she yelled, and chugged after Clarissa.

It was 4:00 by the time Clarissa drove up the circular drive to the Downtown Macon Towers, a hotel distinguished neither by its architecture nor its clientele. The travel agent had told Clarissa about the pool, the sauna, the gym, the wide beds, and the central air, the faux antebellum touches. She told Clarissa she'd love it.

Clarissa hated it.

"You chose the place," ever helpful Gravy pointed out.

"It smells in here," Clarissa said, as they entered their one-bedroom "suite," the suite part consisting of a couch that looked like it had been thrown out of someone's window. During a fire.

"Ugh," Clarissa said, her nose clenched up like a fist, "old lady knee-high nylons and dog hair."

Gravy sniffed the air and sat at the edge of the bed, which was not the double Clarissa had requested but two junior-size singles pushed together. Gravy waved in front of her nose, creating a breeze; she looked as though she were testing a fabulous new Parisian scent.

"Dried semen," she concluded. "Oh, wait, and a hint of fat man B.O."

Clarissa grabbed the hotel phone and held the questionable-hygiene receiver a good six inches from her head as she dialed Cinnamon and Joe Three Mason. She prayed that they had a good attitude and a clean guest room ready to be occupied.

She scratched her arm; a small something had bitten her.

Before they got fleas.

Dead giveaways that one is in the presence of great wealth:

1. An unmarked road that winds through a front lawn; a front lawn which goes on for 3.2 miles.
2. No discernible mailbox.

3. Iron gates that belong, like, outside the Kremlin or something.
4. A sign on the iron gates stating a clever name. Only the stinking rich name their houses.
5. Helicopter pad.
6. Zoo. *Not kidding.*
7. Past the iron gates, past the sign, past all this, the enormous sandstone mansion was another dead giveaway.

These fuckin' Masons were rich. Rich like J.R. Ewing rich. Rich like Hunt Brothers rich.

Rich like the roaring eighties rich and the silicone nineties rich.

This is what Gravy would have said had she been able to speak. Her lower jaw had dropped onto her sternum and remained there until Clarissa, having parked the car (after passing through the gi-normous green acreage the color of leprechaun fantasies—the greenest green—green like, well, old money), pulled her out of her great-wealth-induced coma.

They stumbled from the Mustang to the front steps leading to the entrance. Clarissa counted the steps—one, two, three—she stopped when she couldn't catch her breath any longer.

Cinnamon Mason, a frilly apron around her waist and a freezing martini in her hand, greeted Clarissa at the top of the stairs with such enthusiasm and vigor that Clarissa figured that she must have rung the wrong . . . intimidating iron gate bell.

"Oh, wonderful," Cinnamon said. "Clarissa. Finally."

She hugged Clarissa, quick and hard, and then just as quickly popped her off her chest and shook Gravy's hand so forcefully Gravy later swore her shoulder nearly jerked out of its socket.

"Come in, do come in," Cinnamon said, walking like a peacock into a giant foyer. A butler, an older man with smooth, almost blue-black skin and dramatic, combed-back white hair that looked like sea foam, took Clarissa's and Gravy's coats and purses.

A butler. By the way, another dead giveaway. (Clarissa was pretty certain that she was in the midst of telephone number *plus* area code wealth.)

Clarissa whispered to Gravy, "Eyes back in the head, Miss Sophisticate."

They followed Cinnamon past the ballroom (*ballroom?!*) into an adjacent sitting room. The girls knew the arena with the marble floor was a ballroom because Cinnamon said, "Oh, that's the ballroom."

She said this like saying "Oh, that's the powder room" or "Oh, that's the linen closet."

"Excuse the mess," Cinnamon said, as they entered the sitting room, a tastefully rendered mélange of silk and velvet and fresh-cut roses the color of winter peaches. Clarissa thought she could die happy in this room, even if it were a bad death, like a murder-suicide or choking on a peanut. *God, she was hungry.*

Clarissa looked around for the "mess." There were two magazines lying on an ornate coffee table.

"Joey Très always forgets to clean up after himself," she said, as she scooped up the magazines. Gravy looked at Clarissa. "Aaron's dad," she said. Gravy nodded. She was wearing the face of a startled animal. *Real wealth is too much for some people,* Clarissa thought.

"Please, do have a seat," Cinnamon said. "You must be starved after your long flight." She rang a silver bell that had its very own silver holder, and two maids wearing ruffled aprons and bearing gifts of hors d'oeuvres and various crudités on silver platters silently appeared. Clarissa was beginning to think these people were special effects. "May I get you something to drink, as well?" said Cinnamon.

"Oh, Jesus," said Gravy, looking at the fixings. Clarissa elbowed her in the ribs. It fazed Gravy not in the least.

"I'll have what you're having," Gravy said, eyeing Cinnamon's martini.

Clarissa stamped on her foot. "Water is fine for us," Clarissa said.

"Since when?" Gravy asked, under her breath.

"Dear Clarissa," Cinnamon smiled, reaching out to hold Clarissa's hand. "We have so much to talk about."

"Oh, we do, we do," Clarissa said, smiling. And stuffing several things that looked like tiny hats into her mouth. Whatever they were, they tasted good. She remembered to wipe her mouth with the miniature, square, monogrammed linen napkin. She cursed her parents for not teaching her good manners or enrolling her in an etiquette class.

She made a note for her future child. He or she would know how to act in grandma's house—where, with any luck at all, they would be living.

Cinnamon brushed a nonexistent hair (Clarissa noticed her hair never moved; it stayed obediently in its place, like a well-trained pet) from her preternaturally unwrinkled forehead; she looked like the inside of a lychee nut—shiny and ivory white. "And how is my boy Aaron? I haven't heard from him in . . ."

She gestured with her hand, just like Clarissa's mother; Clarissa wondered if that was the way all mothers eventually communicated.

"Aaron is fine," was all she managed.

Gravy was staring at a lamp with a multicolored hood that looked like an umbrella. "Is that real Tiffany?" she asked. Clarissa thought Gravy was dangerously close to losing all of her "cool" points.

"Why, yes," Cinnamon said. "Are you a collector?"

Clarissa interrupted. "Mrs. Mason."

"Cinnamon, child, please," Mrs. Mason said. Mrs. Mason said "child" drawn out like a high note at the end of a Luther Vandross song.

Clarissa realized Cinnamon was drunk. But she was demure drunk, like a church-going grandmother.

"Cinnamon, there's something I wanted to tell you," Clarissa said. "It has to do with the reason I flew out to your . . . lovely home." *Oh, that's good,* Clarissa thought. *That sounded exactly right—"lovely home."* Nice work. Gravy raised an eyebrow. Not missing a beat with the crudités.

"Of course, of course," Cinnamon said. "I'm assuming you'all will join us for dinner." She said "you'all" with one-and-a-half syllables, not one, as Clarissa had heard of southern people on television and in the movies. Clarissa hoped the accent would rub off on her. She thought of Simon and his English accent, then quickly displaced him from her mind with thoughts of mint juleps and fireflies and warm southern nights.

She felt like Scarlett before that nasty war business.

"For dinner?" Gravy said. "I'm thinking for the next few years. How do you feel about adoption, Mrs. Mason?"

If Clarissa had been packing, Gravy would have been the unhappy recipient of several ounces of lead bullet.

Cinnamon smiled without the use of her eyes. Clarissa studied her. Despite the ruffled apron, "unruffled" was the word that fit her mother-in-law. Clarissa was expert at reading people—she utilized her own, foolproof grid on unsuspecting acquaintances, examining them from head to toe with the force of a neutron microscope. She called it her MGS: Mental Grid System. It had never failed her.

But this one, she was hard to read. Maybe impossible. Suddenly, Clarissa felt something new, something she hadn't experienced since the eighth grade, when Martie Bowers came to school in platform sneakers and a halter top sporting a pair of freshly grown boobs.

Clarissa was intimidated.

"I'm sure you two would like to take a bath, change your clothes," Cinnamon said, smoothing her apron. Clarissa looked at her smooth, pale hands and knew she had never touched a stove in her life. "Our little dinner party is rather informal. Just wear something comfortable. Whatever you have is fine."

"Dinner party?" Gravy said, as they were deposited into a guest room the size of an airline hangar by the butler, who walked with the same gravity as Jesus on the waters.

"I'm confused," Clarissa said, sitting in an overstuffed chair in the corner next to the window. "Why is she being so cheery? She and her husband cut off Aaron because he married me. I wanted to win them over; I was prepared for major mother-in-law–daughter-in-law action. Like WWF stuff."

Clarissa picked up a small, silver-framed picture of a shirtless, teenage Aaron with another boy his age—a fishing picture. Aaron, dark and tawny-skinned and *Teen* magazine handsome, was a head taller than the other boy, who was skinny and blond and wore a pouty expression; their heads tilted toward each other. Clarissa wondered what they had in common.

"Southerners," Gravy was saying, "are always polite. Even if she cut your throat, she'd say 'please' first and 'thank you' after. Remember that."

Gravy went into the bathroom and screamed.

"What's wrong?" Clarissa jumped up—

"Double baths!" Gravy said. "Last one in's a rotten shopper!"

Clarissa shook her head and took off her shoes. She looked at her toes and cursed the fact that she hadn't had a pedicure in weeks. She knew Cinnamon would disapprove, though not to her face; Cinnamon's boy deserved a girl who always has a perfect pedicure.

Clarissa made a vow to herself to sneak into Aaron's boyhood bedroom when and if she had the chance.

And could find it, at the Mason Hilton.

"Come *on*!" Gravy screamed. She was already naked, having thrown her clothes on the floor. She looked sweet and young (and waxed, in the shape of a clover), like the girl Clarissa had first met eighteen years ago when Gravy the Cat, as she was known in junior high, for her cat eyes and slinky walk, had stolen Clarissa's very first boyfriend.

Clarissa peeled off her clothes, which felt, after the long day, as though they were part of her skin, and lamented the growth of her thighs. She felt pounds heavier than the day before.

Clarissa put one heavy foot in front of the other and walked toward the bathroom (fifteen whole, not mincing, steps!), where Gravy, giggling like an eight-year-old, had already submerged herself under bubbles and hot water.

Clarissa caught her reflection in a mirror that was beginning to fog (thank *God*) and thought about who or *what* would be sitting around that dinner table.

After Clarissa and Gravy settled on hair (Clarissa would wear hers blow-dried, straight; Gravy chose to emphasize her curl), they argued about what to wear before settling on white T-shirts, light cotton bebe sweaters and Katayone Adeli flat-front pants. Clarissa wished she'd had pearls; pearls would have been the right touch. She knew that whatever they chose to wear they would be either underdressed or overdressed; there was no getting around it.

They never did find the dining room. They went up this staircase, down that one, across this hall, through that one, into several bathrooms (where they scoured the medicine cabinets), then again into a security bay. Just as Clarissa was ready to burst into starvation- and hormone-induced tears, they arrived at the sitting room to find no one there.

A butler floated in and informed them that the guests were on the veranda, which seemed very nice to Clarissa, but she had no idea what a veranda was.

"It means 'outside,'" Gravy said.

Clarissa nodded. "Big duh. Of course it does."

They followed the butler out, trying to trace his long, noiseless steps.

He opened the double French-glass doors to the outside. On a long patio, overlooking the backyard (*Jesus Christ, was that a golf course?*) were about two dozen people, drinks in hand. This seemed normal enough. What was not normal was that they were as still as a painting, and all appeared to be looking off in one direction—toward the golf course.

Oh. And the women, to the last, were dressed in demure knee-length linen skirts and giant pearl chokers. No one was dressed in slacks.

"Underdressed," Clarissa said, sotto voce, to Gravy.

"Well, we were half right," Gravy replied. "Let's get us a social lubricant."

Just as Gravy turned toward the waiter, who was also looking off, there were two loud gunshots. Gravy and Clarissa screamed and hit the ground and clasped their hands over their heads.

A moment stretched by. The guests started clapping. Gravy and Clarissa, lying supine on the ground, looked up.

"Clarissa, darlin'," Cinnamon called out. "Are you all right?"

Clarissa and Gravy scurried to their feet, helping each other up."Found it!" Clarissa exclaimed, holding up her hand. Gravy looked at her, then grabbed whatever Clarissa had "found" and popped it in her mouth. "Vicodin!" Gravy explained to the crowd.

"Oh, honey, I hope that didn't scare you?" Cinnamon said to Clarissa. "That's my (mah) Joe Three, just doing his thing."

She said "thing" like "thang."

"Hustle on over here, dear," Cinnamon took Clarissa's arm. "He likes to shoot a couple bird before dinner. Quail, mostly; sometimes we get lucky with a duck or two."

"Ducks?" Clarissa said, shaking. "Duckies? Quack-quacks?" Every set of eyes was on her.

"Then Maybelline cuts off their (they) heads, plucks 'em and cooks up a load a chili," Cinnamon said.

"Oh fucking Jesus," Gravy whispered.

"Jesus was a hunter," an eggplant-shaped man in a tweed coat that he would swear fit him in college replied, and he handed Gravy a mint julep as she slumped down, just in time, in a patio chair. If Gravy had turned it over she would have found that it was from the turn of the century. The century that started with seventeen.

The dinner table sat thirty.

Now, look at that again. The dinner table sat *thirty.* That means thirty people (full-grown-adult–size human beings) were able to sit at the dinner table.

Cinnamon seated everyone, moving about the table (this took some time) like a prima ballerina at her Royal Opera House debut; Gravy and Clarissa were seated opposite each other. Gravy was seated between a boy who wore a suit with a string-type bow tie and the eggplant in the tweed coat, who seemed to have a (self) interest in getting Gravy sloshed.

Eggplant Tweed Man had pulled out her chair, startling Gravy so that she hesitated—Clarissa could see that she thought she was about to sit in the wrong seat. Tweed, after an embarrassing moment, motioned to Gravy to sit down. Finally, he was forced to impersonate her sitting down in the chair.

Clarissa laughed. Not to paint an entire species with the same hairbrush, but men in L.A. were, well, allergic to chivalry; they pulled out a chair about as often as they'd pull a hair from their heads. Gravy made eyes at Clarissa and whistled.

Suddenly, a large man with an enormous head of snow white hair bound in, jumping around like a big kangaroo and wearing an orange vest and a hunting cap. And carrying what looked like a 12-gauge shotgun (Clarissa guessed; she'd only seen them in old Burt Reynolds movies and on Fox television).

"Who the *hell* saw that?!" he cried. "Can I get a witness, *people*?!"

Everyone talked *at once,* except for Clarissa and Gravy (who might not ever recover), as he dropped his shotgun on the table with a clatter (Clarissa and Gravy were the only two people to, again, jump and duck) and drank down a brown liquid Clarissa could only surmise was bourbon (again, because of her movie education; all southern-accented men drank straight bourbon), and wiped his mouth with the back of his hand.

"Whoo-whee!" he said. "I am cookin' with gas!" He slapped the table, spilling several water glasses.

"Joe Three." Cinnamon rose at the end of the table. "You sit down this instant. You got yourself all swole up."

Her husband looked sheepishly at his wife. "I'm just feelin' fat and sassy, Sugarbun."

"You are embarrassin' yourself and, more importantly, your wife," Cinnamon said. "Now sit, and behave. Your new daughter-in-law is here, and she's got somethin' to say to us."

The whole table turned toward Clarissa, their eyes wide and expectant.

Expectant, Clarissa thought, *is the right term, all around.*

"Hi, Mr. Joe Three," Clarissa said to her father-in-law. "I'm Clarissa?" She waited for an acknowledgment, something horrible, like a bear hug.

None came. "I'm married to Aaron, your son."

"So I heard. Spit the nuts outyer mouth. What d'you got to say for yourself?"

Clarissa's stomach threatened to empty its contents out on the velvet-backed chairs (ca. 1852). She heard the growl.

"C'mon now, shell down the corn," Joe Three continued.

Clarissa looked at him, stupefied. "Shell down . . . you know what? It's nothing," she said. "It can wait."

"Wait? Waitin's for old dogs and new crops and Christmas mornin'," he said.

Clarissa looked at Gravy, who shrugged. It was clear neither understood a word Joe Three said. It reminded Clarissa of a trip she had taken as a high school exchange student to Kyoto. They didn't speak much English there, either.

Seconds ticked by. All sounds had ceased. Clarissa heard the tick-tock of a grandfather clock (fifth-generation, according to Cinnamon) somewhere in the hallway.

It was as quiet as Barneys the day before their warehouse sale.

Clarissa's brain went into hyperspeed, flipping through possible repercussions for making her "special" announcement at the dinner. She knew she had landed in enemy territory—like a WWII paratrooper on the German countryside—but how deep? Was she closer to the French border or the POW camps? And, she didn't particularly like their clothes. And thus, she did not trust their judgment.

She chose to lie.

Clarissa stood, in a brave, desperate move. "First, I just wanted to say how thankful I am to Mr. and Mrs. Mason, Cinnamon and Joe Three, for welcoming me into their home. So far, it's been more fun than a . . . than a . . . rooster, ah . . ." Clarissa stammered. "I've had a wonderful time. Now I understand why Aaron talks endlessly of his love for his parents."

Joe Three looked at Clarissa like she had just bit off the head of a live rattlesnake. The slightest choking noise came out of Cinnamon's throat. Clarissa wasn't looking but guessed two ounces of gin had just gone down the wrong pipe.

Clarissa had hit pay dirt. She slid her eyes over to Gravy, whose eyebrows had jumped halfway up her forehead. Aaron had never spoken of his parents, except when he had told Clarissa they had cut him off. *Aaron did not like his parents.*

Aaron probably *despised* his parents.

When she wanted to, Clarissa had a mind that worked at warp speed. She just didn't want to all that much.

Clarissa smiled and continued on. "Aaron, who's been working so very hard on his new film, I'm sure you've all heard the gory details from my illustrious hosts," she could tell no one had heard a damn thing, "sent me here as a surprise. He can't get away from his work, as no doubt you can imagine, and he just wanted to send his love through his favorite little homing pigeon."

Now Gravy coughed. Clarissa shot a death ray at her friend, which, instead of turning her into vapor, silenced her instantly.

Tweed Man poured Gravy more wine.

"So, you . . . all. That was my little announcement," Clarissa said.

Twenty-six of the thirty people seated clapped and made polite comments, as though this were dinner theater. Cinnamon thanked Clarissa and sipped at her (latest) martini. Clarissa hadn't even seen the butler slip her another drink.

Joe Three was silent. His hands were locked on either side of the table, as though he were trying to prevent himself from hitting something.

Clarissa scooted her chair away from him. Gravy put her thumb up, giving her high marks.

Then Clarissa heard sobbing. Joe Three was crying into his pecan salad course.

Clarissa panicked and looked at Cinnamon, who was busy conversing with a woman who looked like a peacock.

No one else paid attention to Joe Three except for Gravy, hand over her mouth and shoulders shaking. Clarissa guessed it was from suppressing a nervous laugh, the kind of laugh a child gets when their brother or sister is getting a spanking.

Clarissa spider-walked her hand over to Joe Three's big shoulder and patted it, gently. *Ah, family dynamics,* Clarissa thought. *It's a wonder anyone gets out alive.*

Joe Three sobbed through the entire first course, and was dutifully ignored by his guests, except for Clarissa, who kept a hand on his shoulder the whole time, which made eating the meat course (immediately after the game course, which Clarissa had polished off), somewhat difficult. But not impossible. Clarissa had entered the dining room just good enough to be an "After"; she left as a "Before."

Gravy agreed that Clarissa had handled the situation as well as one could expect of someone with no prior training, while still managing to eat a full meal.

Clarissa decided she would take Cinnamon aside in the morning and tell her about the newest Mason-to-be. And then she would drop a hint about the inheritance. The hint would weigh, if possible to quantify, about eight hundred pounds and be difficult to drive a truck around.

Clarissa had forgotten to peruse (rummage through) Aaron's childhood bedroom but promised herself she'd do it first thing in the morning.

She got a fantastic night's sleep. Being surrounded by wealth beyond one's wildest dreams was, apparently, excellent for one's health.

Sixteen

Good Clarissa Hunting

Morning arrived long before Clarissa opened her eyes and realized she hadn't spoken to Aaron. She checked her phone messages; there were five. She cursed her selfishness, then forgave herself, because her intentions were *always* good, and dialed him immediately. After eating a leftover chocolate.

Aaron was asleep. Of course he was asleep, it was 5:00 in the morning. Clarissa could never keep track of that time change thing—she didn't understand why one country needed several time zones—it'd be so much easier if everyone were on L.A. time.

"Honey," Clarissa said. She put on a pout. "I'm sorry I didn't get a chance to call you back."

"I called you five times; you didn't have a chance to call me back for one minute?" Aaron said. Pissed.

"Emergency. Couldn't be helped. I had to run Gravy to the hospital—try to understand," Clarissa said. She sat up in bed while Gravy snored.

"I understand," Aaron said. "I understand more than you think."

"What's that supposed to mean?" Clarissa asked.

"I know what you're doing," Aaron said.

"You do?" Clarissa asked. She wondered if Cinnamon or Joe Three, in a fit of familial emotion, had called Aaron last night. She wondered how they would have been able to dial, given their alcohol consumption, and then figured they probably had "people" to perform such chores.

"Simon told me everything," Aaron said.

Clarissa had to think a moment.

"Clarissa?"

"Simon who?" Clarissa said.

"You must think I'm stupid."

"Told you what, exactly?" Clarissa asked.

"I don't want to discuss this over the phone." Then, "If you want a creepy English guy, you can have him."

"Simon's not creepy," Clarissa said. "Plus, he's barely English. Look, we're old friends, we had lunch, no biggie."

"I'm not talking about the lunch."

"You knew about the lunch?" Clarissa said. *Suzee,* she thought, *this is Evil's doing.*

"Don't play coy with me; you're too old to play coy."

Ouch. "I am not too old play coy!" Clarissa yelled, causing Gravy not to move even a hair. "I am plenty young enough to play coy, Mister."

"I can't take this, Clarissa. I won't take it."

"Aaron, you're getting all emotional over nada!"

"We'll discuss this issue when and if you decide to come home," he said. And then he hung up.

Clarissa hadn't been hung up on by a man since, using Polo's terminology, the Rachel (Jennifer Aniston's early nineties hairstyle, come *on*). She called Aaron back immediately. "No one hangs up on me!"

He hung up on her.

"Aggghhhh!" she screamed. Gravy rolled over. She slept the sleep of an old, fat dog; the only thing that could wake her was the promise of coffee or oral, and not in that order.

The phone rang. Clarissa answered, "I can play coy with the best of them!"

"Course you can, honey," sang Cinnamon. Her chipper gene was working overtime. "I'm sendin' hunting outfits up—I guessed your size—about a four?"

Clarissa honked.

"We're headin' to the Grande (Something). Joe Three's itchin' for a hunt." Clarissa grunted and hoped they weren't hunting rabbits. She had had a bunny when she was four (Easter gift from felonious dad), and she'd killed it by hugging it too hard. She had, literally, loved the animal to death—yet another childhood trauma to overcome. The list was endless.

Three minutes later Clarissa and Gravy, now awake, were staring at outfits brought up by the (third) butler. It looked like they were to dress for *Vietnam War, Redux*. There were two sets of heavy black boots and combat fatigues: camouflage pants, button-down shirts, parkas, and caps.

Gravy slipped into her outfit as Clarissa lay on her back, face red as a pepper, using a hanger to drag the wheezing zipper up over her belly. Then she rolled sideways across the floor like a sidewinder, and finally, with Gravy's help, came to standing. They looked in the mirror, Gravy's frizzy mop poking out from under her camo cap like a hair explosion; Clarissa's boobs playing tug-of-war with the buttons on her camo shirt—they were expanding like balloons at a child's birthday party.

"We look like ugly trees," Clarissa said, while Gravy stared at her face, lamenting the fact that she had made a smooth transition from acne to wrinkles.

Cinnamon's high-flying voice rang on the intercom with the news that their carriages were about to depart.

A convoy of red Ford 5100 pickup trucks rolled out of the Mason gates like tanks off to a very Garth Brooks war. The license plates started at "Mason I" and ended with "Mason X." Clarissa sat in the passenger seat next to Joe Three, who gulped down a Bloody Mary (easy on the Mary) as he negotiated country roads twenty miles over the speed limit. They passed cops along the way nestled cozily next to the highway like cows sleeping in the tall grass.

Joe Three would wave and wiggle his drink at the cops. And they would wave and holler back. It was like one long-ass block party.

Cinnamon Mason stood with one hand on her hip on the porch of the Grande (Something); she greeted her guests, summoned the help for libation, then steered everyone toward the side of the house. Clarissa and Gravy locked arms and followed, not yet trusting that they, the Beverly Hills Princesses, weren't the huntees.

Clarissa had little experience with firearms; she'd shot off a gun once or twice at the Beverly Hills Gun Club (seventeenth boyfriend—

Tennis Shorts, Clarissa had called him, since he always had dressed like he was on the court. Tragic story; his parents had been killed by a mysterious intruder—intriguing new handicap). Clarissa thought wistfully about their love affair: They drove around in his father's Ferrari; vacationed in Iberia. The only thing that broke them up was the trial.

Parked around the side of the Grande (Something) was a flock of camo-colored ATVs—and two handsome male assistants. "I have to ride one of these?" Clarissa asked. "Course," Joe Three said. "Unless you wanta swim through five miles of marshland to Lake Mason."

Clarissa looked over at Gravy, who was busy talking up one of the assistants.

"Well," she said to herself, "how hard can it be?"

"Holy shiiiiiiiiiiiiiittttttt!" Clarissa screamed, white-knuckling the handlebars, veering out of control, her life flashing before her eyes like a VH1 *Before the Music* episode. She was up to her ears in swamp—grass swiping at her face, mud bombs exploding on all sides. Clarissa had forgotten, in the face of off-road terror, how to stop.

An ATV sped up beside her. Joe Three had lost his hunting cap—his white hairpiece was slapping his head like a seal at a water show.

"Slow down!" Joe yelled. "You'll scare the ducks!"

A large flying insect whapped Clarissa in the mouth; she wondered if she were going to die covered head to toe in dirt and giant insects.

Then she thought of her baby.

"Release the throttle!" Joe Three yelled.

"Throttle?!" Clarissa yelled back. And then, magically, she unclenched her hands.

The ATV lurched and . . . stopped.

Joe Three drove a circle around her. *"Dang!"* he said, while adjusting his hair. *"Dang!"* he repeated. He hopped off the ATV shaking his head, and unhitched his rifle.

"C'mon," he said. Clarissa got off, shaking, and followed. They tramped through more mud and tall grass and eventually found themselves at the edge of a large body of water, where they hid behind something called a "duck blind," an ornate structure forged of leaves and sticks.

Clarissa saw the ducks. There had to be about twenty, a line of ducklings swam close to the edge of the lake, behind their mother. Clarissa gulped as she saw their tiny tails swish by in militaristic duck formation.

Joe Three lifted his rifle to shoot. Clarissa raised her arm, ignoring the fact that he could have rendered her hand a UFO.

"Mind if I shoot first?" Clarissa asked.

"Sure thing," Joe Three handed her his rifle. "Shoot above their heads, that gets 'em in the air. You want to fire north. If you fire south, that'll scare 'em off in the wrong direction."

"North," Clarissa repeated. She smiled. The rest of the party was just coming up. Joe Three motioned for them to stay behind. Then motioned again—*stay way behind.*

Clarissa put the rifle under her shoulder and raised it to eye level, peering at her feathered friends as they played duck volleyball and mallard Marco Polo. The gun felt weighty but surprisingly natural. She wished she could hunt a more sensible target, like rude SUV drivers.

She pointed the rifle north and put her finger on the trigger.

Then she turned, swinging the rifle south while "accidentally" shooting into the air.

Two things happened.

Well, three things happened.

Number one, someone behind them yelled, "I'm hit!"

Number two, the ducks took off in the wrong direction. (*Mission accomplished!*)

Number three, a fat duck fell out of the sky and landed in front of Clarissa's Aryan youth boots. (*Mission unaccomplished.*)

People in combat fatigues and too much orange scurried around Mr. Tweed Man, who was wriggling on his back like an extra in a Frankie Avalon movie.

Clarissa just stared at the duck, dumbstruck, her mouth hanging open like a fish on supermarket ice. Gravy came up.

"I killed a duck," Clarissa said.

"Maybe he fell," Gravy said.

"Flesh wound!" Joe Three yelled from the grass. "The damn bullet fell on him!"

"Look at it this way, C," Gravy pointed out, "you got two fowl with one shot."

Over a barbecued duck, black-eyed peas, corn muffins, sweet potatoes, and peach cobbler brunch Clarissa realized she was a hit with Cinnamon and Joe Three—she was the multiplatinum artist of in-law relations. Aaron's parents and their guests could not stop talking of the kamikaze way she had handled an ATV or the miracle shot that produced both a bountiful lunch and the kind of story that could be told at the dinner table for generations. Even Tweed Man, his side bandaged beneath his shirt, laughed amiably—though doing so appeared painful.

Clarissa had a Sally Field moment. She looked down the long table at the people beaming back at her, their faces reddened with morning sun and exertion.

Even Gravy looked happy. The furrow in her brow, the one that ran from her hairline to her knees, had disappeared.

They like me, she thought about these jodhpur-wearing, Republican-voting, gimlet-drinking, ridiculous-accented people. *They really, really like me.*

And then she thought, *I'm fucked. How can I possibly ask them for money?*

Clarissa decided then and there that she would not. She would do something else: She would tell them she was pregnant and, well, leave the ball in their court.

She stood and tapped her crystal glass with the edge of her sterling silver knife—something she'd seen in movies.

The glass shattered.

Before Clarissa could feel embarrassment, before a guest could emit an attitude or sigh, a servant appeared from the ether and secreted the shards away from the table, and from her wrist.

Clarissa stood there for a moment. All eyes were on her.

"Yes, dear?" Cinnamon said.

"I'm having a baby," Clarissa said.

She was about to sit down as quickly as she had stood when Joe Three enveloped her in the bear hug that she would have earlier rejected but which now she could reside in until "the cows" or whatever-the-fuck came home.

Cinnamon was clapping excitedly—and then she yelped—"Clarissa! You shouldn'ta been out there riding!" She sat back and fanned herself. "Oh my Lord (Lawd), oh my Lord (Lawd)—I coulda lost my first gran'chil'."

Her language was sinking into the road version of *Gone With the Wind.*

"Oh, Mrs. Mason," Gravy said, "don't you worry. Clarissa is excellent at making babies. She's like a scientist."

Clarissa glared at Gravy. "Well, you are, you're like the Madame Curie of conception," Gravy said.

"Joe Three? Cinnamon?" Clarissa asked, eyebrows dancing like flames. "Is there something . . . you'd like to tell me?"

They looked at her.

"Change of heart and all," Clarissa continued. "I mean, given the growing . . . situation."

Cinnamon smiled. "Darlin', I do have an announcement."

She stood. Clarissa smiled, demure.

"This is just the best darn news ever!" Cinnamon said.

Cinnamon and Joe Three bid Clarissa a teary gin-soaked goodbye on the porch of the Grande (Something) and Gravy and Clarissa were driven by one of their many hunky assistants (which apparently were bred on farms, like salmon) to a private airport outside Atlanta. Cinnamon and Joe Three had insisted that Clarissa and Gravy be flown back on their own plane, which they'd dubbed "Goody."

"What is that?" Gravy asked, as they drove onto the tarmac.

"A 727," the driver with the crooked smile said; he looked like something Versace had designed. "You never seen one?"

"That's not Goody," Clarissa said.

"That is," the driver replied.

Gravy and Clarissa boarded, their heads spinning. They were greeted by a stewardess named Lucy Ann bearing ice water and hand towels and a smile that belonged on a Wheaties box. They giggled and put their feet up and hashed and rehashed and Clarissa fell fast asleep shortly after takeoff, not waking until they landed with a bump, in Burbank, where a black sedan with tinted windows and a full cooler, compliments of Cinnamon and Joe Three, were waiting for them.

Clarissa was dropped off first. She hugged Gravy and waved as the car departed. She noticed Aaron's motorcycle parked neatly in his spot; she climbed the stairs to her apartment, her feet heavier with each step.

She was not looking forward to whatever awaited her on the other side of her front door.

Seventeen

Welcome Home, Now Leave

Clarissa realized she'd forgotten her keys; she knocked at the door, and Aaron answered.

You know how they say, in books, "He was more handsome than she remembered."

Well, he was more handsome than she remembered. It had been (barely) two days, and Clarissa had forgotten what her husband looked like.

Aaron opened the door, issuing a small, nondescript hello. "Hi," Clarissa said. She walked over to kiss him, but Aaron slipped away. He stood back and watched her from a short distance, as there was no other kind in this apartment, with a steady gaze, arms folded.

"I'm fine, thanks," Clarissa joked. "And how are you?"

"I haven't slept," he said.

"Ambien, five milligrams," she said. "Ativan, ten milligrams, or Xanax, if you're anxious as well as sleepless. According to Gravy."

"Clarissa."

"I'm sorry you haven't slept."

"You're unbelievable. I'm busting my ass trying to make you a life, and you just take off, with some bullshit lie, and I sit here, like a fool, waiting for you to come home when I have a job to get to—"

Clarissa sat down. She looked at him, nonchalant as a rich woman's terrier, as Aaron paced back and forth, flames practically shooting from his ears.

"I know where you were," he said, puffing like a blowfish. "I don't know what you were doing, but I know where you were."

He continued at this blustery pace. Clarissa looked at her nails. She really, really needed a manicure.

"And I know who you were with, and you know I know, and if you think I'm some wimp who's just going to stand here—"

"I went to visit your parents," she said.

Aaron stopped in a move like that found in a *Road Runner* cartoon—one could almost hear the screech of the brakes on his heels.

"Cinnamon and Joe Three send their love," she said.

"You didn't," he said.

"I did."

"You wouldn't," he insisted.

She raised an unplucked, unwaxed eyebrow. "Wouldn't I?"

Aaron looked at her, his eyes widened like a starlet's, then narrowed. "I don't believe you," he said, finally.

"Of course you do," Clarissa smiled.

Aaron sat down. "Oh my God," he said.

Clarissa put her hand on his. "C'mon, you'all. It ain't that bad. I liked them."

"Did you . . . walk around the house?" Aaron asked.

"House? Is that what you call it?" she said. "My mom's place is a house—houses don't have *names*."

"What did they tell you?" he said.

"Nothing," she said. The fact that this was an odd question flitted through her mind. "What do you mean?"

"I just thought they might have," he continued, watching her closely, "said something to you."

He was hiding something big. Clarissa could tell by the way his pupils dilated.

"You know what they told me," she said. "And I'm very disappointed." *He looked jumpy as spit on a griddle,* Clarissa thought, mentally paraphrasing Joe Three.

"Clarissa, I was going to tell you," he said. "I just thought we needed more time."

"When would you have told me?" Clarissa said, indignant (though she had no idea what to be indignant about). "I don't understand. I mean, I am your wife. Is there any bread in this house?" She was suddenly starving. *Again.*

"You're handling this very well. I thought you'd be more angry," he said. "I would think you'd at least throw a chair or kick the cat or something."

"Aaron. There are many, many things you don't know about me. I am a mature woman, and I am not prone to acts of violence. Now sit down and explain yourself."

He smiled and cuddled up next to her on the red couch, which in the light of a cheap apartment was showing its age. "It is kind of funny, if you think about it, I mean, we sneaked out of our hotel room—they're probably still looking for us."

"That is funny," Clarissa said. Her ears were turning red. "Keep telling me the funny parts."

"How long did it take you?" Aaron said, slipping in next to Clarissa on the red couch, his hand on her belly.

"To what?"

"Clarissa," Aaron said, "you don't know. You really don't know."

Clarissa wasn't about to let Aaron win this battle—she had to find out what he was hiding. She sprang up and darted into the kitchen and started to rummage through the junk drawer.

"What are you doing?" Aaron asked.

Clarissa found what she was looking for: She held up a deck of cards.

"Poker," Clarissa said. "Five-card draw, one hand. You can deal if you like."

"What are we playing for?" Aaron asked.

"The truth," Clarissa said.

"So you'll tell me what you found out from," Aaron stumbled, "from my parents."

"No. You'll tell me what you're hiding from me. Because I'm going to win."

"Oh yeah? You think so, girly. I'm a pretty damn good card player," Aaron said, smirking.

Clarissa looked at him and shuffled the cards with one hand. "Honey, you weren't raised by a man who cried when he walked into casinos and cried when he walked out."

And then she dealt the cards, licking her finger as she snapped them down.

And within five minutes Clarissa had beaten him.

* * *

Aaron studied Clarissa's face while she devoured a box of Frosted Flakes. He put his hand on her belly. "Clarissa." He took a deep breath. "There's something I want to tell you."

She looked at him, her lips covered in sugar.

"I want you to know, I'm not a liar by nature. I've never lied before in my life, in fact—"

"You lied to me?"

"I feel terrible about it, but things sort of got out of hand."

"Aaron. It's about your parents, isn't it."

"Well. Yes."

"You weren't disowned," Clarissa said.

Aaron looked at her, a glint of surprise across his face—and then, a small smile. Slowly, he shook his head from side to side.

Clarissa plucked his hand off her belly and *bit it* as hard as she could without tasting calcium deposits.

"Youch!" Aaron screamed, waving his hand in the air, an orchestra conductor on speed.

Clarissa leaped off the couch and into his face. "You're not disowned?!"

"You bit me!" Aaron had stopped with the waving; he was examining his hand.

"You lied to me!" she screamed.

"Of course I lied!" he said. "Anyone with half a brain knows you married me for my money. I wanted to see how long you'd last if I didn't have any."

"How dare you say that?!" Clarissa puffed up with the extreme indignation of one whose faults have been uncovered. "I *am* the mother of your child!"

"Yeah, until the DNA test clears."

There was a moment of funereal silence; a pall, like the feel of death, hung in the air. Suddenly they were traipsing on Edgar Allan Poe territory.

"What did you say?" Clarissa asked. She was scary calm; she had become Robert DeNiro in *Cape Fear.*

"It was a joke," Aaron said.

"Say it."

"I said . . . ," Aaron wrinkled his nose as though he had stepped in shit. Which he hadn't—he'd jumped in it. "Until the DNA test clears?"

It took Clarissa less than three minutes to pile a week's worth of clean clothes, a set of crystal stemware, all of the gold-rimmed china, including coffee cups and milk dispenser, four sterling silver candlesticks, a large sterling silver serving tray, the matching salt and pepper shakers, her wedding binder, and the white cat into her Louis Vuitton (knockoff) trunk, along with the eight Peanut Butter Balance Bars she'd need for the ride to her mother's house.

"Clarissa, don't," Aaron said, as she attempted to drag her suitcase outside.

The damn thing was too heavy. In her effort to pack all of their wedding booty in one suitcase, Clarissa had miscalculated—she'd need a tow truck to move the thing.

"Let me help you," Aaron said, after watching her struggle. Clarissa ignored him, pulling, pushing, sweating, and finally cursing the case. Despite her effort, she could not budge it. Clarissa became aware that this was not the stoic image she wanted to leave her (former) husband with.

She took a step away from the suitcase and gave him a quick nod, taking a big swallow of her pride; it went down like a spoonful of sand.

Aaron lifted the case with annoying ease and gallantly opened the front door for her. If not for her Stephane Kelians, Clarissa would have planted her foot six inches up his ass.

She walked down the outside stairs to her BMW, head held high, behind heavy sunglasses, images of Grace Kelly and Jackie Onassis instructing her like busy aunts on the correct method of how a "lady" leaves a lying, scoundrel husband behind.

"I'm sorry," Aaron said, "but Clarissa, you have to admit—it is kind of weird that you got pregnant so fast after we were married. And then I find out you had lunch with this Simon person and didn't tell me, and I put two and two together, and man, I think you're trying to make a fool out of me."

Aaron put the case in her trunk, his face close enough to hers that she could see, in the sunlight, the spots he had missed shaving, the rings under his eyes.

He hadn't slept at all. He bent over the passenger seat as she got into her car.

"Clarissa, honey, where're you going to go? You know you can't take care of yourself."

Clarissa blinked. She turned to face him.

"Not only can I take care of myself," Clarissa said, as she grabbed the steering wheel, "I am going to take care of my baby, too. And by the way, you're right: It isn't yours." She patted her stomach. "It's Simon's!"

And then she drove away as fast as she could from the actor's workshop building.

As Clarissa glanced (despite the voice in her head, which sounded not unlike Mr. T, yelling "Don't look back, Fool!") in her rearview mirror at Aaron, his fists deep in the front pockets of his khakis, she wished she could have hated him more.

"Can't take care of myself," Clarissa said to herself. "I'll show him!"

Clarissa dialed a number on her cell phone. She needed her mommy.

Clarissa was forced to listen to a recording of that Donnie Osmond–prototype blind guy who oversings opera on her machine; she hung up before the beep. "Life is too long," she muttered to herself.

She looked at her phone and noticed that she had several messages: the first was from Jennifer, checking in, asking how she was, etc.; the second was from Citibank, checking in, asking where their money was, "You'll hear from our attorneys," blah, blah, blah; the third message was from Simon.

"Just got out of a meeting with (too famous overtly-sexual-but-she's-a-virgin [according to her press] teen singer), and it got me thinking about you," he said, in that funny Anglicized–slash–Rodeo Drive accent. "I have no idea what this means. I find it more than a little frightening."

Clarissa laughed, her first of the day, and dialed Simon up before she realized she had remembered his number.

He answered.

"I need company," Clarissa said. "Bad company, preferably." Then she remembered to be angry with him for telling Aaron about their lunch. "What would possess you to tell my (current) husband we had lunch?"

"Someone else told him," Simon said. "He called me up and asked if it were true, and two words, sweetheart: Nasty Fucking Temper."

"What did he say to you?" Clarissa asked.

"He threatened my life and/or my genitals, words to that effect not remarkably pleasant. I hung up after the fourth motherfucker."

"Jesus. I've never even heard him swear," Clarissa said.

"So, are you running away from home?" Simon asked.

"I'm pregnant," she said, in the interest of full disclosure.

There was a moment of silence. Clarissa wondered if he'd hung up.

"And so, the plot thickens," Simon replied. "I have a full refrigerator."

Clarissa wasn't sure how long she'd cried on Simon's shoulder, but by the time she'd raised her big head, one of the twelve thousand hospital shows on prime-time network television had ended and it was dark outside. Music from a new band played as loud as legally possible in the background.

"He told me I can't take care of myself!" Clarissa yelled over the music. "I've taken care of myself my whole life!"

"Of course you have!" Simon said.

"Not financially, but like, emotionally!"

Simon nodded.

"He thinks it's your baby!" Clarissa said.

Simon looked at her. He turned down the volume with a remote. "It very well could be."

"Simon. I told you. We did not sleep together that night."

Simon put his hand over her lips. "We don't have to deal with that now, if you don't want to."

Clarissa shook her head, as Simon put his arm around her.

"You know, Clarissa, you did jump into this marriage."

"I know," she wiped her nose with the sleeve of her sweater.

"You barely even knew him. He could be some kind of serial killer."

"Point taken," she said. "But the wedding was sensational, wasn't it?"

"It was bound to fall apart, darling. You want to see the new video by Chained Aggression?"

Clarissa tried to bat her eyes and sniffle like Winona Ryder in *Reality Bites.* Instead, she snorted like Arnold the Pig from *Green Acres* (Eva Gabor—fashion icon and acting genius!). There was such a mucus buildup in Clarissa's sinus cavity she felt she would drown in her own snot if she didn't blow her nose in the next five seconds.

Simon must have sensed her discomfort. "Down the hall," he said. He pointed to a dark, narrow hallway.

Clarissa tried to smile. Her face ached. As she walked with dizzy steps down the hallway filled with the gold records found in the hilltop homes of every record executive she'd ever met, she realized she hadn't eaten in hours. She wondered if Simon really did have a full refrigerator.

The bathroom was plastered with old album covers. Here, thought Clarissa, was her childhood. The Stones next to the Beatles next to Led Zeppelin adjacent to Lynyrd Skynyrd. Here and there, in Hollywood columnist parlance, were Duran Duran, Flock of Seagulls, Depeche Mode. A look up at the ceiling revealed REO Speedwagon, Springsteen's patriotic ass, and Aerosmith's wings blending into Wings' *Band on the Run* album.

She sat on the toilet without peeing and wondered about Simon and his passion. Music. How long had he loved music? She wanted to know, suddenly wanted to know everything. But not because it was Simon—she wanted to know more than just a man—she wanted to know where his passion had come from.

Clarissa wanted to know because she didn't have it, this passion that could be turned into a career, a car, a house, a phone system, a full refrigerator, a life.

On a phone stand next to the toilet was a pen and a small tablet of paper that said Simon England at the top. Clarissa didn't have a tablet with her name on it. She didn't have embossed stationery; she was, obviously, not yet a fully formed person.

She took the pen and a piece of paper, and started a list. A list of her passions.

It was a short list.

1. Shopping.

    There was no doubt that shopping was her first love, her end-all and be-all. She remembered back to

> when she was a chubby child carrying her mother's bags through the shoe department at Saks, how lovely the salesgirls were, all rose perfume and pastels, how charming the salesmen were, with their crisp ties and ready smiles.

After five more minutes of thought, Clarissa came up with:

2. Food.
   She loved food; also Subset: Drink.
3. Friends.
   Friends were nice. Clarissa loved her friends. When she could stand them.
4. Sleep.

Clarissa stared at the list. She crossed out shopping and put sleep as number one.

And that was it. Clarissa wasn't crazy about the usual things people were crazy about: She didn't have a favorite book; she didn't enjoy most movies, most music, other people, hard work, easy work, nine-to-five work, volunteer work; she had no hobbies, other than shopping, or its subset, browsing; she didn't particularly care about flowers, activity, sports activity, skill, the environment, free weights, dancing, walking, animals, tennis (except for the clothes), yoga, the beach, talent, or Disneyland, except for the Main Street parade.

There was much Clarissa didn't like.

She was beginning to think there was something wrong with her. She was a twenty-eight-year-old (thirty-one-year-old) woman who had absolutely no interest in the world around her. And there were many, many like her—it was like an army of disinterest. Their mascot would be Monica Lewinsky, waving the flag of the blue dress, whose only talents matched their own: ingrained laziness; a willingness to bestow blow jobs on men in powerful positions; and a sense of entitlement that only the insipid are privy to.

Clarissa looked at herself in the smoky glass mirror befitting a young, groovy, climbing-the-corporate-ladder record exec. She saw a person who cared for nothing but herself and her (very comfortable) survival.

She felt the urge to pee again. *Fucking pregnancy,* she thought. *It's all about peeing and eating and peeing again.*

Clarissa sat down and saw a shadow on the crotch of her thong underwear (she hadn't worn the big cotton "grandma trousers" since the day she saw a Victoria Secret ad when she was twelve). She peered closer. It was a tiny spot. Nothing more than a tiny spot.

It was blood.

"Aw, shit," she said. "*Oh shit.* Already you're fucking with me?"

She dabbed a tissue at herself, which came up with one more spot. Just a spot, nothing more than a spot, she said to herself. "This is completely normal, nothing to worry about," Clarissa repeated, out loud. "It's completely normal that I'm *bleeding to death*!"

She realized Simon probably couldn't hear her, what with the television on and the stereo on and his male ego on. She stuffed enough toilet paper in her underwear to hold back the Hansen Dam and wished she had a doctor, another doctor, not the one she had now, the grayish, owlish, peckish one with the icy hands and muffled voice, the one she'd had since she was a chubby ten-year-old, the one who gave her her first birth control pills on her fourteenth birthday. She wanted another doctor, someone younger, up-to-date, someone who would reassure her, someone who would tell her, over and over, that there was nothing wrong. Someone who had warm hands, blue eyes, and a new condo in the Marina.

Someone who would save her baby's life.

"Oh, snap out of it, Princess," she said to the mirror, which was partially covered with Abba paraphernalia. "I'm keeping this kid if I have to pop a cork in my box."

Clarissa rushed out of the bathroom (as fast as she could with a Costco-size case of Charmin between her legs) to find Simon sucking on a joint, eyes closed, his head, bopping to an unheard beat, encased in giant headphones, an astronaut moored in the Hollywood Hills.

"Simon!" she said. She shook his shoulders when he didn't answer.

"I have to go to the hospital."

He looked at her. "You're pale!" he yelled, forgetting he had headphones on.

"While we're sort of young!" she said, grabbing her purse. "I'm bleeding, you're driving!"

"Bugger!" Simon squealed and jumped up, still attached to his headphones—he was pulled back onto the couch as though he had a giant rubberband attached to his head—it was a moment to be filed under: hysterically funny under any other circumstances.

The emergency room at Cedars Sinai was crowded, but not with broken gang members and mothers with bruised faces; this hospital did not accept the uninsured. Clarissa handed over the insurance card she had with her father's company and prayed that it was still viable.

And then they waited. Clarissa felt sure that she was bleeding to death, even though when she checked (every two minutes, it seemed, in the white, sterile light of the women's bathroom), her body only revealed more spots. No dripping, no release of tissue. Just a couple of spots. Just enough to torture her.

Just enough to realize she cared.

Simon fell asleep in one of the green plastic chairs as Clarissa watched him, thankful (and surprised) that he'd been so responsive.

An hour and a half later, she was seen by a doctor. A woman. Young. Pretty enough to be disconcerting.

"How far along?" she asked Clarissa, as she lay back on the paper, which crinkled at the question.

"Two months," she said, thinking back to her wedding night.

"You're spotting?" said the woman. It was a question, she was looking at Clarissa's information. Clarissa guessed, no, she knew, the woman was younger than her.

"You're a doctor?"

"Resident."

"You live here?"

The doctor looked confused for a second. "No, I . . ." She looked back at the chart. Clarissa shrugged. "I think I'm spotting. I think . . . that's what they call it. It looks like . . . tiny drops of melted chocolate."

The doctor looked at her. Her eyes blinked uncontrollably. "It's probably nothing to worry about," she said, finally. "Let's take a look at you."

Clarissa put her legs in the stirrups.

"Who's your O.B.?"

"My O.B. . . . Well, shit, I don't really have one."

The woman warmed a metal instrument with her hands, then inserted it into her vagina.

"Do you know anyone cute?" Clarissa asked.

"Did you have a prenatal checkup?" she asked.

"You mean like, before I got pregnant?" Clarissa felt like an idiot. She didn't like this feeling. Worse, she felt incompetent. She was already a neglectful mother. Her own mother had waited until Clarissa was at least three to become neglectful.

The woman looked at her. And took a breath. "Dr. Catz. He's got a wonderful bedside manner."

"Okay," Clarissa said. "Is he single?" The woman was still looking around inside of her. Clarissa felt like asking her if she could find any keys, or an old piece of jewelry.

And then the examination was over.

"Everything looks good," she said. "Your cervix is closed. I don't see evidence of a rupture, or a miscarriage."

Clarissa wiped her eyes.

"Your baby seems fine. But I want you to take it easy. I want you to see Dr. Catz as soon as possible."

"I will. I promise."

"And don't worry."

"I won't."

Liar, Clarissa thought to herself. She knew she had entered a world of worry.

"Thank you," Clarissa said. She had grabbed the doctor's arm. "If she's a girl, I hope she's like you." She looked at the doctor's name tag. "What's your first name?"

"Elsbeth."

"Okay, I hope she's like you, but with, like, a real name."

Dr. Elsbeth turned and walked out.

Clarissa watched the door close and sat and wondered what path had led Dr. Elsbeth to her position, why such a pretty girl would sit alone in a room and study for years to become a doctor when it was so much easier just to marry rich and settle down.

And then it came to her.

Maybe it wasn't so much easier.

Maybe the path that Clarissa had chosen—nay, had been *groomed* for—was not the easy one after all.

Clarissa pondered the stages of her existence:

A. She had been born beautiful. Photos to prove it.
B. Grainy videotape documenting her first steps while her father sang "Here She Comes . . . Miss America" in the background.
C. Her first diet at age five. Develops lifelong aversion to cottage cheese—or cottages in any form.
D. In junior high, discouraged by her mother to take the "hard math," even though she had a knack for numbers.
E. At thirteen, told by her father that she would never be a Playboy Bunny if she continued to play soccer.
F. Taken to modeling agencies by her mother at fourteen-and-a-half; embarks on new, bold series of diets.
G. At eighteen, father tells Clarissa she'll never be able to take care of herself, and she should find a rich man. For over twelve years, she had been searching. Twelve years. Longer than it took to become a doctor. *And what did she have to show for it?*

In the stark, small room, the smell of rubbing alcohol in the air, Clarissa vowed to take care of herself and her baby. She would stop running around, find something meaningful to do with her life (with the highest possible salary), and, of course, get her eyebrows done first thing in the morning before they formed a Frida Kahlo.

But in the meantime, she needed a place to stay.

Clarissa toyed with the idea of asking Simon if she could stay with him, but this was just plain dumb. Aaron would find out, and it would perhaps screw up the impending (spousal and child support) divorce. Also, the thought of waking up near the vicinity of Simon while cellulite spread nocturnally in great lumps from her ankles to her armpits served no useful purpose. She wondered if she should call Aaron, but she was still too angry at him, and still too proud.

There was only one thing to do:

Clarissa took a whiff off an open isopropyl alcohol bottle.

"Mama," Clarissa sobbed.

"Wha'?" her mother asked. She sounded tired. Clarissa looked at her watch. It was almost midnight. "*Mija,* is it Aaron?" Now she sounded worried.

"No, Mom," she replied, annoyed.

"Is he okay?" her mother asked.

"Mom. Aaron is fine," Clarissa said.

"You sure he's okay—?"

"*Jesus! Mo-om!*" Clarissa yelled into her tiny cell phone. "Aaron is fine. It's *me. Me!* I'm not okay!"

"Oh," her mother said. "Wha' you do?"

"What did I do?" Clarissa couldn't believe what she was hearing, "What did I *do*?" she took a deep breath. "I flew out to see Cinnamon and Joe Three, Mama, and Aaron called me a bunch of times and I came home and he was so mad, then he confessed he wasn't disowned, then I got really mad, then he made a rude comment, then I packed my bag (*Oh God, the cat!*), then I told him the baby wasn't his, then I went to see Simon (he's been so sweet), then I came *this close* to losing the baby, Mama, and now I'm in the hospital, and I want to go home. I want to go to your house. Are you breathing?"

"The baby's okay?" her mother asked.

"Yes, Mama. The baby's okay."

"Where's Aaron?" her mother said.

"Mama! Haven't you been listening?" Clarissa sighed. "I'm not with Aaron. I don't know where he is, and I don't care!"

"You need to talk to Aaron. He's your husband. He should be with you right now. Not this Simon."

"What's wrong with Simon?"

A man holding his unnaturally bent arm, mouth open in a silent scream, was trying to get into the hospital room. Clarissa put her finger up to signal him to wait and shut the door.

"You know what, Mama? You never liked Simon."

"I don't know heem."

"You never made the effort to know heem."

"Now you making fun of your mother."

"Simon took me to the hospital. He didn't have to do that."

"Pfft. Wha'? He leave you to die in his house?"

"Mama, can I come back home or not?"

"You come back home tonight, but you talk to Aaron tomorrow."

"No, never, I won't. The only way I'll talk to him is if my lawyer is present."

"Where is my Visa card, by the way?"

Clarissa looked at her nails. She needed a manicure this very minute. "I wonder if Le Domaine is still serving," she said to herself, as she hung up on her mother and sashayed out past the man with the silent scream leaning at a right angle against the wall.

Eighteen

Larry the Waiter Reveals All

Clarissa sat on the same ass-wrenching stool at the end of the bar where she had placed herself on New Year's Eve and waited for her waiter to come her way. It was one o'clock in the morning and she had decisions to make and games to play. She had sent Simon home after their trip to the emergency room; there were moments when a person needed a little privacy.

"I need a little time by myself," Clarissa told him.

"I understand perfectly," Simon had replied.

For some reason, his reaction, patient and understanding as it was, annoyed her.

"You don't say," Larry the Waiter said, coming up behind her, carrying a tray deep in gin and tonic. He grabbed a few small napkins.

"I need advice," Clarissa said.

"Don't buy tech for two years, floss once a day, and call your mother," he said. "Let me drop these off at the pathetic-drunk-slash-gold-digger table." He motioned toward a round table filled with tanned women with yellow hair and old men with yellowing skin. "Like herpes, I shall return."

Clarissa was about to order something red and wet and brain-cell annihilating when she recalled she was with child, and so she settled on a cranberry and soda.

She closed her eyes and thought about sleep. Suddenly, the atmosphere of this bar she'd loved just months ago felt oppressive to her; it was too dark, there was too much noise, and someone somewhere was smoking.

Clarissa was a pregnant woman in a sea of noncommittals. She wanted to leave, but the waiter was back and in a mood to chat.

"Spill," he said. "What have you been doing with yourself? And I'm not talking masturbation."

"I don't masturbate," Clarissa corrected. "I explore."

"In that case, you may refer to me as Jacques Cousteau."

"I got married."

"Behold. The Rock of Gibraltar." He picked up her left hand, admiring the Tiffany ring.

"To Aaron Mason."

"My, we are a quick little learner."

"We just broke up. Tonight."

"Maybe not so, so quick."

"I'm pregnant."

"Then again . . ."

"I told him the baby was someone else's."

"My my my my my!"

"But it's not. I mean, it's his."

"And you said this because . . ."

"He lied to me."

"And?"

"And . . . he lied to me."

"Plus?"

"Plus, he also lied to me."

"You have two choices." Larry the Waiter clapped his hands like Yul Brynner in the all-male version of *The King and I.* "One, you get back together with him. Two, you don't get back together with him. That will be forty dollars plus tax, please."

Clarissa looked at her drink and concluded that her life wasn't a movie and maybe she should stop acting like a wide-eyed chorus girl.

"What do you like to do?" she asked him.

"Talk."

"I mean. Do you have a passion for something?"

Larry the Waiter looked at her. "Gay men always have a passion for Something. The foot is always on the accelerator, so to speak."

"Seriously," Clarissa said. "Are you doing what you thought you would be doing when you were a kid?"

"God no. I wouldn't be a train engineer even if I loved the uniforms. Which I do."

"Waiter, you're not helping. What do I pay you all this money for?"

"Okay, sweetheart. Look, I thought I would be an actor. I mean, I'm sadly talent-free, but I love to be on stage. However, this bar, this room, with its gaudy gold fixtures and horrifying beige carpet"—he thrust his arm out, Sir Laurence Olivier performing *Hamlet* at the Royal Shakespeare—"this is my stage. And the clientele, sad and hollow and straight though they may be, they are my audience. I hope there's no alcohol in that drink."

"I can't remember."

"Who can? Try ginseng, fifty milligrams."

"No, I can't remember what I wanted to do. I'm having a kid, and I can't remember what it is I wanted to do with my life. Maybe I never really wanted to do anything. You're talent-free; maybe I'm just goal-free: I'm like, the poster child for underachievement."

"Ambition-challenged," the waiter said. "Let's see. What is your absolute favorite thing to do? Whether you were paid gobs of money for it or nothing at all."

"Shopping."

"So, try working in a store. You're rude enough to work anywhere in the 90210."

"Ah. No. Clarissa Alpert doesn't wait on people. No offense."

"None taken. Neither do I," he said. "They"—there went that Shakespearean arm effect—"wait on me."

Clarissa looked at the scene. The "clientele" looked mighty dry. He had a point.

"I need another idea, Larry the Waiter." Clarissa had no idea what his name really was. And did not want to know; she didn't wish to taint the wise waiter fantasy with visions of his semifurnished single apartment overlooking Thrifty's on Fairfax and Sunset. "My drink is almost finished, and I'm not sure I can afford another."

"A fashion rag."

"A what?"

"Work for a fashion magazine, you know. You never told me what you're drinking."

"Cranberry and soda. What kind of work do you do at a magazine?" Clarissa had never thought about working for a magazine—she didn't think about anyone working for a magazine. She supposed they appeared out of nowhere, from the ether, fully formed with beautiful pictures of beautiful people and expensive clothes and zero conscience.

"C'mon, you open *Harpers* or *Vogue* or *Elle* or whatever, you see lists and lists of names—it's like the Vietnam War memorial, for Calvin's sake."

"I never thought about it," Clarissa said, chewing her lip. "Maybe I could be an editor? What do they do?"

"No, dear heart, not an editor. A *contributing* editor," he said.

"What's the difference?"

"An editor is paid little, is Calista-Lara-week-old-cadaver thin, smokes like Matthew Perry in a recovery ward, and works, baby, works her fingers to her mean, chilly bones. A contributing editor is paid nothing, or next to nothing, is of average stature, doesn't smoke because of the children, works very, very little, but talks about it constantly. It's like having an honorary degree—nothing more than a title, like an ancillary member of the royal family in a small Slavic country. It's the perfect job for you. God, I wish I wore my clogs tonight. My feet are killing me."

Clarissa's head was spinning. Thoughts of seeing her name *in print* on something besides an overdue phone bill bedazzled her. "I've always wanted a title," she said. "I just didn't know what kind of title, until now!" Clarissa stared into the last moments of her drink and formed words on the ice: *Clarissa Alpert Mason*; *C. A. Mason*; *Clarissa A. Mason*; *C. Alpert-Mason* . . .

"You're a genius beyond genius; you're my own personal Einstein." She threw her arms around the waiter. And then she realized, "That would totally blow Aaron's shit, if I pinned down a job like that. Where do I sign up?"

"First of all, don't do this because you want to impress someone, even your hubby. Second, you've traveled every warm body in L.A., Sugar. You'll figure it out. I can only guide you to the trough. My work is done," he said. "Refill? I have to move on before Ears catches on."

Ears was his moniker for the bar manager.

Clarissa slid off the (so-fucking-uncomfortable) stool and into the smoky crowd, visions of the literary life and a new image of herself guiding her into the night.

But first, before driving off, she searched for something in her trunk.

And somewhere on Sunset, convertible top down, she flung the pink wedding binder over her shoulder and into the night.

* * *

Clarissa banged on her mother's door (it was now two in the morning), which was, rightly, dead-bolted, until her mother cracked it open and said, in warm, maternal tones, "Go home."

"Oh, Mommy," Clarissa said, pushing past her mother's tiny but surprisingly strong frame, "I can't, you know that. My husband's there."

"Pfft," her mother replied, as she watched her daughter traipse in. Finally, she sat down on her paisley couch and stared at her daughter.

"I'm sleepy," Clarissa said. She headed toward her old room.

"I want to talk to you (ju)," her mother said.

"In the morning." Clarissa would let her talk all she wanted; she planned on making her escape early. "Where do you keep your magazines?" Clarissa planned on visualizing her name on the *W* masthead before she went to sleep. She was filled with new job frenzy—it was quite the new experience.

"*Ahora.* Now. Sit."

"Mo-om."

"*Sienta se.*"

Clarissa made a big deal out of sitting down. It was like watching a B-actor die in a science fiction film. The action took for-fucking-ever.

"My daughter. You are, how you say, a fuckup."

Clarissa had closed her eyes. They suddenly snapped open. "What did you say?"

"My daughter."

"Not that part."

"You are a fuckup."

"Okay, this is me, Clarissa Regina Alpert, leaving." She got up and headed for the door.

"Where are you going? You got no place to go, remember?"

"I'll stay at a friend's house, I don't care." But Clarissa did care. Her friends were probably asleep and would be very cranky at the idea of opening their door, even to Clarissa, at this hour.

Except for Jennifer, but she had those ugly dogs. Clarissa couldn't abide by ugly dogs.

"C'mon. You sit down."

Clarissa sighed and sat down again.

"I'm saying this for your own good. You are a fuckup and you need to fix yourself."

"How can you say this to me? I'm your daughter!"

"That's why I say it. Because I care. You need to get yourself together. I might have to go to work. I'm looking into a position at Baby Gap. I get a nice discount."

"Please stop talking."

"Your father, he's going to jail."

Clarissa had temporarily forgotten (*thankfuckingGod*) about her father's future housing situation. A strange thought came to mind: *How would he get his hair dyed in jail?*

"You are not a child. You are having a baby, you have a husband. Now, you start your life. You need to be an adult."

"I am an adult. I'm twenty-eight years old, Mama, remember?"

"Thirty-two in Noviembre."

"My driver's license says twenty-eight, my passport says twenty-eight."

"And my vageena, excuse you me, says thirty-one. Now, if you don't get back together with Aaron, you need to get a job. I am not going to support you and the baby. I'll take care of the baby, but I will not take care of the baby's mama."

Clarissa was pissed. "Hey—I was your baby first!"

"This is what I want to say. You need to stay with Aaron and work it out. You do not have options."

"As a matter of fact, I am getting a job." Clarissa said this like "yob" just to bother her mother.

"What kind of yob?" her mother looked at her, trying to find the punch line.

"I'm seriously considering a contributing editor position," she said.

"Wha's that?"

"You don't know what a contributing editor does?"

"No."

"Oh." Clarissa had been kind of hoping her mother would enlighten her. "Well, it's a very important position at a magazine, and I'm taking it under consideration. However, I'm not prepared to make any long-term decisions just yet."

"Clarissa." Her mother sighed. "I feel (fill) I was not a good mother to you. I am saying these (this) things because I want you to be better for your (you) baby. I want you to feel good about yourself (you-self), then you can love your (you) baby with all your (you) heart."

"Are you saying you didn't love me with all your heart? What kind of thing is that to tell a girl at two o'clock in the morning? My own mother!"

"Clarissa. You need your husband right now, not a job." Then her mother gave the kind of sigh only a mother can muster and got up and walked into the hallway to her bedroom; her posture and the act itself said what she did not: "Oy fucking vey!"

Clarissa sat in the dark, grinding her mother's words into dust, and vowed to herself that she would have a job before the day's end. She would prove to her mother that she could be somebody. She would prove that she didn't need her mother, her father, or her husband to pull her along—she could do it herself.

Clarissa sniffed. "Make that before the week's end," she said. No sense in pushing herself too hard.

She heard the toilet flush in the distance of her mother's room and counted to ten, heard it flush a second time, then closed her eyes and saw her mother spinning, spinning down in the blue waters of the basin, surrounded by bits of her flaky pie crust–like shits.

Clarissa, energized by this vivid image of her mother, rose on her heels and started to sift through the magazines stacked neatly under the coffee table. She began writing her name in all its incarnations under the lists of contributing editors in each glossy until fatigue slowed her down, and she fell asleep on the pages of the July issue of *Elle*.

The next day brought Monday morning, which, as Clarissa understood, was a perfect time for a job search. According to her sources it was the first day of the workweek. She ate, standing, out of her mother's refrigerator (shelves of cottage cheese and meat patties—the vestiges of the "lite lunch" on an old coffee shop menu); she sucked down the last of her mother's mango juice and cursed the way her stomach performed rhythmic gymnastics (and *now,* a half-nelson-two-figured-round-off-with-a-twist!) as she tried to quiet it with something resembling food.

Her stomach had awakened her (like vibrations of the pounding of a bass drum a half-inch from one's ear) at 6:00 A.M., and she had followed it, lurching and tugging, toward the kitchen with the stove that had barely been turned on since her father had moved out.

"This," Clarissa said to herself, burping up dry steak, "will *not* do, Pig."

She waited until 8:00, sitting quietly in one of her mother's understuffed chairs so as to not upset the trajectory of her digestion. At the appointed hour she grabbed her mother's phone (her cell had run out of juice—she'd forgotten her battery charger at the Wretched Apartments for the Criminally Untalented) and dialed.

First up, Roberta the Dull. Or Dull Roberta, depending.

"I have to get a job," Clarissa said.

"Fine," Roberta said. "Did you hear? He's having another baby and I can't come within five hundred yards of his mailbox."

"You must know someone at a magazine," Clarissa said.

"Anna, Kate, Mayo, Larn," she said.

"Larn?"

"Do you need publicity? I could help you," Roberta said. "I called him at home yesterday. I hung up. This morning they put call blocking on. Can you believe the paranoia?"

"I've decided to be a contributing editor," Clarissa stated.

"Oh. No problem," Roberta said. "I'll call Page."

"Thanks, my New Best Friend," Clarissa said. "Lunch?"

"Great. I can't go to Chow's, Ivy, Chaya, The Grill, Barney Greengrass, or Locanda. They'll arrest me. Something to do with the letters. Like, you'd think he'd be flattered. But anywhere else is good. Except that new place on Third. Come to think of it, Page is not talking to me right now."

Clarissa paused before asking. "Is there a problem?"

"Oh, same ol', same ol'. Larn told her something about that thing I allegedly did with my car."

Clarissa closed her eyes. "Thing?"

"I ran into him. Total accident, I swear. He should have put Angie on the cover. His arm is like totally healed."

Clarissa murmured a goodbye and opened her Palm Pilot and erased Roberta's name from her address file.

She needed to call Tony B. She needed a job.

Nineteen

The Job Search Continues . . .

Tony B. was bleeding from his eyes.

At least, that's what he told Clarissa. "I'm bleeding from the eyes, here."

"What is your problema?" Clarissa asked.

Clarissa stood over Tony B. as he sat top-half-naked on a rug in his living room, whining like an unpaid hooker. "Haven't you read a paper?" he asked.

"Paper? What paper?" Clarissa asked. "Oh, right, yeah. I read that *213* thing. You know, with the pictures of fat blonde celebrities who look like scary monkeys."

"Jesus!" he cried. "Do you watch the news?"

"Of course, I watch the news. Like that show—the one with the music—da da da dum dum dum."

"*Entertainment Tonight?*" he said. "That is so not news."

"They have reporters. They're reporting stories. Therefore, it's news."

Tony B. looked like he was about to cry. Or throw a tantrum. But Clarissa knew he thought either would make him less attractive.

"Clarissa. How the hell do you get information about the world around you? Like, war, elections . . . ," he asked.

"I meet with the Star Chamber once a week," she said.

"You're an idiot," he said. "Who makes that skirt? It's divine."

"Someone didn't get laid last night. I mean, besides me. Thank God, BTW. I never want to get laid again."

"My stock is in the dumper, honey."

"And that's a bad thing, right?" Clarissa said. "See, I know something. But enough about you and your problems. I'm on a serious time line, here. I need a job."

Tony B. looked at her and laughed. In the background, a male yogi wearing (only) yellow Speedos and body oil went through a sun salutation. His streamlined muscles glistened like a million chrome bumpers.

"Gay?" Clarissa inquired.

"Avert your eyes," Tony B. said. "You're a married woman. My stock dropped from two-sixty to twelve." He looked at the yogi and sighed; his voice dropped to a whisper. "Let's just say I'm seriously considering 91607."

"No!" Clarissa said. "You're supposed to come *from* the Valley—not go back!" To live in the Valley. There was nothing more ignominious to a Westside resider.

"Why do you want a job? You married a stupid rich guy; just settle down," Tony B. said as they stood in his black-and-white kitchen, which had been decorated by the same guy who did the Stars Hotel back when the stock was at 125 and climbing.

"Don't you understand? I need my own identity. Besides, we broke up," she said, drinking Evian from an Irish crystal glass (stock: 150 ¾).

"You're just slightly more self-destructive than I am," he said.

"That's why you like me," she responded. "Now, come on, you know everybody—at least, you know the kind of people who hire people like me."

"People with no skills. The hard-core unemployable."

"I have people skills. Just set me up with an interview somewhere. Do you know magazine people? I really like the idea of being a contributing editor."

"I know someone at *International Male.*"

"This is my face. This is not a surprised expression."

"Okay, let me see what I can do."

"I'm pregnant," she told him. "So nothing too strenuous. Like typing. Or, ah, answering phones."

"Knocked up already?" he said. "And you say you have no skills."

"You didn't hear me. I said I have 'people skills.'"

Clarissa kissed Tony B. goodbye on the terrace of his Spanish-style hillside abode (stock: 221) and drove off in her BMW with the top down, feeling the same optimism as the sun glowing bravely from behind the L.A. afternoon haze.

* * *

She had an interview within twenty-four hours. Tony B. left a message on her mother's phone; after haranguing her about the horrid music on the answering machine (Latin stuff, of course, Mario-Hispanic-something-or-other), he told her to call a guy named Tull Krapinsky. ("Renamed himself after Jethro Tull," he said, "and no, the last name's not a joke. So, when you get there, don't say 'I have to take a Krapinsky.'") He told her that Tull was looking for a people person—someone specifically, he said, with her "people skills."

Clarissa borrowed (stole) her mother's vintage-ish 1977 Diane Von Furstenberg dress, which barely stood a chance against her expanding waistline. While Clarissa was standing in her mother's walk-in closet admiring her taste in borrowed (stolen) clothes, she also noticed a new pair of Prada sandals that were calling her name so loudly she covered her ears; she borrowed (stole) those, as well.

The drive to 31480 Old Malibu Road was as spectacular as the feel of the DVF dress. Clarissa put the top down and tied her hair back and felt like Lauren Hutton in an old Estée Lauder pictorial, except that at her weight, which she was positive had gone up ten pounds in the last twenty-four hours, she felt like two Lauren Huttons with a Rebecca Romaine Lettuce thrown in.

Thankfully, much of the weight had centered in the boob region, which is where any man with the name of Tull Krapetcetera would be resting his eyeballs.

Clarissa was shown into the foyer of a large, Grecian-style home on the beach by a girl with little energy and fewer clothes. The first sign that this would be no ordinary interview was the eight-foot-tall stained-glass "painting" of the abode's owner in the foyer. The colorful artwork depicted a large, bald man surrounded by nude or barely dressed nymphets who, judging by the dimensions of their erect nipples, seemed to have caught quite the chill.

The man was also in his birthday suit, which, as shown, should have been folded up and put away a long time ago. In one hand he held a cell phone (Nokia, black); in the other he held his enormous member. Because of the length and breadth of the piece, it bore a disturbing resemblance to a professional baseball bat.

Clarissa put two and two together (which took some time—"pregnancy brain") and walked out.

"If I'd said he was a pimp, you'd have never gone," Tony B. said.

"That's your *defense*?" Clarissa screamed, and swerved, just missing an RBP—Rich Bored Person—in an SUV.

"You needed a job; I got you one."

"Change the locks on your doors, change your phone number, get a good security system, because if I ever see you again, *I WILL KILL YOU.*"

"I'm having a going-away party," Tony B. switched gears.

"Where're you going?"

"I'm moving out. It's a Chapter 11 bash. Will you come? It's in a few weeks, the day before they foreclose. I'm providing matches and lighter fluid—I'm hoping someone will burn it down."

"Of course I'll come."

Clarissa hung up, depressed. Everything was changing. Tony B. was no longer rich; Simon was no longer just a burning memory; Aaron was no longer her loving husband; and she was no longer the easygoing, fun-loving twentysomething she had never been.

She drove down PCH, passing a minimall where *X* was playing, passing the Malibu Inn, the pier, the working-stiff surfers on nonexistent waves.

Then she dialed 411 for Dr. Catz.

Aaron sat at the bar at the Grill waiting for his lunch meeting to arrive. His first time here, he watched, his gaping awe hidden behind Christian Dior aviator glasses (a Clarissa purchase, four days after they'd traversed the stairs at his erstwhile mansion), his nervousness implied solely in the way his hands played with the keys on his cell phone (Nokia, again, a Clarissa suggestion).

He watched the players, the true Hollywood royalty—the men and women who wave their scepters and make gods out of grocery clerks and truck drivers—the producer who'd won three best picture Oscars in a row, the director who could flit from indies to epics in the same year, the agents—so many of them, and as uniform as Navy pilots—who could make or break, kill or deliver.

Clarissa had introduced him to the Grill. Aaron tapped his fingers, making out Clarissa's cell phone number; the number came easily to his touch—a pianist playing a childhood tune.

He had invited one of the big agents for a lunch meet—young man, ageless ambition, clients who were the crème de la crème of the new crop—and Aaron was wondering how the hell he'd pay for his Cobb salad.

The agent arrived, horn-rimmed glasses both concealing his movie star looks and accentuating them. Aaron wondered if they were prescription or fake. He shook Aaron's hand while looking toward the green leather booths, summing up in ten seconds who was there, who was not, who was anticipated. He turned to Aaron and gestured, with the tiniest nod, for him to follow.

The walk-through would begin.

First booth. "Aaron Mason, you've heard of him . . . ," the agent said to the film producer with the spiky hair and unbroken string of hits. "Oh yeah," the producer said, gulping water, "you're married to that chick, what's her name? She's totally cool."

Second booth. (Commotion as Arnold Schwarzenegger, a rare sighting, but with a movie opening that day, walks in; the dye job is respectable this time.)

"Married to Clarissa, right?" the network chief with the notorious roving eye says to Aaron. "God, she's great."

Third booth. "I hear she's pregnant."

Middle table. "Tell her hi for me."

Aaron smiled and shook hands and repressed the urge to spill the truth; it'd be like inviting an unwelcome guest to a dinner party.

They finally sat down and the agent ordered without looking at the menu (the waiter declared whatever it was "the usual") while Aaron perused the columns and, again, wondered if he had enough to cover the bill.

"You're married to Clarissa?" the waiter asked. "Tell her we miss her."

Aaron placed his order and wished that someone, anyone, drank in Hollywood in the afternoon so he could follow suit.

The agent handed the waiter a credit card—an American Express business card. "I hate to wait for the check," he explained.

Aaron added a hamburger to his salad order and detracted the tab from his list of worries. *One down,* he thought, smiling at the agent, *1,180 more to go. . . .*

"No. My job," Clarissa would say to her mother, who with every sigh, every held breath, every raised eyebrow, and every shouting match, insisted her daughter call Aaron back and mend fences, "is to find a fucking job."

For the next two weeks, Clarissa sat on her mother's couch and dialed everyone she knew every single morning to capture that elusive contributing editor position, while avoiding Aaron's phone calls. Her mother ran for the phone when he called, to complain about her ungrateful, *loca en la cabeza* daughter. By the second week Clarissa didn't care if it was *American Bass Fishing* magazine or *Big Tittie Weekly,* she was determined, like Noah's understanding with God, that if the waiter had deemed something to be true, so be it.

Living with her mother just wasn't the bonding fun fest Clarissa had imagined (*ha ha*); they were getting on one another's nerves faster with each passing day; currently, Clarissa and her mother could spend 5.3 seconds in each other's company before a conflagration began over an incidental, i.e., that Clarissa had eaten everything in the refrigerator, cupboards, under the couch, and in the glove compartment of her mother's car and had yet to replenish a single cocktail onion or Canada Dry tonic water. Clarissa always would come back to the fact(s): a. She had no time to go grocery shopping because job-searching had taken up every spare minute; and b. She had no money to buy groceries, even if she had the time; and c. She didn't know where the grocery store was, and besides, the only kind of shopping she could abide by involved clothes or shoes, in that order.

Meanwhile, to make matters worse (and by this time, it was reaching *Texas Chainsaw Massacre* potential), her mother was rehearsing for her annual Junior Angels charity bash, an event that involved geriatric ex–beauty queens, middle-aged soap stars who hadn't lost their affinity for sixties helmet hair and rhinestoned baseball caps, and senior civilians, like Clarissa's mom, with no discernible dancing or singing talent, putting on a show to raise money for handicapped children. This year's theme was "Stairway to the Stars" and, apropos of the title, the "girls," as they (and no one else) called themselves, had hijacked Led Zeppelin's "Stairway to Heaven" for a song-and-tap-dance number.

Each night her mother would dress up in tights, tap shoes, and top hat, and several of her friends, similarly dressed, plus or minus enough sequins to choke Bob Mackie, would come over and squeal and laugh their old lady laughs and give off their old lady effluvium and practice their musical number, tap, tap, tapping their bunions and their hammertoes until one of them fainted from exhaustion or an overdose of high blood pressure medicine or snapped a hipbone. Clarissa stared at them in disgusted awe while she drank and ate anything that hadn't moved in twenty-four hours and hoped that she would have the grace and decency to die before she was eligible for an RTD discount.

She especially hated when one or two of the women would wax poetic over a spouse who'd been dead since toe socks.

The truth was, Clarissa hated being jealous of the love life of anyone over forty; it strained the laws of nature.

•

"So why don't you just move out?" Teddy asked. He was out on bail, which had been set at $50,000, seeing that he hadn't murdered or raped and wasn't considered a flight risk; he and Clarissa were eating breakfast like any other father and daughter at Nate and Al's on a Saturday morning. They were like any other father and daughter except that he would be in prison by Christmas, and she was pregnant and separated from her husband, with whom she had lived for about three weeks.

"I have nowhere to go, thanks to you," Clarissa said.

"I acknowledge your anger, I feel your anger," Teddy said, "but I will not accept responsibility for your anger."

"What have you been reading?"

"I have no idea what you're referring to." He sucked down his coffee in one long swallow.

"You've been into those stupid therapy books again, haven't you?" Clarissa said.

"I always say, if you learn just one bit of smarts from any of those books, it's worth the price of admission."

"That's weird. I always say that if you need to read those books you're probably a pathetic excuse for a father."

Teddy was too busy grinning at the waitress with the big ankles to lob a comment back over their resurrected father-daughter communication net; his lox, eggs, and onions had arrived. Clarissa reeled at the smell of the dish. At ten weeks along, her nose had become sensitive to certain smells—fish, eggs, onions, and immediate family being the primary culprits.

Shoulders hunched over, fork held like a weapon, Teddy dug into his food; he reminded Clarissa of a gorilla she'd seen once—an old, bored, hungry ape ripping into a clutch of bananas. Her father had spent one meal too many in County.

"What's wrong?" Teddy asked, looking up from his plate. He had a tiny piece of egg hanging from his lower lip.

"Where does one begin?" she asked.

"Did I tell you? Aaron came to see me." Teddy finally licked off the egg, not bothering to use his napkin.

Had Clarissa been eating, she would have choked. "No, you didn't tell me. What happened?"

"Nothing. He just called up, wanted to come over, see how I was doing."

"Who does he think he is?"

"He called me up before you did."

"That's only because he's feeling guilty," Clarissa replied. "I, on the other hand, have nothing to feel guilty about."

"He should feel guilty? Over what?" Teddy practically spit.

"I can't tell you what he said."

"About the baby? That's nothing. You remember how your mother and I used to talk to each other."

"You didn't talk. You yelled," Clarissa said. "Did he tell you what he did to me?"

"Yeah. I thought it was great. Really smart."

"You're on his side."

"Clarissa, I'm on nobody's side," Teddy said. "But you have to admit, he's a gem, this guy. A total gem."

Clarissa could not swallow. A total *gem*?

"Dad. You don't know him like I do, okay?"

Her father stopped eating. He had to stop because he had already finished—convicts are notoriously fast eaters.

"Clarissa," he touched her chin. His hands were smooth, gentleman's hands. This would change once he started working out in the prison yard. "How do you think I'm paying for this attorney?"

"Daddy. C'mon. You have money."

"My accounts are frozen. All of them. What I had left was the five hundred dollars in my condo."

"Mom. She still irons your shirts."

"Nah. I couldn't ask that of your mother. I've put her through too much in her life. Besides, she doesn't have the money."

Clarissa looked at her father. She did not want to say the word. "Aaron."

"Aaron."

"You asked Aaron to pay for an attorney?" Clarissa said. She'd never felt so embarrassed.

"No. He showed up at my hearing. He saw the defense attorney the city provided—the guy couldn't add two and his dick. Aaron wouldn't take no for an answer," her father said. "I'm paying him back, soon as I get out. You eating that?" He pointed at her egg bagel with the cream cheese shmear.

Clarissa shook her head no. As hungry as she was when she'd walked into the deli, her stomach had become bloated with anxiety. "Why would he do that?" she said. She felt anger: at Aaron for being a Goody Two-shoes; at her father for having to be rescued in the first place.

"He's a gem. I told you." Her father stuffed half the bagel into his mouth and washed it down with the remainder of his coffee. Again, Clarissa was reminded of the unfortunate childhood visit to the San Diego Zoo gorilla exhibit: "Come See the Great Apes!"

"Don't tell him I told you, Babycakes. He made me promise."

"And we all know how you are at promises."

"I acknowledge your anger, I feel your anger, but I do not accept responsibility for your anger," Teddy said, stuffing the last half of her bagel into his mouth.

Twenty

The Sighting

Aaron had called Jen from what could be called his corner office but what was really just a corner in the director's production office. He'd had no luck contacting Clarissa (but had learned much about her mother's South American childhood), and though he knew his next move smelled a lot like desperation with a capital *D*, he was willing to take that chance. After all, he *was* desperate.

Aaron met Jen for lunch at the studio commissary—where they sat among the drones, the D girls and boys, whose heads spun like weather vanes every time someone floated past in Prada or Hugo Boss and were quickly enveloped in the womb of the VIP room, where the food, the water, even the air seemed of better quality. *Desperation, indeed,* Aaron thought.

"I'm totally into aromatherapy," Jen said. "You could use a little vanilla in your life. You seem awfully tense." She put a hand on his shoulder, which was somewhere around his earlobe, and pressed down, to illustrate her point.

"Why won't she talk to me? What is she doing?" Aaron knew the questions were sounding quasi-stalkerish, but he didn't feel like wasting time. He stabbed his swordfish, which appeared to be silverware-retardant. He pushed his plate away and went to light a cigarette—which, of course, was an impossibility. So he just sat and scowled.

"Clarissa's hurt," Jen said. "She is practically a human being."

"She's hurt?" Aaron said. "That's funny. That's really funny. I'm the one who should be hurt. She used me, remember?"

"Clarissa Alpert is my oldest, dearest friend in the world, and she may be a liar and a cheat," Jen said, "but she is not a user. You take that back."

Aaron looked at her—the enormous brown eyes, unwavering, threatening to tear.

Of course, he had to take it back.

"I take it back," he said.

"You know, she's been really busy," Jen said. "Clarissa's looking for a job."

"A job?" Aaron said. "Jen, do you realize you just said 'Clarissa' and 'job' in the same sentence."

"Aaron."

"I'm sorry, I'm sorry. I've got lonely curtailed, but not bitter. So, she's looking for a job."

"As a contributing editor. To a magazine," Jen said, accentuating the word "magazine."

Aaron nodded, but he was two steps ahead of the conversation, wondering if he knew anyone, had met anyone in his travels who would be of help.

"So, aren't you going to ask me?" Jen said.

"Ask you what?"

"About the baby?" she said. "I thought that's why you wanted to meet me. Aren't you going to ask me how the baby is?"

Aaron flushed. "I would have asked, but she told me the baby is Simon's."

Jen looked at him, her eyes now taking up half her forehead. "That is so not true, it's untrue." She put her soup spoon down, for emphasis.

"Those were her words—that's what she told me."

"That's impossible. That's like saying, I don't know, there's life on Mars or something."

"There is life on Mars."

Jen looked at him.

"Look," Aaron said, "I thought it was impossible that she was pregnant, period, so I guess anything is possible."

"Aaron. The baby Clarissa is carrying is yours. One hundred and ten percent."

Aaron looked at her. "And you know this, because . . . ?"

"The Star Chamber never keeps a secret when it comes to men," Jen said. "If Clarissa had slept with Simon, it'd be a major news bulletin. Like, that's the top story of the day if I ever heard one."

"You're sure."

"I'm not only sure," Jen emphasized, "I'm positive."

Tony B.'s Friday night Chapter 11 party couldn't have come at a better time. Clarissa was now almost three months along, and she and her mother were down to 2.7 seconds in each other's company before they were sharpening their words like knives on each other's skin. Clarissa desperately needed a night out that wouldn't cost a. money or b. pride, both of which were in diminishing supply.

She looked at the full-length mirror in her mother's bedroom closet while her mother was out at a Junior Angels dress rehearsal at her friend's house. Dressed in a light, summery floral BCBG, with spaghetti straps, that hit just below her knees, Clarissa felt that she looked good. Large, but good. Her boobs were huge and required an underwire "grandma" bra that made them look like she'd swallowed Anna Nicole Smith. But coming right up on her boobs were her upper arms, each of which probably weighed as much as an infant.

She dragged a cashmere cardigan from a padded hanger and draped it around her shoulders, hiding her arms from the judgmental eyes of the Gay Western World. She kicked off her wedge heels (not really "kicked"—she tried to kick and almost landed on her butt) and put on a pair of slip-ons (*thanks, Mom!*) that hadn't made it out of their original box.

She patted her tummy, which hadn't (thankfully) grown in proportion to her boobs, and smiled. For a fat, pregnant, soon-to-be single welfare mom, she looked great.

The Star Chamber was in full effect at Tony B.'s. Jen and Gravy had driven together (Jen was always the designated Designated Driver); Polo had arrived alone and looking like a beautiful, exotic bird in a sarong and a prayer that the scarf tied around her high as hell bosom wouldn't slip; Clarissa was even happy to see Suzee, she of very little body fat and less humanity.

"Lovey!" Suzee squeaked when she saw Clarissa. She hugged her and ran her spider monkey hands down Clarissa's back. "You look amazing—how far along are you? Five, six months?"

"Three," Clarissa replied, so cold she could see her own breath. She squinted at Suzee, peering closely at her face. "Oh my God—are you okay?" she asked.

"Am I okay? Yes, of course, I'm okay," Suzee said, her eyebrows raised as far as the new botox injections would allow. She had "cement head" syndrome.

"Oh, there's Gravy." Clarissa looked past Suzee.

"What? What did you hear?"

"About what?"

"Why would I not be okay?"

"It's nothing. You just look . . . tired."

Suzee's hands went to her eyes in an uncontrollable, Tourette's-like gesture. She turned away, whimpering and patting the thirty-two-year-old bags under her eyes.

Gravy rolled up in a floor-length suede coat with her curly hair sticking out at odd angles and put an arm around Clarissa's waist. "Marvy. eight-point-four out of a possible ten on the insult scale."

"Not an insult. A concern. I just mentioned she looked tired." Clarissa smiled and sipped her Pregnant Girl Cocktail—cranberry and soda with a twist.

"Deadly. Everyone knows 'you look tired' means 'you look old,' like *Three's Company* old." In Star Chamber lingo this meant someone looked old enough to have been a guest star on that 1970s sitcom.

"Is this party fun?" Clarissa asked. "I can't tell because I can't drink alcohol." Clarissa was getting cross; she was beginning to think that the people she knew were only interesting if she had a buzz on.

"As one who can, let me tell you, this party would only suck if it were a million times better," Gravy said. "Tony B.'s lost his touch along with his house: every cute guy here is gay; every woman is a *Vogue* model; every food substance is an appetizer; every drink is watered down; and every drug is legal. I'd sacrifice myself if a bomb dropped in the middle of the living room."

"It's early," Clarissa yawned. She was always yawning these days. "Tony's culling the herd."

Jen came up, requisite Perrier in hand. Polo was on her tail, followed by a rash of male admirers, all of whom were gay or had gay aspirations. They were screaming things like, "Audrey Hepburn and Sidney Poitier's love child!" and "Who does your bone structure?"

"What is this? Crunch: The Party?" Polo asked, referring to the heavily gay-populated gym.

"How's your snatch?" Gravy asked. Polo scrunched up her nose. "Fine. I took a couple of horse pills. Killed everything in my body, but gave me wicked nightmares."

"Tell 'rissa about that guy."

"Lefty?"

"Yeah," Gravy laughed. She snorted and her drink splashed on the floor. She didn't notice.

"What's so funny?" Jen asked. Then started laughing herself.

"I broke a guy's dick," Polo said.

"Oh, please," Clarissa said. "Major overshare!"

"Tell 'em, tell 'em, tell 'em," Gravy said.

"Okay. I drop the fuck bomb on this guy . . ."

"Third date?" Clarissa asked.

"First," Polo said. "Okay, so I was fucking this guy, girl on top."

"Already this is too much work," Clarissa said.

"All of a sudden, the guy screams," Polo continued.

"And she thought it was because she was so good," Gravy said.

"Not only good," Polo said. "Thorough."

"Just ask anyone," Gravy looked around. "And I do mean anyone."

"Meow, hiss, claw," Clarissa said.

"S'okay, Gravy's just getting into her green suit," Polo said. "Jealous, jealous, jealous. Anyway, I did think it was because I was so good. I mean, I was wild on this guy. Sweating, my boobs jumping up and down like slingshots."

"Does that hurt?" Jen asked.

"So, he screams. And flips me off of him, and I look down. His dick is suddenly crooked, and leaning waaaaaay over to the side."

"Like, lying down?" Clarissa asked.

"Like this," Gravy said. She took her lipstick (MAC Deep Throat) and drew on Tony B.'s custom-textured plaster walls (stock: 128).

It looked like this: >.

The girls started laughing.

"I broke his dick," Polo said.

"I've never broken anyone's penis," Jen said. She sounded sad.

"Which is funnier—the head or the shaft?" Gravy asked.

"It's not really broken," Clarissa demanded. "I mean, he can use it again, right?"

"Not with Polo."

"Don't tell anyone; I'll never get laid again."

"Polio," Clarissa said. "You told us. We're your best friends in the entire world, but basically, that's like running it on CNN, *Entertainment Tonight,* the cover of the *Enquirer.*"

"And *People,*" Jen offered.

"Teen People," Gravy added.

"Look, he can use it again. The doctor told him it was some kind of muscle thing—like a spasm."

"A spasm in his dick. A dick spasm."

"Fuck."

The girls all stood there for a moment of quiet contemplation. Then laughed.

Clarissa smiled and looked over at Tony B., who was greeting guests at the door, looking like a tapered-down version of Merv Griffin. He was wearing a white suit with a powder-blue silk shirt and a great big movie-pimp collar. He had dyed his hair a crystalline platinum blond—he looked like a gay snow cone. The woman he was greeting, on the other hand, was a Heart Attack, the kind of girl who gives other women heart palpitations and makes them want to run for cover under a bed of beauty magazines and Julia Roberts (or her evil twin, Sandra Bullock) videos. Even from twenty feet away Clarissa could tell she was born poreless. She shined her radar on the woman and executed her Mental Grid System (MGS):

- 5′7″, No, wait. Fuck, she's wearing *flats*! Modified MGS measurement: 5′8½″.
- Honey-colored hair, coarse, thick, natural wave, no split ends, cut classic, precise: Art Luna.
- Skin untouched by the elements (agoraphobe or Ukrainian?).

- Full mouth but not annoyingly altered to look like pool floats by collagen, saline, silicone, or Gottex (the material stretchy bathing suits worn by scientific anomalies like Elle Macpherson are made of).
- Perfect teeth but not annoyingly bleached, like the hordes of Chiclet mouths seen on daytime TV.
- Long, slender neck. Clarissa pulled her shoulders back and stretched her own neck. Gravy looked over at her mid-sentence. "Cramp?" she asked.
- No boobs. Thank *God.*
- No boobs, because she weighs . . . Clarissa calculated . . . 118 pounds. It appeared to be "natural weight" not "Calista weight." She had good muscle tone in the upper arms (warning: red alert, defcon IV for self-image), her teeth were not gray from throwing up Twinkies, and the way she laughed—she threw her head back in full throttle. No one who laughed like that could be on a diet.

Clarissa's grid, though detailed, worked in mere seconds. She addressed the group, who hadn't noticed her momentary lapse of attentiveness.

"Heart Attack at three o'clock," Clarissa said, the early warning system.

"Holy crap," Gravy said. Gravy annoyed Clarissa by staring too long. Unlike Clarissa, she did not have the requisite KGB-caliber spying skills.

Polo shrugged. Polo herself was Heart Attack material, and had the added appeal of being constantly in need of repair, which men loved; they wanted to take care of her.

Jen turned white as Tony B.'s new 'do. Clarissa looked at her, then glanced back at the girl.

"Ouch," said Gravy.

Standing next to the Heart Attack was none other than: "That monumental fuck job!" Clarissa said.

"Bastard," Polo said.

"There's an explanation," Jen said. "I'm sure!"

"Clarissa!" Suzee appeared, a horrible Pinhead-like apparition. "Have you seen Aaron? He's just arrived!"

Clarissa brushed by Suzee and headed toward the balcony, not knowing whether she would throw herself off or throw up. Either way, it would be messy.

"Think," Clarissa said. "Calm down. Breathe. Think." She was talking to herself, but Jen was already at her side, bearing water and a finely honed sympathetic ear.

"I'll bet she's his sister," Jen said.

"Only child."

"Cousin?" Valiant Jen tried. "Old, dear friend?"

"Earth to Strawberry Shortcake," Gravy said, as she joined them. "Men don't have old friends who look like Barbies. It defies the laws of nature!"

"You know what?" Clarissa replied. "It doesn't matter. We're separated. Our relationship is on life support, and Miss Every Little Thing over there is harvesting the organs."

She took a deep breath. Clarissa was trying to avoid hyperventilating. "Aaron has the right to date. So do I. He just . . . beat me to it."

"Also, he's not three months pregnant. It's hard to date when you're with child." Gravy said.

"Point taken, Gravy," Clarissa said.

"I didn't think he would do this," Jen said, quietly.

"Neither did I," Clarissa said. "But then, that's why people traditionally know each other before they get married, I guess." And she took a big gulp of southern California night air and headed back into the party. She was determined not to let Aaron's presence deter her from having a fabulous time.

She yawned. Again.

As long as she stayed awake.

"Hey," Gravy said, "Clarissa's ultrasound is next week. Be there or be a scum-sucking ho." Gravy put her arm around Clarissa's shoulders. "I'm bringing the wine coolers."

"I'll bring the tissues," Jen said, already tearing up.

Clarissa choreographed the night better than a seasoned Broadway musical director. Whenever she felt Aaron's gaze on her shoulder, his hovering presence, she suddenly would find someone very interesting to talk to on the other side of the room. She managed to look happy and carefree, a twenty-first-century version of Norma Shearer. She even adopted her black-and-white movie star laugh, tossing her head back with glee until her neck almost snapped.

"You look like the Bride of Frankenstein when you do that," Gravy said, having just returned from recon service.

"It's tough, acting lighthearted and gay," Clarissa said. "I'm going to need a chiropractor. What's the report?"

"The 411, you mean," Gravy said.

"Gravy, you are not Lil' Kim and I am clearly not Mary J. Blige. Just give me the facts."

"Suspect is single, gorgeous, available, drives a late-model Lexus SUV, and works out at Sports Club L.A., the disco of gyms, four times a week."

"Really? I wouldn't have pegged her for a gym rat."

"Who's her? I'm talking about Romeo over there. My future ex-husband."

Clarissa looked. There was, indeed, a gorgeous guy talking to a model-type—model-type meaning L.A. runway but not New York, and nowhere in the vicinity of Paris.

"Whoopi, I'll take center square for two hundred," Gravy said.

"Gravy. The girl. The girl. The girl."

"I know. There's no résumé, no CV, no contingencies, no prior knowledge. No one knows her, and everyone wants to," Gravy said. "She's showroom-floor quality, mint condition."

"Fuck squared."

"Second that emotion," Gravy agreed. Then she smiled. "Anyway, here comes six feet of Clarissa salvation."

Simon was making his way toward Clarissa. He was alone, and he looked very *Men's Health* cover boy.

"Love," Simon kissed Clarissa's cheek. "I've called you a million times. Where've you been?"

"Job hunting," Clarissa said, although she couldn't recall fielding a million calls from Simon.

"Perish the thought," he replied. "You're far too Clarissa to work."

"You're so right."

"Baby, we have to talk," Simon said, making the word "baby" sound almost endearing. Almost. "There's a lot of ground we need to cover."

"Simon, I'd love to cover ground with you sometime, but as you know," she gestured toward her tummy, "I'm out of commission."

"A temporary and lovable condition." Simon tapped her belly. "I get a rise out of pregnant women, did you know that?"

Gravy interrupted, "England, you're getting a rise out of me, but I'm talking appetizers." She put her finger in her mouth. "Besides, if I remember correctly, you get a rise out of anything with fewer than three legs."

"Clarissa," someone said. Clarissa turned to see Aaron standing next to the Heart Attack. "Are you leaving already? You can't be done avoiding me yet."

"Aaron," Clarissa said his name as though she were greeting an old friend of her mother's, had she ever been that polite.

"Clarissa," Aaron said. "Simon."

"Aaron."

"Gravy."

"Aaron."

"Well, this is cozy, isn't it," Gravy said. "This is not at all uncomfortable."

Aaron turned to the Heart Attack. "Clarissa, this is Coral. She's an . . . old friend."

Coral smiled and held out her hand.

Faith Hill, who was sitting quietly on Clarissa's left shoulder, brushing her hair and polishing her dimples, told her to smile and shake her hand. Madonna, who was sitting on Clarissa's right shoulder, said, "Tell her to stick her precious hand right up her precious ass."

Clarissa smiled and shook the beauty's delicate hand. "Nice to meet you."

Then she added, "Oral."

"May I talk to you, devil-woman?" Aaron asked, steering Clarissa away as Coral's lower jaw dropped gracefully to the floor.

"I was just leaving," Clarissa said. "Simon and I have a full night ahead, picking out baby names—you know, Celtic? Italian? African is very popular now with Anglos."

"Clarissa. Seriously. We need to talk."

"Aaron. Seriously. We have nothing to talk about." Clarissa said. "Aren't you neglecting your 'old friend'?"

"You are the most stubborn person I've ever met. And I've met a *lot* of people."

"Aaron, do yourself a favor. Don't waste your time calling me again." Clarissa ignored the stricken look on Aaron's face, as she was blinking back her own tears. Her eyelids felt like windshield wipers on high.

"Simon," Clarissa choked out, turning toward him, "are you ready?"

"Ah, of course," Simon said, then he added, to Aaron's Oldest and Dearest Friend Coral, with rapture in his voice, "Lovely to meet you."

Clarissa elbowed him as hard as she could without liver damage, and they walked out of the party.

Twenty-one

Growth Is Hard

Will this hurt?" Clarissa asked. Not that she was worried, but she had chewed through the soft inside of her left cheek. "I'm not a big fan of pain."

"It won't hurt a bit," said a reassuring, radio-worthy male voice. "I promise."

Clarissa wasn't convinced. She looked up at Jen, who gave her a weak smile as the brilliant and without question lovely Dr. Catz with the pale blue eyes and prematurely gray hair and giant-size gold wedding band (worn like a clove of garlic around his neck) smeared lubricant over her white, expanding belly. The Star Chamber, sans Evil Suzee, was in full effect.

Polo smirked. "Ooh. I recognize that stuff."

Gravy stood there, smacking her gum.

"Do you mind?" Clarissa asked her. Gravy swallowed the gum, complete with gagging sound effects.

"An ultrasound is totally painless," Dr. Catz continued, trying to move around the patient and her friends. "I'm just going to move this rubber disk over your belly, and turn on this machine, and we'll see what you've got in there."

"He's cute," Polo whispered in Clarissa's ear. And then sneezed.

The machine started up, making a gentle whooshing sound.

"Okay, we have liftoff," Dr. Catz said.

Dr. Catz moved the disk over Clarissa's abdomen; it felt cold but not unpleasant—much like sex with an investment banker. "How's that feel?" Dr. Catz asked. Clarissa looked at his blue eyes and forgot how to speak.

"Fine," Gravy said. "I feel good."

"Okay, here's the baby," Dr. Catz said. "You see this series of dots?"

The girls bent in, blocking Clarissa's view. "Hey," she said. "It's my fetus—do you mind?"

"That's the spinal cord," he said. "Very neat, nice lineup. Like a string of pearls."

Jennifer started bawling.

"Can you tell if it's a boy or girl?" Clarissa asked.

"Let's see if the baby moves around; I can't tell anything yet."

"I hope it's a boy," Gravy said. "Then he'll never be a single mother."

"I want a girl," Jennifer said.

"You've already been to Baby Gap, haven't you, Jen?" Gravy accused.

Jen nodded, sheepish.

"I feel boy energy," Polo said, closing her eyes and sneezing again.

"I just want a healthy baby," Clarissa said. She almost surprised herself; she hadn't even thought about the sex of the child, yet. "I don't care what it is."

"Well, good, because he or she is not cooperating today. Which one of you is the, ah, partner?" Dr. Catz asked, as he surveyed the room full of women.

The girls looked over at the doctor, then at each other. "We all are," they said.

Clarissa reached up for a tissue, and Gravy grabbed her hand and pressed it to her own wet cheek.

Aaron called Jen the night of Tony B.'s Chapter 11 party to explain and found himself on the other end of a dial tone. He had wanted to tell her the truth—that this girl Coral was not an old friend of his, but one of many girlfriends of someone whom he could not say no to, someone who wanted Coral to have a part in the movie, should it ever be made. She had flown in the day of the party, and it was made clear that Aaron had to escort her around town.

Aaron was relieved, in part, that even Jen wouldn't speak to him. He didn't think he could tell her a fraction of the story without reading her the whole book, and he wasn't prepared to do that, not just yet. But he did want to tell Jen, in the hopes that it would get back to Clarissa, that his director knew someone who knew someone else who was cousins with someone who published a magazine who might just need someone with Clarissa's girl-about-town skills.

For if Aaron could not be a part of Clarissa's life, he could at least be behind-the-scenes talent.

Weeks had gone by without hearing from Aaron, and Clarissa had experienced the five stages of grief: Denial and Isolation, Anger, Shopping, Bikini Wax, and Acceptance. The bikini wax, which was performed by Olga, a large, Russian woman with a bleached mustache and an ax to grind, had hurt about, oh, eight hundred times more than usual because of the heightened sensitivity to pain that pregnant women experience. Clarissa had imagined unhappy face eight on the one-to-ten stages of labor pain in a pregnancy book Gravy had purchased for Clarissa; Gravy had thought she was being a good, supportive friend. The book was called *When You Are Expecting,* but it might have well been called *Expect Everything to Go Incredibly, Horribly, Disfiguringly Wrong*; chapter after chapter delineated every tiny problem that could occur at each week of pregnancy. From the first weeks (spotting: been there, done that) to the fortieth (cord wrapped around neck, emergency C-section, some hideous thing called placenta previa), the book was a lurid combo horror movie/car crash—and every day, Clarissa experienced phantom symptoms.

"I'm swelling, it's totally not normal," she'd tell Gravy, calling her first thing in the morning.

"Of course you're swelling—you're pregnant."

"But it's in my pinky toe," Clarissa said. "According to page ninety-eight, it's diabetes."

Gravy hung up.

"I'm getting palpitations. It's high blood pressure. I'm sure it is."

"Didn't the doctor say your pressure was low?" Jen asked.

"You're no fucking help," Clarissa said, slamming the phone down.

Then she'd call Dr. Catz. In the past week she'd called him, according to the brittle nurse, every twenty minutes, which Clarissa knew was an exaggeration—she'd waited at least a half-hour between calls. After all, she had to eat and sleep.

"He's in with a patient, Miss Alpert."

"Alpert-Mason. I'm still married, even if it's temporary. My water's broken."

"How far along are you?"

"A little under five months. And I'm sitting in a pool of water."

"Where are you right now?"

Clarissa looked around, as though unsure. "I'm at home, I'm in my backyard, sunning, I'm lying down on a very uncomfortable, sticky, green lawn chair." Clarissa felt the seat with her hand. She couldn't look down. She was afraid.

"Is there someone to take you to the hospital?"

"Oh, God, do I need to go to the hospital?"

"If your water's broken, yes. Is there bleeding?"

"I haven't looked."

"You haven't looked?"

"Do I have to?" Clarissa looked down. Her belly was getting big, fast. She moved it to the side. It was something like moving a live jellyfish.

"I've definitely broken my water."

"Is it possible that you've wet yourself?"

"What? Do you know who you're talking to?"

"Ma'am. It's a possibility. At some point, most pregnant women have 'accidents.' It's quite normal."

"That is the number one most disgusting . . ."

"If you broke your water it would feel like a sudden whoosh."

Clarissa thought for a moment. She didn't remember a whoosh. All she knew is that she woke up from a much-deserved nap (after all, she'd been busy growing limbs all afternoon) and she felt, well, wet.

"I'll call back," Clarissa said, hanging up.

She looked at her naked belly, bound by a hapless J. Crew bathing suit from five summers ago (her "chubby June").

Clarissa had wet herself. Was there no end to her misery?

"Clareesa! You friend is here," her mother called from the kitchen.

"What friend?" Clarissa said.

"Doll!" Skinnier-than-you'll-ever-be Evil Suzee appeared. Clarissa nearly vaulted from her seat, which wasn't easy with the extra poundage.

"Evil!" Clarissa recovered, with the requisite double air kiss.

"You're just . . . blossoming, aren't you, you little pork chop?!" Suzee said, sitting down and crossing her legs. They looked like bobby pins. "It feels like I haven't seen you in ages!"

Clarissa wondered why everything Suzee said sounded like it ended in an exclamation point.

Suzee reached over and pinched Clarissa's leg, a faux friendly gesture that could have resulted in bloodshed.

"Suzee, what brings you to my side of town?" They lived three blocks from each other.

"Well, honey, I'm just checking up on my dear old, old, old friend."

There were so many things wrong with that sentence, Clarissa thought. *Starting with "dear," ending with "friend."*

"Cut the crap, Evil. You know we hate each other as only old friends can. Tell me why you're here." Clarissa, lying almost naked in her fat suit, was beyond caring about appearances, even with Evil Suzee. "I'm fat and I pissed myself not ten minutes ago." She smiled and took a deep breath. The truth felt good.

Evil Suzee looked shocked for half a second; she nearly dropped her evil grin. "Lovey," she said, "have you talked to Aaron? You know, your husband?"

"We're separated. I haven't talked to him in a week," she lied.

"Oh, so you don't know?" Suzee said. She put on her best "concerned friend" face. Clarissa steeled her stomach against incoming . . .

"He's hired a lawyer."

Clarissa looked at Suzee, who was struggling with a sympathetic smile. Not her forte.

"I knew that."

"Of course you did. I mean, it happened fifteen minutes ago. Linda Stuber-Meisner, Harry's daughter, the one with all the hair, my very, very dear friend, called me. She's working on the case. She found him very, very charming."

"That's a lot of very, very." Clarissa knew Suzee hated Linda Stuber-Meisner, had since grade school. "You know what else is very, very?" Clarissa said. "This conversation. It's very, very dull."

"I'd love to stay and chat and wipe tears, but I've got to run, Barneys shoe sale; you know how it is." Suzee looked at Clarissa's feet. "I'd invite you, but it looks as though you're a teensy bit swollen."

Clarissa's shoe size had gone up. It was true; she had Shaq feet.

After Suzee left, leaving death and destruction in her wake similar to the destruction of the South after the Civil War, Clarissa sat looking at her enormous clown toes and feeling like 150 pounds (157 ½) of pink, rubbery, nauseated, mirth-inducing failure.

She started to cry. Aaron had hired a lawyer. Clarissa hadn't hired a lawyer yet, hadn't even considered it, to be honest. When she realized why she wiped her tears from her eyes and made her way into the kitchen, where her mother sat, reading the paper. Without her reading glasses on.

"I'm sorry," her mother said.

Clarissa collapsed into her mother's arms as her mother patted her head softly. "Oh, *mija,*" she said, *"mija, mija."*

"I thought . . . I thought he might still love me," Clarissa said. She wondered what evidence she had to support that thought—and couldn't come up with any.

Clarissa saw the motion picture version in her head of the knight in shining armor retreating—and all of her notions of how her life was to be carried off with him.

She had no one to blame but herself. (And, of course, her parents. And society. And men. And that awful high school English teacher.)

And the really fucked thing was, she couldn't take Xanax or Wellbutrin or a glass of chardonnay for that matter. She had to face her stupidity with stone cold sobriety.

Life was truly fucked.

Twenty-two

Makeover Hell

Clarissa was at the hairdresser's with her mother, the one on North Canon in the heart of Beverly Hills (as if there could be a heart, *snicker*) where the ladies who lunch on celery sticks and champagne and painkillers flock in numbers surpassing the Mandarin population.

This was a mistake.

To say this was a mistake would be like saying "Oops, maybe I shouldn't have driven my car off the shoulder into a loaded school bus."

Her hair was cut by a fifty-year-old man with a greasy ponytail halfway down his back (can you say "extension"?) who answered to the name "Joaquin," which he pronounced "Joking." By the time he was finished with Clarissa she'd been cut, blow-dried, and shellacked to look like this week's middle-aged guest star on *Fantasy Island*. Her mother was thrilled; she overtipped "Joking" and thanked him for making her daughter look human. To which Clarissa said, "You've got to be 'Joking,'" but only under her breath.

At this point Clarissa was not up to a fight; the fight had left her, taking its last trip with Evil Suzee as she tap-tap-tapped her stilettoed self off her mother's back patio. Clarissa didn't even have the balls to call Gravy, who had warned her all along to get a lawyer, to protect not only herself (after all, she had been married longer than most Hollywood couples) but her unborn child. Clarissa had allowed herself to be guided along like a prized poodle by her mother, from the hairdresser to the manicurist to the facialist (bad experience involving eucalyptus steam) to Saks, where she watched her ninety-five-pound (when soaking wet) mother try on black tights for her charity show. She accepted her martyrdom; she likened herself to a modern Joan of Arc.

Her cell phone rang (she'd found the adapter, finally, near where she'd found her cat) as she was sitting, draped heavily over a chair, now watching her mother drool over tiny, sparkly Judith Lieber purses.

Clarissa officially had entered the Seventh Circle of Hell. She answered her cell phone.

"'Riss, I just heard the best news," Jen said.

"Aaron got a lawyer," Clarissa said. "That's *my* good news for the day."

Jen didn't reply; she just drew her breath in.

"Don't be so shocked," Clarissa said.

"I really don't think that's true."

"How would you know?" Clarissa said, but hoping that, somehow, Jen *would* know.

"Look, 'riss, I just ran into someone. You know Bebe, well she knows Erica, who knows Lauren, who told Lizzie, who mentioned it to Rachel . . ."

"Jennifer!"

"Right, well, Bebe knows this girl. She's a fashion editor at *Climate*." *Climate* was primarily an entertainment magazine aimed at the West Coast. If *US* was the new *People*, and *InStyle* was the new *US*, then *Climate* was the new *InStyle*.

Or something like that.

All Clarissa knew was she *loved Climate* magazine. It took even less time to read than *InStyle* (and with even less depth) and had even *more* pictures of nail polish and hair accessories.

She *loved Climate*.

"I *love Climate*," Clarissa said.

"Well, I talked to this girl, I called her up, I told her all about you, and she wants to meet."

"She wants to meet *me*?" Clarissa asked.

"Of course."

"Which me? The old me or the new me? Because right now I'm big-fat like the annoying girl from that talk show and I've got a head of hair that could withstand nuclear immolation."

"Hello? Why did God create product?" "Product" meant any substance one put in one's hair. Vaseline could be product; a toddler's lunch could be product.

"I'm pregnant. I . . . I look like boiled crap." Clarissa looked at her ankles. She looked over at her mother's ankles. She wondered how they could be related.

"'Riss. Are you serious? You look fantastic, a goddess, you've never looked better. I always said you could use a little more weight."

Jen was such a terrible liar, but Clarissa didn't care. She loved her.

"When does she want to meet?"

"There's my Clarissa," Jen said.

Clarissa, having hosed down the Richard Meier architecture that was her new hairstyle, went to meet Morgan LeGrange at the *Climate* offices on Wilshire Boulevard in Carthay Circle, a happening enclave of Spanish-style offices and coffee shops where, instead of being served by scowling, rude college students, one could be served their soy double lattes by scowling, rude hipsters.

Clarissa had stepped off the elevators into a world both foreign and inviting—magazine covers framed at odd angles on thick plaster walls, the receptionist with the bold nose ring matched by a tongue stud, the furniture that looked like it was last seen at a poetry reading in Venice.

The place didn't feel like home, but it felt like something better: It felt like discovery.

"Clarissa," a woman dressed entirely in gray (the new pink, which had replaced brown, which had replaced black), greeted Clarissa, who struggled to her feet. "Oh my God, you look freakin' awesome—how far along?"

"Almost five months."

"I would've said three, three and a half," she said. "Freakin' awesome," she repeated.

Clarissa was ready to wash this girl's car, clean her bathroom, read to her children, give her husband or boyfriend a blow—no, hand job. "Thank you," was all Clarissa managed.

Once inside her cardinal red–painted office, Morgan sat on her steel desk cross-legged and said how nice it was to meet Clarissa, she'd heard so much about her, but how they didn't have a job opening at *Climate* just now, but would certainly keep her in mind should something come up.

Clarissa stared at Morgan. "You have no job openings?"

"Not at the moment, unfortunately."

Clarissa tried to sit up but the pillows on the couch were swallowing her like an oyster. "Why are we meeting?"

"I'm polite. I had good parenting. I cover my bases." Morgan looked at her phone sheet. "You never know. Do you have any writing experience?"

Clarissa took a deep breath. "No, but I can be very mean when I want to. And I know how to use a comma."

Morgan smiled. "We don't use commas."

"Where did you grow up?" Clarissa asked.

"Boston."

"Boston. And I bet, like, most of your staffers grew up somewhere else. I mean, so few people are natives," Clarissa said. Morgan just looked at her. "Your magazine feels like a tourist rag—there's nothing insider about it."

"The *New Yorker* uses writers from all over the country," Morgan said.

"Yeah, well, I don't read that magazine. It has something called essays, right? I read yours. You need an insider."

Morgan uncrossed a leg.

"I'll cover parties, charity events, premieres—the whole L.A. scene—from an L.A. girl's P.O.V.," Clarissa said.

"I don't know," Morgan replied.

Clarissa checked her inner Rolodex.

"Edgie Flebedian. This weekend. Holmby Hills," Clarissa said. Edgie was a fortyish producer of fifty-million chock-socky films who also was rumored to be an arms trader—a rumor he was rumored to have started himself. Edgie, an Israeli-Armenian, or vice versa, or neither, was an interesting mix of revolting and amusing and he threw lavish parties, always at the studio's expense.

"You can get in."

"I can get in anywhere. I've owned this town since I'm twelve. Since I went from an A to a spillover C."

Morgan uncrossed her other leg. Clarissa knew she had her. The job fell under the auspices of contributing editor, which, she admitted, meant little money but a nice expense account.

* * *

Clarissa skipped out of the *Climate* offices and practically jumped into her BMW and headed down to Melrose to Oliver Peoples, where she immediately purchased a pair of faux intellectual black-frame glasses (sans corrective lenses—Clarissa was blessed with 20/20 vision) that would befit a "contributing editor"; Clarissa wanted to look the part. She thought of all the great gossip columnists who had come before her; Clarissa could be the next, hetero, Liz Smith or, better yet, the female A. J. Benza.

She was walking in the footprints of giants. The responsibility was awesome.

"I can't believe it!" Gravy said. Actually, she had said this about eight times—

"That's enough, Gravy," Clarissa said.

"Yo, but *Climate* is like the coolest rag."

"So—Clarissa's the coolest girl," Jen said.

"Where's Polio?"

"Bad—"

"Flu."

"Isn't Suzee joining us?" Clarissa looked around, anxious for the first time in her life to make sure Suzee was walking in the door. She wanted to see her face when she told her she was the new West Coast contributing editor for *Climate* magazine. *Wheeeee!*

Gravy was on her third vodka with Red Bull, a cleaner drink, she claimed, than her usual tropical concoctions, something about the clearer the liquor, the healthier it is. Unless, say, you live in Russia or wherever it was people were sucking down vodka like it was Evian. Jen was sipping a Perrier, as usual, and looking off into space; Clarissa was downing cranberry and tonics. The music was making her tummy vibrate.

"Expecting someone?" Clarissa asked Jen.

"No, no, no, why do you ask?" Jen said, her eyes darting around the room. Jen was the sole bad liar in the Star Chamber.

"I can't stay much longer." Clarissa checked her watch. "I've got to be up late tomorrow night."

"Stay!" Jen said, grabbing her arm. "Look, it's Suzee—don't you want to tell her?" Suzee was heading their way.

"Hey, Evil," Gravy said, before Clarissa could open her gloat-filled mouth. "Did you hear about Clarissa's new job?"

"A job?! How exciting!" Suzee said. "Clarissa, I didn't know you were looking for a job—not Burger King, I hope—the uniforms at Taco Bell have more give."

"*Climate* magazine's newest contributing editor," Jen said, with a dash of smug. Clarissa looked at her, surprised. Jen didn't usually talk much to Suzee. And the look in her eye—rather spiteful. Clarissa gave Jen a mental hug.

"Drop dead," Suzee said. This meant, in nicer, more polite circles, *"You're kidding."*

"You first," Gravy said.

Clarissa almost felt sorry for "Pol Pot" Suzee; she'd never seen anyone look so defeated. "Suzee, don't worry, I'll probably be fired in a week."

"Room for one more?" Suzee asked, suddenly perking up.

"We're waiting for someone," Jen said. Gravy and Clarissa looked at her.

"Go ahead. Sit," Clarissa said.

"No. I told you, we're waiting for someone," Jen's voice was rising.

Suzee stood there, her Kelianed, Hard Candy–ed feet glued to the spot; she didn't know what to do.

"Look, I'm leaving. I don't know what she's talking about, but you can have my seat." Clarissa rose.

"No—you can't leave!" Jen said.

Clarissa kissed her cheek. "Make sure Gravy gets home okay," she said in Jen's ear.

"Please don't leave?"

"Baby needs to rest," Clarissa said, patting her stomach. "Big day tomorrow." She pushed her new glasses up the bridge of her nose and made her way through the crowd.

Twenty-three

The Job

This copy's freakin' awesome!" Morgan said. "I love it. It's smart, it's funny, it's . . . completely unusable."

Clarissa had been standing across from Morgan, who was pacing excitedly and waving around an unlit cigarette, Clarissa's coverage of the Edgie Flebedian party in her hand.

"Unusable?"

Morgan at Clarissa, as though surprised she was there. "You're the anti-Christy," she said.

"The anti-Christy? Me? You're comparing me to George Christy?" Clarissa actually felt a chill down her back. George Christy was a legendary columnist at the *Hollywood Reporter* who wrote up the beautiful people—and never printed a bad word about anybody with an income over six figures and a personal plastic surgeon.

Clarissa was thrilled.

"Anyway, what you've written here . . . ," Morgan sighed. "If we wouldn't get sued for slander, which we would, we definitely would, it'd be a total slam dunk. Like your specs, by the way."

"Thanks," Clarissa said. She pushed her glasses up her nose for the one hundredth time that morning. She sorely wanted to sit; her feet were aching and it took all her breath to make it up the *Climate* stairs, but she hadn't been invited to, yet.

Fuck it, she thought. "Morgan, if I don't sit pretty soon, I'm gonna have this baby on your carpet."

"Oh, have a seat," she said. "You want something to drink?"

"No, no thanks. I pee twenty times an hour as it is."

"Did you think this stuff up yourself?" Morgan looked at her. The question sounded like an accusation.

"That's the way my friends and I dish. We're, like, professional dishers."

"Remind me not to piss you off."

Clarissa thought about last Saturday night. The Edgie party would have been a total flop, from the valet parking to the Eurotech-slash-Israeli dance music to the sorry lack of ice, if it weren't for the police showing up at 1:30 to break up the whole disaster. Clarissa, with her lack of experience, judgment, and instruction, had merely written what she observed: three non–English speaking valet parkers for three hundred guests (adding up to a ninety-minute wait for cars afterward); men with toupees picking up girls too young for training bras; very little in the way of food; and too much in the way of drink.

"You can't even use some of it?" Clarissa asked.

"Yeah. Three words: Edgie. Flebedian. Party."

"Fuckme," Clarissa said, totally forgetting about her vow not to swear in front of the baby.

"Well, maybe a few more than that. The writing's terrific—like Dorothy Parker on acid," Morgan was guiding her out.

Who the hell is Dorothy Parker? Clarissa wondered as she left the office. She needed a pick-me-up.

Clarissa would repeat this meeting, give or take a few syllables, each and every week—every week she would attend parties, charity events, or premieres for *Climate* magazine—and each week she would comment on exactly what she observed. It was the irony of ironies that here she was, a person who had groped and clawed her way into every event or premiere she'd ever been to now being welcomed with open arms—and finding the whole thing to be quite dreary. Every charity event was a mimic of the one that had occurred in the same hotel, usually the Beverly Hilton, the week before, maybe with a different color scheme, a different special guest singer (who was always Natalie Cole), a different host (but always with the same I'm-firing-my-agent expression: "What the hell am I doing here? I don't know anything about renal-failure-myelitis-muscular-degenerative-disorder."). Clarissa always would be seated as a guest at someone's table—*Climate* would never buy their own. The tables, which seated eight to ten people, cost anywhere from $10,000 to $25,000 each. At first, being seated as a surprise guest at a table was exciting—especially as a contributing editor to *Climate,* where ne'er was heard a discouraging word. People were willing, even eager, to talk to Clarissa. Sharon Stone had shared a woeful tale of a shag haircut gone tragically wrong; Sylvester Stallone talked incessantly of the existence of UFOs and something called "black helicopters." A tall, blond television host with a midwestern accent tried to pick up Clarissa, even though she was obviously, at almost six months along, very, fatly, pregnant. She didn't know whether to be flattered or repulsed.

Clarissa found, as she'd suspected all along, that most stars were a wacky yet dull lot. After a short while she tired of being around famous people. Playing the rapt fan, the ever fascinated audience member, destroyed what little was left of her energy. And the bottom line was, even though she wrote of her travels honestly and boldly, none of it would ever see the light of day—namely, the pages of *Climate* magazine. "The sitcom star with an ass as flat as Kansas and an obvious botox botch job sat whimpering in her ill-advised sequined halter Donatella Versace (last year's) dress (can anyone say 'bra,' please?), angry at her younger husband's choice of entrée. The boy's crime? Having chosen chateaubriand instead of pasta. The star is an obvious vegetarian; unlike her famous character she has no sense of humor and looks about as healthy as Beth in *Little Women,* from what this reporter remembers of the *Cliff Notes.*"

What *Climate* printed, beneath a picture of the actress, was: "Lainie Gibbons, renowned animal lover and activist, encased in Ralph Lauren, traded pleasant gibes with husband, Gibby Gibbons, over his choice of entrée—steak."

"Are you ever going to print it the way I write it?" Clarissa asked Morgan, as she lay down on the floor of Morgan's office, feet up on her couch to counteract the swelling.

"No."

Clarissa thought about this. She wondered why she was wasting her time. But the truth was, even though she didn't really enjoy the social whirl, she did get a special thrill writing about it. Even if her musings were never printed, at least they had caused a stir around the office. Where her legend was growing. People who were much cooler than she (like, twenty-somethings with goatees and Vicodin addictions) were quoting her lines back to her.

"Please?"

"No. Did you get this week's schedule?" Morgan asked.

"Let me guess. Three shows at the Hilton?"

"One of them should be fun, this one tonight," Morgan tossed a three-dimensional invite shaped like a tuba at Clarissa's head. The thing must have cost a bundle.

"It starts with an auction."

"I hate auctions. They always sell off defenseless Labrador puppies to horrible, nasty children who still have their parents' real noses. I know because I was one of those kids."

"So you don't want to do it?" Morgan asked.

"No, I don't want to do it."

"Word is they give great goodie."

Clarissa's weakness, when it came to these charity dinners, was the goodie bag that was handed out at the end of the night to every attendee. The bag was oversized, usually canvas, the sort of cheap thing one would take to the beach, but no matter. Inside there would be various items: the "book" from the charity bash, stuffed with expensive, full-page gold and silver ads (and cheaper, half-page black-and-white ads, usually from an accounting firm or someone's grandmother), shampoos, conditioners, lipsticks, perfumes, sometimes a silly tchochke that Clarissa could give to her mother. The last one had a porcelain horse on a merry-go-round that played "Raindrops"; hideous, but her mother adored it. Clarissa had seen more fights break out between powerful, rich people over goodie bags than at a televised prison riot. At the most recent event, something dealing with night blindness or prison rape or something (Clarissa could never remember the causes, worthy though they may be), an older woman who wore a little more than millions of dollars worth of diamonds and a savage look on her face actually pushed Clarissa, who bested her on weight, height, and reach, onto the floor to get at the table of goodie bags. No one could resist the pull of a free gift.

* * *

A few hours after her meeting with Morgan, Clarissa was sitting bare-ass naked in her closet at her mother's house, looking not unlike an ultramodern Rubens—a chubby chick with a French pedicure.

And she had nothing to wear.

Seriously. This wasn't Clarissa being cute, like, "Oh my God, I have nothing to wear!" This was Clarissa being stone cold realistic: She *really* had nothing to wear. As of the last twenty-four hours her body had left her closet behind, or rather, her behind had left her closet behind; all of her dresses, even the "fashionable" maternity dresses, made with "breathable" fabric, had mutinied. Clarissa grabbed for the wall and stood up, naked. She had to face facts. She was not one of those cute pregnant women who carried their babies like an accessory—a "basket-ball" pregnancy. No, she was carrying her baby in her stomach, her ass, her arms, her nose, her ankles, knees, toes—suspiciously, even her ear-lobes appeared bigger than normal.

Her nipples looked like the UFOs Stallone had talked about; she half-expected to see black helicopters hovering above her roof.

She called Gravy.

"I'm fat, naked, and late."

"One fact at a time. Yes, you are fat."

"And naked."

"I can only take your word for it. Thank God."

"And late."

"Late to another one of those heinous charity things where rich people get free gifts? Why do you do it?"

"It's my job, my career, *mi vida.* I have an extra ticket—you want to come?" Clarissa asked. Gravy had been to one or two dinners with her but had become fed up when Garry Shandling asked if her breasts were real.

"No."

"You have nothing to do."

"I'll think of something. What's the problem?"

"I have no clothes."

"Black Lycra?"

"I've worn that thing five times in a row. I can't wear it again. I can't." Clarissa looked up at the black cocktail maternity dress; she silently vowed never to wear Lycra again. She ached for cotton, wool. Even acrylic, at this point.

"Clarissa. Do you think anyone notices what you wear? You're pregnant, and you're a civilian. No one cares. If they notice anything, they'll notice the cleavage."

Clarissa sighed; she knew Gravy was right. Her cleavage had reached epic proportions; she looked like the forgotten Gabor sister. The black Lycra would save her again. She hung up after agreeing to meet up with Gravy after the auction and dinner, and smelled the dress. It passed the nose test: no B.O., no cigarette smoke, no Jovan Musk for Men. Only the faintest trace of the last event's chicken dinner. She slipped on her grandma bra, which was constructed of a fabric that could stop a bullet and wires that could hold up the Sears Tower, and then pulled the dress over her head, played with her hair a bit (thicker now, since the pregnancy, the only benefit she had experienced, and one that was wasted on her already thick head of hair), applied MAC Lipglass in a reasonable color, and slipped on shoes that were borderline geriatric.

Clarissa thought she looked horrendous but didn't give a damn; after all, she had never run into anyone she knew at these things—this was a different, more polished crowd. These were the real movers and shakers, the ones who would never give her a second glance.

No one would notice her.

Clarissa, easily the largest female within football field yardage, squeezed her body into the auction room adjacent to the Hilton's ballroom. She carried a small notebook and a pen with a point like a kitchen knife; it worked as both writing instrument and weapon, should someone so much as blink at her at the goodie bag table. Clarissa looked around; all she could see were heads: heads smiling, heads frowning, heads coiffed, heads blow-dried, heads with perfect noses and teeth, heads with eyes that wandered past hers looking for a "face." A recognizable face. A face that could help them in any way at all.

The women were dressed in floor-length gowns; they had taken out their finest jewels and deployed their best hairdressers and makeup artists.

This, Clarissa thought, *is what people think is Hollywood: Everyone here is beautiful.*

Clarissa, ready to do herself in with her pen with a poke at her neck, instead busied herself by studying various items up for auction: A massage for two at the Burke Williams Spa; an extra part on an action film featuring that new, tiny Chinese guy; dinner for eight at Spago; a Labrador puppy.

Ugh, Clarissa thought. She put her name down for the puppy. She knew she wouldn't bid high enough, but she at least wanted a shot at saving the poor thing from an ungrateful kid.

Then she saw it. A small painting. Hidden in a corner, not loud or offensive enough to attract attention, a watercolor of a sailboat. Simple, romantic, lovely, the painting was nothing special.

And Clarissa wanted it.

The minimum bid was $1,250.

A woman nudged Clarissa, as though she, in all her pregnant glory, weren't standing there. "See this, Harry?" she said. "Wouldn't this be great in Josiah's room?"

The woman wrote her name down. With a bid. $1,350. Clarissa looked at her. "Josiah?" she asked.

"My son. He's a collector. He's eight. He loves art. He's already got a Lichtenstein and a who'simicallit."

Clarissa felt sick. She grabbed her pen and wrote down her name, then wrote out a total—$1,500—approximately $1,420 more than she had in her checking account. Hell, she knew she wouldn't have the money, but Clarissa had to prevent little Josiah, the art genius, from running off with her painting.

Afterward, Clarissa made her way through the crowd, finding pockets where she could hide and then emerge, and finally found her table. She then did what she always did: She read every tiny name plate at the table, and breathed a sigh of relief when she realized that no one at table 21 had been on a sitcom, in a movie, or ever sang a song on an album. None of the names was recognizable.

Except for the fact that she, herself, was.

"Oh, mah goodness," the largish man in the tight tuxedo said to her.

"Girl, take a gander at this." He suddenly pulled up his shirt; Clarissa saw a wasteland of stomach with a few moles tossed in like tumbleweeds.

"Stop, I'll do whatever you ask," she begged. "Just . . . put the shirt down."

The man pointed to a red mark on his side; he looked like a paper that had been erased too many times.

"I'm not a doctor; I'm just not that attractive at the moment," Clarissa said. She ripped into a dinner roll. The host, the late-night talk show host with the Dumbo ears and short mouth whose second address seemed to be the grotto at the Playboy mansion, had launched into a diatribe about the current president—Clarissa wondered which president—there were so many studios, but then he mentioned "Republican" being another word for "vicious sea otters" in the Eskimo language, and she realized he was talking about the president of America, or rather, the United States.

"That's where you shot me, darlin'," the large, red-spotted guy said.

Clarissa looked at him. "Shut. Up."

"Keep that girl away from the firearms!" he said, "Say, Frankie, this is the girl I was telling you about."

It was Tweed Man. The eggplant-shaped guy whom Clarissa accidentally had nailed with a bullet at the Mason compound.

"What're you doing here?" she asked Tweed Man.

"Oh, hell, we go to the ball every year," he said. "Frankie here loves the movie stars." Frankie was a smaller version of Tweed, down to the wire-rimmed glasses and bad haircut. He nodded his head and remained silent.

"Well, who doesn't?" Clarissa said.

"How's mah boy Aaron doing?"

Clarissa put her hand over her left ring finger. It was bare. "Fine, fine. Great."

"How's your friend, Alexandra?"

"How's your wife?" Clarissa asked.

"Divorce was final ten days ago," he said. Then he took a breath, as though thinking something that shouldn't be said out loud. He looked up at Clarissa, a serious look on his face; he had wrestled that demon. "Maybe you could give me Alexandra's number. I think she's a . . . an interesting girl. I'd like to look her up while I'm here." And then, a torrent of cordial inconsequence: "I'm staying at the Four Seasons. I like the Four Seasons, don't you? Nice bath towels. Good service, food's pricey, though, pancakes for twenty-five dollars, what's that about? Say, where is Aaron—I saw him in the auction room—he's somewhere around here, isn't he?"

Clarissa must have gone white.

"You okay, Miss?"

"Baby's kicking."

He looked down at her stomach, surprised. "I thought you were looking a little healthy. Congratulations!"

"Thank you."

"I can't wait to slap ol' Aaron on the back—where's he at?"

Clarissa, desperate, pointed suddenly at the stage, knocking over her glass of water. "Oh my God, look! Shania Twain!" One could almost hear the *clap* of silent Frankie's neck as he snapped his head around.

The host, after the dinner (fresh-some-time-ago salmon, mixed greens, a dessert involving chocolate coins and peach soup, proving two rights do indeed make a wrong), named off the auction winners. Screams abounded, followed by laughter, the laughter of rich people, which was different from other types of laughter—calculated, measured, emerging from the upper regions of the body, not the lower.

And finally, it came down to the painting. The watercolor.

The host did not appreciate the watercolor. "Do people get paid for this?" he cried. "I've got a five-year-old (or so the paternity suit claims) . . ."

Clarissa tuned out, momentarily engaged in a battle with the gold wrapping on one of the chocolate coins.

"And the watercolor, 'Sailboats at Dusk,' goes to . . ." Clarissa found herself holding her breath.

"Aaron Mason."

She felt Tweed Man's eyes on her, his round head turned her way. "You won!" he yelled. "Gotdam, girl—you won!"

"Over here!" The Tweed Man turned and screamed at the host. "This little lady! Over here!"

The table erupted in cheers—everyone (except for the two empty seats on her left) was smiling, enjoying Clarissa's good luck with the sudden camaraderie of teammates. She felt the woman on her right, a society maven, widow of a sixties movie star who probably hadn't touched another human being in twenty-odd years, pat her on the shoulder.

"Congrats! I think my five-year-old could've done better, but hey, there's no accounting for taste. Where're you gonna hang the thing? May I suggest Poughkeepsie?" The host turned, gathering up artificial laughs from the crowd.

Clarissa looked up at Mr. Potato Head as he thrust the microphone in her face, a huge strobe light momentarily blinding his prey.

"Hey Aaron," Mr. Tweed Man yelled, "you won!"

"Shit!" a voice yelled back, "Course ah did!"

Clarissa turned to see a young man coming up behind her: small (unlike Aaron) and sandy-haired (unlike Aaron) and decidedly inebriated (unlike Aaron).

And a complete *stranger.*

"Anyway, this my seat?" the man asked Clarissa, the exchange playing out over two concert-size screens at the front of the room. The host was shaking his head, wheels spinning, figuring out how to milk the moment.

The stranger pulled out a chair and picked up a place card from the floor. "Oh yeah," he said, "tha's me, Aaron Mason—right, baby?" He turned to a blonde behind him, who looked like she'd been poured out of a bottle. She giggled.

"So you're the man who bought this thing?" the host said. "No wonder you're drinking."

Then this Aaron Mason person looked at Clarissa, as though remembering his strange-fat-girl manners.

"Anyway, Aaron Kingsley Mason," he said. "How'd you do?"

He spilled a glass of water that landed in Clarissa's pregnant lap as he extended his hand toward hers.

Tweed Man stood up, annoyed, shaking his head, waving a napkin toward Clarissa. "Damn, Aaron, stop playing. You know how she is—that there's your wife."

Twenty-four

Stranger, Then Fiction

This particular Aaron looked at Clarissa, computing whatever information he could given that his brain was taking a bath in tequila, and Clarissa did the only thing she could do, given the increasingly hostile environment.

She ran.

Now, even under the best (or worst) of circumstances, Clarissa was hardly a runner. However, she had been a runner as a young girl, was actually the fastest runner in her class, boy or girl, in sixth grade; she weighed more than most of her classmates, her thighs were naturally built and strong. But she'd given up running when her father said that something called her "quads" were getting too big, and that she wasn't some black kid, and that running was a man's sport. So she hadn't run since then, even the time when, after a summer of growing boobs in seventh grade, Joey Lester had popped her bra and called her "Mongo Bongos."

But tonight she ran like the little girl in those new, white as rice Adidas. Seven months pregnant, big as the proverbial house, Clarissa knocked down several evening gowns and one or two tuxedos, and, apparently, table 108. It was fight or flight, her body told her, and Clarissa had chosen flight.

The girl could still run.

She made it outside the building in under a minute, eliciting stares but little else from onlookers; they were probably afraid she was going into labor and would ask someone for a ride.

Clarissa finished hyperventilating and slipped off her shoes and headed out, head held high, past the valet parking to the bargain four-dollar parking where she had left her BMW (*Climate* didn't pay for valet).

The second she heaved her body into her car (annoyed by its cramped single-girl style), she dove into her purse for her cell phone and started dialing.

Gravy wasn't home. Her cell phone went to voice mail. Her pager was turned off.

Jennifer wasn't home. Her cell phone went to voice mail. Her pager wasn't working (washer/dryer incident).

Polo wasn't home. She answered her cell phone, and then was immediately cut off. She never took her pager with her.

Simon wasn't home. Clarissa hadn't programmed his cell phone into her phone yet. And she'd forgotten the number.

"Conspiracy theory!" Clarissa cried. She was almost desperate enough to call Suzee (after all, this was *news* with a capital *new*), then thought better or it.

Finally, when all options (including the fraternal twins, Suicide and Homicide) were spent, she started to cry. One lonely tear was joined by one more, soon to become a salty torrent; Clarissa was a wet, blubbering, stranger-marrying mess.

She had the presence of mind to look at herself in the vanity mirror—she was not one to have mascara running down her cheeks, after all. Even when one's life is on the verge of becoming an "It Happened to Me" story in *Glamour* magazine, one still had to look good.

And that's when she started laughing. A chuckle became a giggle, merging into a genuine guffaw—she ended up hitting the steering wheel with her head, she was laughing so hard.

On an emotional level, this pregnancy thing was one rough road.

Clarissa had come to realize: She, the master manipulator (Clarissa) had been masterfully manipulated (Pseudo Aaron) and she had no one to blame but herself. It was clear, from Eggplant Tweed Man's reaction, that the real Aaron Mason was now enjoying a "fresh" salmon dinner, the cheerful haze of a pickled brain, and the breathy attentions of a Pamela Anderson double—leaving Clarissa with one question:

"Who the hell fuck is Pseudo Aaron?" she said, aloud. "Who on earth have I married?"

All she knew was that the little fucker had kicked her sedan-size ass, and now, to quote Ricky Ricardo, he had some 'splainin' to do.

Clarissa's emotions swerved, making a detour at the signpost that read "manic."

"Screw Pseudo Aaron!" she yelled as she drove away. "Screw his dimples, screw his narrow waist, doubly screw his broad shoulders, and screw his club-fucking-foot! Who needs it?!" she screamed. "I can fucking run like a fucking gazelle! I don't need him! I don't need any man! I can take care of myself!"

As she drove east on Wilshire, Clarissa's only regret was about the goodie bag she'd left behind; but then, she took her forgetfulness as a good sign. Maybe she was growing up.

Twenty-five

Hey, Ricky!

Pseudo Aaron would have been awakened at 4:45 that morning, except he was already awake, working on the first draft notes for the *Gay Divorcee* (working title) script; it had come in two days ago, and the director had called a script meeting in the morning.

The script was awful, as Pseudo Aaron knew it would be. The studio had hired a screenwriter who was notorious for two things: Not writing his own scripts—they were written by a committee of USC and UCLA starry-eyed coeds—and taking credit where credit was not due (and suing when credit was not forthcoming; among his charms was that he was a former contract lawyer). He had earned an Oscar nod earlier in his career (as a cowriter—no one could figure out what he did with the body of the other guy) and had dined out on it ever since, to the tune of a second apartment in Paris, a third in New York, private schools for the kids, and dental work that made his teeth look like an igloo.

I've taken dumps, Pseudo Aaron thought as he forced his eyes into the second act, *but never this big . . . and never this expensive*. The script had cost the studio upward of seven figures, to quote Army Archerd's *Variety* column.

He had sixteen pages of handwritten, single-spaced notes, and he hadn't finished reading yet; he rubbed his eyes and finally answered the phone. He had thought the ringing was all in his head.

On the line was Aaron Mason. The real Aaron Mason.

"Hey, man!" the voice said. Drunk or stoned or somewhere in between or beyond. Pseudo Aaron heard giggling in the background. "Anyway, I'm in town! Party's starting!"

Pseudo Aaron gasped, nearly losing his bowels along with his temper.

"What are you doing here?" Pseudo Aaron demanded. "You can't be here—we had an agreement."

"I jus' wanta get in on the fun, dude." Genuine Aaron said. "Anyway, hey, you know where we could score some shit—my driver doesn't seem to understand the urgency of a gentleman's requirements." And then, Genuine Aaron burped.

Pseudo Aaron rubbed his head, staving off the inevitable stress migraine. This is just what he needed, just when he was starting to get a handle on the process of moviemaking (endless, tedious, without mercy), just when he thought he could work things out with Clarissa . . .

He needed time to think.

"Look, why don't you go to, I don't know, have him drive you to the Peninsula—no, not the Peninsula, L'Ermitage," Pseudo Aaron said. Clarissa had told him the L'Ermitage was known for its discretion. It specialized in "postoperative" clientele. "Go there, tell the driver to take you there, he'll know where it is; we can have breakfast tomorrow."

"Breakfast?" Genuine Aaron said. "Wha's that?"

"Just go, please," Pseudo Aaron said. "I'll call you in the morning. I can't believe you came out here. You're going to fuck everything up."

But Genuine Aaron had already hung up, leaving Pseudo Aaron to his lousy script and his empty apartment and a whole slew of new problems. He wished he had someone to call to commiserate with, but he knew he couldn't talk to Maxi Reese or any of the other agents he'd befriended. The minute they heard he was not who he said he was—well, he was toast in this town, instead of the toast of the town.

He wished he could call the one person who would find this mess amusing (after she killed him and hacked up his body and tossed the pieces onto the 405)—Clarissa. But she wouldn't talk to him, and besides, he thought, feeling self-righteously bitter, she married him under false pretenses and, despite Jen's assurances, wasn't even carrying his baby.

But that didn't change the fact that he still wanted to talk to her.

An exhausted Pseudo Aaron sank into a fitful sleep on Clarissa's red couch surrounded by his stuffed pals and wishing there were a different kind of softness there to comfort him.

* * *

At an Emergency Meeting of the Star Chamber (menu: Starbucks caramel macchiatos, Twix, and one jar of Skippy creamy-style peanut butter) held at Clarissa's mom's house, Clarissa discussed options.

"Shoot him," Clarissa said. It wasn't a question.

"Untidy and impolite," Jen said.

"We don't own a gun," Polo pointed out, through clogged sinuses.

"I do," Gravy volunteered. The girls looked at her.

"Turn him into the police?" Clarissa asked.

"For what?" Gravy said. "Pretending to be someone else? We're all pretending to be someone else."

"I don't care if he is a total sociopath. He's sweet, and he has nice hands." This, of course, from Jen.

"I feel like a human chew toy," Clarissa groaned.

"He could be a serial killer," Polo said.

"No way. He doesn't have that kind of charisma," Gravy said.

"Excuse me?" Clarissa said. "I think he's totally serial-killer charismatic."

The girls looked at her, eyebrows jumping off their foreheads.

"He scared Simon," Clarissa said, as an example.

"Jen's dogs scare Simon," Gravy pointed out.

"Look. Just because I want him dead doesn't mean I dislike him," Clarissa pointed out. "Besides, he is the baby's father."

"Why don't you tell him that?" Jen said. "He thinks it's Simon's."

"How do you know he thinks it's Simon's?" Gravy asked.

"Because. Because, that's what Clarissa told him, and you know how psychic I am." Jen turned to Clarissa.

"It's the fluoride," Polo said. "The fluoride in the L.A. water has this effect on men. They're all insane."

"I say we lay low and gather more information before we make our next move," Gravy said.

Clarissa agreed, mainly because she was tired and emotionally spent and had to take a pee every few minutes.

She was in the bathroom doing just that (and reading an ancient issue of *Architectural Digest* featuring Michael J. Fox and his wife and their farmhouse) when the phone rang.

"Do you miss me?" it was Simon.

"Simon," Clarissa said. "I miss you like I miss seeing the top of my feet. I miss you like I miss bending over without farting."

"We have to talk, Clarissa," he said. "I'm feeling almost ready to commit."

"Commit what?"

"You know . . . ," Simon said. "Commit to . . . the idea of . . ."

"Simon, you don't have to commit. Nobody's asking you to commit."

"Wonderful. Can I come over?"

"I'm having a meeting."

"What did you call me about last night? You sounded upset."

Clarissa had forgotten that she'd called him, in her manic-pregnant-married-an-unknown-factor stage. "It was nothing. Nothing important."

"I'll call you later, love," he said. "I've got to hear some tracks at the studio."

"You do that, you go hear those tracks, you knock yourself out with those tracks, Mister Trackman," Clarissa said. She hung up, grateful with the realization that she no longer cared nor counted on Simon calling her back.

In the morning, Pseudo Aaron rode his motorcycle to L'Ermitage, contemplating the fact that his carefully constructed life in L.A. was about to meet its bitter demise.

He'd lose his job, he'd lose his contacts, there would be no returned phone calls, no two-hour lunches at the Grill, he'd be run out of town like the penniless loser wannabe he was. He could only imagine what people would be saying about him—how he had fooled everybody—and nobody. People would be livid. There may be lawsuits.

He was dead in this town.

He thought it'd make a good story.

But what about the love angle? Pseudo Aaron could imagine a development executive asking him, a year from now.

Pseudo Aaron knew how the love story would end: Clarissa would never forgive him. She would never see him again.

He had gambled. He had lost everything.

* * *

The Aarons met over an unmade king-size bed, several pizza boxes, two still-burning roaches, numerous empty champagne bottles, and one rambunctious blonde at the Presidential Suite at the L'Ermitage.

Genuine Aaron, half-naked and barely able to lift an eyelid, never made it out of bed. And so, Pseudo Aaron sat in an overstuffed chair in the bedroom gathering up his composure like so many loose marbles while he tried to ascertain why Genuine Aaron had come to Los Angeles.

"What happened to Nepal?" Pseudo Aaron asked.

"I got arrested, had to leave the country," Genuine Aaron said. "I tried to get a couple Buddhist monks high on Pakistani hashish."

"Thailand?"

Genuine Aaron looked up as the blonde rolled out of bed, naked and lush, and into the bathroom.

"I picked up a little souvenir in Thailand," he whispered.

"Nothing antibiotics won't cure, I hope," Pseudo Aaron said.

"Good as gold," genuine Aaron smiled.

"Russia?"

"The women are very strong. The vodka is stronger—and their boyfriends. Incredible Hulks, down to the last Igor."

"You got rolled."

"I made it out of the country with a pair of biker shorts and a passport. Anyway, somebody else's passport, but that's another story."

"Germany?"

"Germans."

"London?"

"Wet."

"Paris?"

"Smoky."

"Amsterdam? C'mon, I know you loved Amsterdam, you could've stayed in Amsterdam."

"Sadly, I couldn't keep up, my friend. It's like . . . you finally make it to the candy store, you can get all the candy you want, and it just makes you sick."

Pseudo Aaron just shook his head.

"Nice threads, by the way," Genuine Aaron said. "Anyway, who is that, Hugo Boss?"

"Dries Van Noten."

"You have a very generous expense account."

"Once upon a time. Living like Aaron Kingsley Mason is hard on the wallet."

"Where're you staying? I want to check out the homestead. I'm tired of hotel living."

"A one-bedroom apartment. Up in Beachwood Canyon."

Genuine Aaron made a face. "Well, what are you driving? Tell me it's the Bentley."

"I got rid of it. The lease was more than my rent."

"Dudeman, that's part of the whole deal, the Bentley. That's what Aaron Mason would drive if Aaron Mason lived here. Shit, I wanted to take it for a spin this weekend."

"I've got a motorcycle. She might even fit on it," Pseudo Aaron said, regarding the blonde.

"Christ. Hot Christ," Genuine Aaron looked at him with genuine sorrow. "Anyway, okay, just tell me. What happened to the money? It is drugs? You're totally strung out, right, am I right? It's coke, right? It's that devil coca."

"No."

"Good. I can barely handle my own little Betty Ford situation," Genuine Aaron said. "Gambling. Like your old man. You got the fever. You're gambling."

"Only with my future."

"Anyway, it's women, then. Prostitution?"

"Hell, no. I don't pay for it."

"Really?" Genuine Aaron asked. "Hookers cost less than girlfriends, and they don't complain. How much you got left?"

"If I had a dog, I'd have to eat it."

The blonde sauntered back into the room. Pseudo Aaron tried to look anywhere else but her aggressive breasts; it was no use. He gawked like a choir boy until she got back into bed.

"Look," Pseudo Aaron said. "I wanted to save you money. I mean, it didn't seem necessary to be living in that house and driving that car.

And I started to feel bad about your parents, not knowing what's going on here."

"It's my job to feel bad about my parents, and anyway, I don't. It's more healthy that way."

"A friend of mine got in a bind."

"Oh, Christ Hell," Genuine Aaron grimaced. "You gave it away."

"A retainer. Attorney's fees. He's going to pay it all back. He's totally untrustworthy, but he's good to his word."

"Anyway, dude. Good news. I'm waiting on some good news. You are, like, wearing me out," Genuine Aaron sighed.

"The good news is, we have a director, we have a writer, we have a shitty first draft, which the studio will like because that writer is under a three-picture deal and they have to like it. And you, you'll be getting your money back, one way or the other."

Genuine Aaron seemed soothed by this. He started making out with the blonde. Pseudo Aaron looked at the ceiling.

"So," he finally said, "what brings you here, anyway? Checking up on your investment?"

Pseudo Aaron was acting cool. He wanted to deal with Genuine Aaron in such a way that he would leave town quietly—and, also, he didn't want to be late to his notes meeting.

"My business brings me here."

"There's always email, telephone," Pseudo Aaron said.

"Anyway, I thought I'd take a meeting or two while I'm here, you know, hang out, have lunch, put my two cents in," Genuine Aaron said. "Anyway, you know, I think I'm ready to start working. Isn't that right, baby?"

The girl giggled and reached under the sheets.

Pseudo Aaron looked at Genuine Aaron. Here, wrapped in sheets and a woman and the afterhigh, here was the man whose money had brought him to L.A., the man whose money had paid for the rights to *The Gay Divorcee* (which Pseudo Aaron had found), the man who agreed to pay expenses for a set period of time. All of which Pseudo Aaron had accepted, because while Pseudo Aaron had desire and knowledge and commitment and would work the endless hours necessary to build a company, he did not have a plugged nickel to his name, as his grandmother would have said. When he left Georgia he'd had $180 in the bank—barely enough for the plane ride out.

He thought back to months ago, before he'd come to L.A. The final caveat in their business agreement had been put to him in a room filled with bong smoke.

"Anyway, you have to pretend you're me," Genuine Aaron had said.

"What are you talking about?" Pseudo Aaron had just finished packing his duffel bag with a couple of pairs of tennis shoes, his favorite boots, two pairs of pants, flannel shirts, and seven stuffed animals (which he had packed first, hidden from view).

"My parents are about to disinherit me," Genuine Aaron had sniffed. "Their only son, you believe that? Anyway, they think I'm a loser, they think all I want to do is get high and get laid, you believe that shit? Anyway, I told them I'm leaving for L.A. I'm going to set up a megaproduction company, I've already got the rights to an old movie, etcetera, totally . . ."

"Did you remember the title?" Pseudo Aaron had asked.

"Hell Christ no," Genuine Aaron had said. "What the fuck. I made one up. Anyway, that's the deal. Take it or stick it."

"I have to pretend I'm Aaron Mason," Pseudo Aaron had said. He sort of laughed. He'd been pretending he was Aaron since the Scooby Doo years—which he would watch with Genuine Aaron on his *color television set* in his *room*!

"Tha's right," Genuine Aaron had said, smiling, as smoke filtered out of his nose.

"And where will you be?" Pseudo Aaron had asked. The idea was intriguing to him.

"I'm gonna take off, man, see the whole fucking Christ crazy world, who knows when I'll be back. Anyway, I got lots to do. I got the three necessities of life: Money, Time, and Wasted Youth. And I'm aching with ambition."

So they shook on the deal. Genuine Aaron cut him a check, with numbers Pseudo Aaron couldn't say out loud without choking; the next day he left for L.A. with a new identity and virgin credit cards.

Pseudo Aaron must have been staring into space and his recent past a long time. Genuine Aaron was almost asleep, the giggling blonde was not giggling anymore, only snoring. Pseudo Aaron looked at him and smiled, as a thought formed. Once Genuine Aaron realized that people in the movie business work hard, harder than most—well, he'd find his way back to Amsterdam or Iceland or Bali before he could say "turn-around."

"All right, Aaron," Pseudo Aaron said, waking him. "I've got a notes meeting after lunch, why don't I leave the script here—you take a look at it, and come on in to the office—I'd love to get your notes, you know, see what you have to say. The second act is long, the third act is soft."

Genuine Aaron looked at the script. "How long is it?"

"One hundred and fifteen pages, it's nothing. It's a fast read."

"Oh," Genuine Aaron said. "Oh."

"So I'll see you later?"

"Sure, anyway, yeah, sure."

Pseudo Aaron was almost out the door.

"Hey, did you get married, man?"

Pseudo Aaron did that thing where he stopped in his tracks. He felt like one of the six "Friends."

"Ah . . . why?"

"Anyway, boy, the air's a little foggy up here," he tapped his head, "but, was it last night? I was at this awards thing—I don't remember. Anyway, I met this girl, and she's like, out to here, man—she's totally knocked up—and some guy, you remember that guy with the—he tells me that's my wife, man."

Pseudo Aaron felt the blood drain from his face to his feet—which responded by growing two sizes.

Genuine Aaron laughed. "Anyway, I thought it was real interesting. Just don't saddle me with no paternity suit, man, those are a bitch. I learned my lesson the first two times."

Pseudo Aaron was out the door and passing the valet station on the way to his motorcycle when he thought about the best way to approach Clarissa (besides wearing Kevlar). He'd have to call Jen and tell her everything.

He knew Clarissa would never hurt Jen.

You know how it is. You've reached rock bottom—the nadir of your (relatively) short life—and yet, for no reason at all, you're feeling on top of the world, superior as a French *Vogue* cover. You laugh gaily at the slightest amusement and notice the beauty of all that is natural—a sunrise, a perfect wave, bratwurst. And you wonder how it is you ever forgot these things, or never knew them. And then they're all there, right in front of your curious, magnetic eyes, and you, this supreme human form, the person who can do no wrong, who has all the answers, the master of the "in my opinion," she who is completely in control, suddenly gets a phone call which, in the course of minutes, nay, seconds, wipes all of the beauty away, every sparkle, and leaves you, this person with a formerly full plate of life, nothing but the ashes left of crumbs.

"That's exactly what I'm talking about," Clarissa said. She was curled up in a semifetal position (semi, because of the pregnancy thing, stomach and all) on her mother's couch, unable, and moreover, unwilling, to move.

"So then, what did he say?" Gravy asked. She was sitting nose-to-nose-job with Clarissa, who was speaking in such a soft voice Gravy had to tell her she wasn't a lip reader and she had better speak like a human being.

"He said that two people got injured," Clarissa said. She gulped. Literally. "Table 108."

"Holy shit. Not table 108—"

"I was running pretty fast," Clarissa said. "Apparently, some woman's got this thumb thing—I don't know. A sprain. They're suing the magazine."

"Fuck 'em, let 'em sue. Not your problem," Gravy said.

"I'm fired," Clarissa said. Her chest heaved like a broken accordion—nothing in her breath was rhythmical. Clarissa was having a nervous breakdown. "I'm fired, I married a fake person, I'm pregnant, I might as well be dead. Gravy, I can't take care of myself, Pseudo Aaron's right. And if I can't take care of myself, how do I take care of this?" She pointed to her belly.

"First things first. Yes, you did marry a fake person, but that could happen to anybody," Gravy said, taking Clarissa's face in her hands. "But they can't fire you! Think about it. It's an unpaid position: How can they possibly fire you? Fuckers! Take that!" Gravy kicked in the air as she sometimes did when she had "figured it all out."

Clarissa bawled. "I'm such a *loser*!"

"You," Gravy said, "are many things. Many things. Some of them bad. But not one of them is a loser."

Clarissa sniffed. "Gravy, I'm going to have a baby. I don't even know the baby's father's real name, and meanwhile, he's dating a physical specimen seldom seen in nature, and I don't have any money, and I finally had a good job, found something I was actually good at, and I just got fired. There's no mystery here, this is not an episode of *CSI*—I fit every definition of the word "loser."

"Every great female name in history has had a setback," Gravy said. "Name anybody."

Clarissa looked at her and raised her head, just enough to breathe normally, if breathing normally were possible for a pregnant woman. "Oprah?"

"African American, poor, zaftig except for that Optifast week, and plus, remember, she was raped," she pointed out.

"Really?" Clarissa said, with hope making a surge.

"Go on. Give me another one."

Clarissa smiled. Sometimes Gravy was so wise, like a hip Dalai Lama. "Madonna?" she whispered.

"Michigan working class, mother died when she was young, came to New York with no money, fucked every stepping-stone."

"And she winds up marrying the cutest guy in the whole world who's not, like, a trainer."

"See?" Gravy said.

"And two kids."

"And two kids."

They sighed.

"Hillary Clinton."

"Obvious. She, the smartest girl, married the smartest guy with the most wayward dick. But hey, she lived in the White House for eight years, how cool is that."

Clarissa had to agree.

"You need a vacation," Gravy concluded.

"Of course, I need a vacation," Clarissa said. "How am I supposed to pay for a vacation?"

"More than a vacation. You need a spiritual awakening," Gravy continued.

"I had one, weren't you listening? I almost killed two people."

"You know how Polo goes to these retreats."

"The yoga retreat? The one where the teacher fucks all the married female students and drives their cars?"

"No, no," Gravy said. "This is a 'silent retreat.'"

"I don't like the sound of that," Clarissa said. Beat. "Get it?"

"You can't talk for a week."

"We'll never make it."

"It'll be good for us."

"Since when are you interested in doing something that's good for you?"

"Since I have no more alternatives," Gravy admitted. Clarissa thought about this; she decided it was true. Gravy had worked her way through most of humanity's known vices; she had never, however, performed in hard-core porn. To Clarissa's knowledge.

"You won't last."

"I'll last if you'll last."

"I won't last. Where is this place?"

"Ojai. It's like a two-hour drive," Gravy said. "C'mon, I need to shut up and so do you."

Clarissa was all set to argue this point, but thought better of it: *Gravy, as usual, was right.*

Twenty-six

The Silence Is Deafening

The retreat was held in an old monastery ensconced in the womb-like setting of verdant rolling hills. The summer had been mild enough that the hills were a deep, soothing green, and the trees, abundant, were just turning color at the edges in anticipation of autumn.

"Fuck, this is fucking beautiful," Gravy said, with her usual poetic style.

A small, hand-printed sign led them to a room where about a dozen people sat on metal chairs listening with rapt, polite, anxious attention to a man with a graying beard who wore the sort of clothes that bore no visible seams. "New Wave, Ex-Junkie, A.A., Hippie Born-Again Buddha Man," Gravy said, too loudly, as she and Clarissa, hiding behind aviator glasses, clattering on their high heels, mooning needy folks with their low-slung Seven jeans (Clarissa, pregnant as she was, tucked them under her belly), found seats in the back of the room, four rows behind any other human being.

They were the equivalent of the bad kids in algebra one, and people stared at them from behind thick glasses and unruly hair and middle age.

"COPs," Clarissa said to Gravy, speaking sideways like a stroke victim. "Creepy old people."

Someone shushed them as Gray Beard continued his speech on not speaking. "What are you trying to find? Inner peace? Truth? The reason your husband/wife/mother/father/son/daughter left you?" He took a beat, as Clarissa smirked and looked over at Gravy, who was staring intently at Gray Beard. Clarissa, bored with anything that didn't involve eating, tried to find something interesting to focus on: the thick white walls were bare; the back of other people's heads became her focal point. Clarissa stared at one after the other, deciphering lives by the color and texture of hair, the curve of a shoulder, the tilt of a neck.

She decided this group was a bunch of losers. The retreat already was making her feel better.

"The only way to find answers is to look within yourselves. The only way to look within yourselves is to block out the excessiveness of our everyday lives—too many words, too many images, too much sound, too much." He looked directly at Clarissa and Gravy. "For seven days, you will not utter so much as one syllable to your neighbor; for seven days, you are freed from the sound of your own voice."

"What about food?" Clarissa's mouth opened before her hand had shot up.

"Believe it or not, we have food," he said, and he smiled, which spread across his face, the warmth dulling his sharp features. "Breakfast, lunch, and dinner. Three vegan meals a day. You'll find the schedules in your packets."

"What's a vegan? Is that like a Lisa Bonet thing?" Gravy asked.

"It's like when Polo stopped eating chicken and wearing leather for a week. What if you want seconds?" Clarissa asked Gray Beard. By the sound of their laughter, some people found this question amusing. Clarissa just found the question one of practicality and survival.

"I can see why you would ask," he said, "and congratulations on making this trek during this special time for you. Your baby will thank you."

"When do we start being quiet?" Gravy asked.

"In about five minutes," he said.

After the introductory seminar, Gravy and Clarissa walked, serenaded by their heels, to their room. Gravy wiggled her eyebrows, gesturing toward Gray Beard. Clarissa shook her head and wagged her finger at her. They entered room number 12, a small room, dark wood, two twin beds. Doll beds.

"Seven days," Clarissa said, looking at the room.

"Shh," Gravy said.

* * *

Dinner was held in a small cafeteria setting that sported a salad bar similar to Denny's on one end and a soup bar on the other, which held brown, gray, and green liquid inventions. Which was fine for Clarissa, because she would gladly have eaten the rubber off her tires by the time dinner started (7:00, as per the schedule).

In an empty cafeteria, silence sounded something like twenty or so strangers chewing, slurping, coughing, sniffing, sighing, and performing almost all manner of bodily function, an orchestra of gurgles.

Clarissa and Gravy were halfway through a dinner item enthusiastically deemed "Veggie Tofu Grill!" which tasted like burnt sponge and bell pepper when Gravy's cell phone rang, with its familiar, to Clarissa, "I'm Too Sexy" ring. The entire room, sixteen people (including Gray Beard and another counselor, a woman who was dishwater from her hair to her Birkenstocks) turned and looked at Gravy in an inseparable, unspoken censure: *That phone was supposed to be turned off, unplugged, not on your person at any time throughout this week. If an emergency situation arose, it would be handled by the front desk.*

Gravy didn't move. She glanced at Clarissa and the two held each other's eyes as the phone continued its mid-eighties siren dance.

A side door opened, snapping the tension, and a figure appeared, a small-boned silhouette wearing half a head of sunglasses and wrapped almost to her delicate toes in a cashmere pashmina that had the look of being thrown on in half a second yet was camera-ready for the fashion pages of *Harper's Bazaar.*

This apparition, Clarissa thought, had to be Someone Famous. "Thank God," she said aloud, incurring the wrathful looks of her silent comrades. Even the lowest celebrity was better than no celebrity at all.

Clarissa espied a glint of blonde hair under the shawl.

"Madonna," Gravy said, using sign language from a junior high school course they had both taken. Her hand signals actually spelled something like "mad janitor," but Clarissa was twenty paces ahead. She shook her head no. She stared at the figure, at the patrician nose with the trademark superior arch poking out from under the dark . . .

"Zoë," Clarissa mouthed to Gravy, aware of Gray Beard watching them watching Zoë Monroe, the girl *People* magazine had ordained

"Not the Next Big Thing, but the Big Thing." At age twenty-five, barely out of Yale Drama School, she already had been nominated for a Tony, had performed in several Merchant-Ivory films, was in negotiations to be the next Austin Powers Girl, had dated Gwyneth Paltrow's ex-boyfriend and stolen Winona Ryder's ex-ex-boyfriend, was currently working as the voice of the Fairy Princess in the DreamWorks animated Thanksgiving movie, and had not one but several documented stalkers.

Gravy looked to the sky, somewhere beyond the primitive, pitched wooden ceiling, as if to thank God for this blessing.

Clarissa smiled at her victory at breaking the celebrity code and commenced to eating her tofu and was happy that her attentions were elsewhere and not on her taste buds.

As Gravy snored the snore of skinny people—which, in Clarissa's experience, was much louder than any heavy person—Clarissa wondered at Zoë's presence at the silent retreat. She remembered Guru Oprah saying every chance meeting had meaning; Zoë being there, of all places, held meaning for Clarissa, and all she had to do was find out what that was.

Clarissa lay awake under the weight of her baby and rolled over in her bed, a piece of furniture that was as hard as it was small, and listened to Gravy's grunting and decided that she was not going to sleep, so why not take advantage of the safe environs of the monastery. She arose, wrapping herself in Gravy's robe, which was nicer than her own, sneaked out the door, and padded down the hallway. There was a bench outside, bathed in moonlight, with her name on it.

For a moment Clarissa thought about how romantic it would be to walk the path with Pseudo Aaron, to sit in the dark with her beloved, her head on his shoulder, feeling his chest lift with each breath.

Until she remembered that she wasn't speaking to him.

Clarissa, who'd neglected to bring a flashlight, emerged from the path and managed to find her bench, only to discover someone else felt the same way about it: There was a shadow, the telltale eraserhead of light—someone was smoking a cigarette on *her* bench!

Clarissa stopped short, then decided she hadn't walked all the way out here to be a wuss. She made enough noise to not startle anyone, but the shadow smoker nonetheless jumped, and Clarissa was suddenly face-to-face with Zoë Monroe.

Who is actually much smaller in person than one would expect, Clarissa thought.

They stood, staring at each other. One would start to speak, and then the other, neither one wanting, for some stupid reason, to break the code of the silent camp.

And so, finally, they both sat down. Zoë put her cigarette out when she noticed the breadth of Clarissa's midsection wasn't due to poor genetics, and they sat for what seemed like hours, but which in reality was forty-five minutes, in complete silence, watching the play of the moonlight against the trees, which moved regularly and softly in the breeze, like a heartbeat. And still, they managed to communicate.

Zoë was the first to rise; she smiled at Clarissa and left behind an air of sadness and also her pack of Salems, which seemed to Clarissa an unusual choice of smokes for a skinny white girl, but who was she to judge Zoë, anyway?

Clarissa couldn't wait to tell Gravy that Zoë was her new best friend, then realized she couldn't actually tell Gravy, but thankfully, she could write it down.

Five-thirty A.M. (as per the retreat schedule; apparently Buddhists don't sleep in). Here is the note Gravy awoke to:

.yvarG reaD

dna dneirf tseb ym neeb evah uoy ,wonk uoy sA
comrade (and co-Star Chamber President) for years and
years and years, however, I must inform you that as I am
now best best friends with Zoë, your services are no
longer needed.

C ,evoL

Gravy read the backward note with the ease of a practiced eye; she and Clarissa had exchanged backward notes constantly in Mr. Rippey's seventh-grade homeroom. Before she could demand information from Clarissa, who was already dressed, Clarissa held her finger to her mouth, and Gravy grabbed a pencil and threw it at her, and Clarissa wrote down all she could remember from the night before.

Gravy begged, in writing, to join her that night; Clarissa wrote back that she would think about it, but as her friendship with Zoë was in its tender, nascent stage, she had to protect it by all necessary means. Gravy objected profusely, again, in writing, and then they headed to the cafeteria for breakfast, where they quickly realized (by din of the state of the cafeteria, enormous in its emptiness) that the 5:30 wake-up horn was meant to signal a time for breathing and meditation; breakfast was at 7:00.

Upon this realization, Clarissa began to conjure ways in which to escape—but not until she and Zoë had bonded.

Meanwhile, in the day and a half since they arrived at the silent retreat, Gravy had become a fearsome acolyte of Gray Beard; this womanchild who would not awaken until 11:00 on most days, was up at 5:30 for meditation; this girl who was not in bed before 3:00 A.M. (on most days) was now asleep by 8:45. The upshot to all this clean living? Gravy refused to let Clarissa drive back to L.A. in her car—Clarissa was stuck. None of her credit cards were in working order and she had about twenty bucks to her name, but after the second day of silence and Seitan Stroganoff, Clarissa was desperate to get out.

Clarissa plotted her breakout, waiting for her new best friend on the bench where they sat the night before. Zoë did not disappoint. She appeared, halfhearted smile across her lips, barefoot, wearing an item, practically a spider's web, as wispy as its owner, moments after Clarissa arrived.

Zoë sat and curled her legs under her, as only thin, beautiful, winsome actress-types can do (Clarissa had tried this maneuver before and had pinched a nerve in her back), and a look of appropriate distress rose in her lovely face, enveloping her features, rendering them . . . even more fucking perfect. *Method feeling,* Clarissa thought. *Nothing under a size four could be that depressed.*

Minutes meandered by, Clarissa aware of every breath her celestial benchmate took. Each sigh, every murmur, the occasional soft moan. She recognized the tenor of her new best friend's sadness, for it mirrored her own. Soon they were matching each other, sigh for sigh, groan for groan, and finally, tear for tear.

Clarissa was crying, sobbing, on a bench, in the middle of the night, in the middle of nowhere, with Zoë Monroe.

And they were crying for the same reason: *men.*

On the third day, after lunch, Gravy raced in her yoga wear to something called Cosmic Colon Cleansing; Clarissa, having plodded her way through Onion Surprise, raced to something called Gravy's Car Keys.

She ran to room number 12, shut the door, and began rifling through Gravy's effects: tampons, fossilized mints, scraps of menus with ring designs scribbled on them, pennies, condoms (wishful thinking!), hazy photographs, and keys.

Keys.

Clarissa wrote a hasty note to Gravy on the retreat stationery, which came in the recycled color, bits of wood pulp ingrained in the paper to remind the writer of its superior lineage.

> yletulosba ,ot evah ,yrros ,uoy evol ,yrros ,syek kooT
> .C ,sessik ,yroslupmoc
> !llihC .syad ruof ni pu uoy kcip lliW .S.P

Clarissa's bags (there were three; she had, as per usual, overpacked for a trip in which clothes were not only irrelevant, but disregarded) were packed already, meaning her clothes had been thrown in the bags that morning. She exchanged flip-flops for sneakers and tried to figure out how to get the bags out of the room and into Gravy's car without appearing as though she were sneaking out. She decided to toss them out the window. They managed, somehow, given their girth, to land on the ground below without killing anything.

Clarissa stepped into the hallway and was caught in a wave of human traffic heading toward the main "healing room"—a large, pentagonalshaped room filled with pillows. She moved with them into the room and sat on the floor nearest the doorway, figuring she could make an escape halfway through the midmorning meditation. Gray Beard stood in the front of the room and banged a large gong and they all sat there in silence while Clarissa concentrated on when she could sneak out and how to keep from making embarrassing gastrointestinal utterances.

Five minutes in (hard to tell, as there were no clocks and watches were discouraged), the door burst open and Aaron was standing there, breathing as though he'd just run a marathon.

Pseudo Aaron, that is.

"Clarissa!" he said, "Jen told me where you were. I can explain everything." He started to walk over to her, trying to maneuver through the sea of pillows and people.

Gray Beard shot up and waved his hands, and Pseudo Aaron waved back, in greeting.

Clarissa, stunned, stood, teetering, and tried to answer him without talking.

"I know you don't want to talk to me," Pseudo Aaron said. "I know you think I lied to you, well, okay, I did lie to you, but we're splitting hairs here."

Gray Beard's face was red; the silent campers were in a silent seethe.

"We can't go on like this forever," Pseudo Aaron said, as Clarissa gestured for him to shut up. "Clarissa, I demand that you talk to me!"

Gray Beard went over to Pseudo Aaron and tried to escort him out by the elbow.

Big mistake.

Pseudo Aaron pushed his way back in. "I have a right to be here—that's my baby!" he said, as Gray Beard started to wrestle him away.

"That is not your baby," someone else at the door said. "Clarissa, love, are you all right? Suzee told me this lunatic was going to harm you." Simon was dressed like he was attending Wimbledon. "She gave me directions to this place, she said it was a spa, is this a spa? People don't look very happy here. Do they have shiatsu?"

"What is he doing here?" Pseudo Aaron demanded.

Clarissa didn't answer. She didn't know what to say; she was mesmerized at the train wreck that was unfolding in front of her, and also, she was at silent camp.

"I have every right to be here," Simon said. "I am the father of her child."

And that's when Pseudo Aaron lunged at Simon, and Simon jumped to the right, so Pseudo Aaron landed on a Silent Camper, a middle-aged woman who, as it turned out, had quite the left hook. She punched Pseudo Aaron in the face as Simon took the opportunity to jump on his back.

And that's pretty much when, as they say, all hell broke loose—pillows flying, Silent Campers jumping in the melee—and the only ones yelling, still, were Simon and Pseudo Aaron.

Clarissa watched, debating whether they were fighting over her or their own pride. Either way, she and her little package weren't going to stick around for the outcome.

As Pseudo Aaron grabbed Simon and spun him like a white-crew-socked top, Clarissa made her escape.

Clarissa ran out the main entrance and over to the spot where she had thrown her luggage. And heard a loud grunting sound, like a horny baboon on the Nature Channel. She looked up to see Zoë, staring down from the second story, her face a *TV Guide*–worthy question mark.

Clarissa sighed, and made a gesture with her thumb. "I'm eighty-sixing this asylum," she said, without saying the words.

Zoë put her hands up in a frantic gesture; Clarissa thought she was going to try to "talk" her out of going, and stood there, frozen in her curiosity to find out how Zoë, her new best friend, would attempt this feat without speech, and then worried that her new best friend would snitch on her and Clarissa wouldn't see red meat again for days.

As Clarissa pondered the implications of half a week of soy sausage, she heard a commotion—and wondered if the fighting had spilled outside. A car had swerved into the parking lot and was expelling its passengers without having bothered to stop. They looked, at first glance, to be armed terrorists hoisting Kalashnikovs, and at second glance to be photographers with cameras that had zoom lenses the size of compact cars.

Clarissa looked up at Zoë's window and realized what had happened: Zoë, like Clarissa, had been ratted out.

Clarissa ran to Gravy's car, passing the photographers as they ran in the opposite direction—big men with mincing, careful steps, hugging their camera equipment against their bodies like newborns—started it up, and raced around to the front of the monastery, where she knew Zoë would be rushing out, unaware and defenseless.

She circled the front of the parking lot as fast as she could with all four wheels on asphalt; Zoë ran out alone, toting a piece of luggage so unencumbered by design it must have been very expensive. Clarissa braked right in front of her. "Hurry!" Clarissa yelled, thrusting the door open. "They're onto you!"

Zoë looked at her, concerned, her foot caught midstep. Clarissa could feel her hesitation, understood the origin. "Photographers!" she yelled, explaining her morbid exuberance. "I saw them heading toward the entrance!"

Zoë, to Clarissa's surprise, did not run to the car. She looked around, with a hand over her unfreckled face to shield it from the sun. She was curious, unafraid.

"Oh, well," she said, and opened the back door to put her luggage in. "I guess I just missed them."

Zoë and Clarissa were sitting outside a McDonald's halfway between Ojai and Los Angeles surrounded by small children and blue-collar mothers—and no one recognized Zoë. Clarissa surmised it was because the moms were too tired and Zoë was the type of movie star who'd never had a hit.

"I'm sorry about you and . . ." Clarissa had forgotten his name. She thought of the ax-head actor, interchangeable with any number of young, arrogant, future E! channel–exposé types.

"I thought it might help if the photographers caught me on film and he could see how sad I was," Zoë said, eating Clarissa's French fries and a Big Mac. Clarissa noticed that Zoë ate like a twelve-year-old boy; she wished she could hate her as much as she did when they hadn't bonded like sisters.

"You can do better," Clarissa said. "I have to believe that, because if you can't, nobody can."

Zoë just nodded, as though the act were a physical feat. She reached over to Clarissa's hand. "No ring?" she asked.

"Long story," Clarissa replied. "Okay, I meet this guy, we get married, I get pregnant, we separate, I find out he's not even who he says he is, I get a job at *Climate* doing dish, I'm really good but I get fired, also a long story, and then I end up at this retreat with my best friend, and while my soon-to-be ex-husband who I still like even though I'm mad at him and don't know his real name, and my ex-boyfriend who's a catch but a commitophobe, are engaged in a silent pillow fight, I steal her car and escape with Zoë Monroe."

Zoë looked at her for a second, then started laughing.

Clarissa shrugged, enjoying the wind chime quality of her new best friend's laughter. Zoë looked at her watch (Cartier, platinum tank, leather band) and crushed her perfect eyebrows into a frown. "I've got Yun at 4:30."

"Yun?"

"The best waxer in L.A.—he's a magician."

They picked up their trays, vestiges of their semi–Happy Meals, and headed over to the trash bins.

"Hey," Clarissa said, as they walked out, "you want to come to my baby shower?"

Twenty-seven

The Baby Shower from Hell

One o'clock in the afternoon on a bright southern California Sunday, an hour into Clarissa's baby shower (the first ever for a member), and the Star Chamber was still arguing over the invitations.

"Who got conned into picking these?" Polo said. "They're so Laura Ashley, 1982."

"I designed them myself," Jen said, looking at the white invite with the fancy lettering and lace borders.

"If you didn't like them, Polio, you should have said something at the first meeting," Gravy said. "Where's Evil?"

"She said she'd be late, she's got a surprise," Jen said.

"Polo's too busy screwing to concentrate on invites," Clarissa said. She looked over at the four tables, which seated six each; she noticed that several women were checking their table seatings. She saw one woman, whom she recognized as a distant (but rich) cousin, pick up her name card and switch it onto another table.

"You got that right. I'm single-parked, double-parked, and triple-parked," Polo agreed. "I met this new guy, nothing to look at but his diplomas and his digits."

Clarissa couldn't take her eyes off the tables. Another woman, a girl Clarissa had known and disliked as much as anyone since junior high, was moving her name around.

"If we're going to discuss love lives," Gravy said, "I'll need another." She started off in search of a mimosa, but Clarissa grabbed her arm.

"Look at this, look what's happening."

The girls looked over at the tables; more women gathered. Each had shoulder-length, blow-dried hair by Melina, thighs by the Zone, eyebrows by Anastasia or Faith, laser by Lancer. Though they ranged in age from twenty-five to fifty there was no discernible difference in their manicured facades. And, like a Balanchine performance gone mad, each woman was picking up her name card when she thought no one was looking and exchanging it for another at a different table. Misty Anderson (thirty-five, pregnant for four years straight, attorney husband cheats with her pregnancy yoga instructor) was trading her card with Tabitha Yancy (twenty-nine, single, TV agent, angling for engagement to short, angry studio executive); Eve Smooty (forty, blonde, pig nose, MWC but screws anything not bolted down) placed her name card, inexplicably, next to Gravy's seat.

"What is she doing? I hate that woman. She makes me talk about my dad every time I see her," Gravy said. "Major cuntastrophe."

"Someone got the place settings wrong," Polo said. "No one likes to be seated next to someone they hate."

"All the best people hate everybody," Clarissa offered.

"I went over these place settings eighty times," Jen said. "I spent nights and weekends on those place settings."

More women were gathering at the tables, looking for their names, and rearranging accordingly.

"Screw it," Clarissa finally said. "I don't care who sits next to me, I'm . . ."

"Starving?" the Star Chamber submitted.

Clarissa and the Star Chamber split up, one at each table, and quickly realized the name card antics had not worked—the cards wound up in the exact same spots as they started, and everyone seemed satisfied.

Twenty minutes later Clarissa was eating a tiny waffle along with mini–bacon strips (minifood for a minibaby, get it?) and trying to figure how to finagle about, oh, a dozen more out of the chintzy waiter, when Evil Suzee dropped in, carrying a Diaper Genie.

"Doll!" Suzee said. "Sorry I'm late, I am just crazy busy!"

"Hi, Evil," Clarissa said. "There might be some toadstools left; go check in the kitchen."

"I brought the game!" Suzee said.

"Game? What game?" Clarissa said, looking over at Jen, who was deep in conversation with one of the blow-dried, freeze-dried guests. "I specifically said no games."

"You weren't specific. Besides, it's just a little crossword puzzle, took me forever to figure it out," Suzee said, starting to pass out pages to each of the women.

"A crossword puzzle?" Clarissa asked.

"It's got the name of every one of your boyfriends, dating back to preschool," Suzee said. "First table that fills it out correctly wins a vanilla-scented votive candle!"

"Gravy!" Clarissa shouted. "Did you okay this?"

"Not guilty," Gravy said, as Clarissa waved the paper at her. Gravy waved her empty mimosa glass back.

"What's the worry? It's all in good fun," Suzee said. "Although it might take us a while to figure out. There were so many, many . . . many . . ."

Clarissa blocked Suzee out and peered over at Jen, who was now talking on her cell phone and heading into the living room. Polo was having a sneezing attack; she looked over at Clarissa and mouthed the words "hay fever."

Clarissa placed her head on her hands and wished for sleep as she listened to the women around her laughing and calling out the names of her old boyfriends, some of whom she couldn't remember and most of whom she had tried to forget. She remained in this semicomatose state until she realized she was hungry again, and not for tiny food. She shifted her chair out to head into the kitchen, and she was bumped from behind.

She looked up to see Pseudo Aaron, clean and buffed (even with the shiner), holding a gift. Jen was standing next to him, a hopeful look on her ever hopeful face. "Look who's here?" she said. "Isn't this nice?"

"Nice? *Nice?*" Clarissa said. She looked around. The eyes of twenty-three women and two waiters with attitude were glued to her. "Kitchen! *Now!*"

And Clarissa got up (well, almost got up, with Pseudo Aaron and Jen's help), and Gravy, Polo, and, finally, a skipping Suzee, followed them into the kitchen.

* * *

"Is this some sort of plan to humiliate me?" Clarissa asked, humiliating herself further by stuffing tiny sausages from a frying pan into her mouth.

"How could I have not thought of this! It's geeenius!" Suzee exclaimed.

"I didn't know about him coming here," Gravy said, sticking her thumb in Pseudo Aaron's direction. She wore one of her new designer thumb rings, a heavy silver band with a mathematical equation etched onto it. The ring was bulky, impractical, and unattractive, and would be a huge seller.

"Neither did I," Polo said.

"I only wish I'd planned it!" Suzee said.

"Stick it, Evil," Clarissa said. "Jen? Did you know Pseudo Aaron was going to show up and ruin my wonderful day?"

"May I say something here?" Pseudo Aaron said. "Since this does concern me."

"Oh, don't start with the concern, Mister fake-Aaron, bring-a-perfect-girl-to-a-party-to-make-your-wife-feel-bad," Gravy said.

"First of all," Pseudo Aaron said, "that girl is a friend of Aaron's."

But Clarissa wasn't paying attention to Pseudo Aaron—her focus was on Gravy.

"What do you mean, 'perfect girl,' Gravy?" Clarissa said. "You thought she was perfect?"

"Well, you said it first . . ."

"I have the right to call her perfect, you don't. It's like, if I had a nose like Suzee's old one, I wouldn't want someone else to point it out."

"Well, I just know I didn't have anything to do with this," Polo said.

"Of course you didn't. You're too busy worrying about getting laid." This, surprisingly, from Jen.

"What?" Polo said.

"What?" Gravy said.

"I just wanted to drop off a gift, Clarissa," Pseudo Aaron said. "I just want to do the right thing."

"Right thing? What's this 'right thing' bullshit?" Gravy said. "We don't even know who you are!"

"Clarissa and I will discuss that matter—it's our relationship, not yours," Pseudo Aaron pointed out.

"Clarissa's my best friend," Gravy said.

"I thought I was your best friend," Polo said.

"She tells that to everyone," Jen said.

"What?" Gravy said. "Is it Jump on Gravy Day? Did I miss the CNN Special News Report?"

"No one's jumping on you," Clarissa said.

"Not for months, baby," Polo said, her speech as languid as her form.

"This is why men and women cannot live together," Pseudo Aaron offered. "Does anyone have a cigarette? I'm going outside."

"You are a total bitch," Gravy said to Polo.

"I learned at the foot of the expert," Polo said.

"That's not fair, Polo," Jen said. "Gravy may be a bitch, but she's our bitch."

And then there was no turning back. Gravy was arguing with Polo, who was arguing with Jen, who in turn was arguing with Gravy. Clarissa stood with greasy fingers and puffy ankles and tried to break up the ensuing melee while Suzee sat comfortably on the chopping block in the middle of the kitchen and watched with a satisfied expression on her face and drank leftover champagne and Pseudo Aaron threw up his hands and said, "I give up!" and gave new meaning to the overused filmic term "stormed out."

A half moment later, Polo or somebody said, "I never want to see you again," to which Gravy or someone else said, "I never want to see any of you again," and Clarissa begged Jen to reason with them but she had had her fill as well, and soon enough, Clarissa was left alone with Suzee, who was sipping her leftovers and swinging her skinny legs and wiggling her skinny eyebrows as far as she could, given the botox.

"Do you want to open the gifts?" Suzee said.

"Clarissa, baby," Simon walked in, squeezing through the kitchen door with an enormous yellow duck. *What was it,* Clarissa thought, *with men and stuffed animals?* "I hope I didn't miss anything."

Suzee took one serpentine look at Simon, wriggled off the chopping block, snaked her arm around his waist and maneuvered him toward the patio. "Where should I begin?" were the last words Clarissa heard from Evil Suzee as she sank to the floor, all 167 (170) pregnant pounds of her.

After a moment of intense self-pity she looked up at the kitchen counter. There was the gift that Pseudo Aaron had left.

Clarissa stood, which took some time, and walked over. The present was wrapped carefully. It was a flat package, from the weight of it, a picture frame. Clarissa smirked as she began to open it, pulling at the lilac tissue paper—a picture frame from her baby's father. *How professional,* she thought.

And then, there it was: the painting. The watercolor that had been auctioned off at the last horrible charity event. The one she had wanted, the one that Genuine Aaron had won.

"Sailboats at Dusk" was hers.

Clarissa set it down on the counter and stared at it for a long time, this simple watercolor that she somehow fancied, and wondered at how different her life had become in the last year. And she thought about who she was when she had started out, and wondered at who she was to become.

And then she ate a plate of very small blueberry muffins.

Twenty-eight

Birth of a . . . Well, What Is It?

Teddy's big day in court came and went with nary a ripple—except for the fact that he was sentenced to six months in federal prison. By sheer luck he was ordered to start his sentence in a week, so he was able to attend the Junior Angels Gala at the Stardust Palladium in downtown Hollywood with his daughter to watch his ex-wife dress up in tights and a top hat and perform with twenty other senior citizens seemingly unending tap dance numbers to showtunes that were old when they were new.

"It could've been worse," Teddy said, as he drove Clarissa down Hollywood Boulevard toward the venue. "Thank God for Aaron. That lawyer he got me, the man's a goddamned human jackknife."

Clarissa rearranged her seatbelt so it rested underneath her huge belly. An elbow or a knee was jutting out under her belly button. She rubbed the protrusion and shifted her hips. She hadn't yet told her father that Aaron wasn't Aaron—his life seem complicated enough, already.

"Either way, it won't be as long as this show."

"Clarissa. That's enough. You have to be supportive of your mother."

"I think it's plenty supportive that I'm showing up to this thing."

"She's been taking care of you all these months. Show her some respect," Teddy said. He glanced over at her.

"What's gotten into you?" Clarissa asked. She looked at her father; his face was serious.

"What's gotten into me?" Teddy shook his head. "Clarissa, I'm a sixty-year-old man who's going to prison for the second time in his life. I have an ex-wife I cheated on for half our marriage and a daughter who views me as little more than a nuisance, except when she wants money."

"And whose fault is that?" Clarissa asked.

"Mine, Clarissa," he said. "It's my fault."

"You don't mean that. I know you, Teddy."

"You don't have to believe me, Clarissa," Teddy replied. "I just think you should treat your mother a little better, that's all."

Clarissa sank down in her seat and looked out the window: here she was, a twenty-nine (thirty-two)-year-old woman who was about to pop out a kid, and suddenly she felt very much like a punk twelve-year-old who's been reprimanded by a parent.

"You're sulking," Teddy said.

"I'm not sulking," Clarissa said, while she continued to sulk. Teddy reached over and grabbed her lower lip, like he used to do when she was a child.

"What's that?" he said.

"I not sulting!" she sulked.

The Junior Angels show was a mélange of red lips and powdery faces and legs that looked twenty-five years old but had been around for at least fifty. When Clarissa's mother came out, all five feet of her, Teddy yelled like a high school sophomore on his maiden trip to Hooters. Clarissa looked over at her father, clapping and whistling, his eyes lit up without benefit of loads of alcohol, and realized that Teddy loved her mother, even after they had put each other through every natural disaster possible. He still loved her.

Clarissa wondered what made her feel worse: that her mother and her friends made her look like a bowl of mashed potatoes or that her parents, who had driven her and each other crazy for so many years, still had the hots for each other. It was enough to drive a perfectly sane person to bed for a week.

In the middle of the big patriotic number, where all the gals wore red, white, and blue hats and sequins and ribbons and, incidentally, enough perfume to burn the hair off one's body, Clarissa felt her stomach tighten and motioned to Teddy. "I'm heading to the bathroom," she said. "I've got to walk around; it's Braxton-Hicks." Clarissa was referring to the false contractions that had kept her in a constant freak-out zone for the last week. Teddy nodded sympathetically. "I know, my back is killing me, too." Clarissa looked at him and shook her head and left the table, careful not to step on anything with a heartbeat.

The trip to the bathroom offered no respite from her false contractions, sadly, and Clarissa started thinking about other possibilities, like, say, *real labor.*

"It's not labor," she said, from inside the stall, on her cell phone to Gravy. Even though they were not speaking, they continued to talk every day.

"How do you know it's not labor? Have you ever been in labor?" Gravy said.

"Not recently," Clarissa groaned. She cradled her stomach as it tightened again.

"How close together are your contractions?"

"They're not contractions, you idiot!" Clarissa screamed from the bathroom stall. "They're Braxton-Hicks!"

"Are you done in there?" someone asked. "There's a line out here."

"Christ," Clarissa said. "I'll call you back."

She got up and exited the stall; a long line had formed for the two bathroom stalls that constituted the women's restroom for the five-hundred-seat theater. Women stared at her with arms crossed over their grandmotherly bosoms.

"You okay, honey?" one of the women, with a snake brooch pinned to her chest, asked.

"It's nothing, just a little, I don't know, like—" Clarissa made a squeezing motion with her hands, then suddenly noticed the line of women looking at Clarissa's shoes. She followed their curious gazes—and realized she had peed on the floor of the bathroom of the Stardust Palladium.

Would small, needling humiliations never cease?

"Someone get a doctor!" she heard a woman with a warbly voice cry.

"I'm fine," Clarissa said, with some annoyance. "I'm fine."

"Sit down, dear," the woman with the snake told Clarissa, as she put a surprisingly strong arm around what once was her waist. "Your water just broke."

Clarissa looked into the woman's blue, marbled eyes which she now, looking at them closely and from a vantage point of extreme panic, regarded as beautiful, and nausea enveloped her body from her stumplike, swollen ankles to the top of her full head of bountiful pregnancy hair.

And she sank to the floor like an anchor off a cruise ship docking at Mazatlán.

"Hold on, Babycakes!" Teddy yelled, as he sat next to her in the back of the ambulance.

"Dad, I'm in labor, I'm not deaf!" Clarissa yelled back. Her mother sat across from her, still in her tights and red, white, and blue sash, holding her hand and yelling at the driver in Spanish to go faster.

"OOOOHHHSHIT!" Clarissa yelled. "That one hurt! That one hurt!"

"It's okay, baby, is okay," her mother said, as she stroked Clarissa's forehead. "The contractions only last a little while."

"Aaaaaarrrrrgggghhhh!" Clarissa replied, though she had never used the term "argh" previously in her life. And then she thought about Gravy and the rest of the Star Chamber.

"Mommy, my phone." Clarissa grabbed at her purse.

"You want to call someone now?"

"Phone!"

Her mother looked through her purse. She found Clarissa's Nokia, and Clarissa grabbed it and pressed redial and waited. "Gravy!" she said, when Gravy answered, "I'm having this baby right now and I swear to God if you and the rest of the team don't make up and get here quick, not only will I rescind my offer to make you the godmothers, but I will never tell you the name of the man who asked about you the other night who is now officially divorced!"

And then she yelled, once more, a short, hoarse yell, like a cough, and threw the phone to her father, who caught it, and issued instructions to Gravy on where to meet them.

The ambulance sped into the Cedars Sinai emergency room driveway, and Clarissa was taken out of the back by a pair of hunky paramedics, and she tried to implant their names, displayed on their name tags, into her brain for future reference (the well-established and respected Hero Fuck) before she went into a complete, labor-induced meltdown.

Her screams could be heard, as legend tells the tale, from Santa Monica to Long Beach.

"You're only at two, Clarissa," Dr. Catz told her. His eyes twinkled.

"Two centimeters?" Clarissa moaned, "That's *it*? I was over one centimeter dilated a month ago."

"I have to wait to give you an epidural until you're at least a four," Dr. Catz said.

"Let me tell you something, Doctor," Clarissa grabbed his collar. "When you go into labor, you can wait for four. I want that fucking pain killer *now*!"

Dr. Catz calmly untangled himself from Clarissa's grip with what appeared to be a practiced, Ninja-level move.

"I'll be back," he said, smiling. And he walked out of the room. Rather quickly.

"Malpractice!" Clarissa yelled after him. She turned to her mother. "Is it too late to fire him?" she demanded. And then she grabbed her mother's tiny birdlike hand and screamed again. Teddy suddenly stood up and followed the doctor out of the room, "Videotape!" he said, waving his hands in the air. "I'll be right back!"

Clarissa looked at her mother, her stage makeup sinking into the soft folds of her skin. "You'll destroy the tape, right, Mom?" Clarissa said. Her mother smiled and nodded.

"Good," Clarissa said.

Her mother sat there and held her hand. Neither of them, for the first time in months, spoke.

"This is so hard," Clarissa said, looking up at the pocked ceiling.

"I know, my daughter," her mother said. "But just wait until it becomes a teenager."

Let's talk about the four stages of labor. The early phase of the first stage is where light contractions start, say twenty minutes apart, dilating the cervix from one to four centimeters. For Clarissa, the first stage was fainting in the bathroom in front of a group of strangers. The active phase of the first stage is when labor becomes more intense, and the cervix dilates from four to eight centimeters. For Clarissa, the active phase was broken up into two parts: a. lunging at Dr. Catz's carotid artery with a bent straw until he agreed that three centimeters was plenty dilation enough to warrant an epidural; and b. dishing dirt with the Star Chamber, who arrived en force, luckily, five minutes after the epidural was administered. The transition phase of the first stage was watching a *Facts of Life* rerun with her girls and debating which child star on that show would most likely be performing in soft-core porn today. At the second stage, which involves the birth of the baby, Clarissa was so numb from the epidural her game of Celebrity with the girls had to be interrupted just as she was guessing that Matt Perry was the "Friend" who had had a chin job to be told that her baby was about to emerge from her vagina.

It was then that she noticed that Dr. Catz was no longer wearing his wedding ring.

"Push, Clarissa!" Dr. Catz said.

"I'm pushing!" she yelled back.

"You're not pushing. *Push!*" he yelled.

"*Push,* Babycakes!"

Clarissa realized her father was in the room. With a video camera.

"*Dad!* Get *out of here!*"

"Push, Clareesa!" her mom yelled.

And then everyone was yelling *"push!"*—Gravy, Jennifer, Polo, even Suzee, who had come late but fashionably dressed with the fall season's newest over-the-knee alligator-skin boot.

Clarissa screamed one last time and pushed, though she could barely feel anything below her belly button, but she pushed as though the fate of the nation depended on it, or at least a few people in the room, and out he came.

Out came a baby boy.

"He's a boy!" Dr. Catz yelled.

"A boy! I got a boy!" her father yelled. "Good going, Babycakes!"

Her mother was smiling and teary-eyed and mute. The girls were squealing. "He's totally hung!" Gravy said. "Look at the size of those balls!" Polo said. Jennifer just cried.

"A boy?" Clarissa said. "Are you sure?"

"Well, I'm pretty sure," Dr. Catz said. "He's got all the equipment, as your friends just testified." And he put the newly wrapped baby on her chest. "You want him on your breast?" a nurse asked.

Clarissa surprised herself by nodding. She had not planned on breast-feeding but suddenly found her body throbbing, wanting, needing to feed her baby. *What am I going to do with a boy?* she suddenly thought.

"Can I please . . . be alone?" Clarissa said, her voice light and scratchy. She realized she was very thirsty. No one heard her over the fray as they congratulated themselves on the new baby. "I'd like to be alone with my son," Clarissa said, stronger now.

Dr. Catz looked over at her. "Okay, everyone, let's leave our new mother alone. Seems she'd like to get acquainted with somebody special."

He winked at her and Clarissa wondered about the wedding ring again. But then, she just thought that he probably took it off when assisting in births. After all, who'd want placenta bits all over their wedding band?

Her mother kissed her and kissed the top of her baby's head and was the last to leave.

And Clarissa was alone, as the baby nuzzled his way across her huge, momentous breasts and began to suckle.

"I see," Clarissa said. "So this is what it is."

The baby made little piglet sounds as he ate his first hot meal outside the womb.

"Who are you?" Clarissa asked, looking at this boy. She realized she hadn't thought up a name for a boy; only girls' names had entered her repertoire, she was so convinced she was carrying a girl. Clarissa ran down a list of names in her head and realized they were all ex-boyfriend names. She even thought of naming him after her father until she remembered that in Jewish tradition one names a child after a dead relative. Then she thought that could be arranged.

She thought about naming him after Pseudo Aaron. However, she *didn't even know his name.*

"Well, shit," she said to the fuzzy little head. "We'll just wait and see who you are, okay?" she told the tiny, 7.5-pound fleshy mound. He squealed and shifted and Clarissa took this as agreement and smiled for the first time since the birth. They were already getting along.

* * *

"So, who's divorced?" Gravy wanted to know. She was holding Baby X, as he was known, rocking him in a surprisingly gentle manner.

"Tweed Man," Clarissa said, as she sucked a pink liquid through a straw. It could have been lemonade; Clarissa wasn't sure and didn't care. Gravy looked confused. "He's shaped like an eggplant and has a Texan accent and a flesh wound?" Clarissa continued.

"Oh. Ugh," Gravy replied. "N.I." Not interested.

"At that charity function—the auction one—he was there, he asked about you. Said you were . . . interesting."

"I am interesting," Gravy said. Beat. "He said I was interesting?"

"That's what he said. Can you . . . he's wrapped too tight."

"Shh. I know what I'm doing."

"He's hungry. Give him to me," Clarissa said.

"You fed him ten minutes ago."

"He likes to eat; he's my son."

Gravy made a face, then handed the baby over. Clarissa's parents had gone off to get a bite (and, per Clarissa's instructions, to bring back bulk in the way of deli food), and the other girls were out making phone calls to everyone Clarissa wanted to make jealous. Even Suzee offered to make phone calls to several of Clarissa's ex-boyfriends.

No one mentioned Pseudo Aaron; no one asked where he was. These were good friends.

Gravy pulled up a chair and watched and sighed as Clarissa fed her baby.

"I want one of those," Gravy said.

"Really huge boobs?" Clarissa asked. "You can have 'em, after he's done." Gravy went to pinch her friend, just as a voice called out . . .

"Beautiful," Pseudo Aaron said. "You look so beautiful."

He was standing in the doorway holding a hospital bouquet and a large blue teddy bear. He was dressed in a bright green shirt and a dark brown leather jacket. He looked older, more mature, and fashionable. Just looking at him made Clarissa want to dive under the bed, baby, stitches, and all.

"The sperm donor's here," Gravy announced.

"Gravy. That's your cue," Clarissa said. Gravy nodded and left the room without so much as a sneer; Clarissa was quite proud of her.

"Can I . . . ?" Pseudo Aaron asked. "I'm dying to see him."

"Let me check his schedule," Clarissa said. She lowered the blanket covering her son's head and out came a dome of fuzzy blackness.

"He looks like you," Pseudo Aaron said. "He's so beautiful. Motherhood becomes you."

"Bull-oney. He's the spitting image of you, and you know it," Clarissa said. "Just my luck, huh?" She felt naked and vulnerable and tired at the thought of conversation with Pseudo Aaron; the moment felt like the exact opposite of what she had wanted and anticipated.

"Clarissa," Pseudo Aaron said.

"Pseudo Aaron," Clarissa said. She closed her eyes as a wave of fatigue washed over her; her adrenaline was starting to wear out. She thanked God she had remembered to blow her hair dry that morning.

"What do you want?"

It was such a simple question, and Clarissa could have answered it so easily only months ago. *What do I want?* she thought, looking at Pseudo Aaron, and then at the baby. *What* do *I want?*

"I don't know," she replied. "Wait, I do know. Sleep. I want to sleep."

"We have a baby, now, Clarissa," Pseudo Aaron said. "We have to think of what's best for . . . what's his name?"

"Blank. I don't have one. As far as I can tell he doesn't need one until the fifth grade anyway."

"We've got to give the boy a name—he needs a name."

"And I suppose you have a suggestion?"

Pseudo Aaron looked at her. "James, Junior. James B. Tanner, Junior."

"That's your name?" Clarissa said. "James?"

"Yes," James said. "That's my name." He looked at her face. "What's wrong with 'James'? 'James' is a king's name."

"And the 'B' stands for?"

"Barnard."

"Next."

"What's wrong with . . ."

"Next."

"He's my son, too, you know."

"Oh, no—don't you start. After you manipulated me into marrying you under false pretenses."

"Well, now, who could do such a thing?"

"And, you hired a divorce lawyer."

"What?" James said. "I didn't hire a lawyer—I couldn't afford to hire a lawyer."

"Well, it's obvious you want a divorce."

"Who said I wanted a divorce?" James said.

"You just said it."

"I never said that," James said. "But, Clarissa, you must admit, we do have more than our share of troubles."

"I'm sorry our marriage got in the way of your dating."

"*My* dating? First of all, I wasn't dating . . . and what about that English . . . that . . . dandy . . ."

"Simon's not a fag, Aaron—James, I mean," Clarissa said. "He's a fashion-savvy heterosexual."

"Hello! Is this the right . . . room?" Simon appeared, toting a huge bouquet of balloons.

Clarissa hated balloons.

Simon could barely squeeze them through the door.

At least this aspect of her future was suddenly clear: Clarissa could never be with a man who gave her *balloons*.

"Get out," James said to Simon.

"I am not getting out. Clarissa and I are getting married; you might as well get used to it." Simon puffed his chest out. He was wearing a sweater vest, a clothing item Clarissa hadn't seen since fifth grade.

"Who's getting married?" Clarissa sat up, as though someone had put a hot iron up her ass. "And the vest, Simon . . ."

"You like? It's Fall 2002, brand new."

"That's it," James lunged at Simon, trying to grab him through the huge plumage of balloons.

"Crazy man! Crazy man!" Simon yelled as he scurried around the bed, hiding behind Clarissa.

"Simon, please get out of here!" Clarissa yelled. "I just had a baby! Don't you know birth is fucking sanctified?"

"You heard her," James said. "My wife said get out of here!"

"Now, wait a minute, Aaron/James, we haven't finished discussing . . ." Clarissa was cut off by Simon.

"She's only saying that for your benefit. I've known Clarissa forever.

I'm the one who'll stick by her no matter what, I don't care how big she is." Simon ducked as James grabbed his hair and tried to drag him out from behind the hospital bed.

"What?" Clarissa screamed. *"I just had a baby, you twit!"*

"I'm the one sticking by her!" James said. "That's my job!"

"Excuse me! Baby, mother, sacred time?!" Clarissa said. "Simon, please. Aaron/James . . . he is the father of my child. We need to be alone."

"But . . . I thought I was the baby's father."

"Simon, I told you. We never had sex that night!"

"Fine, if that's what you want to believe," Simon said, finally. "Where do you want the balloons?"

Clarissa looked at the balloons. "The children's ward is upstairs," she said.

Simon stiffened. "Well," he said, "well." And then he walked out, dragging the balloons with him, squeezing them through the doorway.

Clarissa looked down at her baby. He had slept through the whole ugly encounter; she was thankful he'd have no memory of it. James sat down, breathing heavily.

Clarissa then pinched the baby, to make sure he was still alive. "I know divorce never solved anything, James," she said. "Look at my parents. On the other hand, we may be past the point of civility. I could hate you. I could put tacks in your driveway and not think twice. I could take a crap on your dash—"

"Enough," James said. "Not in front of the child. He shouldn't be exposed to an overdose of his mother yet."

"Maybe I do hate you, but I just pushed a freakin' watermelon out of my vagina, and I'm torn from one end to the other because of his big head, and I'm high on Vicodin (thank God) and I can't think straight."

"Not my fault, Clarissa," James said. "You're the one that has a head with its own zip code."

"Climate, you mean. More current joke."

James smiled.

"Besides," Clarissa said, "you don't want a wife who'll never sleep with you again. And I am *never never ever never, ad infinitum* putting anything down there except an ice pack."

James smiled again. He stood and kissed Clarissa on the forehead and kissed the baby on the top of his fuzzy head. "I love you, little James," he said.

Clarissa slapped James' hand.

He grinned at her and got up, walking to the doorway. "I'll be back. I'm going to get you something sweet and gooey and . . ."

"Chocolatish?"

"Beyond," he said, and he walked out, blowing her a kiss at the same time.

"Fucking dimples," Clarissa said to herself. "Oops, sorry, Baby X," she corrected herself.

Then she looked for those same dimples on the baby's cheeks, and when she found them, she smiled.

She had exactly fifteen seconds of quiet time before she heard "Babycakes, guess what?!" as Teddy strode in as though he'd won the California lottery by legal means. One of his arms was wrapped around her mother's shoulder. She was looking up at him, beaming. "We're getting married!"

Clarissa closed her eyes again.

Twenty-nine

The Long, Exotic Trip

Clarissa wasn't a person who liked surprises. The unexpected held no excitement, no interest for her. And the shitty thing about an unexpected death is that it's, well, unexpected. A surprise.

Her mother died two weeks after the baby was born, before he even had a name. Clarissa had been living, still, in her mother's house; her mother had insisted that until she figured out what to do with Pseudo Aaron, Clarissa and the baby live in the house as long as she needed. So Baby X slept in a bassinet next to Clarissa, who slept in her childhood bed. And her mother cooked every day and every night, all of Clarissa's childhood favorites—which she never cooked when Clarissa was a child—and helped her diaper the baby in the middle of the night, and encouraged her daughter when her nipples were sore and the baby had gas and, somehow, seemed younger than she ever had, even when Clarissa herself was young.

In other news, Teddy had entered state prison to start his term, but after it was over, her parents were to be married again.

She had never seen her mother so happy.

There's a lot of ways to die. Most people die of natural causes, in their old beds and bodies; most deaths are noteworthy for their relative normalcy.

Clarissa's mom died on the toilet. Like Elvis, like that bloated Hollywood producer who looked like a tanned balloon, her mother expired early one morning after one too many shits. Clarissa found her leaning back against the basin as though taking a nap, a magazine (*Martha Stewart*) two inches from her outstretched hand.

Clarissa, sleep-deprived after nursing half the night, thought her mother was sleeping. Not wanting to disturb her, she went back to bed.

Until she woke up an hour later, and her mother was still there. Clarissa had screamed and almost dropped her precious bundle and slammed the bathroom door behind her and immediately called Gravy.

"My mom's dead!" Clarissa screamed.

"Holy crap, you're kidding!" Gravy said.

"Why would I kid? Why?"

"I'll be right over," Gravy said.

Gravy was over within ten minutes, Clarissa not asking how she made it so fast, being that her house was twenty minutes away. Clarissa had waited for her, sitting on the porch, holding her baby, rocking like an extra in *The Snake Pit.* She just pointed to the house. "She's in there."

Gravy went in, came out thirty seconds later. "Yeah, she's dead," Gravy said. "I'll call her doctor."

The doctor, a man with bald forearms and a high-pitched voice that made everything he said a whine, stated her death was probably due to a potassium deficiency, an electrolyte imbalance that leads to heart failure; he had been warning her about the effect of her dietary habits on her heart.

Her mother, literally, had shat herself to death. That special tea that she drank, day in and day out, had caused her heart to stop beating.

Clarissa looked at the whiny doctor and handed Baby X off to Gravy and ran into the kitchen and dumped all the tea in the cabinets into the trash can, then threw the trash can out the back door, not caring that its contents had spilled all over her mother's flower bed, because, after all, who was going to yell at her now.

Clarissa stood over the garbage and realized she had to break the news to her father, who every day, twice a day, had called, even though the lines on the "floor" were an hour long, and he, inevitably, had to wait behind someone with a drippy jheri curl or a detailed Aryan tattoo to talk to his new (old) bride, to whisper in the ear of his new grandson.

Clarissa wasn't sure how to tell him. She sat down with the Star Chamber, who had hurried, beautifully attired in all forms of black, to her side, and came up with a plan.

"Tell him straight out," Gravy said. "It's always best to be direct."

"No," Jen said. "It could kill him."

"Tell him when he gets out," Polo said. Clarissa looked at her. "So what do I do for the next six months?"

"Tell him she's taken a trip," Suzee said. "A long, exotic trip."

"Yes, yes. She wants to get her last trip in, before their wedding," Jen said. "Oh . . . where were they planning on getting married?" Jen was starting to well up again.

"The backyard," Clarissa said. Her mother's backyard was beautifully landscaped. Her mother had spent many days toiling away in the garden working off excess sexual energy.

The phone rang. 10:30, as it had every day since her father had been put in the "slammer" (his word).

"Babycakes," Teddy said, "how's my girl?"

Clarissa looked at her friends. She nodded and motioned for them to leave the room. No one budged.

"Fine," Clarissa said, still motioning for them to leave. "How's the big house?" Jen finally got up to go into the kitchen, but Gravy, Polo, and Suzee were staying put. Clarissa just glared at them.

"They got me on the run here, baby. How's my boy? He got a name yet?"

Gravy wrote the word "roommate" on a piece of paper and held it up. Clarissa stared at her.

"Who's your bunkmate, Dad?" Clarissa asked.

"I don't know. Some guy. Sad sack, big complainer. Where's my bride?"

"What's he in for?" Clarissa said. "Financial thing or something else?"

"I don't know. I think he killed somebody. Anyway, he's totally out of shape. That's his problem," Teddy said. "I got two minutes; where's my little Cuban cupcake?"

"Bolivian, Dad," Clarissa said. "Bolivian."

"I know, I know. You think I don't know? I've known that girl over half my life," Teddy said. "Where's my Alejandra?"

Clarissa took a deep breath; she looked at her friends. "Dad," she said, "I found a name for the baby. What do you think of Alejandro?" She shook her head, trying to stem the tears that were beginning to roll down her face. Gravy grabbed her around the shoulders, holding her up as she bent forward.

"Oh, that's beautiful, sweetheart," her father said, quietly. "What does your mother think of it?"

Clarissa couldn't say anything. She held the phone for a moment, aware of the time between them ticking away.

"Dad," Clarissa finally said, looking into Gravy's eyes. "Mom is . . . she's . . ."

Now Teddy took a deep breath. Clarissa could hear him catching himself, not wanting to say any words.

"I'm here," he said. "I'm here."

"She's dead," Clarissa said. "Her heart . . ."

And then Clarissa waited while her father sobbed with his whole big-shouldered, flawed being and the Star Chamber gathered around her and rocked her and listened to her father, until he told them that he had to go, and that he loved her very much, and she told him she loved him very much, and that little Alejandro would be awaiting his call, as usual, that afternoon.

Clarissa hung up and lowered her head into Gravy's lap, who stroked her hair as she cried.

"I'm not strong enough, Gravy," Clarissa said.

"You don't have to be," Gravy said. "I'll be strong for you."

Later, Clarissa pumped milk from her engorged breasts as the Star Chamber took turns holding the baby and sometimes her hand when she would break down, which, from the beginning to the end of the horrible day, occurred every five minutes.

Clarissa tried to insist on being left alone that evening, just her and Alejandro, but the Star Chamber wouldn't hear of it and insisted on spending the night, and as many nights as she needed them to, and Clarissa, in the morning, wound up waking up in her mother's bed, her mother's pillow in her arms, moist with her tears.

She didn't know how she got there.

James appeared the next morning, at the same time as her mother's newspaper. Holding a paper bag with red lettering, containing what looked like two large coffees, he walked over to Clarissa and said he loved the name Alejandro Mason, that nothing made him happier, and he insisted on taking his wife and child out to breakfast, even if she didn't want to go.

"My mother," Clarissa said to him, pulling her mother's robe tight around her body.

"I know," he said. "Let's eat. You have to eat."

"I don't want to eat," she said. "I just want to cry."

"Then I'll stay here," James said. "And cry with you."

Clarissa looked at him. *How could she trust him? How could they trust each other?*

"I liked your mother, Clarissa, very much. I'd like to mourn with you."

Clarissa took a deep breath; it felt as though it was the first time she had breathed that morning.

"I can't prevent you from spending time with the baby, but I've got too much to deal with to even begin to think about the ramifications of you standing here the morning after my mom's death," she said. "I am so far from having healed, emotionally, spiritually and physically . . . I mean, I am ripped from here to China, if you get the picture."

"I get the picture," James winced.

"Anyway, the bottom line is, I'm not ever interested in seeing or talking to or touching a man again, except for Alejandro."

"Do you want coffee or not?" he asked.

"Is that Peets?" Clarissa said, eyeing the bag.

"Yes."

She opened the door for him. But not, yet, her heart.

Thirty

The Funeral

Thirty-six hours later Clarissa heard her mother's voice throughout the entire funeral, even as the rabbi, a young woman who was hip enough to be a Star Chamber sister, asked Clarissa up to the podium to say the Kaddish, the special Jewish prayer for the deceased. With every step Clarissa heard "Those roses are too pink, an' why's she bringing flowers to a Jewish funeral anyway?" or "Oh, Clareesa, why you don't put your hair back, is more sophisticated."

But she also heard, as she stood, facing the standing-room-only crowd of sad but carefully plucked, tucked, and sucked faces, "Nice turnout, eh?" and "My beautiful grandson, look at heem, he has my eyes. He has my mother's eyes."

And then the rabbi reached over to tear Clarissa's dress at the right shoulder, and Clarissa grabbed her hand, and the rabbi explained that this was tradition, the tearing of the Kria, and Clarissa hissed that she could shove that tradition somewhere deep inside those robes, and the rabbi eventually dropped the whole concept and gave Clarissa the floor.

Teddy and Clarissa had decided to bury Alejandra Vera de la Cortes Alpert at Mt. Sinai Cemetery, the nicest Jewish cemetery they could find, situated in Beverly Hills Adjacent, within shopping distance of Rodeo Drive and eating distance of Spago Beverly Hills.

Her mother would have been very pleased.

Clarissa made it through the Kaddish (which she, inadvertently, shortened by half) and stepped down and took her place next to Gravy, where they had a short and mild tug-of-war over Alejandro, which his mother won.

As Clarissa cooed, quieting the baby, she turned her head, her eyes dashing over faces, finally resting on the one she was hoping to find. James was here; he was in the back, standing against the large double doors. He was wearing a yarmulke, which made him look like a very hot, very goishe rabbinical student. Clarissa felt very Barbra Streisand within arm's length of cutie Mandy Patinkin. At her own mother's funeral she was experiencing the hots for her (soon-to-be) ex-husband. Her mother noticed: "See, my son-in-law, he shows up, but where is your Simon friend, eh?"

Clarissa hated when her mother said "eh." But she did have a point—Simon was nowhere to be seen.

Teddy gave the eulogy; he allowed Rabbi Pearl to tear his black Carroll and Company suit; *but after all,* Clarissa thought, *it was at least ten years old.* Teddy had been given twelve hours off, and was to be escorted by a parole officer to make certain he didn't run off to Mexico or Canada, which is preposterous, because, as anyone who knew Teddy could tell you, he'd never go anywhere that didn't have wall-to-wall sushi restaurants and golf shops.

He walked up to the podium, wearing a yarmulke stuck on his head with what appeared to be paper clips. Clarissa had never seen him wear one, and it gave him an air of piety and ridiculousness in equal measure that suited him well.

"Alejandra Vera de la Cortes Alpert," Teddy said. "A lot of names for a lot of woman."

Clarissa almost choked. Gravy squeezed her elbow.

"She was a wife, my wife, off and on, as most of you know, for twenty-four years," Teddy continued. "She was a mother. She was, as of three weeks ago, a grandmother. She was a good friend. An athlete. A dancer. A volunteer. But she was not just the sum of all these parts. Alejandra was more, much more than that."

Clarissa breathed, relieved. Alejandro squirmed.

"I heard this woman, over thirty years ago," Teddy continued, "before I even saw her. She was a little thing, barely five feet, and so she always wore these incredibly high heels, and I mean they were spiked and shiny, and she loved them. And I'm sitting in a restaurant, in the middle of the city, and I hear this tap, tap, tap, and it's the sexiest sound

I've ever heard before or since, just this fast, tap, tap, tap, and I'm thinking, who does that sound belong to, because I want some of that."

Clarissa stiffened slightly.

"And I turn around, and there's this . . . in movies, they talk about beauty and grace and . . . this . . . this was a vision. Like staring at the sun, I could barely look at her face. From her toes to the top of her head, she was perfection. But you know, it's not about the looks part, in the end, I mean, in the beginning it is, of course."

This got a few laughs. Teddy was doing just fine.

"It went beyond looks. She was kind. I could tell she was kind. Her smile was big and her eyes were bright. She felt to me, before I even knew the name Alejandra Vera de la Cortes, she felt to me like a soft, warm breeze."

By this time, half of the room was in tears, the other half biting their lips and the inside of their cheeks to resist their inevitable onslaught.

"I said to my friend, a business associate," Teddy continued. "I said, that is the closest facsimile to heaven on earth I have ever seen, and if I'm lucky enough to get her number, I'm going to make her marry me." He paused. "I didn't get her number, but I got her brother's number, and eventually, I did get her to marry me."

He took another breath.

"My wife was always a good woman to me, but sometimes I was not a good man to her. I was lucky enough, recently, to ask her forgiveness, and she forgave me." Teddy barely got it out. "I was lucky enough, recently, to ask for a second chance with my sweetheart, so that we could live the rest of our days together. And she said yes."

And now, Teddy started to cry. Clarissa sat straight up, watching her father, this strong male figure, as he melted into a sad little boy. She was reminded of childhood photographs of her father, in dress shorts and shiny shoes, his mother's arm protective around his shoulders.

"I am a lucky man, but only because she was here," Teddy said. "But you're still here, Alejandra, you're still here, always here," he rubbed his chest, "always in my heart."

Clarissa handed Alejandro off to Gravy and ran up to the podium and wrapped herself around the crouching figure that was her father, and they both cried, for her mother, his wife, themselves.

"Not a dry eye in the house," Gravy said later, in the black stretch limo that escorted them home, "except for that cunt Suzee, and who cares about her. Did you see what she was wearing?"

Clarissa had looked out the window and watched in awe at the typical sunny California day evolving in disregard to her mother's passing. "Life goes on," she said to Gravy. "And I don't want it to." Gravy just nodded and held her hand.

Clarissa sighed and thought of James. She wondered about the eulogy he would say for her, what words he would choose—what he would say—what he wouldn't say.

Sadly, Clarissa realized her own husband probably didn't know her well enough to say her eulogy.

After the funeral the large group of people who bid her mother goodbye at the funeral home came to what was now Clarissa's house in the lower flats of Beverly Hills to help her sit shiva. Clarissa thought of the various places her family had lived as she was growing up, from a one-bedroom apartment she and her mother shared a half-block from the freeway in Santa Monica after her father went to prison (the first time) to the mansionette he bought on Bedford with an interior straight out of Ali Baba two years after he was out (the first time) to this modest, neat, Spanish-style bungalow. Clarissa had found much about this house to be ashamed of when she was growing up: the slight frame; the compact lawn; the reedlike lap pool that screamed "We can't afford a real swimming pool." All of Clarissa's friends had lived in better, bigger houses; they had real pools, some with diving boards (which they would use—cannonballs when younger; drunk and halfhearted dives as they aged); her friends and associates—even her enemies—had had everything she wanted and felt she deserved, and Clarissa had sworn, as a young girl, that one day she would get everything—*everything*. Her list grew as she grew. At age eight, she wanted Gravy's canopy bed, her pink carpeting with its thick tufts of wormlike fabric, and those shoes; at eleven, she wanted tennis lessons, like Polo complained about, from the pro every teenaged girl and every mother had a crush on, and those shoes; at thirteen, it was stereo equipment that would cover half a wall, along with those shoes; at thirty-two (copping to her age, but only in the privacy of her own mind), Clarissa wanted nothing but her mother back.

And maybe those shoes, Clarissa thought, looking over at Polo, who was wearing black sling-backs that were, at once, Hepburnesque with a peppery touch of Frederick's of Hollywood thrown in.

Clarissa sat back on her mother's paisley couch and placed her hands on her belly, which had, with the help of the stress of her mother's death and marathon breast-feeding, retreated down to a reasonable size.

And she took a breath.

Thirty-one

The Wedding

My God, the wedding was beautiful. On the same day, in the same setting that Alejandra de la Cortes Alpert was to remarry her husband, Theodore Alpert, Jennifer Ellenbach took her gardener, Pablo Ramirez, as her lawful wedded husband.

And Clarissa could not have been happier.

Her mother's garden had been tended beautifully by Pablo for the last months after her mother's death—and, under his mindful tutelage, it was as though spring had burst forth with a vengeance. Clarissa could see her mother in every color—in the orange poppies, the yellow buttercups, the lavender daisies.

Jen had approached Clarissa about her wedding about a month beforehand; her parents didn't approve of her choice of fiancé; they were still hoping for that doctor, that lawyer, shit, that high school teacher. But a gardener? No, uh-uh. So she asked Clarissa if she could be married in her mother's backyard (and Clarissa still felt it was her mother's, after all—it was always her mother's) and, well, how could Clarissa turn her down?

And so Pablo's family came, and came, and came (we're talking a *big* family), and Jen's friends were out in full force, and there had never been, in Clarissa's experience, a happier yet more wistful day. Because it only served to remind her that she and James were never going to be together; that though she had his child, she did not have his love. James loved the baby, she could tell that. He would come over and hold him (the wrong way), and talk to him (inappropriately) about trucks and motorcycles, and change his diaper (backward), and Clarissa would avoid contact. She would be polite and invisible. She had experienced birth and death in one fell swoop, and so she steeled herself against heartbreak. She became something she'd never mastered: aloof.

Jen threw the bouquet, and Clarissa flashed on the fact that only a year before Jen had caught Clarissa's bouquet. Clarissa stood out during this part of the ceremony; after all, she was still, officially, married.

She stood to the side, holding the baby. She watched how high Gravy (who now insisted on being called Alex) leaped—what was it called? A vertical leap. Alex could've been called up by the pros, it was that high.

Alex caught the bouquet and waved it at the man she had brought with her to the wedding—Tweed Man, he of the freckled forehead and lust for Four Seasons bath towels. Oh, and Digital Annex Computers, the second largest manufacturer of computer parts in the *universe*.

Polo was, as usual, surrounded by a flock of men, all ages, sizes, breeds, colors, religions; she would always be surrounded by men; they found light in her reflection—who didn't? But also there was Dr. Catz, whose wedding ring, it turned out, was not lost somewhere in Clarissa's uterus, but had been removed permanently by his soon-to-be-ex.

And we all know how Polo feels about doctors.

Suzee was there, too, with Simon, who finally accepted, after seeing Alejandro, who looked like James Mini-me, that he was not his father. Clarissa was surprised at her surprise at how well Evil and Simon fit together: Simon was a self-indulgent pain in the ass, and so was Suzee. Also, they were both as thin as whippets and in constant twitch mode.

And Clarissa was with Alejandro, holding him in her arms, the love of her life, her man, and as long as she was . . .

James was walking into the backyard. Clarissa could feel her face flush starting somewhere around her kneecaps.

She decided to buck up and show him she wasn't embarrassed to be a single mom, that she wasn't embarrassed about the extra ten (fifteen) pounds, nor about the fact that she'd forgotten how to put on mascara, that her shoes were rated either comfortable or uncomfortable, that the clothes she wore yesterday were the ones she wore today. She was a new mom, after all. And she was proud, damn it, she was pr—

"Clarissa," James said, "game over. I'm sick of coming here and holding the baby while you avoid me and then having to leave and sit in my stupid apartment night after night, sleeping with a used onesie and a picture of you. I don't want to leave; I don't ever want to leave again. I belong here. And by the way, you're not getting rid of me."

Clarissa looked at him. "I'm thirty-two years old," she said.

"Like, duh," James said.

"I'm sorry," she said. "I shouldn't have lied to you."

"Ha. You call that a lie?" James smiled. "How's this one? I never had any money; I grew up in the servants' quarters of the Mason compound. My alcoholic father was responsible for the care and feeding of Joe Mason's firearm collection. You have no idea how exciting it is to grow up in a house with a drunk who cleans rifles on the kitchen table."

"Well, you're right, that is one big fucking lie," Clarissa conceded.

"Oh, it's not over yet," James said. "It's just getting good. After I graduated SMU film school, Aaron Mason and I struck a deal: While he was off getting high from Amsterdam to Zimbabwe I'd pretend I was him, set up a production entity in Hollywood with his start-up money, and protect his inheritance by making his parents think he was doing something productive with his life."

Clarissa nodded, then shook her head, then nodded again.

"It's like something I read about Hollywood: 'If you're going to lie, lie big,'" he said.

"You succeeded."

"But I didn't feel right being in on the lie anymore, especially with his parents, and then it turned out that he wanted to be in on the action. Just like everyone else."

"So you're out of a job, correct? Which would make you just the perfect man for me right now."

"No such luck," James said. "After a few days, Aaron realized that people in Hollywood work harder than anyone on the planet. So, he's somewhere in India, or the Himalayas, or wherever the drug laws aren't so inhibiting."

"I'm disappointed. You're not going to jail?"

"No, I mean, this whole 'mistaken identity' thing was a scandal for about a minute. I was fired, thrown off the lot, told I'd never work in this town again, but it turns out people here love a good story. So I sold the rights to Paramount."

Clarissa looked at him, her mouth dropping open. "You are good. You are really good."

James took a bow.

"Three questions," Clarissa said. "Why did you marry me?"

James looked at her, his expression solemn. "Honestly, at first I didn't take you seriously. But when it became clear that you were going to get married, whether you knew me or not, I took it as fate. I wanted to live an interesting life—and I knew you could provide that. Plus, you helped me get situated here. You knew everybody, and you were fun, and you were using me, and I . . ."

He stopped. "I was using you."

"That is so romantic," Clarissa said.

"But then, you were really funny, and on top of that, really hot, and I just, I don't know, I went along for the Clarissa roller-coaster ride," James said. "I dove in, and then I dove deeper. And I don't regret it. Not one bit."

Clarissa looked him in the eye. "Love Fuck," she said.

"I know exactly what you mean," he replied.

And he put his hands on her cheeks and they held that kiss for the longest while.

"Wait a minute," James said. "You have two more questions."

"The painting. Aaron gave that to you, I presume?"

"He didn't like it, once he sobered up."

"Slocum."

"Slocum?"

"That lawyer who got a free show out of me? The one with the prenup—"

James started to laugh, "Old college buddy. He's an aspiring actor. He was good, wasn't he?"

And Clarissa punched him in the arm with her free hand without even waking the baby.

Thirty-two

The End / The Beginning

Okay, you know how life is, right, like you're sitting on your dead mother's ugly couch, the baby's crying (gas bubble), your nipples are cracked, your husband, though adorable, is getting on *your very last possible nerve*—the nerve you didn't even know you had anymore (until he brings you, without you even having to ask, water, no ice, and the remote)—

And then the phone rings, and within minutes, nay, seconds, your whole life is transformed, and all is right with the world.

"Clarissa?" the voice said. Familiar voice, Clarissa thought. Morgan LeGrange from *Climate* was calling.

"Clarissa, I'm sorry I haven't called."

"If this is about the lawsuit, I have absolutely nothing at all to add."

"We need you to write an article."

"What?" Clarissa stood up, almost knocking the baby over.

"It's a cover article," she continued. "Are you sitting down?"

Clarissa sat down. Almost on the baby.

"A cover article on Zoë Monroe. She wants you to write it. She asked for you. Specifically." She drew out the word specifically as though painting it onto a canvas. "Get this—she likes your voice!"

Clarissa hung up the phone without answering and started speed-dialing the Star Chamber; they had to be the first to know. They always had to be the first to know.

And then she put down the phone.

And looked at her husband. Her wonderful, tolerant, hunk of a husband. "James," Clarissa said, "Zoë Monroe wants me to write a cover story on her—for *Climate*!"

And after he hugged her and danced around the room, Clarissa resumed speed-dialing the Star Chamber.

"Guedegess whadigat?!" Clarissa screamed.

The young waitress at the Coffee Bean and Tea Leaf on Sunset Plaza had noticed the pink binder on the sidewalk as she got off the bus on the way to her early morning shift. She'd picked it up for no reason but the color—Pepto Bismol pink—such a happy color, it cheered her out of her gray mood. She'd been in town from Montana not four weeks and was already homesick for what had been a dismal past.

She read the binder on her breaks, pink cover to pink cover, fascinated by the dedication and one-mindedness of its owner. She'd tried to reach Clarissa Alpert, whoever she was, to return the binder, to no avail. Finally she'd put the binder away, only to be pulled back into its pages by a force stronger than she, stronger than her strict, fear-of-God upbringing.

Soon, she found herself spending money on shoes in stores with silk walls, not rent or acting classes. She dyed her mousy hair blonde and got twice-monthly manicures she could ill afford. She flirted with customers.

She dated for leftovers.

She married a rich man.

And one day, she tossed the wedding binder onto Sunset Boulevard from her Jaguar convertible, on a bright southern California morning that could only have been invented in the movies.

About the Author

Gigi Levangie Grazer is the original screenwriter of *Stepmom*, which was made into the Columbia TriStar movie starring Julia Roberts and Susan Sarandon. The feature film rights for *Maneater* have been sold to Mandalay Entertainment and will go into production in early 2003. Her previous book, *Rescue Me*, currently is being developed into a film at Fox Searchlight. Gigi lives in Pacific Palisades, California, with her husband, producer Brian Grazer, and their three children.